MYTH MAKER

MYTH MAKER

MYTHICAL MENAGERIE SERIES BOOK 3

SUNEÉ LE ROUX

Strawberry Moon Press

Copyright © 2025 Suneé le Roux

All rights reserved.

For permission requests, contact the author at contact@suneeleroux.com.

This book is a work of fiction. Names, characters, places, incidents and dialogues are used fictitiously. Any resemblance to actual people, living or deceased, is coincidental.

ISBN (Paperback): 978-1-83491-129-8

Author's Note

The stories that make up the Mythical Menagerie series were written in serialised short-story form. Each story contains its own complete arc while contributing to the larger narrative of the series as a whole. Think of them as very large chapters in a single story.

This collection brings the episodes of the third series together into one continuous reading experience.

This novel makes use of UK English spelling and syntax.

TABLE OF CONTENTS

PART 8

SERPENT'S STRIKE

"Watch it!"

I lurched aside, narrowly avoiding bumping into a man twice my size sporting a military buzz cut, his bare arms covered in tattoos. For a moment, the world tilted around me as memories flooded my vision of another man in another place, his predatory grin exposing oversized canines. Of my sister laying in an alley, her blood on my hands.

"Hey, buddy. Are you alright?"

I blinked the past away and focussed on the man in front of me. He was buff, like someone whose paycheque depended on the size of his biceps, but his canines were a perfectly acceptable length and the concern etched across his face was hardly threatening. He looked familiar, and it took me a moment to realise that I knew him. Sort of. He had been in the helicopter that had brought me to the Repository from Dubrovnik this morning. In fact, I think I was wearing his black bomber jacket…

"Sorry, yes," I said, sliding a hand across the smooth stone wall of the underground corridor outside Amari's – no, *Father's* – office, letting the cold surface banish my momentary vertigo. Norton – the werewolf – was dead, and things have changed inside the mountain fortress.

I leaned the *rogatina*, the modified spear I had taken from Nadiya before we'd been separated, against the wall and shrugged the jacket off. "This is yours, I think. Sorry, I didn't catch your name…?"

"Clint," the man said, grinning. "And you're

the boss' son."

I winced. "Ambrose," I replied as I handed the jacket over. "Do you know where Stavros is?"

"The chimaera?" Clint asked as he pulled the black bomber on. "Yes, he's in a holding cell. Want me to show you?"

I shook my head. "I know where it is, thanks. Hey," I said just as he was about to walk away. "How long have you...? You know, worked with mythical creatures?"

Clint cocked his head, as if trying to do difficult math. "Been hunting them most of my adult life," he finally said with a shrug.

He fell in beside me as I picked the *rogatina* up again and started walking towards the temporary enclosures. "I worked for Marco Mazzoni for many years, but when he disappeared, I was sort of drifting around, not knowing what to do with myself. Thought about going back to the army, but the pay's not as good as I'm used to. Was glad when your father called the old team back together again. And this place!" he exclaimed as we turned the corner into the corridor where Amari had kept new acquisitions while she worked on their enclosures. "Who knew about this? An entire mountain full of them!"

A loud trumpeting greeted us as five elephant trunks reached through the bars of the closest cell door. Clint batted one of the airavata's trunks away. "I don't have any on me," he said, his voice laced with laughter.

I shot him a quizzical look and he explained: "I'm the one who brings him his jackfruit every morning. Big guy has a sweet tooth. Come, the other one's towards the end."

I shot the airavata a last glance as we walked on. It looked much too big for the cell it was confined in. "It's been more than a month since he came here. How long are you guys planning on keeping him inside that tiny cell?"

Clint shrugged. "As I understand it, the previous Keeper left without telling anyone how to make new enclosures. I say, just throw him in one of the existing ones, but the boss reckons we won't know how the creatures will react when they're put together like that. So... he stays where he is."

I felt a tightness wrap around my chest. The airavata was here because of me. Granted, it was better off than having its heads mounted on some rich guy's wall, but it didn't deserve this either.

My ears pricked at the sound of a goat bleating forlornly. I hastened my steps as we passed several empty enclosures until we reached the one where Stavros was being kept. The vice around my chest tightened. The chimaera lay slumped on a bed of hay in the cell's corner, the dead snake tail hanging still. Stavros lifted his leonine head to look at me, his yellow eyes filled with sadness. He whimpered and, before I knew it, I'd dropped my spear and whispered the Word to open the cell door. I was crouched beside the chimaera before Clint could stop me.

I ran my hand through the coarse hair of Stavros' mane, inspecting the wound on his chest where Nadiya had sliced him with the *rogatina*. It looked better already, the healing magic of the Repository working its wonders. But guilt still tasted bitter in my mouth.

"You don't like being cooped up in here, do you?" I murmured. "All you wanted was to get back home, and now you're confined here."

The goat bleated softly and the lion's head just slumped back onto the hay again. The creature's misery was almost palpable.

When I'd brought him here, I'd thought Amari

was in charge, and that she would take good care of him. I'd had little opportunity to see how Father ran things now, but I had a feeling his priorities were going to be different from hers.

My hands clenched into fists as I pushed myself to my feet again. "I'll make this better. I promise."

My words sounded hollow in my own ears. Without Amari's expertise, there wasn't much I could do for the chimaera, short of breaking him out of the Repository again. My shoulders slumped in defeat. Much as I hated it, there was nothing else I could do for it now.

Stavros lay listlessly as I exited the cell and clicked the gate shut behind me again. Clint's face was pale as he handed me my spear. "You have balls of steel, Ambrose, I'll grant you that."

I stared at him for a moment, wondering why he'd said that, before I realised that Clint still saw Stavros as a monster, something to be feared. I'd thought so too at first – but I knew better now.

If there's one thing I'd learned during my time working for Amari, it was that monsters came in all shapes and sizes – and it wasn't always obvious which was which.

Clint pulled a pair of sunglasses from his pocket and placed them on top of his head. He laughed as my eyes narrowed in a questioning look, my confused face reflecting back at me in the polarised lenses. "I was on my way to clean out the basilisk's enclosure. Damn thing's gaze can turn a person to stone, or so they say. Better safe than sorry, right?"

He gave me a friendly clap on the shoulder. "Hey, you seem to have a knack with the beasts – want to come with me?"

"Sure," I shrugged. I had nothing better to do right now, anyway. "Let me just put this spear away.

Not much point lugging it around inside the Repository."

Clint grinned. "The boss will have your hide if you harm one of the creatures, that's for sure. Go on, I'll meet you downstairs."

We parted ways at the end of the corridor with the airavata's trumpeting ringing in our ears. I headed to the room Father had said I could stay in. I'd left Dubrovnik so abruptly, I hadn't had a chance to retrieve my things from Nadiya's house, and I was pretty sure her less-than-warm welcome would be lethal this time round. It definitely wasn't worth my skin to go back for the few sets of clothes I'd left behind, but that meant I had nothing to unpack once I reached the room.

I leaned the *rogatina* against one wall and quickly pulled my mobile phone out. My fingers hesitated as I opened a chat with Amari. Father had told me what had happened: she'd lost control and killed Norton – and nearly the unicorn too! – before fleeing with all the Keeper's knowledge, leaving him to take over from her.

Hell, I could understand if Norton had driven Amari to do something drastic. There was no doubt in my mind on which side of the monster-not-monster side he stood. But it wasn't like her to just leave the creatures behind. Father had mentioned some of the new reforms the Council had enacted – the so-called 'voluntary donation' – which sounded to me like exactly the kind of thing Amari would be opposed to. Father said it was for research purposes only, but I doubted that would be the end of it.

No matter how many times Amari had called the Repository a haven, this was exactly what Daniel and so many like him had been afraid of.

And Amari had just walked away from it all.

I put my phone away again. I needed Amari to

keep my promise to Stavros, but I'd try contacting her again when the tightness in my chest had loosened a bit. She would know what to do.

If she still cared.

✷✷✷

I wandered past the enclosures in the main cave, trying to remember which one the basilisk called home. The plain concrete walls gave few clues from ground level, but I think it was just left of the nymphs' enclosure…

A bloodcurdling scream rent the air, almost drowning out the cacophony of noises escaping from the other pens. Adrenaline flooded my veins and my sneakers slapped against the stone floor as I ran towards the sound. The voice had definitely been human, and it had come from outside an enclosure, which could only mean one thing. Something had escaped.

I turned a corner and stopped dead in my tracks.

An enormous snake was wrapped around Clint, the scales of its sinuous body glinting an iridescent green in the ambient light as its coils constricted around the man's body. The snake's hood was flared as it stared intently into the mercenary's eyes. It opened its jaws and revulsion shuddered through my body – it was going to swallow the man whole.

I lurched forward and heard a crunch underneath my feet. I looked down to see Clint's glasses shattered on the ground.

Frantically, I looked around for a weapon, wishing I still had the *rogatina* with me. There was nothing to hand. A strangled croak drew my eyes back to the struggle. The snake's jaws were already grotesquely wide, and Clint's face was turning an alarming shade of purple.

"Hey!" I shouted. "Over here!" I waved my hands, hoping it would distract the snake.

It worked!

The reptile's jaws snapped shut and it turned its head towards me.

"Shit," I mumbled, as my vision started blurring. I stumbled as the world lurched around me, a shade of purple weirdly tainting my sight. I shook my head, trying to shake the dizziness, but I lost my balance and stumbled to the floor. My right hand closed around the broken sunglasses.

I shoved them onto my face. A headache exploded behind my eyes as my vision snapped partly into focus through the cracked lenses. The snake's body still coiled around Clint, but its head was focussed on me, swaying back and forth in a creepy hypnotic dance.

Pain seared through my brain. I lashed out impulsively, kicking at the snake. My sneaker connected with its taut body and it hissed angrily, jerking towards me. As I recoiled, my foot slipped out from underneath me and I tumbled to the ground. The glasses slid off my nose and clattered onto the smooth stone floor, skidding out of reach.

I clamped my eyes shut as I fumbled around blindly, searching for the glasses.

Instead, my fingers found cold scales.

Horror pulsed through my bones as I felt the pressure of the reptile's coils wrapping around me.

Shit, shit, shit.

A gunshot rang out, and my eyes snapped open. The snake hissed as it released me, slithering away as more shots followed. It moved faster than I would have given it credit for, disappearing around a corner as Clint emptied his magazine on empty air.

The mercenary had a look of pure horror plastered across his face, his handgun clicking empty as he continued to fire at the shadows into which the snake had disappeared.

I could hardly blame him. By now, I'd seen my fair share of screwed-up shit, but nearly being devoured by an enormous snake definitely topped my list of unwanted traumas.

I climbed to my feet, still unsteady as the world teetered around me. The pounding behind my eyeballs had faded to a dull throb, but I still felt like I'd been tossed into my dryer's spin cycle, the one that set the entire machine shaking as it tried to run across the laundry room floor.

"What the hell was that?" I asked as Clint finally holstered his gun. I noticed his hands were shaking just as bad as mine.

"Lamia," he spat, like the word left a foul taste. All traces of his earlier joviality were gone. He bent to pick up his ruined glasses, crushing them even further in his clenched fist. The purple tint had left his face, leaving it an angry shade of red instead.

"And this is why we rid the world of these monsters," he snarled. "They don't deserve what they have here."

He stomped off, leaving me to stare after him, speechless.

My knees wobbled as I climbed the steel stairs leading up to the administrative wing. I hadn't expected Father's mercenaries to care for the creatures like Amari had, but I'd thought they understood their importance, at least.

But what worried me more was that I *did* understand. And right now, I felt the same.

✳✳✳

"Do you know there's a lamia loose in the Repository?"

Father didn't look up from the book that was spread open across Amari's mahogany desk.

"I suspected as much," he said. "Norton left a trail of corpses behind when he escaped. A regrettable waste." He shook his head, still engrossed in his reading. "The lamia wasn't among the dead, however."

"That lamia nearly killed me, and one of your men!" I slammed my hand on the desk and Father finally looked up, adjusting his reading glasses as his lips pulled down in a frown. "You could have warned me about the enormous man-eating snake prowling the corridors."

"It tried to eat you?"

I flopped down into a chair, exasperated, as his eyes took on that far-off look that meant his scholarly curiosity was taking over.

"Did you look into its eyes?"

"Yes," I sighed. "It gave me one hell of a headache and made everything look purple."

Father grinned eagerly. "So it's true!" he exclaimed, nearly bouncing with excitement in his chair. "It does have a hypnotic gaze – I wondered about that. Did it bite you? I read somewhere its venom can cause hallucinations."

He stared at me expectantly, and I felt my shoulders slump as my anger faded. There was no reasoning with Father when he was like this. Academic fervour always trumped paternal concern. I'd learned that many years ago.

"No, it didn't bite me."

Father turned towards the bookshelves behind him, but not before I saw a look of disappointment cross his face. I liked to tell myself he cared about my welfare. Just perhaps not as much as he cared about his work.

As his hands skimmed lightly across the spines of the old tomes, my eyes drifted to the place where a painting of Diana, a bygone Keeper, had once hung. A garish silver frame with a picture of a much younger Cassie and me was suspended in its place.

"That's new," I said.

Father glanced at it. "I wanted a reminder of what's important to me. So I don't lose my way again."

I had little to say to that. You'd think he wouldn't need that kind of reminder.

"Ah, here it is."

Father pulled a book from the shelf and returned to the desk. He opened it at a place bookmarked with a silver ribbon and turned it so I could see the illustration decorating the left page. It was the lamia, alright: an enormous hooded snake with spirals drawn inside its eyes. The text beside it was in Greek and although I could probably have deciphered it given the time and inclination, I had neither of those in abundance right now.

"Give me the CliffsNotes," I said.

Father tutted as he pulled the book back towards him. "According to legend, Queen Lamia had been one of Zeus' many conquests. Jealous Hera responded the way she usually did when she learned of her husband's deviance and cursed the woman, driving her insane and turning her into a monstrous snake who devoured her own children. Since then, the lamia has been associated with nightmares and childlessness."

I grunted. "And how true are the legends?"

Father shrugged. "Who knows? If you could recapture it for me, then I can study it and find out."

I straightened in my seat. "You want me to

hunt it down? Why? Don't you have a team of men to take care of it?"

Father huffed. "Paid muscle, that's all they are. Not one of them has the wits to outsmart any of the sentients in here. I'm amazed I haven't had more casualties."

"Casualties?" I asked, startled. "Men have died?"

"Just the one," Father said quickly. "And he was an idiot. Waved his gun around like it could solve everything. Let's just say the dragon didn't care much for that kind of behaviour. I chalked it down to learning experience, but it does mean that the old beast will have to fend for itself from now on. It won't let anyone enter its enclosure. Not that any of the remaining men are willing to try, mind you. No matter how many incentives I dangle in front of their dim-witted noses."

I sat back in stunned silence for a moment. When had Father become so callous about losing human lives?

Then it hit me. "The dragon? You mean Kentigern Mor?"

"Yes, that one," Father said irritably. "You know, Nessie, or whatever it likes to call itself. Bloody cranky bugger. I don't know why Amari bothered to visit it as often as she did."

"Perhaps she cared," I mumbled, still shaken by the thought of a man being killed. I knew first-hand how dangerous the creatures inside the Repository could be, but I'd never felt unsafe inside the mountain before today.

"Yes, well," Father huffed, pushing the book about the lamia aside and pulling the one he'd been reading earlier closer again. "If she'd cared, she wouldn't have run off at the first hint of trouble. Did you know Norton was the last of his kind?"

A hard knot formed in the pit of my stomach.

"Does that mean…?"

Father nodded. "It does – we lost a trait. I've been trying to figure out which one, but the literature on werewolves is unreliable, at best. Most of what we think we know comes from popular culture, and nothing remotely credible mentions a possible trait." Huffing, he slammed the book shut.

I winced, wondering what Amari would think if she knew how he was treating her books. She'd always been very protective of the old tomes in her library.

"And for some reason, I just can't seem to concentrate on my research," Father complained. "It's not just the interruptions – even when it's quiet, my mind wanders. I used to be able to focus for hours. Now… I lose steam after ten minutes."

A soft squawk sounded, as if proving Father's point, and he reached down for something behind his desk. When he straightened, he held a little bird in his hands. Sleek crimson feathers covered its tiny body and a golden crest stood erect on top of its head. Father ruffled the soft feathers at the bird's nape affectionately.

I leaned closer to have a good look at it. "Is that…?"

"Nusku," Father confirmed, a hint of pride in his voice. "The little phoenix. He likes to play in the bottom drawer while I'm busy in the office. If I let him wander around on my desk, he nibbles on my notes."

The little phoenix nuzzled Father's fingers, squawking a bit louder. Father pulled a Tupperware box from the top drawer of Amari's desk and plucked out a dead cricket, which he fed to the chirping phoenix. The baby bird gulped it down greedily.

"He's grown quickly," I marvelled. "What do

you plan to do with him?"

"Do?" Father peered at me over the top of his glasses. "Nothing. He's not a danger to anyone. When he's old enough, I'll get him a stand and he can perch here by my side while I work. You'd like that, wouldn't you, Nusku?" He popped another bug into the bird's mouth, before putting the box away again and tucking the little phoenix back into the desk drawer.

Then he turned his attention back to me again. "So, what do you say? Think you can catch that lamia for me?"

I shuddered. I'd almost forgotten about the snake. "Not sure I'm the right guy for the job."

"Nonsense." Father waved my objection away. "If you can catch a werewolf, you can catch an overgrown snake. Just don't look into its eyes."

"Right…" I rose reluctantly. The last thing I wanted was to come within ten feet of that thing again. But if I didn't catch it, who knew what might happen? I'd never be able to live with myself if someone was hurt because I didn't feel like facing the lamia again.

"And remember," Father added just before I left the room. "I want it alive. The Council is keen to explore the possibilities the creatures present. Imagine what we could do with the lamia's venom! It might be a powerful hallucinogenic."

I hesitated in the doorway. "To do what with?"

"Recreational drugs, my boy! Oh, don't look at me like that. The research must be funded somehow. Besides, I won't let them sell anything with too many adverse side effects."

My breath hitched in my throat. Suddenly, everything Amari had ever said about creature parts came into sharp focus. She'd been right all along.

And she'd still left.

A sour mix of guilt and anger swelled in my chest – guilt for brushing off her warnings, and anger that she hadn't stayed to fight this with me. Had she known this would happen? Had she given up on everything she stood for so easily? I didn't want to believe it.

I pushed the questions down, forcing myself to focus.

There was still one snag. "Didn't you say the new policy stipulated that those parts had to be provided willingly? How are you going to get the lamia to give you its venom voluntarily?"

Father touched his nose, a knowing smile playing across his lips. "Oh, there are ways. Don't worry about that."

Honestly, I was getting more worried by the minute. Amari wasn't here to curb Father's enthusiasm. Who was going to ensure the creatures inside the Repository were treated fairly?

I strode out of the office – not to go in search of the lamia – but to go see the one person in here who weighed heaviest on my conscience.

※※※

I swallowed nervously, watching the ripples on the pond's surface coming closer. The heady scent of holly permeated the air, its spicy fragrance mingling with the earthy aroma of damp soil. A nightjar called somewhere out of sight. I took two steps backward as the asrai's head broke the surface. I wasn't fool enough to come within her reach again.

My skin crawled as the asrai's pale eyes lingered on me, a smirk distorting her otherwise flawless beauty. The memory of her icy touch on my skin sent shivers down my spine – and not the good kind.

"I wondered if you'd come see me again," she said, her voice husky. "One would think you'd know better by now."

"I do," I said, my mouth suddenly dry.

She stepped out of the pond, water cascading down the intricate lacework of her Victorian gown, accentuating the curves of her shapely body. I took another step backwards and she laughed, a sound like crystals clinking against ice. She turned away from me and made herself comfortable on a rocky outcrop, her head tilted towards the sky as she studied the pale sliver of moon illuminating the perpetual twilight of her enclosure with an eerie, otherworldly glow.

"I'm here on behalf of a friend."

"You should choose your friends better."

The asrai pulled a bone-white comb from the folds of her dress and started untangling the snarls from her long, pale hair. I swallowed loudly as I watched her, my breath hot in my chest. Even though I knew she'd kill me given half a chance, I had to keep myself from imagining our bodies intertwined.

"You can't have any of it," she said abruptly, watching me from beneath hooded eyelids.

"Have what?" I asked, confused. I was suddenly very aware of my hands and how sweaty they were.

She shot me a pointed look and realisation suddenly dawned. "Your hair? Is that what they want?"

"Ever since the previous Keeper abandoned us."

She plucked a single strand from the brush, twirling it deftly around her slender fingers. "Such a small thing in exchange for safety, don't you think?"

I frowned. "Your safety's never been in question

here, has it?"

The asrai shrugged. "As long as I comply. Give them what they want."

I shook my head. "That's not how this is supposed to work."

"Don't be so naïve," she retorted. "Amari may have been idealistic, but at least she had principles. Our new Keeper has targets."

"That's... not true," I floundered. For all I knew, he very well may have.

"Believe what you will," the asrai pouted.

She stared at me for a moment, her gaze calculating. Then she held the single hair out to me.

"Here. For my keep."

I noticed her hand was trembling.

"Keep it," I said, turning towards the enclosure door. "If they want it, they can come get it themselves."

※※※

My heart was still pounding by the time I reached the second enclosure. If the asrai was frightened, then everything else in here had to be terrified.

Still, I wasn't sure if I could trust her. It may all have been a ploy to lure me into her clutches.

But there was someone else here in the Repository who I was sure wouldn't try to deceive me. I just hoped he wouldn't eat me before I'd had a chance to speak to him.

I stepped through the gate and nearly lost my balance as my foot found no resistance. "Whoa!"

Windmilling, I managed to grab the doorframe and steady myself before I nearly fell into what looked like an infinite lake. The sky above was grey and cloudy – much like it had been that day on the banks of Loch Ness when I had first met Kentigern Mor.

The water rippled as the dragon's head breached the surface, his scaly face contorted into a vicious snarl, fangs the length of my forearm filling my vision.

"Get out!" he roared, his sinuous blue body swirling through the stormy waves.

I retreated, stumbling back into the safety of the Repository. Water splashed through the open doorway, drenching me and plastering my clothes to my body.

"Great Mor!" I shouted from outside the enclosure, holding up the mackerel I'd had the foresight to raid from the kitchen before coming here. "I bring a gift!"

"Ambrose Davids?" The dragon sounded startled. I heard him sniffing the air, and then: "What gift?"

I risked stepping back into the doorway. The enormous dragon was right up against the opening. If I wanted to, I could reach out and touch the scales sparkling across his torso.

I held the fish up. "It's not haddock —"

"It will do," he rumbled eagerly. I suppose he must get tired of eating the same thing all the time.

I tossed the mackerel into the air and the dragon snapped it up before it could fall into the water. It disappeared down the great beast's maw and Kentigern Mor smacked his lips in appreciation, before turning towards me again.

"Speak quickly, Ambrose Davids, while I still have patience. At least you haven't come to threaten me with a gun."

I decided not to waste words. "Is it true that the new Keeper demands a keeper's price?"

An ominous rumble emanated from the great dragon's throat. "It is true."

His words hit me like a punch in the gut. I clutched onto the doorway, afraid that my knees would give in and I'd tumble into the endless lake.

"Willingly?" I croaked, the word nearly sticking in my throat.

Kentigern Mor reared up before me, his powerful body roiling through the tumultuous waters.

"Do you truly believe anything can be taken from me by force?" he bellowed. "I am the Ceann-Cinnidh, the Chief of Chieftains. Your puny weapons are no threat to me!"

"Peace, great dragon," I said, holding my palms up. "I meant no offence."

I swallowed nervously as the dragon lowered his head closer to me. If he wanted to, he could swallow me in one gulp.

My eyes darted away from his penetrating stare. "I've failed you."

"How so, little human?" Kentigern Mor asked, and I looked up again, startled. His eyes narrowed and his head tilted to one side as he regarded me, as if I were a puzzle that baffled him.

My shoulders sagged. "I asked the Keeper to bring you here. It's my fault."

Kentigern Mor huffed. "I made my own choice, Ambrose Davids. I came here willing. And so, it is only fair that I pay for my keep."

"But…" I hesitated, afraid to risk the dragon's ire again. "Don't you feel…?"

His eyes bored into mine and my throat was suddenly very dry.

"Exploited?" The word came out in a register much higher than my normal timbre.

The dragon harrumphed. "If I did, I would leave."

I stared at him. "You can leave?"

Kentigern Mor's laughter washed over me.

"Of course. Do you think anyone on the other side of that door can stop me? Or perhaps you think I don't know something as simple as the Word for Opening?"

Heat rushed to the back of my neck. Of course he could leave.

"Then why do you stay?"

"Because Amari gave me exactly what I asked for. I am happy here." He growled ominously again. "As long as they don't pester me."

"But Amari isn't in charge anymore."

"No, she isn't." There was genuine regret in his voice. "And, while I don't particularly care for the new Keeper and his minions, I can be patient. Their lives are but a moment in the span of a dragon's years."

I blinked. I hadn't thought about that.

"But what of the payment?" I asked, troubled.

Kentigern Mor swirled languidly through the choppy water. "What do I care?" he asked. "What is a tear or a loose scale to me? I have all I need."

I shook my head, amazed. "Thank you, great Mor," I said, bowing before the swirling dragon. "Next time, I'll bring something better than a mackerel."

"Come again, Ambrose Davids," the dragon said as he dived back into the lake. "But not too soon," his words carried as he disappeared into the deep.

I shut the enclosure gate behind me and winced as my wet sneakers squeaked on the smooth stone floor.

Although my chest felt less constricted, I still had that uncomfortable feeling – like ants under my skin – that what was happening here wasn't right. The dragon was clearly more than willing to pay the price – and the asrai grudgingly did the same – but were all the creatures in the Repository as amenable?

I tramped up the steel stairs and came to a stop on the landing overlooking the main cave. From here, I could see a snapshot of each enclosure.

The cyclops was sitting beside the entrance of a cave, beaming blissfully as a burly man clipped his toenails. I grimaced as the man carefully caught the clippings and deposited them into a little plastic bag. The cyclops wiggled his toes, and then eagerly placed one hand in front of the man, clearly eager to get a manicure too.

Maybe I was wrong. Maybe asking the creatures to part with bits of skin and scale was not as distressing for them as I thought it should be. Maybe the Council's price was small enough in exchange for the safety the creatures enjoyed in the Repository.

But a few pens over, little Caerus crouched behind his mother while his two older siblings bunched in protectively on either side. The big male griffon, his tail whisking in agitation, screeched as the griffon family crowded around a man reaching down to pick up a blue feather laying on the ground. Leonine paws clawing at the ground, the griffon patriarch suddenly reared up on his hind legs, his wings flapping threateningly. He snatched the feather from the man's grip, his razor-sharp beak nearly severing a few fingers in the process. The man yelped and backed away as the female and the three little ones took off.

A token not freely given, then.

In the dryad grove, another man was sweeping up leaves in the forest. Of the usually carefree nymphs frolicking around the river, laughing and drinking ouzo, there was no sign.

And in the unicorn enclosure, the moon glinted off Una's sparkling white horn as she thrust it at a man brandishing a syringe. The man narrowly avoided being skewered, and his syringe remained empty as he beat a hasty retreat.

I clamped my jaw shut so tightly my teeth ground together painfully.

Clearly, not all the creatures were willing to pay the keeper's fee.

For now, the rebuffed men left empty-handed. How long would it be before they resorted to taking what they wanted by force?

I'd had my reservations about working for the Council in the past, but my decision was crystal clear now – I could no longer be a part of this.

It was time to say goodbye to the Repository.

✕✕✕

Father waved me into his office, a frown creasing his forehead as he looked pointedly at the *rogatina* in my hand. The spear tip was retracted so that it looked like a simple walking stick.

"Don't tell me you're leaving?" he asked.

"I am," I replied. "And I'm taking Stavros with me."

"Ha!" Father snorted. "Not likely. The chimaera belongs to the Council now. Besides," he added as I was about to protest. "It's still recovering from its wounds – wounds that you helped inflict, I might add."

He peered at me over the top of his reading glasses. "Come now, Ambrose. You know the best place for it is inside these walls."

I swallowed my guilt down. He *was* right. Stavros was better off recuperating under the effects of the Repository's healing magic.

And, if I were honest, I had no idea what I was going to do with an enormous lion-slash-goat-slash-snake-like-monster out in the world. I might attempt to return him to his home, but then what?

Leave him to terrorise the locals? Give another hunter the chance to capture him, and maybe sell him to the highest bidder?

My shoulders slumped in defeat. "You're right," I admitted.

Father shot me a look that shouted of course he was right.

Then he cleared his throat. "And then there is the matter of the lamia."

"A matter your own men will have to take care of," I said quickly. I ran a hand through my hair, feeling sheepish. "I just want to go home. See if Cassie's alright."

"Well, I won't say I'm not disappointed." Father's mouth pursed into a thin line. "I'd hoped you'd stay here and help with the animals. You do seem to have a knack for them. Take after your old man."

"I've been offered this choice once before. I turned it down then, too."

"Fine," Father huffed. "Go home. Keep your sister out of trouble."

His eyes took on that faraway look again. "I have big plans for the Repository. It has so much potential! And that damn snake isn't going to stop the Council's new vision for this place." He slammed his fist on the table to punctuate his words.

My stomach churned. Nothing good could come of this 'new vision', I was sure of it.

And Stavros was here because of me.

And Kentigern Mor.

Hell, even the asrai would still be living her best life drowning innocent bystanders in the lake at Hyde Park if it hadn't been for my interference.

No. None of my business. Not anymore.

All I wanted was to go home, kiss my girlfriend, give my sister a hug, and play a game of squash with my best friend. The mythical world must sort itself out for once.

If Amari could walk away, then so could I.

"Well… I'll be off then…" I said awkwardly.

"Do you need a lift home?" Father asked.

"No, I can manage."

Father's brows furrowed and I realised he didn't know I could Travel. Well, whether I could actually make the jump from here to London was still up for debate, and whether I could do it at all without life-threatening danger nipping at my heels remained to be seen.

Either way, for some reason, I didn't want to share this new skill with him.

"I'll walk down to the village and catch a train." His eyebrows lifted into his hairline and I shrugged, trying my best to look carefree and spontaneous. "I've always wanted to travel."

"You have," he agreed, as if he actually knew that about me. "Want me to walk with you?"

"No, I can find my way. I know where the West Gate is."

We stared at each other awkwardly for another moment or two, then we both tried to speak at the same time.

"Take care of Stavros —"

"Give my regards to your sister —"

I turned on my heels and strode out of the room, my knuckles white around the *rogatina*'s shaft.

✳✳✳

Outside in the corridor, the far-off bleats from the chimaera's goat's head and the airavata's trumpeting echoed down the hallway to compete for the sound most likely to let me lose my resolve. I couldn't help but feel like I was running away from my problems.

But I just didn't know what I could do about any of it. Fixing what was wrong with the Repository was too big a job for me on my own. The best I could do was find Amari and hope she'd know what to do. I wasn't running away at all.

If I just kept repeating that thought, I might actually believe it at some point.

I hurried down the tunnel, guessing at the direction I needed to take. I'd lied when I'd said I knew where the West Gate was. The mountain was a warren of tunnels I couldn't keep track of. But I hadn't wanted Father to accompany me on my way out.

I found the kitchen, which was rowdy with some of Father's men, although I didn't see Clint among them. They pointed the direction out to me, and I wandered along a long corridor in what I hoped was a westerly direction.

My footsteps echoed down the long tunnel. It was dimly lit, with lights suspended from the ceiling only every few feet. Blackness pooled in the bits in between, and my imagination threatened to run away with me. It was the kind of corridor where you'd expect something fatal to happen to a minor character in a horror movie.

Something caught the corner of my vision. I spun around, clenching the *rogatina* so tightly my fingers cramped. There was nothing. Frozen in place, I strained my ears listening for any kind of noise, but all I could hear was my own, slightly startled, breathing.

I continued on my way.

The sound of something scraping on stone sent my heart rate racing. I turned around again. A lightbulb flickered on the far end of the empty corridor.

"Who's there?" My question reverberated off

the cold stone walls.

Spooked, I flicked the switch on the *rogatina*, letting the spear tip slide into place. Sweat made the weapon's shaft slippery in my hand. Blood pounded in my ears as I waited for something to jump out at me.

Nothing happened.

Taking a deep breath, I turned around again and started walking once more, a little faster than before. I needed to get out from underneath this mountain. My imagination was playing tricks on me.

The knot in my stomach untwisted as the tall steel doors of the West Gate finally came into view. Amari had said that a powerful spell of protection prevented anyone but the Keeper from Travelling inside the Repository's walls. I'd need to cross the threshold before I could attempt to make the jump home.

My free hand brushed across the smooth surface of the enormous gates. There were no door handles.

The hair on the back of my neck sprang to attention as that scraping noise I had heard before sounded behind me.

Brandishing the *rogatina*, I spun around, feeling the air escape my lungs as the lamia slithered out of the gloom. It lifted itself up, hood flaring, and I swallowed loudly as all moisture suddenly left my mouth.

A headache slammed into my frontal cortex and I wrenched my gaze from the lamia's luminous purple eyes. The snake's body was swaying slowly from side to side. I held the *rogatina* out in front of me, feeling like I'd forgotten everything Nadiya had ever taught me.

When the lamia struck, it was so quick I nearly missed it. One moment it was still a few feet away

– the next its jaws snapped inches away from my face.

I batted it away with the wooden shaft of the *rogatina*, grunting at the lamia's weight.

It coiled upon itself, its tongue tasting the air as it watched me, poised to strike again.

Without taking my eyes off the lamia, I fumbled with one hand behind my back until I felt the West Gate against my palm. Between gritted teeth, I muttered the Word for Opening.

A click sounded, and the door swung open behind me.

The lamia hissed threateningly as I stepped backwards.

Just as my feet crossed the threshold, the snake lunged at me.

I screamed the Word and nearly collapsed with relief as the world exploded into white light.

✳✳✳

I felt the pressure around my leg before I could see again.

Thrusting blindly with the *rogatina*, I was rewarded with an angry hiss, just as the searingly bright light faded and the world came into view. The weight fell from my leg, and I stumbled backwards, tripping over something and landing gracelessly on a gravel pathway. It took me a moment to get my bearings.

The cloudy sky glowed with the reflection of city lights. Trees hanging overhead hardly stopped the soft drizzle from plastering my hair to my head, filling my nostrils with the scent of wet earth and mulch. Somewhere nearby, a car horn honked angrily.

I was in Hyde Park.

My stomach twisted as movement caught my

eye. I whipped my head sideways just in time to see the end of the lamia's tail disappearing into the underbrush.

Shit.

Scrambling to my feet, I clutched the *rogatina* so firmly I was surprised it didn't snap under the pressure. I attacked the bush as if it had said something offensive about my mother, but my spear met nothing but leaves and broken twigs. I flanked the shrub, searching for the lamia, but there was nothing. My gaze roved across the grass, and I cursed the darkness that shaded everything in black and grey.

There was nothing to see. The lamia was gone, and it hadn't even left so much as a trail in the dirt behind. Just a smear of crimson blood on the tip of my spear.

Shit.

I stood motionless for a few moments, weighing my options. The lamia was loose in London, and it was my fault. If it hurt someone…

The responsible thing to do would be to hunt it down immediately, while it was wounded and confused, but hell, I was tired. I didn't want to stay out here in the rain and get soaked for the second time in a day.

And I sure as hell didn't want to deal with a cranky snake in a dark alley somewhere, if I happened to find it.

No, best to go home now, get some rest in. I'd be better prepared to face the lamia tomorrow.

Maybe in the warm light of day.

Maybe with a team of well-armed mercenaries beside me.

Maybe I'd even get lucky and find its corpse washed up at Dead Man's Hole underneath Tower Bridge.

Snorting, I flicked the *rogatina*'s switch and turned

it back into a staff.

I was lucky, but not *that* lucky.

✖✖✖

I half expected Amari to be sitting on my couch, but my apartment was empty when I walked in. I stood the *rogatina* in one corner of the lounge, kicked off my shoes and slumped down on the living room couch. The beige ceiling glared back at me belligerently.

I should be out looking for the lamia. The thing was my responsibility – and I knew exactly how dangerous it was.

But it just seemed like such an effort.

No. I had to go out and find that snake now, before someone was hurt. If I hurried, I might still catch it somewhere in the park. I just needed to pull my sneakers back on again and go.

Instead, I pulled my phone out and texted Sarah.

-- Back in London. Want to come over for coffee? --

Her response came quickly.

-- Wish I could, but on my way to a crime scene. Call you when I'm free? --

I sent her a thumbs up and returned to staring aimlessly at the ceiling. It occurred to me that the full moon had come and gone, and Cassie had said she was fine, but I hadn't had much time to check up on her. The memory of her laying in that alley… It sent a shiver down my spine.

I pulled my phone out again.

-- Hey, I'm back in town. Everything still alright? --

I didn't expect an immediate response – final exams were right around the corner and Cassie had a habit of partying late and then going radio silent while she crammed for the next day. I'd probably only hear from her tomorrow afternoon, after she'd slept it off.

The unexpected ping from my mobile startled me.

-- If you're still wondering if I have fangs, then you can rest easy. My canines are as cute as always. --

I chuckled.

-- Glad to hear it. Does that mean I have to return this dog collar now? PS: How're the exams going? --

Her response wiped the smile from my face.

-- No more exams for me! Dropped out of uni. Too much hassle! Gotta go now. Speak later. --

My fingers punched the next message frantically.

-- What do you mean you dropped out of uni?? --

Frustratingly, Cassie didn't respond.

I dialled her number but ended the call as soon as it went to voicemail. I knew I should press her – but I also knew she'd just get upset with me and shut me out.

I sighed, a mental shrug. What was done was done. There was nothing I could do about it now. I'd probably have more luck convincing the lamia to go vegan than I'd have trying to push my sister into doing something she didn't want to.

Speaking of…

Huffing, I dragged myself off the couch and picked up the *rogatina* again. I flicked open the blade, grimacing at the dried blood stuck to the spear tip. I rubbed at it with my thumb, hoping it would come off easily, and swore loudly as I nicked my thumb on the edge of the blade. A bubble of red blossomed on my finger, and I stuck it in my mouth instinctively, sucking the pain away.

I realised my mistake almost instantly.

My vision blurred as the world started spinning. I grabbed for the wall to brace myself as vertigo threatened to overwhelm me. A face swam into my vision. I blinked until it solidified and Sarah's moss-green eyes stared at me from behind her black hipster glasses. My breath hitched in my throat. She looked scared.

"Ambrose." Her voice was accusing. "Ambrose – you did this."

"No," I said, shaking my head. This wasn't real. It couldn't be. Fear seized my heart in a stranglehold.

"You did this, Ambrose. This is your fault." Sarah's eyes were filled with hate.

"What?" I whimpered, clutching a hand to my aching head. "What did I do?"

Sarah's face flickered, and then a cascade of images bombarded my beleaguered eyes. A man strapped to a bed. A sobbing woman. White surgical gloves. A pale girl with freckles lying motionless in a hospital bed – Caitlynn.

Then, Cassie's sightless eyes staring at nothing.

"You did this, Ambrose," Sarah's voice echoed around my skull until it felt like my head would explode.

"No!" I shouted – and then my knees gave out and I tumbled to the floor.

Gasping for breath, I crouched on the ground, shaking as the fog lifted from my eyes and my living room came back into focus.

Five things you can see, I reminded myself as my heart tried to gallop out of my chest. The geometric pattern of the parquet floor. The dust bunnies collecting underneath my couch. A strip of wallpaper curling loose from that time I'd left the window open and a torrential downpour had warped the paper.

I climbed back onto my feet. My chest was still heaving, but a few deep breaths later I felt composed enough to realise that none of what I'd seen had been real. I'd imagined it all.

I glanced at the spear lying on the floor, its tip still covered in the snake's blood. That damn lamia had poisoned me! Somehow, its blood had twisted every fear I had and made it look like reality.

If that hallucination was what happened when the lamia's blood had entered my system, then I'd better get rid of it before anything like that happened again.

With the beginnings of what promised to be one hell of a headache pounding at my temple, I fetched a damp dishcloth from the kitchen and carefully wiped at the congealed lump stuck to the tip of the blade point. It was remarkably difficult to get off.

I swore under my breath as I rubbed at it, getting more annoyed by the second. In a fit of anger, I tossed the cloth onto the floor and was about to fling the spear too, before I caught myself just in time.

Why was this such a struggle?

I glared at the *rogatina*. I needed to get the damn thing cleaned. Not only was the leftover blood dangerous, but with my luck, it was probably acidic enough to burn into the metal. I bent down to retrieve the cloth and half-heartedly dabbed at the splotch again. Aversion filled me with every swipe.

This was just too much effort.

Disgusted, I flipped the switch and watched the blade disappear into the shaft. I could do this some other time.

I left the weapon and the dirty cloth on the dining table and went to take a shower, scrubbing at my skin as if I could wash away the horror of what I'd imagined, the terrifying images still burnt into my retinas.

Bloody Norton went on a rampaging killing spree, and yet he left that bloody lamia alive.

Bloody bastard.

✕✕✕

I woke up still groggy from headache tablets the next morning and avoided looking at the *rogatina* or thinking about the serpent on the loose while I spent the morning lying on my couch browsing the internet on my mobile, somehow convincing myself I was doing 'research', but mainly falling down a YouTube rabbit hole as I watched one video after another of crazy people baiting more conventional snakes.

Around noon my stomach reminded me I was more than a pair of eyeballs and a scrolling finger, and I dragged myself off the couch and out the door. I sent Sarah a quick text, asking if she'd join me for lunch, but I'd walked halfway into town before her response turned me down.

-- Wish I could, but I'm swamped. I'll catch up with you later, promise. --

Disheartened, I grabbed a seat at a busy coffee shop and whiled away an hour or two nursing a cup of disappointing coffee and gnawing on a lacklustre sandwich while I considered my options.

As I saw it, I could either go looking for the lamia – by now as hard to find as an empty seat on the Tube during rush hour – or I could wait it out and hope it would reveal itself somehow.

The latter seemed like the easiest option, but to appease my conscience, I decided to have another look at the place where I'd last seen it – and maybe pick up a trail I'd missed last night.

So resolved, I paid for my lunch and set out.

I swear I was on my way to Hyde Park, but somehow my feet carried me around its outskirts and the next thing I knew I was dodging the tourists clustered around Big Ben and found myself outside a certain shoemaker's shop. Twin rainbows arched across the cloudless sky as a bell tinkled and I entered the shop.

Caitlynn looked up to greet me and I staggered backwards as – for a moment – Sarah's voice howled around the inside of my skull again and images of last night's hallucination superimposed themselves over Caitlynn's features. Somehow, it seemed like she was both sleeping and screaming.

"Ambrose!" Daniel exclaimed, shattering the illusion and pulling me back into the present, blinking. "Just the guy I need to help me talk some sense into this one."

It took me another moment to notice the tension in the room. Caitlynn's hands were crossed, her posture strained, while my friend's freckled face was tinged with red. It looked like I'd caught them in the middle of a fight.

Before I could say something, the bell tinkled again and the door opened behind me. The way Daniel stiffened told me things were about to get worse.

"Oh, hey, Am."

I spun around to see Cassie standing in the

doorway. At least, I thought it was Cassie.

My sister was dressed in tight leather pants and a black tank top. Her shoulder-length brown hair had been slicked back, and her eyes were so heavily made up it looked like she'd escaped from an eighties pop video. Black knee-length boots completed the picture.

I cleared my throat, wondering how to ask the question tactfully, but instead it just dropped from my lips: "Did you join a biker gang, or is there a costume party I wasn't invited to?"

"What?" She gaped at me for a moment until the penny dropped. "No, silly, of course not. This is how I dress for work now."

"Work." I swallowed uncomfortably. "From the… nearest street corner?"

"If only!" Daniel huffed. "Your sister thinks she's Batman or something. She has this fool idea in her head of 'protecting the city'," he said, his fingers shaping air quotes. "And she's dragging my sister along for the ride!"

"It's not a foolish idea!" Cassie objected, and Caitlynn said at the same time: "I want to help!"

The look Daniel shot me spoke volumes – mostly about how this was my fault, and I'd better talk some sense into them.

"Hang on!" I said, turning towards Cassie. "You dropped out of university to do what, exactly?"

"I want to make the world a safer place," Cassie said, slowly, as if she were trying to explain something difficult to a toddler. "Look, Am – ever since I came out of hospital, I've been feeling…"

"I knew it!" I said, casting about for something made from silver.

"No! Not that," Cassie retorted, rolling her eyes at me. "Nearly dying makes you reconsider your life choices – and it feels like I've made all the wrong ones so far. I don't want to waste my time sitting in front of a computer all day doing things that will soon be done by AI anyway."

"And instead you're going to…?"

"Do what you do. Hunt creatures. Protect people. I listened to Father's stories too, when we were little. I'm just as qualified for the job as you are."

"Cassie…"

She folded her arms across her chest. "It's not your decision. It's my life. I decide."

"It's mine too," Caitlynn added. I turned to see her staring daggers at Daniel. "I didn't leave the farm just to be coddled by you instead."

"Fine," Daniel threw his hands into the air. "Let's assume I am coddling you – I'll stop. But that doesn't mean you get to chase after danger, too. You know how important –"

Caitlynn lifted a threatening finger at her brother. "Don't you start with that! I've had years of Mother telling me how important I am – for *raising babies*. I'm more than a set of ovaries."

"Of course you are," Daniel replied, flushing. "It's just that –"

"No!" Caitlynn stamped her foot and Daniel's mouth snapped shut. The two redheads glared at each other, neither willing to concede to the other.

I cleared my throat uncomfortably, turning back to Cassie. "What does Pavi think of this?"

Cassie pursed her lips, scowling. "It's not up to Pavi either."

Her expression softened, almost turning wistful. "She doesn't know," she admitted. "She's in India at the moment. Family crisis, or something."

She shrugged. "And she doesn't need to know, either. Not right now, anyway. Besides, Pavi doesn't know about werewolves and everything else, remember?" Cassie shot me a threatening look.

"And you're not going to tell her either. I'll tell her when the time is right."

I sighed. I knew exactly what that kind of secret did to a relationship.

Before I could object though, Caitlynn stormed past me.

"Come on, Cassie. Let's go. We don't need their permission."

My sister nodded, and the bell tinkled just before the door slammed shut behind them.

I turned towards Daniel. "What the hell?"

He sighed. "I know."

He slumped down onto the stool behind the counter. "The thing is, I agree with her. With both of them. They *do* get to decide for themselves. But this is not a good decision."

"How do we change their minds?" I asked, stomping irritably around the small space, resisting the urge to swipe shoes from their shelves in a fit of pique. How is it I'd seen a vision of both women in danger – and now this was suddenly happening?

"If I knew that, mate, my sister wouldn't be out there courting trouble right now."

I stopped dead in my tracks as it suddenly occurred to me just what flavour of danger they might come across. I swore loudly.

Daniel grimaced. "Something tells me I don't want to hear what you have to say."

"There's a lamia loose in the city."

Daniel cursed in Gaelic, and I nodded in agreement. I clearly didn't need to tell him how dangerous it was.

"It attacked me as I left the Repository, and I accidentally brought it with me. I lost track of it somewhere in Hyde Park."

"That's… not good." Daniel rubbed at his temple with one hand. "How do we find it?"

"We?"

"Yes. My sister's out there too, Ambrose."

"I don't know," I admitted. "My plan was just to go looking for it. You know – poke every bush in the park. Maybe look for tracks?" It had been a while since I last felt such a lack of ideas.

"Trust the luck?" the leprechaun asked drily.

I nodded. "Trust the luck."

Daniel rose to his feet. "Come on then. Let's get started. Sometimes you have to make your own luck."

✕✕✕

"If you were an enormous magical snake, where would you be?" I said as we wandered aimlessly through Hyde Park, half-heartedly peering into bushes and up trees.

It was a balmy late afternoon, the sounds of the city nearly drowned out by birdsong, and it seemed like half of London was taking the opportunity to enjoy the pleasant weather. We dodged joggers along the path, nodded politely at a patrolling policeman on his horse, and twice I had to kick a football back at a group of kids playing on the grass.

"How did it get out, anyway?" Daniel asked.

"Norton must've set it free when he escaped. It's been harassing everyone in the Repository ever since."

Just the memory of the snake's coils wrapped around me sent a shiver down my spine. I remembered the way its jaw had unhooked as it tried to devour Clint, and how it had jumped out from the shadows just before I'd reached the West Gate.

Something rustled in the tree above me, and I froze, my heart suddenly in my throat. I looked up just in time to see a shadow lunge towards me.

Yelling, I threw my hands up to protect my face. Whatever it was hit me full on – all claws and fur and teeth. I fought like a man possessed, lashing out with my hands until I grabbed something solid and tossed it away from me.

Panting, I gaped at Daniel, who was laughing so hard tears were rolling down his freckled cheeks.

Frowning, I turned towards the thing that had attacked me. It scrambled to its feet and scampered back towards the nearest tree, its little limbs carrying it quickly out of sight.

I huffed. A grey squirrel.

I'd been assailed by nothing more than an irritable rodent. Bloody pests.

The corners of Daniel's mouth twitched as he fell in beside me again, and I had to give him credit for trying to keep a straight face.

"So, Norton?" he asked as if nothing had happened. "That's the werewolf, right? What happened to him?"

"Amari killed him."

That sobered him up quick enough. "And you're still telling me the Repository is safe for my kind?"

"It's not like that," I said. Then I sighed. "To be honest, I don't know what's going on. I've been trying to find out the truth, but it's been so difficult. Everything feels difficult lately – you know what I mean?"

Daniel nodded. "I've noticed that, these past few days. I've found myself struggling with stupid things."

He prodded at a particularly lush patch of vegetation and we both held our breath, and then released it slowly when nothing else jumped out at us.

"There's this thing with Caitlynn, of course,

but even just work. I find myself giving up easily when the soles just won't line up as I'm trying to repair shoes. And the other day, a customer refused to pay full price – and I didn't argue with her. I just let her go."

His expression was pained, and I knew how difficult it must have been for a leprechaun to let someone walk away with money that was rightfully his.

"Amari said the world lost a trait when Norton died. I just wish I knew which one – it might explain all of this."

Daniel's eyes widened and I suddenly did know which trait had been lost.

Tenacity.

Daniel shot me an exasperated look. "It's tenacity, mate. I could have told you that. And that does explain a lot."

He shook his head, annoyed. "You have one wish left, by the way. Don't waste it, too."

Damn. I'd forgotten about the three wishes Daniel had given me when we'd first met. I'd used the first to inadvertently save myself from drowning, and now I'd squandered the second.

Still, it felt good finally knowing why I'd been so unfocussed the last few days, and why Cassie had given up on her studies. If I could somehow get the trait back into the world, perhaps I could get her back on track again too.

My phone buzzed and I pulled it out to see Sarah's name on the screen. Maybe she was finally ready for that coffee.

"Hi!" I answered, a smile already forming.

"Ambrose." My stomach dropped. Her voice was tight – something was wrong. "You'd better come to St Thomas. Bring Daniel if you can."

The smile slipped from my face as I glanced at Daniel.

He caught the look and his expression tensed. "We're on our way."

※※※

Sarah was waiting for us in the hospital foyer, her face drawn and her eyes rimmed red with exhaustion. She shot to her feet when she saw us and hurried over.

"Cassie?" I asked before she could even greet me, my heart thumping against my ribcage.

I hated this place with its minimalist furnishings and sterile white walls. I didn't want to remember the way my sister had looked that night when Norton had nearly killed her and she'd ended up here, fighting for her life. That night when it should have been my blood splashed across an alley's walls, not my sister's.

"She's alright," Sarah said, giving me a quick hug. The knot in my gut loosened slightly as her citrusy scent filled my nostrils, calming my rapidly beating heart.

But her face was grave when she pulled away from me and turned towards Daniel. "It's Caitlynn."

My friend's face paled visibly. "Where is she?" he rasped.

"Come, I'll take you to her."

We followed Sarah down a long corridor, my sneakers squeaking against the worn linoleum floors as I tried to keep up with her hurried pace.

"She's stable and out of the ER," Sarah said over her shoulder as we walked. "They've moved her into one of the bigger rooms, along with the others."

"Others?" I asked, shooting Daniel a confused look.

"That's why I'm here," Sarah said as she stopped

outside a closed door. "Multiple people have been attacked in various separate incidents since last night, all displaying the same injuries and symptoms. It's… unusual. I think the girls were just in the wrong place at the wrong time. Bad luck, more than anything else."

I winced at Sarah's choice of words, and saw Daniel clenching his jaw in response. He visibly steeled himself as he pushed the ward's doors open. I followed close behind him.

Maybe I should have expected it, but I wasn't ready for what I saw.

There were six beds in the ward, all filled with patients in various states of distress. Two of them were lying still, staring off into space with vapid expressions, but the man closest to the entrance was strapped to his bed, writhing frantically against his bonds while a nurse wearing white surgical gloves tried to hold his arm still enough to administer an injection.

Just like my vision.

Horrified, my gaze wandered to the woman in the bed across from him. She was scratching at her arms as if they were covered in thousands of mosquito bites, and the woman next to her was wailing loudly while she pulled at her hair. A beleaguered male nurse tried his best to calm her – unsuccessfully.

"There!" Daniel said, and I swallowed back bile. I already knew what I'd see.

Caitlynn lay in a bed in the far corner, her hair a red smear across the white hospital linen, her face nearly as pale as the sheets. Her eyes were closed. Bandages were wrapped all along one arm.

Cassie sat beside her, holding the hand of the unafflicted arm. The heavy black mascara she'd worn earlier traced dark rivulets down her cheeks, but otherwise she seemed uninjured.

I swallowed back a sense of guilty relief. At least that part of my vision had been wrong.

Daniel rushed over to his sister. "What happened?" he asked, his voice trembling.

Cassie glanced at me, shaking her head as a teardrop traced the shadowy path already drawn down her face. I was beside her in an instant, wrapping my arms around her as she came in to hug me. Her shoulders shook as she cried silently.

"It's alright," I whispered as I stroked her hair like I had when she'd been hurt when we were younger. "It's alright."

I held her until she stopped shaking.

Then she pulled away from me, wiping at her eyes, and turned to Daniel, who had taken her place beside his sister, his hand firmly clamped around Caitlynn's.

"It happened so fast," she said, her lower lip trembling as she fought to control her emotions. "Caitlynn saved me."

She turned towards me again, her bruised eyes sad. "She saved me."

Sarah put a comforting hand on Cassie's arm. "Tell us what happened," she said softly.

Cassie nodded, taking a deep breath, as if trying to find courage. "We were on our way to this cool pop-up art installation I'd heard about," she began. "We'd just come out of the Tube when we heard someone scream. A woman. I thought…" She bit her lip, grimacing. "I wanted to help. No –" she said as tears started leaking across her cheeks again. "I wanted to prove a point. Don't tell me I should have known better. I know I should have."

Her voice faltered for a moment, and her chin quivered. "Then a woman ran out of an alley, and I… I ran towards it. That's when… when it grabbed me."

She shuddered again, the horror of the memory

written across her tear-streaked face. "It was enormous. Some sort of... snake?"

Pain seared through my stomach, as if someone had punched me in the gut. I stared at my sister, my chest aching so intensely it must surely be bruised on the inside.

"It coiled itself around me," Cassie continued, her face blanching. "I couldn't breathe. I couldn't think. All I could see were its eyes. They were so... purple. And the only thought in my head was that I didn't want to die like that. Not like that."

I tore my gaze from my sister's stricken face and met Daniel's eyes. His jaw was clamped firmly shut, but I could read the accusation in his glare. I wanted to run away from my best friend's fury.

If only the lamia had eaten me in the Repository, then none of this would have happened.

"But you're alright," Sarah said softly, squeezing Cassie's arm again. "What happened next?"

"I don't know," Cassie replied. "One minute it was all I could do not to pass out, the next it was gone. My legs gave in, and I fell. And then Caitlynn screamed."

Cassie's voice was raw, and tears welled up in her eyes again as she looked at her friend. "The thing's fangs were in her arm, and she was screaming and screaming. I didn't know what to do. All I had on me was some pepper spray. I think I emptied the entire bottle in its eyes, and then it let go of her. It must have fled, because it was gone then, but she kept on screaming. I couldn't get her to stop, no matter what I said. That's when the police showed up. They brought us here."

I glanced at Sarah.

She confirmed with a nod and wrapped her arms around Cassie. My sister slumped against her, looking exhausted.

Daniel slammed the side of his fist into the wall, making us all jump. "My sister's been poisoned by a lamia," he snarled. His eyes bore into mine. "A lamia!"

It felt as if the universe convulsed into a funnel that pointed straight at me.

This was my doing.

I'd brought the lamia here, and I'd let it escape.

I could have prevented this, but I didn't.

Because it had felt like too much effort.

"What's a lamia?" Sarah asked.

I dropped my head into my hands as Daniel explained, his words clipped with anger. "A mythical snake. Deadly. Its venom causes hallucinations that can drive people mad."

Daniel was pointedly not looking at me, and yet his every word was a noose around my neck. "One recently escaped from the Repository."

To her credit, Sarah took the news of a supernatural snake loose in the city in stride, but a frown still pulled her brows down. "The Repository?" she asked, her eyes flicking towards me. "But that's somewhere in the mountains, isn't it? How did it get here?"

I knew what was going to come next. I'd already seen it in my flat while cleaning the snake's blood off the *rogatina*.

"I did this," I said, my voice hoarse. "This is my fault."

"Yes, it is," Daniel said, his words falling like a judge's gavel upon my conscience.

I wanted to run – away from my friend's anger, and away from the consequences of my decisions.

And then Daniel's gaze whipped towards Cassie. "Both of yours. If you don't mind, I'd like some time alone with my sister now."

Cassie's face was stricken, but she nodded and

pulled me away from the bed. I felt Sarah tucking her arm into mine as I followed my sister out of the ward. Like the lamia, guilt tried to swallow me whole as we passed the other victims. Most of them had quietened down now – probably drowned by sedatives – and laid in insensible stupor while the nurses checked their vitals.

"Are they all the same?" I asked Sarah as we stepped out into the hallway. How could the lamia have attacked so many people in such a short time?

She nodded. "We didn't know what to make of it. I should have known it was something… unusual."

"I'll fix it," Cassie declared. "Caitlynn saved me – and I can't just sit around and do nothing to help her."

Her face was streaked with tears, and I'd never seen her look so dishevelled, but I knew my sister and I knew that tone.

"No, you won't," I said adamantly. "I brought the lamia to London. I'll get rid of it."

She crossed her arms. "We can work together."

"No!"

I took a deep breath as Cassie scowled at me, anger blooming across her pale cheeks.

"No," I repeated, more calmly this time. "I don't want anything else happening to you."

"I'm not a child, Ambrose," she said, which convinced me even more that she had no idea what she was getting herself into.

"I know that," I said, trying to placate her. Huffing, I ran a hand through my hair. "Look, even Father said he didn't want you anywhere near the Repository. We just want to keep you safe."

That was the wrong thing to say.

Cassie let out a cry of frustration, and I saw a nearby nurse glaring in our direction.

"You don't get to decide for me!" Cassie screeched.

The nurse looked like she was about to come have a word with us.

Embarrassed, I tried to calm my sister down by reaching to pull her into a hug.

Cassie pushed me away with a huff before turning on her heels and storming off.

I tried to go after her, but Sarah caught my hand. "Let her go," she said softly.

"She'll get herself killed!" I protested.

Sarah's hand was warm in mine, but her tone was firm. "I know you want to protect her, Ambrose, and I get it. But this isn't the way. She needs to make her own decisions."

"But I –"

Sarah pressed a finger against my mouth. "If you want to keep her safe, go find that lamia before she does."

I blinked at her, my head trying to make sense of it all, but failing miserably. I felt numb, wracked by grief and shock and guilt. All I wanted to do was pull my girlfriend closer and forget all of this had ever happened.

As if sensing my thoughts, Sarah leaned into me, letting me put my arms around her. We stood there for a moment, her citrusy scent enveloping me as I tried to come to grips with everything.

She was right, of course. About all of it.

Someone cleared their throat, and we pulled apart to see a nurse sticking her head out of the ward.

"Detective Inspector?" she said, exhaustion audible in her voice. "Patient Three's awake again. She's talking, but I can't make any sense of it. I thought you'd want to hear for yourself?"

"I'm coming," Sarah said, and the nurse nodded before disappearing into the ward again. Sarah turned back to me, a question in her eyes.

"I know what I have to do," I said, sounding

much surer than I actually felt.

Sarah nodded, giving my hand a last squeeze.

"Stay safe," she said, and then she was gone.

I was halfway down the corridor before I realised that not once had Sarah said that any of it was my fault.

My vision had been wrong.

※※※

How do you find a mythical snake in a city like London?

The lamia could be anywhere, and with no clues to follow, it was like searching for a needle in a haystack. The only confirmed sighting was when it had attacked Cassie, but she hadn't been clear about exactly where that had happened.

I was sitting on the edge of one of the fountains in Trafalgar Square, watching the evening's stragglers make their way home. The last time I'd been here, Norton had tried to kill me.

My hand tightened around the *rogatina*'s shaft.

Norton. I didn't want to blame all of this on the dead werewolf…

But who was I kidding? I really did.

But I couldn't help but wonder how much the loss of Tenacity was influencing the world in general – and me in particular. If we'd still had the trait, would I have listened to Father and taken care of the lamia while it was still in the Repository?

Maybe Cassie wouldn't be in danger now.

I glanced down at my phone again. My sister still hadn't responded to any of my texts. I could tell she'd read them by the blue tick marks next to each message – so at least I knew she was still alive – but she steadfastly refused to respond.

For all I knew, she was back in that alley, trying

to confront the lamia on her own.

My head jerked up as a scream rent the air.

I was on my feet and running towards the sound before I knew what I was doing. The gleam of the Charing Cross Station's sign illuminated a girl – about Cassie's age – with her back against the base of some forgotten general's statue, clutching her purse – and a guy threatening her with a knife.

"Let her go," I said, suddenly so angry my hands were shaking. I was trying to save the city from a damn snake so large it could swallow a person whole – and this jerk was just making the world a worse place.

He turned towards me, all pumped up from adrenaline and who knows what. With a five o'clock shadow roughing his cheeks and a port wine stain splattered across his left eye, he looked like nothing so much as the nameless goon from a bad cop movie.

"Yeah?" he sneered, waving the knife in my direction. "And who's gonna make me? You? Big guy with a stick!"

Somewhere at the back of my head, a voice was warning me of potential death, murder, mayhem – but honestly, by this point, I was over it. A man with a knife was nothing compared to a psychotic werewolf, or a raging chimaera, or a vengeful asrai.

The *rogatina*'s spearpoint flicked into place, dried droplets of the lamia's crimson blood glinting in the light from the station's sign.

The goon's eyes widened. I could see him weighing up his odds – comparing his weapon with mine.

"I'm not going to ask again," I said through gritted teeth.

I don't know what he saw in my face or heard in my voice – or maybe the loss of Tenacity was finally working in my favour – but the man's face paled and he lowered his knife.

"Alright, alright," he said. "Take it easy, man. I didn't mean no harm."

And then he bolted, sprinting past the railings and down the steps, and disappeared into the Tube station.

I turned to the girl. Her mascara was leaking across her cheeks – much like Cassie's had earlier – and I waved her off.

"Go home," I said with a sigh. "But – don't take the Tube."

The girl nodded, her bottom lip quivering. She tightened her grip on her purse and scurried off.

I gritted my teeth as I watched her go. This could so easily have been Cassie, preyed upon by some random ruffian in the dark. And now she thought she could catch the lamia!

Frustrated, I pulled my phone out again. Still no response from my sister. She could stumble upon that snake any moment now and I didn't even know where to look for it!

I needed help, and there was only one person I could think of.

I dialled Amari's number. It went straight to voicemail. I sent her a message instead.

-- Father told me what happened with Norton. Good riddance, if you ask me. Can you call me? I desperately need your help with something that escaped from the Repository. --

I watched the screen for a moment. One tick showed the message was sent, but the second tick to confirm delivery didn't appear.

Wherever Amari was, she was not going to come to my rescue.

Huffing, I put my phone away and dipped the

rogatina's blade in one of the square's fountains, watching with a grim satisfaction as the last of the snake's blood dissolved into the water. That, at least, was something I didn't need to worry about anymore.

Much as I hated the thought, Cassie was just going to have to look after herself tonight. I wasn't going to accomplish anything more. Might as well go home.

Maybe my luck would be back by morning.

※ ※ ※

If the triple rainbows arching across St Thomas were any indication, luck was in abundance the next day.

Whether or not that luck was good was debatable, judging by the glower with which Daniel greeted me as I hesitated in the doorway of the private room he'd had Caitlynn moved to.

I fidgeted with the bouquet of daffodils I'd brought, wondering if I should go. To my relief, Daniel's face smoothed out into a haggardness that looked more tired than mad. He beckoned me in, and I swallowed a relieved sigh.

"How is she?" I asked as I placed the flowers on her bedside table.

"Not good," he said, knuckling his eyes. "She woke up screaming twice during the night. The doctor had to sedate her. And now she's in an induced coma."

The words drained the strength from my limbs. An induced coma. It sounded like surrender, a last resort when nothing else could be done.

I hated how easily I sank into the second chair by her bedside, how I didn't argue or demand more answers. I should be out there fighting for her, like my sister was. Instead, I just sat there, too numb to do anything but stare.

Caitlynn lay very still – as pale as the hospital sheets tucked around her – but her eyes twitched beneath closed lids, caught in some fevered dream. Or maybe a nightmare.

"It's the visions," Daniel said, as if reading my thoughts. "Lamia venom causes hallucinations. If left untreated, they can lead to madness."

I tasted guilt again. "What can I do?"

"I don't know," my friend said, a tremor in his voice that he tried to hide behind a yawn. "I don't know what the cure is."

"But you must know someone," I said, frustrated. Daniel always knew someone.

He shook his head. "Not this time. Not for this."

"What if we…" I hesitated, not sure I wanted to upset my friend even more than he already was.

He shot me an enquiring look.

"What if we moved her to the Repository? Hear me out –" I said as his eyes filled with alarm. "It has a powerful Word of Healing over it. I should know – it saved my life when the asrai's curse was still flowing in my veins. Nobody needs to know what she is while she's there."

It's a measure of how desperate he was that he actually took a moment to consider the idea.

Then he shook his head. "No, I can't risk that. If the Council somehow found out… No. She'd be trapped even worse than she had been at the farm – and it would put the whole family in danger, too. Thank you. I know you mean well – and I trust you, but I can never trust the Council."

I nodded before slumping back into the seat. Was I imagining it, or did it feel slightly warm? Like someone else had been sitting in it recently.

Daniel yawned again, and I said: "Why don't

you go home? I can stay with her for a bit while you get some rest."

To my surprise, Daniel nodded. "Thanks," he said. "But you don't have to stay."

"I want to," I replied – maybe a little more forcefully than I'd meant to, because Daniel's forehead rumpled into a frown as he stared at me.

"Look, I know you blame me for what happened. And you're right!" I added hastily, before he could protest. "It's my fault the lamia is here. I should've taken care of it when I could, and I didn't. I'm sorry. I'll understand if you don't want to leave Caitlynn alone with me, but you're my friend and she's my responsibility too."

A twinkle of humour returned to Daniel's blue eyes and a smile tucked at the corners of his mouth. "Thank you, Ambrose. That means a lot to me. But you really don't have to stay."

His eyes focussed on something behind me and I heard someone clearing their throat.

"You're a good friend, Ambrose – and Daniel is lucky to have you."

I turned around to see Mary Brady standing behind me, holding two cups of steaming coffee. Even though I knew she must have travelled through the night and very early this morning to be here now, having come from the family estate in Ireland, only the lines around her eyes betrayed the worry Daniel and Caitlynn's mother must have felt. Her greying auburn hair was tied up in a neat bun and her lacy sleeves were pulled up, as if she was about to pull a freshly baked loaf of bread from the oven.

I jumped up off the seat. "Mrs Brady! I didn't realise... I'm so sorry about what happened to Caitlynn!" I stammered, offering her the chair. "I promise I'm going to make this right again."

"I know you will, Ambrose," she said, accepting

the seat and handing the second coffee to Daniel. "Because I know you understand just how important Caitlynn is to us. She should never have come here."

"Not this again, Ma," Daniel sighed.

"Yes, this again!" Mary exclaimed. "You should have sent her home the moment she arrived. She doesn't belong here."

"She has a right to her freedom," Daniel said, his freckled face taking on a reddish tinge. "You couldn't keep her locked away forever."

"At least she was safe there," Mary fumed. "Your father and I were just about to send out invitations to her debutante ball when she ran off. It's all the Families have been talking about for months."

"I don't care about the gossip, Ma!" Daniel exclaimed. "She's more than an asset to be sold off to the highest bidder! She's your daughter!"

Mary's face went cold. "How *dare* you?" she said, her voice low and her body rigid with barely controlled anger. "You have no idea how much I care about her."

I shifted uncomfortably. "Perhaps I should go…"

"No," Daniel said, rising to his feet. "We'll both go. You're right – I need to get some rest. I'm sure Caitlynn will be perfectly safe while Ma's at her side."

He stormed through the door, leaving me alone with his mother in a moment of uneasy silence. I turned to Caitlynn again, oblivious to the family drama playing off around her. For a moment, I wished I could drop into a coma too to escape the awkward situation.

"I'd better go…" I said, turning towards the door.

Mary took a deep breath and ran her hand down the front of her dress, smoothing the fabric down. "You know what lamia venom can do to a woman, don't you, Ambrose?"

I cast my thoughts back to the conversation I'd had with Father, not too long ago.

Nightmares and childlessness.

A chill of realisation spiked down my spine. Caitlynn had been cloistered on the farm because female leprechauns were so rare. The only daughter in a family of seven children, Mary was worried about more than just her daughter. She was concerned about the very survival of their kind.

My horror must have been visible on my face, because Mary said: "I know you'll do your best to save her in time."

Something was lodged in my throat, and all I could do was nod wordlessly. I don't know if I said goodbye or not, but I stumbled out of the waiting room in a daze and wandered towards the exit, barely aware of my surroundings.

Daniel hadn't waited for me, thankfully. I didn't know how I'd face my friend, knowing what I knew now.

And it was too much.

I'd said I'd fix it, but I didn't know what to do. I didn't know where the lamia was, and I didn't know how to cure Caitlynn from its venom before... Before it was too late. For all I knew, it was too late already.

An anguished yell pulled me from my own tortured thoughts, and I realised I was standing just outside the ward where the lamia's other victims were being taken care of. I ducked my head in and saw Sarah talking to a tall, but slightly stooped man wearing a white lab coat that had seen better days. Thin, wire-framed glasses perched on the bridge of his sharp, angular nose, and his wavy blond hair had a slightly unkempt look.

Sarah waved me over when she noticed me, her voice briskly professional as I gripped the man's hand in greeting.

"Dr Elliot Grayson, this is Ambrose Davids, a private investigator helping me out on this case."

The man's pale blue eyes narrowed as he assessed me with an almost clinical intensity – and I felt for all the world like a lab rat under a microscope. When he spoke, his words were clipped but laced with an underlying curiosity. "It's not often that the Metropolitan Police consult with civilians."

"It's not often they have to deal with anything as unusual as this," I said, wondering how much Sarah had told the man. Did he know the victims had all been attacked by a supernatural snake? If so, he was playing it pretty cool.

"Ambrose is somewhat of a specialist," Sarah said, giving me a significant look. "Dr Grayson is a forensic toxicologist. He's helped me in the past with cases that involved unusual poisonings."

"Unusual, indeed," Dr Grayson said, turning towards the patient in the bed. "I've worked with cobra venom, batrachotoxin, and ricin, but I've never seen anything like this. Hallucinations, severe fever and manic delirium – caused by neurotoxin, hemotoxin, or something else? By all rights, this man should be dead already."

I turned towards the patient, straining against his bonds while his eyes moved rapidly behind closed lids. I inhaled sharply as I saw the red stain across his left eye.

"I know him," I said. "He was in Trafalgar Square last night, harassing a young woman."

"That checks out with the paramedic's statement," Sarah confirmed, glancing at her notepad. "They brought him in after someone found him lying on the platform at Charing Cross."

"But what did this to him?" Dr Grayson asked, running his fingers through his hair. He was staring at the patient as if he were a puzzle to be solved – and I wasn't quite sure if he was frustrated, or intrigued.

I shot Sarah a glance, and she nodded, slowly. She seemed to trust Grayson, but I still wasn't sure how much to tell him. I might not be working for the Council anymore, but my promise to Amari and my duty to the creatures inside the Repository still weighed heavy on my conscience.

Still, the man couldn't help us if he didn't have the facts.

I cleared my throat. "We think it was a lamia."

Dr Grayson turned to me, his brows furrowing. "A what?"

"It's a… type of snake. Exotic. Very rare." I resisted the impulse to run my hands through my hair too. "Highly venomous."

"I can see that, Davids," he replied irritably. "But I've never heard of a – what did you call it? – a lamia? What's its scientific classification?"

"I have no idea," I admitted. "But is that really important? All we need is a cure for its bite."

Grayson huffed. "How do you expect me to do anything if I don't know what I'm dealing with? I'll need a sample of the venom at the very least. Without that, all I have is observation and speculation. Hardly enough to work with."

"Ambrose will get it," Sarah said confidently.

I grunted. If I hadn't cleaned the *rogatina* in the fountain last night, we'd be halfway to a cure right now. Now I'd have to come up with a different plan.

"Let's say I manage to get my hands on some of its venom…" I said, an idea forming. "How long would it take to develop a cure?"

The toxicologist shrugged. "Hard to say at this point. Bring me a sample, then we'll find out."

Right. I didn't know where to find the lamia, but getting my hands on some of its venom might be easier than hunting the creature down.

All I needed to do was make a phone call.

※※※

Signal inside the Repository was unreliable but, to my surprise, Father answered his phone almost immediately. "Ambrose! I was just thinking of you this morning. Are you still travelling or have you made it back to London yet?"

"What?" I asked, leaning on a railing next to the Thames. A cool mist wafted from the river, and I zipped my jacket up to keep the chill out.

It took me a moment to realise he didn't know about anything that had happened since we'd last talked. He thought I was making my way leisurely back home by train.

"Oh, no, I'm in London." I cleared my throat guiltily. "Have you noticed the lamia is no longer in the Repository?"

A pause on the other end of the line. Then: "No one has seen it in a while. I assumed it was lying low somewhere. Something tells me that's not the case."

"It's loose in London," I said, and heard him gasp.

"How?" he demanded, sounding more intrigued than worried.

I waved my hand in the air. "Not important. What is important, is that it's attacked several people. I need to know: is there a cure for its poison?" It was worth a shot.

"If there is, I haven't found mention of it in my research."

I grimaced. "Then please tell me you have a sample of its venom?"

"No," Father huffed. "Amari never allowed it while she was still in charge, and I didn't have the opportunity after she'd left."

I felt my hopes plummet down a long chute and dash to pieces at the bottom.

"Tell me – these victims…" Father continued, unfazed. "Are they suffering from hallucinations?"

"I think so," I said. "They're keeping them sedated mostly, but you can see them dreaming behind closed eyes."

"Fascinating," Father breathed, and I felt annoyance crawling like ants underneath my skin. It's as if he didn't care that there were real people suffering.

"Look, I have to go…" I said, pulling a hand through my hair. My easy solution was a dead end, and I was rapidly running out of time.

Caitlynn was running out of time.

"I trust you to return the lamia to where it belongs, Ambrose," Father said. "Just pop me a text when you have it. I'll send a team to come pick it up. And Ambrose…" For the first time, a hint of worry crept into his voice. "Keep your sister safe."

"Of course," I said, trying not to choke on guilt before ending the call.

I groaned as I stared at the water of the Thames, hoping to find an answer in its murky depths. It felt like there was an airavata sitting on my chest, weighing down on me until it was almost too difficult to breathe.

Everything was too difficult. I couldn't bear it any longer.

I needed a break.

I needed a good long walk to clear my head.

※※※

The sky was a cloudy grey as I strode aimlessly around the streets of London.

The lamia's victims had been found in various places around the inner city. It could be anywhere. How was I to know where to look? From what I'd seen in the Repository, it liked to hide in the shadows before it attacked. Would it even come out during the day? Was I wasting my energy trying to find a supernatural snake while the sun was out?

Suddenly, a scaly green serpent caught the corner of my eye, and I flinched, my body freezing on instinct. Around me, I heard people huffing as the river of pedestrians swerved to avoid me. I swallowed down my embarrassment as my heart rate recovered. It was just a banner flapping in the breeze.

Before me stood the gates leading to the British Museum. The snake that had startled me was just one of many writhing on the head of a woman with angry, blazing eyes, her mouth agape in a silent scream.

Medusa.

It was an advertisement for the museum's current special exhibition.

Was it just me, or were there too many snakes in town right now?

At the same time – in the reflection of a shop window – I noticed that someone else had stopped in their tracks when I had. Coincidence? Or was someone following me?

I thrust my hands into my jacket pocket and started walking again, slowly, trying to keep an eye on the people around me.

Abruptly, I stopped and dropped to my knees, pretending to tie a shoelace. I glanced behind me, ignoring the angry mutters of people veering past me again, just in time to see someone ducking out of sight and into an alley.

I was definitely being followed.

Rising slowly, I considered the situation. It could be my old friend, Stalker, the rogue Procurement Specialist who kept popping up whenever he was least welcome. He might be after the lamia too, following me with the hope that I'd lead him straight to it.

Honestly, if he wanted it – he could have it.

Or perhaps it was the Huntress? It wouldn't be the first time that she'd swept in and taken care of something I was supposed to handle. I wouldn't mind her help – but I couldn't let her take the lamia before I took a sample of its venom first.

Either way, it was probably best to confront whoever it was first, before we came to blows. We might be able to work together to capture the monster.

I stepped into the alley, too.

Cloaked in shadow by overhanging buildings, all I could see were a row of skips lining one side, their metal lids dented and rust-streaked, the stench of rotten cabbages emanating from them warring with the stink of urine permeating the small space. Somewhere in the distance, a siren wailed, its sound bouncing between the buildings before fading into the London hum.

Something darted past and I nearly cried out before the cat, its black fur matted and smeared with grime, disappeared behind a stack of wooden crates. It knocked over a discarded glass bottle that rolled noisily along the uneven pavement and came to a stop beside my feet.

I tensed.

This was the perfect place for an ambush, and if the lamia was lurking nearby, I'd just stepped into its hunting ground. My hand strayed to the silver whistle I still carried around my neck. I don't know who'd come to my aid if I were to blow on it, but it felt reassuring to have it with me, just in case.

"I know you're in here," I said, more confidently than I felt. "Come out now and we'll talk this through."

Silence.

And then a shadow extricated itself from behind one of the skips. I held my breath as it moved closer. The figure lunged – or maybe just shifted – but it was more than my nerves could handle.

Adrenaline spurted through my veins – and I moved before I could think. I slammed into the figure, pushing it up against a wall.

I recognised her an instant too late.

Pain exploded between my legs as she kicked me in the groin and – as stars flooded my vision – she shoved me roughly. I slipped on the slick pavement, damp with what I hoped was just rainwater, and crashed into the stack of crates. The cat screeched, and pain blossomed across my hand as it raked its claws across my skin. Then it darted back into the shadows with a ferocious hiss.

"What the hell, Ambrose?" Cassie yelled, glaring at me with her hands on her hips.

"Sorry, sorry!" I said, wincing as I rubbed my injured hand. What was with the random violence from small animals these days? "I didn't know it was you."

"Well, who did you think it was?" she demanded, still fuming.

I grunted. "Not important. What were you doing following me?"

"I told you: I want to help catch the lamia."

I shook my head. "It's too dangerous."

She gave me an incredulous look. "I think I

can take care of myself," she retorted, eyeing me meaningfully, still slumped over in pain.

"Point taken," I groaned. "I'm sorry I attacked you."

A smile tugged at the corners of her lips. "And I'm sorry I kicked you... there." I winced, but managed to stand upright again. "Are you going to be alright?"

"I'll be fine," I muttered. My ego was more bruised than anything else, really. She fell into step beside me as I hobbled back to the main street.

The first thing that caught my eye again was the banner of Medusa, still flapping in the breeze. Legend said she'd been cursed by the gods, twisted into something monstrous. Wasn't that what had happened to the lamia too?

"All I'm saying is..." I said, turning my attention back to my sister. "I don't want you to get hurt. Seeing you in the hospital like that nearly broke me. I can't let that happen again."

Cassie nodded. "I get it, Am, I really do. But I'm not a porcelain doll. You can't keep me wrapped up in bubble wrap."

"Damn, I'm going to have to cancel my bulk order then," I quipped.

"I'm serious, Am!"

"I know, I know," I said, lifting my hands in surrender. I still had no intention of letting her get anywhere near the lamia – but perhaps she could help in other ways. An idea sparked and a smile slipped across my face.

"What do you say we go do some research? Learn more about mythical snakes?" I nodded toward the museum.

Excitement sparkled in Cassie's eyes as her gaze caught the banner. She'd been just as enthralled by Father's stories as I'd been when we were little. I knew she couldn't resist.

"Good idea!" she said. "I'll race you to the foyer!"

She sprinted across the road, her brown hair bobbing as she ran.

I chuckled as I set out after her.

Perhaps I could keep her safe a little longer after all.

✳✳✳

Everywhere I looked, images of snake-haired Medusa confronted me. She was on vases and urns, her belligerent gaze glared at me from both classical and contemporary paintings displayed on every wall of the special exhibition wing, and there was even an enormous rug woven from a collage of book covers retelling the myth for a modern audience.

"Over here," Cassie said, grabbing my arm and pulling me towards a small auditorium to one side where people were already taking their seats.

I paused in front of a noticeboard: *Medusa, Misunderstood Monster.* Apparently, a Dr Sarff from Cardiff University would be telling us more about the myth in a few minutes.

I already knew the story, but I settled into a chair next to Cassie towards the back of the room.

It wasn't long before a coffee-skinned woman wearing glasses with polarised lenses and a green headwrap stepped up behind the podium. When she spoke, her voice had more than a hint of a Welsh accent to it. I frowned. She looked strangely familiar.

"Welcome, ladies and gentlemen," she began. "I'm Dr Rhiannon Sarff and you're here to learn more about Medusa – the fearsome monster with a head of snakes and a gaze that turned her enemies to stone."

Her own hidden gaze swept across the small crowd, and a shiver crawled down my spine as it paused on me for a second before moving on. Where did I know her from?

"For those of you not familiar with Medusa's story," Dr Sarff continued, "let me give you a brief overview. She was a priestess of Athena – the Greek goddess of wisdom – and known for her beauty – especially her beautiful hair. You know how the story goes: she caught the eye of a god." The crowd chuckled knowingly. "Poseidon – god of the sea – wouldn't take no for an answer and had his way with Medusa in Athena's temple. As you can imagine, the virgin goddess was none too pleased with her place of worship being defiled in such a way, and so she cursed her priestess and turned the once-beautiful girl into the monster we all know today."

Beside me, Cassie's hand shot into the air, and I tried to disappear into my chair as Dr Sarff's gaze focused on my sister.

"Go ahead," the speaker said.

I shuffled my chair a little to the side as everyone turned towards Cassie.

"Why would Athena punish her priestess?" she asked, and I sighed. It was a question that had bothered her ever since we'd been children. Father had never really had an answer that had satisfied her. "Medusa was a victim. She didn't deserve to be cursed. If anything, Poseidon should have taken the blame."

"What makes you say Medusa was punished?" Dr Sarff asked.

Cassie stared back at her, for a moment at a loss for words. "Well, snakes for hair?" she said tentatively, and I saw a few other people nod emphatically as they agreed with her. "And she killed anyone she looked at it. Sounds like punishment to me."

"Does it?" There was a hint of annoyance in Dr Sarff's tone. "Some would say Athena gave Medusa a formidable power with which to defend herself. She was not a helpless girl anymore – she was an intimidating monster. A woman not to be trifled with. What the goddess gave Medusa was empowerment. She would never be a victim again. Instead, she'd be the one to decide who lives or dies. Sounds like a gift to me."

A murmur rose as the crowd considered these words. I sat back in my chair, feeling like I'd been struck by a bolt of lightning.

Choice. This was what it was all about – the freedom to make your own decisions.

That's all Cassie wanted.

And, come to think of it, that's also what the asrai had been trying to tell me all this time. When I'd put her in the Repository, I'd taken her right to choose away from her.

I shook my head. No, the asrai had given up any rights she might have had by trying to kill me. She deserved to be locked away.

But she didn't deserve to be exploited any more than Medusa had deserved it.

"You don't agree with me, sir?"

My attention snapped back to the moment, and I saw all eyes in the room turned towards me.

Dr Sarff was leaning forward on the podium, and although I couldn't see her eyes behind the tinted glasses, I somehow felt like she was glaring at me. Almost as if I'd personally offended her.

"No, I agree," I blurted. I caught Cassie's eye and knew she was thinking the same thing as I was. The lamia hadn't exactly endeared itself to either of us. And before that, I hadn't been overly fond of Stavros' serpent-headed tail either. "But… snakes?"

More people laughed in agreement.

Dr Sarff's pose relaxed. "Not an uncommon objection," she acknowledged. "Snakes have had a bad reputation ever since the Garden of Eden. And yet, you might find it interesting to know that in Greek mythology, they were associated with the gift of prophecy. Remember the Oracle of Delphi?" Her gaze swept across the room again, the audience once more quiet in rapt attention.

"The Oracle – also known as the Pythia – was named for a monstrous snake that had been slain by the god Apollo. The rotting vapours from its decomposing body was said to have induced the trance from which the priestess prophesied."

"Are you saying Medusa could see the future?" I asked, stunned. Belatedly, I lifted my hand and then dropped it sheepishly again, as a smile tickled at the corners of Dr Sarff's mouth.

"Perhaps," she said. "A helpful gift, wouldn't you say?"

"Not helpful enough," Cassie spoke up. "It didn't save her."

"And this is where a Greek hero enters the story," Dr Sarff said, her chin lifting to an almost haughty angle. "Perseus – son of another woman who had caught a god's eye – was sent to kill Medusa. With the aid of a reflective shield provided by Athena herself, he crept up on the sleeping Medusa and lopped off her head. Hero, indeed," she added drily.

I shifted uncomfortably in my seat. When we were little, Father had let us watch *Clash of the Titans* one Sunday afternoon. I still remembered clearly how terrified we'd been, watching Perseus and his men creep into the monster's lair – and how she'd picked them off one by one until he was the only man left. In the movie, Perseus didn't kill Medusa while she was asleep, but he also didn't confront her heroically. He hid behind a pillar and just chopped her head off as she happened to slither past.

I'd been so disappointed by this anticlimax that I didn't even watch the rest of the film.

"And so, to commemorate this heroic act of bravery…" More chuckling from the audience. "Athena placed the image of Medusa's head on a shield and gave it to Perseus as a gift. It became his personal emblem – and her power became his instead."

Cassie's hand was in the air again. "If – like you said – Athena didn't punish Medusa, why did she help Perseus kill her?"

Dr Sarff shrugged. "The Olympians were not all-powerful. They had laws, politics, rivalries. Athena couldn't openly defy Poseidon – a fellow Olympian, and one of the three most powerful gods in the Greek pantheon. But she could shift the balance in Medusa's favour – and so the goddess transformed her. And when a son of Zeus set out to kill Medusa, Athena couldn't directly oppose him without risking the wrath of the king of the gods. So, what did she do? Instead of letting Perseus erase Medusa – she helped immortalise her. She took her likeness and placed it on her shield, the very emblem of divine protection. A symbol that could strike fear into her enemies. Do you see? Medusa did not disappear – she became a legend. She became a weapon of the gods. And even today, her name is not forgotten."

Someone at the front of the room raised their hand to ask a question, and as Dr Sarff responded, I let my mind wander. Something about the woman's words unsettled me.

Or maybe it was just her.

I played distractedly with the silver whistle tied around my neck, wondering where I'd seen her before.

And then something in the air changed. Dr Sarff faltered.

It was brief – so quick that most of the audience wouldn't have noticed – but I caught it. Her lips parted as if she'd lost her train of thought, her fingers tightening subtly on the podium's edge. Her head tilted, just a fraction, in my direction.

A prickle ran down my spine.

Slowly, her gaze swept the room again, but when it passed over me this time, it lingered.

Was she looking at me? No, at... I glanced down at my hand, where the whistle gleamed under the auditorium's lights. I tucked it out of sight, but it was too late. Dr Sarff's reaction was unmistakable.

She straightened abruptly, tugging at her headwrap. "Well, I believe that's all we have time for today. Thank you for your attention."

The audience murmured in confusion as Dr Sarff turned away, her movements stiff and precise. Without another glance at the room, she disappeared through the side door, leaving behind an air of unfinished business.

Cassie frowned. "That was sudden."

I nodded, still feeling uneasy. "Come on, let's go look at the rest of the exhibition."

I left my sister to study the oil paintings on her own – she'd always been more interested in art than I had – while I wandered over to the ancient relics section.

I drifted past a display case housing a set of bronze helmets, their surfaces dulled with age and etched with a relief of Medusa's severed head. A plaque explained that warriors once believed her gaze could still turn enemies to stone – even in death.

Beyond the helmets stood an amphora depicting

Perseus in mid-stroke, Medusa's eyes wide and fearful as she watched the descending blade. I moved on, drawn to a fragment of marble taken from an ancient temple. It was smoothed by time, but you could still make out snakes coiling around a beautiful woman's head.

I wondered how much of the legend was wrapped in fear – fear of the unknown, of powerful women, of creatures that defied the expected norms? Misunderstood monsters, indeed.

As I studied the artifacts, my attention caught on a small room off to one side, its entrance barred by a velvet rope. A placard beside it read: *Gorgoneion. Strictly special ticket holders only.*

I glanced around. No one was watching me, or the door.

Curious, I slipped past the barrier and stepped inside.

A single glass display unit stood in the middle of the room. Inside it, on a marble plinth, stood an enormous bronze shield, polished until it was almost as reflective as a mirror. It was embossed with Medusa's anguished face, her lips contorted in a scream. Lightning bolts shot from her eyes and a myriad of snakes writhed around her head.

"Beautiful, isn't she?"

Goosebumps broke out across my skin as Dr Sarff stepped out from behind the shield. My own startled expression was reflected back at me in the polarised lenses of her glasses.

I cleared my throat to hide my unease. "Is this Perseus' shield?"

My eyes followed her as she walked past me and softly closed the door. I turned away from the shield to face her. I had a very bad feeling about this.

"Tell me, Hunter," she said as she slowly started

to unwind her headwrap. "Why are you here?"

My throat dried up as she removed the material and a nest of emerald snakes uncoiled from around her head.

Snakes, instead of hair.

Fear somersaulted around my insides as I suddenly realised why she'd looked so familiar. I'd seen her once before, sitting at the bar of the *Dragon's Roar* in Cardiff.

I took a step away from her, unable to wrench my eyes away from the serpents writhing across her scalp. "You're a… a medusa," I stuttered.

Sarff sighed, exasperated. "Medusa died a long time ago, as you should be well aware after my talk earlier. I am what she was turned into – a gorgon. And I am not going willingly into the Council's prison." She reached for her glasses.

"I'm not looking for trouble," I said, quickly averting my eyes, my heart banging against my chest. I had no wish to end up a stone statue in the museum's classical section. "I'm looking for help."

"Why should I help you?" I watched Sarff in the glass display's reflection. My stomach churned at the sight of the snakes coiling about her head. "You wear the Council's whistle. And…"

I risked a glance at her face. Her lips were turned down in distaste. "And I've seen a vision of you, armed with a bloodied spear. You bring only death. I should rid the world of you now."

She plucked the glasses from her face, and I snapped my eyes shut, sucking in a breath. It had never occurred to me that someone would see me as the monster to be slain. I didn't care much for the thought.

"I don't work for the Council," I said. Every muscle in my body was tense, and my ears strained to listen for movement. It took all my willpower not to open my eyes and make a run for it. "I'm only trying to save a friend."

"Why should I care about that?" she shot back.

"Because you're not the monster they make you out to be."

Silence followed, in which the hissing of her snakes suddenly seemed deafening in the small room. A bead of sweat rolled down my back, and my palms were slippery with fear.

When she finally spoke, her voice was grudging. "Tell me more."

I exhaled slowly, and risked opening my eyes, although I kept my gaze on her reflection in the glass display case. A good thing too, because she hadn't put her glasses back on. She stood with her arms folded across her chest and – more disconcertingly – the snakes' heads were all turned towards me, unblinking, as if waiting to hear what I had to say.

I swallowed some moisture back into my throat. "There's a lamia loose in London."

Sarff tensed, and her snakes burst into agitated motion around her face. "So that's what you're hunting. And you'll kill it when you find it." It was not a question.

Of course not. She'd seen it happen in a vision.

I felt the air grow heavy with the potential for violence.

"It doesn't have to come to that," I said carefully. "But it can't stay in London. I have to take it back to the Repository."

"No. I can't allow that."

She glared at me, and I watched her hands carefully, ready for the moment when she'd try to attack me – or force me to look straight into her eyes.

My fingers twitched. If I reached for the silver whistle now, there'd be no going back.

"Ambrose?" My eyes snapped towards the

door as it opened. Cassie popped her head in. "Are you in here?"

"Don't come in here!" I said – but it was too late.

Cassie stepped into the room, her smile slipping and her eyes widening as she saw Dr Sarff's exposed snakes.

She froze.

And then her skin started blistering with patches of grey. I watched in horror as the grey spread rapidly until her entire body was encased in stone.

"No!" I roared.

I slammed my elbow into the display case, hoping to smash it and grab Perseus' shield, but my elbow just bounced off the shatterproof glass. I grunted in pain.

Clenching my eyes shut again, I reached for the whistle.

"Don't be a fool, Ambrose!" Sarff's voice was in my ear, her icy hand clamped around my wrist. The hissing of snakes right next to me sent a shiver down my spine. "I'm sure we can come to some sort of agreement."

"You killed my sister!" I spat.

My entire body was shaking with shock and rage. Blood rushed in my ears, almost drowning out the hissing.

Why did I not have my *rogatina* with me? I wanted to slice those slithering serpents from Sarff's head, the way I'd sliced off Stavros' tail.

"Calm yourself," the gorgon said, her voice as cold as the blood running through her veins must be. "She's not dead."

I stilled. "What?"

"Open your eyes," Sarff said. "It's quite safe."

My eyelids snapped open – and my knees threatened to give in as my gaze landed on Cassie.

She was a perfect statue, carved from rock as if Michelangelo himself had created her. Her eyes stared back at me sightlessly – accusingly.

Just like in my vision.

Sarff released my wrist and I stumbled towards my sister. I flinched at the cold stone that met my fingertips.

"I can tell you how to reverse the curse. If you do something for me."

I spun around, barely able to keep a rein on my anger.

The gorgon faced me calmly. My own face, flushed red with anger, stared back at me again in the reflection from her lenses.

I took a deep breath. "What do you want?"

The gorgon's lips curled into a cold smile.

⁂

"Are you alright, mate?"

I blinked the world back into focus and found myself standing in the doorway to Caitlynn's hospital room. A faint antiseptic smell filled my nose and the steady beeping of a monitor showed that Daniel's sister, at least, was still alright – for now.

Daniel's lips were still pursed in permanent worry, but he looked much better after he'd had some rest – his eyes weren't bloodshot anymore, and he'd changed his clothes into something a little less rumpled.

"Of course he's not alright. Just look at him!" Mary's gaze swept over me, her lips thinning. She stepped closer, concern lining her face. Then she put a motherly arm around my shoulders. "Tell us what happened, Ambrose dear."

"It's… Cassie," I managed, swallowing back a sob.

I pulled away from Mary and went over to Caitlynn's side. Her face was calm, and if it hadn't been for her fluttering eyelids, I'd have thought she was just asleep. But I knew she must be screaming on the inside.

Just like Cassie was.

"Ambrose?" Sarah strode into the room. She was by my side and had her arms wrapped around me before I could say anything. "I came as quickly as I could. Where is she?"

"Still at the museum." I cleared my throat, but my voice still came out hoarse when I spoke. "She's part of the display now."

Daniel was on his feet. "What are you talking about? What happened to Cassie?"

I took a deep breath and told them everything. When I came to the part where Cassie was turned to stone, Mary gasped out loud, her hand flying to her mouth, while Daniel's face paled visibly. Sarah squeezed my hand, her lips pursed into a thin line.

"It's fine," I said, willing myself to believe it. "I need to catch the lamia, anyway. We need its venom for the antidote. For Caitlynn."

"Antidote?" Mary's eyes lit up. "You've found a way!"

"We're still working on it," Sarah said quickly. "I don't want to get your hopes up, Mrs Brady – I assume. Sorry, we haven't been introduced yet. I'm Sarah, Ambrose's girlfriend. I'm with the Metropolitan Police."

"Delighted, dear," Mary said. "Daniel told me you were here when they brought Caitlynn in after she was attacked. I'm very grateful to you."

"Of course," Sarah said, flushing. "Both Caitlynn and Cassie mean the world to me. As Ambrose was saying – I'm working with a toxicologist to develop an antidote. But he needs the lamia's venom before he can do anything else."

"We need to find that damn snake!" Daniel said, his hands balling into fists. "Everything depends on it."

"I may be able to help with that," Sarah said, reaching into her coat pocket and pulling out a piece of paper. "Have a look at this."

She spread the paper out across the overbed table and Daniel and I leaned in closer. It was a map of the inner city, with various locations circled in red.

"These are all the places where people displaying the same symptoms as Caitlynn have been found," Sarah said. "You notice anything in common?"

I studied the map. Trafalgar Square was marked – and I remembered the goon I'd chased off had been found at Charing Cross Station. I gasped as my eyes flitted across the other circles. "They're all close to Tube stations."

"Exactly," Sarah said.

"It's travelling by train?" Daniel asked, looking uneasy at the thought.

"Not by train," Sarah said. "But it is moving through the Underground. Possibly the service tunnels. Look at this." She pulled a pen out and connected all the red marks. It formed a roughly circular area centred around Hyde Park.

"Of course!" I said, feeling like an idiot for not realising it any sooner. "That night I brought it here – I lost it in the park. It must have found itself somewhere to hide. But where…?"

I bent lower over the map, trying to trace the pattern in my mind. The lamia would have wanted somewhere dark and secluded, easy to escape from. My eyes skimmed over the Tube stations, a jumble of interconnected lines and red circles, and suddenly I felt overwhelmed by the sheer number of options.

What if I was wrong? What if we were too late

already?

I stared at the map, unable to concentrate. My thoughts slipped sideways – Cassie frozen in stone, Caitlynn fighting for sanity, the weight of failure pressing on my shoulders like a dead water-leaper.

I shook my head sharply. No. I had to pull it together.

I forced myself to breathe, to think.

The lamia was clever, but it would still need a place to nest. My eyes scanned the map again – then I saw it. A blank spot on the map. Most of the stations in the area were still in use, but there was one… One that looked like a hole in the map. A forgotten place. The perfect hideout for an enormous snake.

"Here!" I pressed my index finger onto the map. "Down Street Station. It's been abandoned for years. I'll bet an entire pot of gold that's where we'll find the lamia."

Sarah's gaze met mine, excitement twinkling in her eyes. "I think you're right," she said. "Let me make a few calls. I'm sure I can find someone to get you into the station." She stepped out of the room, her phone already against her ear.

"What are we going to do when we find it?" Daniel asked.

I looked at my friend, surprised. "We?"

"Of course," he said, shrugging. "I have your back."

A swell of gratitude rose in my chest. After all that'd happened, I hadn't been entirely sure where our friendship stood. Volunteering to face down a mythological monster with me was more than I'd hoped for.

"But what about Caitlynn?" I asked. "Are you sure you want to leave her side?"

Mary grunted, startling me. I'd nearly forgotten

she was here.

"There's nothing more he can do for her here. I'd feel better knowing there's two of you taking the creature on."

"She's right," Daniel agreed. Then he grinned. "Besides, I can't let you take all the credit. When Caitlynn wakes up, I want her to be proud of me, too."

I was about to tell him his sister was already proud of him, when Sarah re-entered the room.

"It's all sorted," she said. "A man from a tour company will meet you at the entrance in half an hour."

My stomach clenched into a knot. I wasn't sure if it was from fear or anticipation. I had the sudden urge to tell Daniel to go on without me. Heat crept up the back of my neck.

Some friend I turned out to be.

I squared my shoulders. "Let me just go fetch something from my apartment."

My sister would be proud of her brother too.

⚹⚹⚹

Two men were waiting for us outside the redbrick building that housed the disused station. One was a short, stocky fellow with an impressive handlebar moustache. The other was Dr Grayson.

"What's this about, Davids?" the toxicologist asked, eyeing the bricked-up station entrance with trepidation. "Inspector Miller said you'd have the venom I asked for. She didn't mention anything about a historical tour."

"We're not here for the tour. We just need access."

"Good," the other man rumbled. He was wearing a blazer that had the logo of the London Transport Museum embroidered on one shoulder.

"The tour's been cancelled until further notice. Our best guide is currently in the hospital. They say she's had some kind of nervous breakdown, but I reckon she saw something down there – in the dark." He shivered, the points of his moustache wobbling for emphasis.

I shot a look at Daniel, who nodded back at me. We were at the right place.

I tightened my grip on the *rogatina*'s shaft. I had to do this. For Cassie, and for Caitlynn.

"We don't have the venom yet," I told Grayson. "But if we're right, the snake we're looking for has made its lair inside the abandoned station." I inclined my head towards Daniel. "This is Daniel Brady. His sister needs the antidote."

Grayson grunted. "What are we waiting for, then? With an unknown toxin, every second counts."

The man from the museum pulled out a bunch of keys and turned towards the steel door barring the public from entering the old station. He fumbled with the lock for a moment, probably unnerved by the mention of a dangerous reptile ensconced on the other side.

Finally, the door creaked open, revealing a darkness so black I might have likened it to a gate leading down into the depths of hell – if I had a flair for the melodramatic.

The guide stepped inside, and I couldn't help but hold my breath. What if the lamia was right there, ready for us? What if it was already wrapped around the man, his enormous moustache tickling the lamia's fangs?

Then a low buzz sounded, and the lights flickered on, illuminating a dusty corridor covered in graffiti.

The man stepped back into view. "You're on your own from here," he said. "That cop said I only needed to open for you. She didn't mention anything about catching poisonous snakes."

"Venomous," Grayson muttered, but the man just shrugged.

He pressed the bunch of keys into my hands. "Lock up when you're done and leave the keys at the shop next door. I'll get it there tomorrow morning."

I thanked him and he scurried off, clearly eager to get away from here as fast as possible.

I could hardly blame him.

"Come on, then", Grayson said, stepping through the door. He obviously didn't know what we were dealing with yet, or he wouldn't be so keen.

Daniel and I followed him more carefully.

The corridor was small and dusty, the tiled walls coated in grime. The yellow tube lights flickering overhead gave the place a slasher film vibe that set my nerves on edge. Brick stairs at the end of the corridor let down into the darkness. I scanned the walls. There was no light switch.

I guess this part of the station wasn't on the tour.

A dim ray of light suddenly pierced the dark. I turned to see Daniel wearing a headlamp and a perturbed expression. "I only brought two," he said, holding out another lamp and looking pointedly at Grayson.

The toxicologist was eyeing the darkness with distaste. "Davids can have it. I'll wait for you here."

I shook my head. "You don't know what we're up against. It's best if we stay together. Let him have it," I said to Daniel. "Just stick close to me."

Reluctantly, Grayson pulled the second headlamp on. "What kind of snake are we really dealing with? What is it you're not telling me, Davids?"

The man had a point. And if he was going down into the darkness with us, he'd soon see for himself. Better if he was prepared.

"It's a mythical creature," I said as I flipped the switch on the *rogatina*'s shaft. The spearpoint flicked into place and Grayson's eyes nearly bulged out of his head. "Large. Big enough to swallow a man whole."

A condescending smile slipped across the toxicologist's face. "Snakes that large aren't venomous."

"This one is," I said, grimly. "Its venom doesn't kill, but causes hallucinations. You've seen them in the hospital – those people were suffering from visions so horrendous that they lost their grip on reality. Oh, and the lamia's gaze is hypnotic. Not the kind you see in magic shows and makes you cluck like a chicken in front of strangers. The kind that gets you eaten while you stare stupidly at the pretty purple colours. I know that firsthand."

Grayson scoffed. "Stories. I'm a man of science."

"It's true," Daniel said softly. "But you don't have to believe us. You can go back to your office and your scientific journals and your ignorance. Or you can come with us and help us catch a myth. Help us save my sister." He glanced at me. "And his, as well."

Grayson stared at us, scepticism warring with his curiosity. For a long moment, the only sound was the quiet hum of the lights behind us. Then he exhaled sharply through his nose and adjusted the strap on his headlamp.

"Fine," he finally said. "But if this thing bites me, I expect naming rights when they write the case study."

He stepped forward, flashlight beam cutting ahead. "Let's go find your monster."

※※※

I descended the stairs slowly, lungs complaining as I inhaled stale air. The stench of decades of decay clung about me like a cloud of filth. My hand was wrapped tightly around the *rogatina*, its spearpoint reaching for the dark as if I could slice through my fear with it.

"Remember," Daniel muttered from somewhere close behind me. "We don't want it dead. We just need to catch it and milk it, somehow."

The toxicologist grunted. "If you catch it, I'll milk it."

I clenched my jaw. Both Cassie's and Caitlynn's lives depended on us. Not to mention the other victims still strapped to their hospital beds, fighting for their sanity. We couldn't afford to mess this up.

The corridor widened out when we reached the bottom of the stairs, opening into a forgotten service tunnel thick with dust and silence. Daniel swept his headlamp across the walls, revealing crumbling brickwork and an alarming number of cobwebs that glistened in the beam like trap wires.

I stopped short, dismayed. Facing a mythical snake was one thing, but spiders too?

For a moment, I seriously considered turning around and going home.

Then, from somewhere deeper in the Underground, the distant rumble of a train approached. A sudden rush of sound and motion followed as it thundered past a nearby platform, its headlights cutting through a side grate and throwing flickering bars of light across the tunnel. The illumination lasted only seconds, but it cast long, eerie shadows that did nothing for my state of mind. Then it was gone, plunging us back into oppressive darkness.

Against my better judgement, I stepped into the tunnel.

The lamia pounced immediately, its coils wrapping around me so fast I didn't have time to defend myself. I cried out as the *rogatina* pressed uselessly against my body. The snake's coils tightened. My breath rushed into my throat as, with a crunch, the spear's shaft splintered and cracked in two.

"Mother of —" Grayson's voice cut off as two glowing purple orbs filled my vision. I felt my limbs slacken, my resolve petering out, as a profound weariness washed over me. It was all so pointless. We were all going to die anyway – why fight it?

In a corner of my mind, a little niggling voice told me to snap out of it, to fight back. But it was such a small voice, and I was so tired. It was just easier this way.

Through the purple haze, I saw the lamia opening its jaws. I wasn't afraid. I was… nothing.

And then something struck the side of the snake's head, breaking its eye contact.

Abruptly, the purple miasma was gone and I shook my head, trying to clear it.

The lamia hissed as something else hit it, and its coils loosened a little. I twisted my body and managed to squirm out, dropping to the ground and rolling back onto my feet.

The tunnel shook as another train zoomed past. Beams of light briefly painted a hellish picture: the enormous lamia darting back and forth as it tried to evade whatever Daniel was throwing at it. Grayson stood with his back pressed up against a wall, his face contorted with shock and fear. I grimaced as the light from his headlamp blinded me.

Bits of debris rained down from the roof, and

I glanced around, looking for something I could use as a weapon. Piles of rubble littered the floor, a bucket and a mop, and some tools that must have been left here from when the tunnels had been used as bunkers during the war. I grabbed the mop just as the lights went out and swung at the lamia. It hissed as I felt the handle connect with something solid.

"Ambrose!" Daniel shouted a warning.

I jumped backwards, hearing the snake's jaws snap shut inches from my face.

The beam from Daniel's headlamp swerved, and I saw the lamia's tail hit him across the chest. The leprechaun was thrown against the far wall. He cried out as a pile of workmen's tools clattered over him.

I didn't have time to worry about my friend as the lamia lunged towards me again. Gripping the mop with both hands, I fended the monster off.

The snake darted towards me, and I ducked and rolled out of its reach.

My eyes lit upon the broken *rogatina*. I dropped the mop and lunged towards the smashed spear. My hand closed around the shaft and I spun around, but not before I realised that I'd grabbed the wrong piece.

The broken end with the spearpoint on it was still on the floor – out of reach.

The lamia struck again.

I stuck the splintered shaft into its gaping jaws, turning my head quickly to avoid eye contact.

Light from Grayson's beam reflected off something – a large shard of mirror lay on the floor where it must have fallen off the wall, a decoration from decades ago.

With a cry of fury, Daniel appeared out of the dark, swiping at the lamia with a rusty wrench.

I stumbled backwards as the snake let go of its

grip on the *rogatina*, and I tripped over something, gasping as I nosedived onto the floor. The broken shaft slipped from my grasp, clattering out of reach.

Swearing, I fumbled around for something else I could use as a weapon. My fingers closed around the thing that had tripped me over. A length of chain!

Suddenly, I had an idea.

"Daniel!" I shouted, holding the chain up for him to see.

"Little busy, mate," he shouted back as he swung the wrench again.

The lamia snapped at him, driving him back against the wall. Daniel was in no position to help me right now.

"Grayson, catch!" I yelled, tossing the chain at the petrified toxicologist.

The man grunted as it hit him in the chest, but I didn't have time to spell the plan out for him. I ran towards the mirror I'd noticed earlier.

My hand closed around it just as the lamia's coils wrapped around my leg. It wrenched me off my feet and I dropped the mirror. It shattered into smaller pieces.

By the light of Daniel's headlamp, I saw him lunging for the shards of the mirror. He recoiled, swearing. Blood dripped from his hand where a jagged edge had cut a gash into his palm.

The lamia reared up before me, its hood flared.

I clamped my eyes shut before it could hypnotise me again, my fingers searching for the mirror. My hand clamped around something cold and smooth just as the sound of rattling chains reached me.

Grayson's guttural war cry startled my eyes open as the lamia suddenly released me again.

A beam of light illuminated the tunnel as

another train shot past. Grayson was on top of the lamia – a cowboy on a bucking bronco – trying to pin it with his body while entangling the creature with the chain.

For a moment, I didn't know whether to laugh or applaud.

Then the lamia shook the man off and reared up before him. The toxicologist froze, the chain dropping from his hands as he stared into the lamia's eyes.

"Shit," I said. If something happened to Grayson, I'd have another soul on my conscience.

Adrenaline surged through my veins as I propelled myself forwards, jumping in between the lamia and its prey. The snake lunged at me, and I thrust the piece of mirror towards it. It stopped abruptly, stunned by its own power as its gaze was caught by its own reflection in the mirror.

"Quickly!" I said through gritted teeth.

Daniel appeared out of the shadows, grabbing the chain Grayson had dropped and wrapping it around the stilled snake's body. He crouched down and fiddled with the chain. When he stood up again, I saw that its ends had been fused together seamlessly.

The lamia was trapped.

I breathed a sigh of relief. Behind me, I heard Grayson panting loudly.

"Well done," I said as Daniel slumped down onto the ground.

He shot me an exhausted look and winced as he cradled his injured hand against his chest.

"How's your hand?" I asked.

"It'll be alright," he replied, smiling wanly. "I'll bet it's worse than it looks."

"Here," Grayson said, handing Daniel a handkerchief. He knelt down and inspected the wound. "Keep it wrapped up. We'll need to get you to a doctor to see about stitches."

"Great," Daniel sighed. "Another mark to commemorate the day."

I grinned. "Well, you know what they say…"

Daniel grimaced. "I've yet to meet these scar-loving ladies you keep going on about."

"They're out there, I'm sure of it," I laughed.

Grayson turned towards the lamia, still enthralled by the mirror I was pointing at it. He whistled softly. "This… was not what I was expecting."

He rubbed at his temples, as if trying to get rid of a headache.

"Think you can extract its venom for us?" I asked. "I'm not sure how long I can keep it docile like this." My arm was already feeling the strain of being held in one place for so long.

Grayson's eyes widened, but he nodded. He pulled a glass phial from his coat pocket. Slowly, he walked towards the lamia. Daniel had managed to wrap the chain through the creature's maw, leaving its fangs exposed. Grayson eyed the snake, clearly intimidated by the size of it.

He pulled a pair of blue latex gloves from his pocket and put them on as he leaned closer to inspect the lamia.

"It's even more unbelievable now that I can get a good look at it," he said. "Definitely not in any textbook I've read. But the principles are sound – pressure the venom sacs, avoid getting bitten, don't die. Same as usual."

The toxicologist knelt beside the creature, his movements precise but wary. He placed the glass phial carefully beneath the creature's exposed fangs, then reached in, manipulating the snake's venom sacs with careful pressure. His brow furrowed in concentration as he worked.

The low hiss of the creature filled the air. A thin

trickle of a glistening white liquid began to drip into the glass, and Grayson glanced up at me briefly, his lips tight. "We're in business," he said, his voice low but assured.

"Just like milking a cow," I quipped, watching the phial fill with morbid fascination.

"I've milked a cow before," Daniel said, also coming in for a closer look. "This is nothing like it."

"There," Grayson grunted, stoppering the phial. "Let's get this back to my lab. It should be enough to synthesise an antidote."

Hope flashed briefly across Daniel's face. He looked at me. "Mind if I...?"

"Go with him," I agreed. "Get the antidote to Caitlynn as soon as possible."

"Will you be alright on your own?" He eyed the lamia doubtfully. "I can stay and help you move it –"

"I'll be fine. Go."

Daniel pulled off his headlamp and handed it to me.

Grayson gave me a brief nod – this time with a glimmer of respect I hadn't seen there before – then turned and followed Daniel.

I watched their light bob away up the stairs before fishing out my mobile.

There was only one bar of signal down here, but it would be enough. I sent a quick text and watched my phone anxiously as I waited for a reply.

The lamia's tail undulated, and I wrenched my arm back up into place. I'd nearly let the creature's gaze escape! It stilled again and I swallowed back the spike of fear that had nearly choked me.

My phone buzzed, loud in the quiet Underground tunnel. I risked taking my eyes off the lamia to look at the response. A pin drop, along with a brief message.

-- Meet me here in 10 minutes. --

I stared at the phone.

I didn't have Amari's ability to Travel via GPS coordinates, but fortunately, this was a place I knew all too well. What was it about Hyde Park that drew the mythical world closer? Was it a vortex of magic or something? A place where the veil between the mundane and the mythical was wearing thin? It was a fascinating idea I wished I could discuss with Amari sometime.

If she ever responded to my texts again.

I looked at the lamia. Daniel had tied it quite securely, but I had no doubt that if I let the mirror drop, it would find a way out of its bonds somehow.

Its tongue flickered out, as if testing the air. It could probably taste my fear, even through its mesmerised haze.

The last thing I wanted to do was touch it.

Avoiding the inevitable, I let the headlamp's beam swipe across the tunnel floor until I located the discarded pieces of the broken *rogatina*. A part of me wanted to retrieve them and see if I could get the spear repaired, but something stopped me. It had been Nadiya's weapon, and I'd never quite felt comfortable wielding it. She'd tried to teach me violence, but in the end, Stavros had taught me compassion instead. Perhaps it was best if I left it there.

I looked at the lamia again and shuddered. Not all mythical creatures were monsters, but maybe this one was the exception.

Carefully, I inched closer to the creature, bracing myself.

Its scaly coils rippled beneath my touch, and I

shivered, repulsed. Before I could change my mind, I let my arm drop, still clutching on to the mirror.

Fear was a gut punch as the lamia's eyes regained focus. Its hiss slithered down my spine as it readied itself to strike.

I said the Word, and the world was washed in white.

※※※

A woman's scream pierced the air as soon as my vision cleared.

I'd placed myself and the lamia close to the Horse Head statue across from the entrance to the Mayfair car park, and spitting distance away from a woman carrying her groceries home. She stared at the chained-up snake with horror-filled eyes, a ripped Sainsbury's bag dangling forlornly from her hand as tins of tuna rolled down the length of the pedestrian walkway.

Shit. No one had ever been around when I popped out of thin air before…

The woman gripped her remaining bag to her chest and turned around, running as fast as her stubby legs could carry her.

"It's not real!" I shouted after her. "It's just your imagination playing tricks on you!"

Somehow, that spurred her on to run even faster. I didn't know her, but I was fairly sure she was going to self-medicate herself to sleep tonight.

I spun around as the squeal of tires announced the arrival of a panel van that came to a stop with one wheel up on the curb just before the ramp leading down into the parking lot. Sarff, her uncanny hair once again wrapped up in a headscarf, jumped out of the vehicle. She was wearing her tinted glasses and an air of satisfaction.

"Oh my," she gushed, spotting the lamia. "She's beautiful! Just look at those iridescent scales! And still alive as agreed, I see."

"Of course," I spat. It was a good thing I'd left the *rogatina* behind, because I really wanted to stab the gorgon through her oily heart right then.

"Quick," she said, ushering me towards the back of the van. "Let's get her out of sight."

Fortunately, dusk was settling and anyone driving past had their eyes on the road and their thoughts elsewhere. If any of them happened to see us manhandling an enormous snake, I'm sure they convinced themselves they'd seen something else. Londoners were good at pretending weird things didn't happen. I figured they'd chalk it up to a trick of the light, or just a long day. Still, it was best to get it done quickly.

Sarff opened the van's back doors to reveal a long wooden crate lying in the hold. Its similarity to a coffin sent a sharp, stabbing pain through my chest. My fingers twitched to open it, but Sarff tutted and pulled out the trolley lying next to it first.

Grimacing, I manoeuvred the bound lamia onto the trolley. It was heavier than it looked and still tried to snap at me, even with the chain running through its maw. I couldn't wait to get the damn thing out of my life.

Once it was on the trolley, Sarff helped me lift it into the back of the van.

Then we took the crate out and deposited it on the grass. The gorgon put the trolley away and locked the van up again as I opened the lid of the crate. The sight of Cassie, petrified and wide-eyed, sent a jolt of anguish through me.

I swallowed back the lump in my throat. "Alright, you have what you want. Now turn her back."

"Oh," Sarff said, her red lips puckering into a sardonic smile. "You must have misunderstood, my dear. I said I'd return your sister to you. I didn't say *I* could bring her back to life."

"What?" I stammered as fear rippled down my spine.

"I'm sorry, Ambrose," the gorgon said. "I thought you knew your mythology. There's nothing *I* can do for your sister." She headed towards the driver's side of the van. "But don't worry about the lamia. I'll take good care of her."

"No," I said, shaking my head, unable to believe what was happening.

"No!" I pulled the silver whistle out from beneath my shirt and blew on it.

Sarff's smile faltered. She jumped into the van and turned the engine on. I had time to slam a fist futilely against its side before she sped off, ignoring the screech of cars slamming on their brakes as she swerved out in front of them, horns hooting furiously.

I sank down onto my knees beside the crate. My fingers curled around Cassie's outstretched hand. It was smooth as stone, and just as cold.

The wind tugged at my hair, but I didn't move. Grief crashed over me in silent, suffocating waves.

I'd failed her.

I'd chased monsters, made deals with gorgons, and still – I couldn't save her. My vision blurred as I pressed my forehead to her unmoving hand, the jagged edges of despair cutting deeper than any fangs or claws ever could.

Cassie was gone. And I had nothing left to bargain with.

The crunch of footsteps cut through my pain and I felt a stab of annoyance flash through me. Had Sarff come to gloat? I didn't have the strength to face her again – or anyone else.

"Ambrose?"

I blinked back tears and looked up to see Amari standing a few steps away.

A breathless, incredulous laugh escaped my lips. After all the time I'd spent trying to reach her, all I'd had to do was blow the damn whistle.

Amari's dark curls were wind-tossed and tangled, half tucked beneath the hood of a weathered jacket. Fatigue shadowed her eyes, and though she stood tall, there was a heaviness in the slope of her shoulders, like someone who'd gone too long without rest. Dirt stained the hem of her jeans, and the leopard-print scarf tied around her neck was frayed at the edges.

Her lips were pursed into a thin line. "What happened to Cassie?" she asked.

I cleared my throat, trying to scrape together enough voice to answer. "Gorgon," I managed, the word a curse on my tongue.

I couldn't wrap my head around it – Cassie was gone.

My little sister, full of life and laughter, who only ever wanted to chase joy on her own terms. She'd been my anchor through everything – when the job nearly broke me, when Rachel left, when I'd hit rock bottom and didn't know how to climb back out. Cassie had been there. Always. With a sharp joke, a warm hug, a quiet kind of strength that never asked for anything in return.

And now? Now she was a statue.

Because I hadn't protected her. Because I'd failed.

A sob tore out of me, raw and ragged, and I folded forward, the grief too heavy to hold up any longer.

A warm hand settled on my shoulder, steadying me. I looked up through blurred vision to find Amari crouched in front of me, her dark eyes locked onto mine with quiet intensity.

"She's not gone," she said gently, but firmly. "Ambrose, I know how to bring her back."

For a second, I just stared, the words not quite landing. Then I blinked.

"You do?" I croaked.

A faint smile curved her lips. "Yes. But I can't do it for you. You'll need your father's help."

※※※

Father's face blanched as I opened the crate's lid to reveal the statue Cassie had become.

"Leave us," he ordered, a tremor in his voice – and the three men who had helped me carry the crate to Father's office filed out the door.

"This," he said, pulling his glasses off and rubbing the lenses vigorously with a handkerchief. "This is why I didn't want your sister to become involved with the mythical world."

"Do you have what I asked for?" I asked as I surveyed the room. The hearth was still cold, but Amari's mahogany desk had been pushed to one side and the thick Persian carpet was covered with a layer of black refuse bags.

"Yes," Father replied, putting his glasses back on and retrieving a large glass bottle filled with a viscous yellow liquid from his desk. "I just hope it's enough. Fortunately, the basilisk's been in a foul mood lately." The new Keeper unscrewed the top off the bottle and a sulphurous stench assailed my nostrils. "It's been spitting up so much bile I was wondering if I needed to find it some antacids. Need a hand with your sister's statue?"

I grunted as I lifted Cassie's petrified form from the crate and gently placed it upright on top of the black bags, propping her carefully so she wouldn't topple over.

Father handed me the bottle.

Carefully, I poured the oily, foul-smelling liquid over the statue, watching as it glistened and spread, coating every inch of the cold stone.

My hands trembled as I stepped back, wiping my palms on my jeans. I couldn't stop staring at her – at the sheer wrongness of seeing my sister frozen like that.

My heart thudded against my ribs. What if this didn't work? What if we were too late?

"You're sure this is going to work?" Father echoed my thoughts. He adjusted his glasses and stepped closer to peer at the statue. His concern faded as professional curiosity took hold, his gaze lingering on the statue's intricate details.

"I guess we'll find out," I said, afraid to hope – but more afraid not to. Even though Amari had assured me it would work – and sheepishly confessed that she'd been revived this way a few times herself – I still couldn't help but worry.

I stared at Cassie's statue, hardly daring to breathe, willing – begging – it to move.

Then, to my utter disbelief, her chest rose with a slow, shuddering breath.

The rigid stone began to soften, colour returning to her cheeks. Her fingers twitched. She blinked once, then again, dazed and unsteady. In the next moment, she was lurching to her feet, wiping at her face with a grimace.

"Ugh," she muttered, looking down at the thick yellow slime clinging to her clothes. "What the hell is this?"

I didn't answer. I just pulled her into a hug, holding on like I'd never let go again.

When her arms wrapped around me – solid, warm, *alive* – I nearly collapsed with relief.

"Remarkable," Father said as I pulled away from her.

Cassie smiled back at me, and I swear it was like coming up for breath after nearly drowning.

"Did you catch it?" she asked, her voice scratchy but eager.

"I did," I said. "You won't have to worry about the lamia again."

Her shoulders sagged with relief. "And Caitlynn?"

"We have someone working on the cure. It should be ready soon."

Cassie exhaled a long, shuddering breath. Her hands trembled slightly as she wiped at her face, tears spilling across her cheeks. I reached for her hand and held it tight.

"Come," Father said gently, placing an arm around her shoulders. "Let's get you into bed. A night's rest in the Repository and you'll be as good as new by morning."

Cassie leaned into him, her movements still cautious, like someone relearning how to exist in her own skin.

As they reached the door, Father paused to look back at me. He met my gaze and gave a small, approving nod, before they disappeared into the corridor.

My heart swelled, pride and relief crashing together in a tide so strong it nearly knocked the breath from my lungs. For the first time in days, I let myself believe everything was going to be okay.

My phone pinged, and I pulled it out to see a message from Sarah blinking on the screen.

-- *It's ready.* --

Shrugging off my exhaustion, I tucked the phone away again and ran for the West Gate.

⁂⁂⁂

Tension hung heavy in the air as I pushed open the hospital room door.

Inside, the atmosphere was taut with hope and fear. Mary Brady stood nearest to the bed, wringing her hands, her eyes locked on her daughter's motionless form. Daniel was beside her, one arm wrapped protectively around his mother's shoulders.

On the other side of the room, Sarah looked up as I entered, her face pale with worry. She stepped toward me and squeezed my hand, her voice barely above a whisper. "Cassie all right?"

I gave a small nod, unable to trust my voice just yet.

Grayson, standing near the foot of Caitlynn's bed with a small medical case in hand, cleared his throat. His eyes swept over the room, taking in each face, each of us holding our breath, waiting for a miracle. "I want to reiterate that this antidote hasn't been tested yet, and that it was synthesised under rushed circumstances. Are you sure you want to proceed?"

"It's the best shot we have," Daniel said, nodding grimly. "Do it."

The toxicologist pursed his lips but didn't argue further. "We'll need her out of the coma before I can administer this," he said. He stepped out of the room and returned a moment later with a nurse in tow.

The nurse gave Mary an encouraging smile as she adjusted the IV drip. "We'll reverse the sedation slowly. It might take a few minutes for her to regain partial consciousness."

We waited in breathless silence as the machines beeped steadily. A flicker of movement twitched across Caitlynn's brow. Mary gasped and clutched Daniel's hand.

When the nurse nodded, Grayson stepped

forward, swabbed Caitlynn's arm with alcohol, and carefully injected a clear liquid into her vein. Then he stood back, his eyes fixed on her face, watching for the first signs of change.

Slowly, colour returned to Caitlynn's cheeks. Her eyelids fluttered and she opened her eyes. She looked dazed, disoriented, as if unsure of where she was. One trembling hand rose to her temple.

"I've had the most horrible dream," she rasped.

Around the room, everyone seemed to exhale at once.

Mary let out a sob and threw her arms around her daughter, holding her as though she'd never let go again. Daniel sat down hard in the chair beside the bed, hands over his face, shoulders shaking. Sarah gripped my hand tighter, tears glistening in her eyes.

I couldn't speak. Relief flooded through me so fast it left me dizzy.

Grayson gave a small, satisfied nod, then leaned in to speak quietly with the nurse. She gave a soft reply and slipped out of the room. A moment later, he caught Sarah's eye and tilted his head toward the door. She gave my hand one last squeeze before letting go and following him out.

Sensing that Caitlynn and her family needed this moment to themselves, I stepped out a minute later and found Grayson and Sarah waiting in the corridor. Grayson was pacing slightly, his brow furrowed.

"I'll make sure the antidote reaches the other patients," he said without preamble. "There should be enough to treat the whole ward, but that's it. I've used up every drop of venom from the sample I took."

He turned to me. "Any chance of securing more?"

I shook my head. "No. The lamia's gone. For good." I didn't care what Sarff did with it, as long as I never saw the creature again.

Grayson let out a long breath, running a hand through his hair.

"Gone," he echoed. His voice was tight – equal parts relief and frustration. "Well... perhaps it's for the best. Dangerous creature. But it does mean this cure is a one-time miracle."

He gave Sarah a brief nod. "Keep me posted on the patients."

Then he glanced at me. "Davids."

With a final look – somewhere between approval and exhaustion – he turned and walked down the hallway, his white lab coat flaring slightly behind him, like the cape of a superhero.

Sarah watched him go, then turned to me with a small smile. "With the patients in recovery, all that's left now is the paperwork."

"How are you going to explain any of this?" I asked, raising an eyebrow.

She shrugged, the corner of her mouth quirking wryly. "Oh, you know. Gas leak, tainted medication, mass hallucination... I'll figure it out."

Then she stepped forward and wrapped her arms around me. "Now let's get you cleaned up," she murmured, her nose wrinkling as the stench of basilisk bile reached her. "And after that, I think you owe me a drink."

I smiled, the weight on my chest lifting. "Best idea I've heard all week."

※※※

Amari was already waiting on a weathered bench in Hyde Park when I arrived the next day. Morning mist hung low over the Serpentine, the water rippling gently in the breeze. I sat beside her, staring out across the lake, the memory of the asrai surfacing unbidden.

None of this would've happened if I hadn't tried to save a drowning girl in these waters.

"The bile worked," I said quietly. "Thank you."

She glanced at me, one brow raised in invitation.

I hesitated, then ran a hand through my hair. "I thought you didn't approve of using creature parts."

Amari let out a soft laugh. "I don't. But trust me, the basilisk isn't exactly shy about sharing. He doles it out quite willingly, whether you want it or not." Her smile faded slightly. "I'm not against using the gifts they offer freely. It's the exploitation I can't stand. Most people are far too good at convincing themselves they're doing good when there's power or profit on the line."

My gaze dropped to my hands. "You think my father and the Council will cross that line?"

She didn't hesitate. "They already have. But that's a battle for another day. Right now, there's something more urgent."

I turned toward her, curious. She met my gaze evenly.

"The trait we lost," I said. "Tenacity."

She nodded, understanding sparking in her eyes. "You think that's what it is, too? I've been scattered – unfocused – lately," she admitted. "It's not just inconvenient – it's dangerous."

My heart thudded. "Do you know how to get it back?"

Her expression turned wry. "Not exactly. But I have a lead. Remember the autopsy on Norton's victims? The hybrid DNA?"

"Human and wolf," I said. "From that rare Bavarian breed."

She nodded. "Wolves that carry a strain of

werewolf taint in them. That's unique. And perhaps we can use it."

A slow grin spread across my face. "You want to track them down."

"I want us to track them down," she corrected. "We'll need all the focus we can get, and I think the key to reclaiming what we lost might lie with them."

I stood, stretching my legs and rolling my shoulders. The wind stirred the leaves above, rustling them in a whispering chorus. Sunlight dappled through the canopy, warm on my skin.

"Well then," I said, smiling. "Germany awaits."

She chuckled. "Let's just try not to get anyone turned into statues this time."

"No promises," I replied, grinning.

PART 9

WEREWOLF'S GIFT

The scent of geraniums wafted from windowsill flower boxes as I dropped my shopping bags on the floor and sat down across from Amari.

"That should be everything," I said as I grabbed a fork and tucked into the *apfelstrudel* waiting for me. "Sleeping bags, trekking poles, water bottles, a flashlight each, and some toilet paper." She lifted an eyebrow and I shrugged. "You never know!"

I smacked my lips as I sat back and appreciated my surroundings. We were sitting outside on the terrace of a charming bakery café in the heart of a picturesque little town on the edges of the Black Forest in southern Germany. Half-timbered medieval buildings painted in warm shades of orange and yellow adorned with colourful shutters lined the attractive square, and I smiled as an old gentleman wearing traditional *lederhosen* ambled past. He tipped his hat at me with a friendly *"Grüß Gott!"* before continuing on his way.

"Did you get our food supplies?" I asked between mouthfuls of the delicious apple tart.

"Of course," Amari replied, taking a sip from one of the two glasses of amber liquid sitting on the table. "But I hope we won't be hiking for too long. I only bought enough to last us two, maybe three, days."

"Should be more than enough," I said, reaching for the other glass. I took a long gulp and then spluttered at the sharp taste spilling across my tongue. I gave Amari a sidelong glance. "Apple juice? We're in Bavaria, Amari. We should be drinking beer!"

She levelled a stern look at me. "After we've done what we came here for. We're here to find wolves – not for sightseeing or to enjoy the local brew, but because the fate of the world depends on it." Then she smiled, softening somewhat. "Call it motivation, if you will."

"Alright…" I said, pushing the juice to one side. "And what exactly is our plan? Do we have any idea where to look for the wolves?"

Amari shook her head. "No. I've asked at the hotel, and they say no one has seen them for a long time now. I just hope we're not too late."

She pulled a map of the area out and smoothed it down on the table. "Here," she said, pointing at a green section intersected with thin brown lines. "These are all the hiking trails through the forest. I reckon if there are still wolves around, they should be somewhere along here." Her fingers lingered on a section that had no trails running through it.

I frowned. "I'm the last person to be accused of planning ahead, but even I think this is a long shot."

"It is," Amari agreed, folding the map away again. "But do you have a better idea?"

I sighed. "No. Trust the luck, I guess…"

"Excuse me?" Amari's eyebrow was raised once more.

"Nothing," I replied quickly. "Just something a friend of mine always says."

She eyed me for a moment longer, before pulling her plate of apple tart closer.

"What do we do when we find the wolves?"

Amari calmly finished her tart, then said: "Then I'm going to let one of them bite me."

For a second, I couldn't breathe. I just stared at her, the sound of café chatter around us suddenly muffled like I was underwater. "What? You can't be serious?"

"I'm perfectly serious," she replied. "What did you think was going to happen, Ambrose? Someone needs to take over where Norton left off, and I don't think the werewolf infection is passed on with an affectionate lick."

I stared at her, dumbstruck for a moment. We obviously needed a werewolf to get the trait back, but I hadn't considered the implications before now. I just sort of assumed we'd somehow get the werewolf DNA and then let a scientist sort the rest out. Maybe someone like the toxicologist – Grayson. A man in a lab coat who'd had a fling with the mythical world.

But Amari, a werewolf?

Norton had been dangerous enough – an ex-soldier with a bad attitude, murderous at the best of times. But Amari? She was formidable in a very different way. She could literally set things afire with a click of her fingers, and who knows what other Words of Wonder she had in her arsenal? If she turned into a monster with that kind of power…?

I wasn't sure whether the world would be better off if that happened.

"There must be some other way…"

"What would you have me do, Ambrose?" Amari huffed. "This is not the kind of thing you ask someone else to do – and who'd volunteer for the job, anyway? Not you?"

I nearly choked as a bit of tart went down the wrong way. Norton still haunted my nightmares. The last thing I wanted to do was become him. Coughing, I tried to force the suddenly tasteless pastry down.

Amari chuckled, handing me a serviette. "Relax, I'm not asking you to do it," she said, and

I couldn't help but sigh with relief. "I'm the reason we lost the trait. I have to make it right."

Pushing my plate to one side, I reached for the juice. "Are you going to tell me what really happened?"

She rose to her feet. "Maybe some other day. It's getting late. I'll see you for breakfast bright and early. The bus leaves at seven o'clock, sharp." She slung her satchel across her shoulder and strode quickly towards our hotel on the other side of the square.

I looked up at the blue sky, and then glanced at my mobile phone. It was only four o'clock in the afternoon.

I shrugged. We'd have plenty of time on the trail to talk things out. No point trying to push too much too soon.

Grabbing my bags, I smiled at the waitress who came to clear our table as I stood up. I was in Germany, it was a beautiful day, and saving the world was tomorrow's worries.

I dropped the gear off in my cosy hotel room before heading out on a quest of my own: to find a pint of the local brew.

※※※

The sun was setting slowly behind the snow-capped mountains as I sat on my balcony, my feet up on the wooden railing, swigging a cold draught, when my phone rang. It was Daniel.

"How's Caitlynn?" I asked immediately.

My friend sighed. "That's why I'm calling," he said, voice tighter than usual.

I sat up a little straighter, worried. "Is she alright?"

"I don't know. I want to say yes, but... she's having visions, Ambrose. Real ones."

"Visions!" I frowned. "You mean hallucinations? Did the cure not work, then?"

"The cure worked," Daniel replied. "But the lamia's venom has left some side effects. What she sees are definitely not as intense or as frequent as the hallucinations had been while she'd been infected, but they are visions. They come true."

I grunted. I remembered the vision the lamia's blood had given me, that time I'd been careless enough to get myself cut with the blood-splattered *rogatina*. If Caitlynn's visions were anything like that, then the poor girl was still suffering.

"She had one about you."

I slopped beer all over myself as I nearly fell off my chair. Putting the half-empty glass down, I wiped my hand on my trousers while I tried to regain my composure. "What did she see?" I stammered.

"She said to tell you this: '*Circles will lead you nowhere. Only the White Lady can show you the way. Beware the monster inside.*' Mean anything to you?"

I swallowed back trepidation. I've encountered my fair share of mystical women in white, and they usually meant trouble. "I don't know, but I don't like it. How do you know her visions are true?"

"Well, last night she saw a coffin covered in clover, and this morning I received a letter from Ma to tell us Bessie had died."

A twinge of sorrow pierced my heart. Bessie, the family cow who'd nearly munched on my lucky four-leaf clover. "I'm sorry to hear that. What happened?"

"She was old, it was just her time," Daniel said sadly. "But there was truth in Cassie's vision – and there could be truth in the one she saw for you, too."

"I'll keep that in mind," I said, uncomfortable at the thought of another White Lady crossing my path. "Did she say anything else?"

"No, but have you seen the news tonight?"

I hadn't. I went inside and turned the telly on, skipping channels until I landed on Sky News. The logline running across the bottom of the screen read: *Thousands desert army, while school and university dropouts increase.* A lump formed in the pit of my stomach. What were they all doing instead? Drifting, aimless? Getting into fights? Wandering into places they shouldn't?

"You think it's because we lost Tenacity?" I asked.

"Undoubtedly," Daniel replied. "I don't know how you're going to fix it, Ambrose, but you need to fix it, somehow. The world needs it, and it's only going to get worse the longer we go without it."

"No pressure, then," I said wryly.

"Good luck, mate. The fate of the world rests on your shoulders," Daniel chuckled as we ended the call.

I turned the telly off again, a bitter taste in my mouth that had nothing to do with the beer I'd savoured earlier. Damn Norton for leaving me with this unwanted obligation.

And Amari as well. Until she decided to talk to me, I only had Father's version of events to go by – and if he were to be believed, she'd run away that night. She'd killed Norton and left the creatures in the Repository – and the world in general – to fend for themselves.

How could I trust her after that?

But what worried me most was Caitlynn's words. *Beware the monster inside.* Was there something dangerous inside the Black Forest?

Or did she mean something inside of me?

After a restless night in which I didn't sleep much at all, I missed breakfast entirely and found Amari already waiting for the bus in front of our hotel. Like me, she was dressed for the hike in boots, jeans and a T-shirt. But whereas I had opted to travel as light as possible, her backpack looked like she'd packed for the both of us.

"I nicked this for you from the breakfast buffet," she said, handing me a paper bag from which the smell of freshly baked bagels wafted. "And here's the bus. Lucky you didn't miss it."

My stomach growled as I tucked the bag into my backpack and followed Amari onto the bus. It was surprisingly crowded, filled with people outfitted much like us, presumably also on their way to go hiking in the Black Forest. Why anyone would choose to be up this early while on holiday was beyond me.

Amari paid for both our tickets and we walked towards the end of the bus, where we dropped into the last available seat at the back. I shuffled, trying to get comfortable with Amari's overfull backpack pressing up against me.

"What do you have in there, anyway?" I asked as the bus started moving.

"Oh, odds and ends," Amari said vaguely as she pulled her gaze from the window to look at me. "I'm used to a certain level of comfort, you know." She chuckled, a little self-consciously.

"Did you pack the minibar, too?" I muttered, shifting in my seat.

"I just wished we had a tent," Amari said. "What?" she laughed when she saw the look I gave her. "I don't particularly like getting my hair wet, is all."

"We're going hiking in the deepest parts of the Black Forest to find —" I lowered my voice, looking to see if anyone was listening, but the other tourists were all too occupied staring out the window or talking amongst themselves to pay us any attention. "To find werewolves. Your hair is the least you should be worried about."

Amari nodded thoughtfully. "I *am* pretty worried about snakes," she admitted.

I chuckled. "You've handled worse than snakes, I'm sure."

She shuddered as I felt my own skin crawl. I'd be happy if I never saw anything scaly again.

Finally, somewhat comfortable, I pulled the bagel out of my bag and attacked it with the ravenous ferocity of a pack of werewolves while I watched the scenery sweep past through the window. The bus trundled through the scenic medieval town, winding through narrow streets lined with postcard-pretty buildings, flower boxes overflowing with brilliant red geraniums. A little stream gurgled its way through town, with early-morning cyclists zipping along beside it on dedicated bike paths.

It must be all this fresh mountain air.

Not long after, the bus escaped the town limits and the scenery shifted. Rows of houses and cobbled streets gave way to open fields stretching to the foot of far-off mountains. Rolling meadows dotted with wildflowers sparkled under the sun, while clusters of timber huts with red-tiled roofs lay scattered along the landscape. In the pastures, cows with glossy tan coats grazed lazily, their copper bells clinking as they looked up to gape at the bus as we passed by.

Ahead, the road curved gently toward the edge of the Black Forest, where dense clusters of dark, towering pines and firs cloaked the hillsides in shadow.

Beware the monster inside.

Shivering, I turned my attention to the former

Keeper instead. She was staring out the window, a wistful look upon her face. After spending so many years hidden away inside a mountain fortress, she was probably glad to have her freedom again.

"Penny for your thoughts," I said.

She turned towards me, blinking, as if pulling herself back to the moment from a very long way away. "Oh, I was just thinking that I've always wanted to travel," she replied. "There were so many places on my bucket list when I left home, and none of them have been crossed off yet. Things didn't really go the way I'd planned."

"Is that why you left the Repository?"

Her jaw tightened. "I left because I had no choice."

"That's not how Father tells it."

Amari snorted. "James can be quite creative with the truth, when it suits him."

I wanted to push her for more, but the bus eased to a stop, its doors hissing open.

"We're here," Amari said, rising to her feet as the rest of the passengers started spilling onto the tarmac.

A breeze ruffled my hair as I climbed down the bus steps. I breathed deeply, inhaling the scent of pine and wet grass. The sun was already half-way up the clear blue sky. It was a beautiful morning.

The bus had dropped us off at an unremarkable gap in the shrubbery lining the road. There were no signboards to welcome us to the Black Forest, no stalls littered with touristy trinkets. Just a thin dirt track leading over a small meadow and off into the trees. A cluster of hikers were already walking resolutely towards the woods.

Amari paused to pull her map out again. "I think we're here…" she said, pointing at a small trail at the southern edge of the forest. "We can follow the path up to here, and turn off onto that one, and somewhere before we reach that turn, we go off-trail."

"Oh no, you mustn't go off trail," someone with a thick German accent said from behind us.

I turned to see a man, last off the bus, frowning at us. His boots were scuffed and stained with mud, and his lined face was weathered by many days spent outside in the sun.

"It's forbidden."

"Forbidden?" I asked, glancing at Amari.

The hiker nodded. "To protect the animals and the forest. And also, yourselves." He leaned in closer and whispered: "There are stories about the things that live in the deepest, darkest parts of the *Schwarzwald*."

My chest tightened, and then he shrugged and smiled. "Of course, these are just folktales. But you know there is always a grain of truth in all the old tales."

"Tales of what, exactly?" Amari asked. We both knew fairy tales shouldn't be so easily dismissed.

"Oh, you would laugh at an old man if I told you," he said, chuckling.

Amari smiled encouragingly. "Indulge us, please. I love a good story."

"Alright," the man said, clearly pleased by her interest. "There have always been *waldgeists* and *wichtels* – forest spirits – who protect the woods. They might help or hinder you, depending on how the mood strikes them. But legends tell of more sinister creatures as well. Nightmare creatures – we call them *alps* – and *doppelgängers* who would lure you deeper and deeper until you are lost forever." He scratched at the white stubble on his chin. "And then there is Frau Holle."

"Who?" I asked.

"Frau Holle," the old man repeated. "An old woman of the forest. Some say she lures people into her house and make them clean it for her. And if she is satisfied, then she will reward you. But if she's not…"

I grunted. Let's hope the fate of the world didn't rest on my housekeeping abilities.

"Thank you," Amari said. "We will respect the old tales and watch out for forest spirits."

Pleased, the man reached into his backpack and pulled out two large ginger biscuits.

"*Lebkuchen*," he said as he handed one to each of us. "In case you do meet something unexpected." He tipped his hat at us, and then sauntered down the path, whistling as he headed towards the forest.

"Well," I said, pocketing the biscuit. "That was… interesting."

Amari rolled her eyes. "Superstitious nonsense."

I gaped at her, and then had to hurry to catch up as she started walking towards the trees too. By now, we'd lost sight of all the other hikers who'd been on the bus with us.

"You don't think there was some grain of truth in that?" I asked.

Amari laughed. "Nightmares and *doppelgängers* and an obsessive-compulsive neat freak forcing hikers to clean for her? No, I think it's just stories. I expect there might be a dryad or two in the woods, but they'd know better than to show themselves to us."

"I don't know," I muttered, running a hand through my hair. "Just seems like a good idea to listen to what the locals have to say." If there was one thing Father's stories had taught us when we were little, it was to heed the warnings given by passing strangers. That, and not to mess with powerful women in disguise.

I wanted to argue the point further, but my breath rushed out as we stepped into the forest and the trees closed off the light coming in from overhead. It felt like we'd stepped into a realm of perpetual twilight, where anything could happen. I was suddenly even more inclined to believe old folktales and stories of spirits and ghosts.

The forest wrapped around us in shades of deep green and shadowed grey, with towering spruce trees and ancient firs stretching high overhead, their branches weaving a dense canopy that filtered the sunlight into faint, dappled patches on the ground. The air grew cool and damp, carrying the earthy scent of moss and wet leaves, mixed with a faint hint of pine resin. Further on, the trail turned from packed dirt to a carpet of pine needles, crunching softly underneath my boots. A bird warbled, hidden somewhere in the foliage, and the scurry of small creatures rustled the underbrush.

"Did you feel that?" Amari asked, her eyes wide. She had stopped short, her body rigid with pent up energy. A vein was pulsing in her temple.

"No…" I said, alarmed. "Feel what?"

Amari stood frozen for a moment longer, and then her body visibly relaxed. "Nothing," she said, shaking her head. "It's nothing. I just thought… No, don't worry about it. It's nothing."

"It's clearly not *nothing* if you had to repeat yourself three times," I said, eyeing the surrounding trees with a sudden trepidation.

"I just thought…" She took a deep breath. "It just felt like we'd crossed some kind of border. Almost like when you step into an enclosure." She laughed nervously. "Ignore me. I'm probably just imagining things. Let's move on."

"Alright…" I said, shrugging.

She hoisted her backpack to a more comfortable position on her back before continuing along the path, while I brought up the rear.

Maybe Amari was just skittish. I certainly hadn't felt anything, although now I jumped at every rustle – a squirrel darting up a tree trunk set my heart rate racing, while the flutter of unseen birds shifting in the foliage nearly had me reaching for a branch or something I could use as a weapon. I strained my ears, listening for any unusual sounds – the howl of a wolf, maybe – but who was I kidding? It was all strange to my ears. I was out of my depth in this forest. I was a city boy, always had been.

Apart from the adrenaline-inducing rustling of small creatures and our own stomping steps, the quiet beneath the trees felt quite profound. It was a stillness that seemed ancient, as though the forest had stood this way for centuries, untouched by the world outside. Despite my best intentions to stay on high alert, I felt my shoulders relax, my worries evaporating, as I drank in the beauty of our surroundings.

Branches swayed in an unseen breeze overhead, and the gentle murmur of water betrayed the presence of a stream hidden somewhere out of sight behind the greenery. Every so often, shafts of sunlight broke through the canopy, illuminating the small pockets of the forest floor where ferns and delicate wildflowers took root, their pale petals and fronds vibrant against the dark, damp soil. I felt a childlike excitement as I spotted white caps clinging to the base of a tree, and brilliant orange and red toadstools peeking out from the shadows like hidden gems.

And, finally, I could definitively confirm that Sarah's eyes were indeed moss green.

As we moved deeper, the trail narrowed and twisted, weaving between thick tree trunks and clusters of bushes that brushed against us as we passed. We clambered over large tree roots protruding from the muddy ground and – gasping for breath – crossed a fallen log like a bridge over the hidden stream, revealing itself to be a modest brook.

On its other side, we stopped in a small clearing, a tantalisingly familiar scent wafting from delicate white flowers sprinkled on a few bushes on its outskirts.

I sank down onto a likely-looking rock, my legs suddenly making it known that walking along Hyde Park and hiking in the forest were two very different forms of exercise, while a sudden, insistent hunger started to nag at my stomach. I took a swipe from my water bottle while wiping perspiration from my brow. Then Amari tossed a protein bar at me, and I spent the next few minutes eagerly devouring every crumb.

Satiated for the moment, I sat back on the rock, stretching my legs out and reaching with my arms into the air. I froze, mid-stretch.

"Umm…" I swallowed, my throat suddenly bone dry. "How long have we been walking?"

"Couple of hours?" Amari replied, distracted by her map. She was turning it this way and that, as if she wasn't quite sure what she was looking for. "This can't be right…"

"Amari…" Engrossed in whatever was confounding her, she didn't respond. "Amari!"

"What?" she snapped. Her words were clipped when she said: "I think we might be lost."

I pointed up at the sky, and her eyes widened as she finally looked up. It was night and a full moon was beaming down upon us, basking the clearing in a pale light I'd mistaken for sunshine dappling through thick foliage.

The former Keeper said a word I didn't recognise, but by the sound of it, it probably wasn't something one uttered in polite company.

"We can't have possibly…" she faltered. "Did we…? How…?"

I shook my head. "Not only that, but I've been paying attention lately, and that full moon isn't due for another week or so." A shiver ran down the length of my spine. "I hate to state the obvious, but something very weird is going on."

"Look," Amari said, holding the map out at me as she slumped down onto a rock beside me. "There's no river marked anywhere near the trail we started out on. I don't know where we are, Ambrose, but it's not where we thought we were going."

"Do you think –" I started saying and then stopped abruptly as a wolfish howl lifted the hair on my arms.

Amari's eyes widened as many howls suddenly rent the air.

"Quick!" she said, scrambling to her feet. "The sooner we find them, the sooner we can get out of there."

"Amari, wait!" I shouted, but it was too late. She'd left her backpack on the ground and disappeared into the woods. Swearing, I ran after her.

It was dark underneath the trees, but I could hear Amari somewhere ahead of me, crashing through the underbrush. Another howl rose to the left, and then from somewhere behind me. A chill ran down my spine. There was something very primal about that sound.

More howling echoed through the trees from my right. Shit. They had us surrounded.

Were they hunting us?

Fighting rising panic, I dashed in the direction I thought Amari was going. Like a fool, I'd brought nothing to defend myself with – Amari had insisted that we wouldn't need any weapons. My walking poles were still somewhere in that clearing, and the *rogatina* was long gone.

And I'd seen enough David Attenborough documentaries to know that fighting off a pack of ravenous wolves with my bare hands was probably not going to go my way.

Suddenly, I tripped over a tree root and careened forwards, knocking into Amari and bowling her over. We landed, hard, on the moist ground and I felt a sharp pain shoot through my ankle.

"Ambrose!" Amari hissed, her eyes wide. "I think they're hunting us."

"No shit," I muttered, rubbing at my ankle. It wasn't broken, but I might have sprained it. I'd seen what happened in those documentaries – the old and the injured, they were eaten first. Well, I wasn't going to go down without a fight. I stood up, wincing as my ankle complained.

Howls rose from all around us. Any moment, a pack of ravening beasts were going to descend upon us. Amari was on her feet beside me, her hands clenched into fists. She wouldn't go down easy, either.

And then… quiet.

I glanced at Amari. She was still braced for violence, but a small frown of confusion clouded her face. Her head was cocked to one side, as if she was listening intently.

"Are the wolves… gone?" I asked.

Amari exhaled slowly. "I don't think they were ever here. Look."

All around us, little white lights bobbed into existence. They floated lazily past us for a moment before dispersing into the trees. A lonely howl echoed in their passing, and then they were gone.

"*Waldgeists,*" Amari huffed. "We've been tricked."

A hollow pit formed at the base of my stomach. "And now we're lost."

"Well, more lost than we were before," Amari said, wryly. "And with nothing to show for it."

"What do we do now?"

Amari shrugged. "We start over."

She placed her hand on my arm and I closed my eyes, expecting the blinding white light to whisk us away. After a moment, I opened one eye to have a peak. Nothing had changed. We still stood in the middle of the forest.

Consternation was plastered all over Amari's face.

"This... has never happened before," she said, and if I didn't know her better, I would have thought there was a hint of panic in her voice. "Let me try again."

I didn't bother closing my eyes this time. I watched with growing alarm as Amari's grip on my arm tightened. By now, I could see the panic in her eyes. Her hand started trembling and I felt a sudden heat bloom beside me. I looked down to see fire blossoming from her other hand.

"Stop!" I shouted. I wrenched myself free from her grip and grabbed her shoulders, angling her body so she faced me. "Amari, stop," I said gently.

"I've lost it," she mumbled, her eyes slipping away from mine. "I can't do it anymore."

"You haven't lost anything," I said, urgently. "And you're about to set the forest alight. Look!"

I grabbed her arm and lifted her hand up to her face. Heat spilled from her fingers, and for a moment the image of a dryad, ablaze inside the arena of the Colosseum, flickered across my vision.

"Nothing's changed," I insisted as Amari's stricken face came back into focus. "We just can't

121

Travel from here, that's all."

Amari stared at her flaming hand. And then she blinked and seemed to snap out of it. She flexed her fingers and the fire was gone, leaving the air around us feeling suddenly much colder.

I let out a relieved breath and released the former Keeper.

She wrapped her arms around herself, her head down, staring at the leaf-strewn ground. She was still trembling, and I didn't know whether I should give her a moment to compose herself or wrap my arms around her.

I was still trying to decide when she seemed to pull herself together and looked up at me.

"It's this way," she said, pointing off to my left. "The clearing where we stopped earlier – it's back that way."

"How do you know?" I asked, glancing around. Every tree looked exactly like the next one, to me.

"Your footprints," Amari said, and I nodded, finally understanding. "They came from that direction."

I hobbled into step beside her as she started retracing our footsteps. My ankle still hurt, but luckily, it wasn't sprained too badly. I was probably going to have an impressive bruise in the morning, but at least I could still walk on it.

Still, it was aching like hell by the time we finally stumbled back into the clearing. I let the scent of the surrounding white flowers waft over me as I sunk gratefully down onto my rock, loosening the laces on my boots. It might not be evening yet in real time, but my aching body clearly wasn't used to this kind of exertion. What I needed now was a warm cup of tea and a good night's sleep.

"I'm sorry I lost my head back there," Amari

said as she sat down on a fallen log across from me. "I don't know what came over me."

"Don't worry about it," I said, attempting to pull my boot off without aggravating my injured ankle any further. "We were both spooked."

I gingerly wriggled my sock off and inspected my foot. There was a bluish tint to it, but I would probably survive. Just.

Amari cleared her throat. "Do you think we should keep looking?"

"Hell no," I said. "At least not right now, in any case. I reckon we set up camp here and rest and recover. The world can do without Tenacity for one more day."

She shot me a relieved smile. "I was hoping you'd say that."

She looked around the clearing, a small frown creasing her brow. "I was also hoping I could jump back to the hotel every night and sleep in a comfortable bed. But I guess we'll have to make do."

She stood up and walked over to where her backpack still lay undisturbed. After some searching, she pulled out a small camping kettle and two enamel mugs. A look of alarm crossed her face as she rummaged through her bag. "I forgot to bring the tea," she said, dismayed. Her eyes widened. "And I also thought we could have dinner at the hotel. I only brought snacks to tide us over while we walked."

"Snacks? You were in charge of the food, Amari," I snapped, suddenly irritable.

I rose to my feet, ignoring the twinge of pain shooting through my ankle. "Let me find some wood and we can at least make a fire." I glanced up at the starry sky, still dark despite my internal clock's protestations. "It might get cold tonight."

Grumbling under my breath, I limped along

the edge of the clearing, scanning the forest floor for anything that looked like it wouldn't explode, bite, or poison me. The cool moss squished between my toes, and every broken twig I collected felt like a fragile truce with the surrounding woods. If there were dryads watching, I hoped they'd see I was only taking what was already dead.

A rustle came from the bushes beside me.

I froze, heart hammering against my ribs.

My eyes searched the shadowed undergrowth, every part of me tense.

Something was out there. Watching.

Caitlynn's words surfaced in my mind like a whisper through the leaves: *Beware the monster inside.*

I held my breath.

No movement, no sound. Just that low, persistent gut feeling that we weren't alone.

"Ambrose?" Amari's voice cut through the tension, sharp and concerned. "Everything okay?"

I forced air back into my lungs and tore my gaze away from the brush. "Yes," I called, louder than necessary. "Just a trick of the light."

I clutched the gathered kindling tighter and limped back into the clearing.

"I'm sorry about the food," Amari said. She was kneeling near a cleared patch of earth, arranging stones in a circle with careful precision.

I dropped the twigs beside her and crouched, my ankle flaring in protest.

"We'll do without," I replied, trying not to sound as resentful as I felt. "Incentive to finish what we came here to do."

She nodded.

I stacked the firewood like I'd read about in books – twigs at the bottom, thicker pieces crisscrossed above.

When it was ready, Amari leaned in and whispered

a Word. The spark caught instantly.

Relief swept over me. No food – but at least we had heat.

The fire crackled to life, golden light dancing across the gnarled tree trunks surrounding us. A hush fell over the woods, sudden and complete.

And then the forest exhaled – an icy breath that doused the warmth in my bones.

Behind us, a voice like rustling leaves spoke, low and sharp: "Put that out."

I shot to my feet so fast my ankle screamed.

Amari rose more slowly, but I could feel her body tense beside me.

The speaker stepped into the firelight, and my breath caught.

She was tall and lean, her limbs more branch than bone. Bark-like skin knotted across her shoulders and arms, her hair a cascade of dark green leaves threaded with moss and thorns. Antler-like boughs crowned her head, and vines wrapped around her torso like a living corset. Fury burned in her chestnut eyes.

"We need it," Amari said, her chin lifted in a stubborn tilt. "You have nothing to fear from us. I can control the fire."

Vines lashed forward from the dryad's arms, hissing through the air. I staggered back, nearly losing my balance. One vine coiled toward my leg like a striking snake, and I barely managed to hop clear.

Amari moved faster, sidestepping one tendril and lifting her hand in the same breath. With a clenched fist and a Word, she froze the vine midair.

The dryad snarled, her body suddenly seized in place, limbs rigid with magical resistance.

Behind her, the forest came alive.

Ten, maybe twenty, other dryads stepped into

the clearing. Some leafy and lithe, others hulking and rough, their roots cracked the earth as they advanced, bark creaking, vines whispering across the ground.

One root caught my foot. I kicked it off and limped forward, stomping the fire out with frantic, panicked bursts. Sparks hissed and died beneath my heel.

"Enough!" I shouted. "The fire's out!" I turned, breath heaving, and yelled toward the crowd of dryads. "We meant no harm or disrespect. We only wanted to keep warm."

"Fire is forbidden in the *Schwarzwald*," the first dryad spat, still paralyzed in Amari's hold.

I looked at Amari, my face grim. "Let her go."

She hesitated – just long enough to make me nervous – then unclenched her fist. The vines dropped and the dryad crumpled to the mossy earth with a thud, her leaves rustling like brittle parchment.

The other dryads stepped closer, forming a wall of gnarled limbs and shifting shadows. I felt Amari's back press against mine, her posture stiff.

"I could have handled them," she hissed without turning.

"They're not the enemy," I shot back. "Remember why we're here."

The leader finally rose, brushing mulch from her vine-wrapped limbs. "Why are you here?" she asked, eyes narrowing. "It is rare for humans to reach this part of the forest."

"And rarer still that they leave," another dryad muttered, her voice like grinding stone.

"We're here to –"

"Our business is our own," Amari cut in. "Let us be, or the Elder Council will hear about this."

I wanted to kick her in the shins. This wasn't the Repository. She was going to get us killed.

Sure enough, another dryad stepped forward, her bark peeling in curling strips. "Only if you live long enough to tell them."

Amari tensed and I could feel static building in the air.

"We're here for the wolves," I said quickly. "We're trying to fix what's been broken."

The dryads stilled.

A susurration moved through them, a whisper spoken through leaves and branches, like the wind carrying secrets.

Finally, the leader stepped back.

"You will not find what you're looking for here," she said coldly. "We will allow you to rest in this clearing for a few hours. There will be no fire." Her eyes narrowed at Amari. "Not a spark. And then, you will leave."

Amari opened her mouth – probably to argue – but I elbowed her, hard. She grunted.

"No fire," I said quickly. "Understood."

One by one, the dryads melted back into the trees, but the air still felt thick, like we were being watched.

When they were gone, Amari rounded on me. "I could have handled it."

"No, Amari, you couldn't have. You're not the Keeper anymore, and we're not inside the Repository. Things work differently in the real world."

She crossed her arms, grumbling something under her breath.

I sighed and sat down, exhausted, my ankle throbbing.

"I'll take the first watch," I muttered. "Get some sleep. We'll figure it out later."

To my surprise, she didn't argue. She just pulled out her sleeping bag and flopped down with a weary exhale.

An awkward silence stretched between us as I kept my eyes on the treeline, still haunted by the way the dryads had emerged from the dark like ghosts. The immediate danger had passed, but the memory of it still smouldered in my mind.

"I left because I'd failed."

I turned towards Amari. She was propped up on her elbows, staring up at the night sky, her features washed in moonlight. Guilt etched every line of her face.

"It was my job to protect the creatures in the Repository. All of them. And I killed Norton. I didn't even hesitate."

I snorted. "He probably more than deserved it —"

"Yes, he did," she said, cutting me off. "He was going to kill Una. But if I'd been more careful... If he hadn't escaped his cell in the first place..." A tear traced a shining path down her cheek.

"I knew the moment the bell tolled that I'd made a terrible mistake," she whispered. "And that I needed to fix it. James wanted to detain me, and I knew the Council's endless bureaucracy would tie my hands. I had to leave. I had no choice."

Heat flared in my chest. Father had said she'd lost her temper. He'd made it sound like she'd struck out recklessly and run away to avoid facing the consequences. I should've known better. She'd been carrying all this guilt on her own all this time.

"I get it," I said quietly.

And I did. When Cassie had been lying in that hospital, fighting for her life because of me, I would've broken any rule to save her. But Amari didn't know what her absence had cost.

I cleared my throat.

"What is it?" she asked, picking up on my hesitation. She leaned over and pulled her backpack closer, unwrapping the *lebkuchen* before taking a bite.

I rubbed the back of my neck, reluctant. "Things have changed in the Repository since you left. There's a… Keeper's fee."

Her eyes widened, horror dawning on her face.

"The amendment…" she breathed. "It goes against everything the Repository was meant to be. Tell me it hasn't been implemented."

"It's still voluntary – for now. But I don't know how long that'll last."

Her jaw tightened. "It looks like the Council was playing a long endgame," she muttered. She shook her head slowly, fury simmering just below the surface. "One thing at a time. First, we fix this. Then I'll make damn sure they regret ever passing that amendment."

There was steel in her voice now, a quiet, dangerous conviction. I almost felt sorry for the Council. Almost.

A nearby owl gave a sudden hoot, shattering the silence. We both jumped.

"Are you sure you want to stay awake?" Amari asked.

Glancing around the clearing, my skin prickled at the thought of watchful trees. "I can't sleep right now. I'll wake you in an hour or two."

She nodded, then finished off the last of her gingerbread before turning onto her side and pulling the sleeping bag tighter around her.

I settled back against a moss-covered rock, my ankle throbbing softly. The cold crept in without the fire, threading into my sleeves and under my collar.

But that wasn't what kept me awake.

It was the feeling of being watched – not just by dryads, but by the forest itself. This place was alive in ways I couldn't name. And we were trespassers.

As Amari's breathing evened out beside me, I

kept my eyes on the shadows. Sleep would have to wait. Because something about this perpetual night – the hush between trees, the air heavy with judgement – told me we weren't out of danger yet.

✷✷✷

The crackle of dry leaves snapped me awake. I jolted upright, heart hammering, eyes straining into the trees.

I breathed a sigh of relief. It wasn't a murderous dryad come to finish us off. Just a small brown deer, nose twitching as it snuffled around our makeshift camp. I noticed my pack was open, and the *lebkuchen* packet was empty, crumbs scattered around my bag. The deer looked directly at me for a heartbeat, ears flicking nervously, then bounded back into the shadows without a sound.

Still shaking off sleep, I turned toward Amari – and froze.

Her eyes were closed, but her body was twisting restlessly, her face contorted in distress.

A nightmare, I thought. Until I saw what was crouched on her chest.

It looked like a child, but not one that belonged to this world. Its hair was a filthy tangle of mud, twigs, and leaves, and its skin had the waxy, grey pallor of something long dead. Streaks of dirt smeared its face and arms, like it had been dragged through the forest floor.

Its hands – long, spindly fingers like skeletal branches – pressed hard against Amari's shoulders. With each breath she took, it leaned in closer, feeding off her somehow.

My skin prickled. The air grew colder.

Then its eyes met mine.

The thing grinned – an awful, jagged stretch of yellowed teeth stained dark with something I didn't want to name.

Without thinking, I lunged forward and slammed into the creature with a hoarse yell.

It flew backward, but landed on its feet with eerie grace, like a feral cat. It hissed and launched itself at me, crashing into my chest before I could brace myself.

We hit the ground hard. The stench that came with it – damp earth, rot, decay – clung to my throat like mildew. I gagged. Its razor-sharp fingernails dug into my chest, impossibly heavy, as if its weight grew with every breath I took. A low, warped lullaby spilled from its cracked lips, thick with malice and madness.

And then the nightmare swallowed me whole.

My hands – no, claws – were drenched in blood.

The taste of it coated my tongue: metallic, hot, alive. I wanted more.

Tangled black fur blanketed my arms. A body lay crumpled at my feet. A girl. Short brown hair. Green eyes now glassy, staring through me with frozen terror.

Cassie.

I'd killed her. My sister.

I tipped my head back and howled.

Then pain stabbed through my chest and the nightmare shattered. I sucked in air like I was drowning, heart splintering with each breath.

"It's not real," I gasped. "It can't be real."

A shout snapped my head towards Amari.

She had the creature by its matted hair, holding it at arm's length as it thrashed and clawed at her, screeching like a banshee. Her face was pale and drawn, but her gaze was steady – furious.

Then, in a flash of fire, the creature ignited in her grip.

Its shriek was brief, but the scent of scorched rot hit me like a blow. I gagged again, eyes watering.

131

And then the roar came – deep, primal, furious. It tore through the clearing like a war cry.

Amari's eyes met mine. "Run!" she shouted.

And then the dryads were upon us.

I turned on my heels and ran, not caring in which direction I was heading, swearing under my breath and wishing Norton had lived to a ripe old age at some comfortable retirement home, playing bingo every Tuesday night.

The trees blurred past me as I sprinted, half-hopping over roots and ducking under branches, Amari's voice already lost in the chaos behind me. Pain lanced up my bad ankle, but adrenaline kept me going. I ran until my breath was ragged, and then I ran some more.

The forest seemed to shift around me. Trees I could have sworn I'd passed before loomed again, their gnarled limbs stretching wider, closer. Shadows bled into one another, distorting the narrow trail I thought I'd been following. I turned left and pushed forward, only to emerge in the exact same thicket I'd just fled.

My heart pounded faster. The trees were moving. I was sure of it. How could I escape the dryads if the forest itself was herding me?

I crashed through a tangle of undergrowth and stumbled into open space – a clearing bathed in the familiar scent of delicate white flowers blooming on the surrounding bushes. A stream burbled past and in the centre a sleeping bag and two backpacks lay discarded around the scorched remains of a campfire within a small stone circle.

My breath caught in my throat.

Had I run in a circle?

Circles will lead you nowhere.

A rustle behind me made me spin. One of the dryads – the first one, the furious one with the antlered crown – stepped out from behind a tree.

Her eyes glowed faintly in the dim light, and the vines on her arms twisted like snakes.

"You were told to leave," she hissed, raising a hand.

Panic surged in my chest. I didn't wait for her to finish whatever punishment she had in mind. I turned and bolted.

I veered sharply away from the clearing, pushing through low branches that clawed at my face. Thorns snagged my shirt. My ankle protested every step, but fear outweighed the pain.

Faster. Just keep running.

The trees seemed to close in again. Branches bent lower. Paths twisted impossibly. I ran left, then right, then ducked beneath a fallen log and scrambled over a mossy rise.

And burst out into –

The same clearing.

Same stone circle. Same scorched ground. Same forgotten sleeping bags. My own footprints overlapped in the dirt.

I gasped, my chest heaving. "No," I whispered. "No, no, no."

The white-flowered bushes rustled.

I turned and ran a third time. I wasn't even sure I was choosing directions anymore. My body moved on instinct – anywhere but here.

The canopy darkened, branches knitting together above me like grasping fingers. Every sound around me was too loud – my panting breath, the crunch of underbrush, the thunder of my pulse in my ears.

And then – again – I crashed into the clearing.

I skidded to a halt, heart hammering, lungs burning. For a moment, I couldn't move. Couldn't think.

Standing at the edge of the clearing, her gown as pale as starlight, was a woman with hair like snow and eyes that shimmered like frost.

Only the White Lady can show you the way.

Amari emerged from the opposite side, hair mussed, face flushed with exertion. She pulled up short when she saw the woman. Her eyes darted to mine, wide with uncertainty.

"The *Schwarzwald* doesn't take kindly to strangers," the woman said, stepping gracefully toward the blackened stone circle Amari had laid out earlier. She sank onto the fallen log as though it were a throne in a woodland court. A small fire sparked to life in the pit.

I stiffened, eyeing the surrounding trees, but the dryads remained out of sight.

The woman turned her gaze to Amari. "I believe you brought a kettle."

Amari blinked. "Yes. Yes, I did." She hurried to her backpack and retrieved the kettle and the two enamel cups, then dipped the kettle into the stream.

"I find elderflowers make a fine tea," the White Lady added, glancing at me.

Elderflowers.

Of course. My ex-girlfriend Rachel used to drink elderflower tea obsessively. She'd made me scour all of London to find a specific German import. I couldn't believe I hadn't recognised the scent earlier.

I knelt by the bushes and carefully picked a handful of blossoms, placing them into the kettle once Amari set it to heat over the fire. The White Lady nodded approvingly.

When the water boiled, she poured the tea and handed us the cups. I offered her one in return, which she accepted with a quiet smile. Amari accepted the second with a murmured thanks. I didn't take one — Rachel's memory had long since soured the taste.

The White Lady sipped and sighed. "A beautiful brew." Her Bavarian accent curled softly around her words. "Now. Why are you here? Most hikers have the good sense to stay on the trails."

Amari's gaze flicked to me. I knew she wasn't sure whether we could trust this woman. I hadn't told her about Caitlynn's vision.

"No offence, ma'am—" she began.

"You may call me Berchta," the White Lady interrupted, gently but firmly. "And truth would serve you better than pretence. Unless you've particularly enjoyed your time among the forest's guardians. I know the *alps* in particular can be quite disturbing – especially if you don't have any gingerbread to hold them at bay."

My stomach turned. The deer. The crumbs. The empty packet. We'd lost our protection without even knowing it.

"We're looking for wolves," Amari admitted, flinching as she realised her mistake too.

Berchta's expression turned wistful. "Then you are four years too late. The last of our wolves was lost when a hunter from across the sea came seeking a rare pelt."

Norton. My fists clenched. The bastard's reach extended beyond death.

"They're all gone?" I asked. "Every last one?"

"I'm afraid so," she said softly.

Silence stretched between us, heavy as a dragon's judgemental gaze. Amari and I exchanged a look. This was it. Our final lead – gone. The wolves had been our last hope.

Amari buried her face in her hands. "This is my fault," she whispered. "I should have been more careful."

Berchta took another measured sip of tea. She didn't interrupt, but watched us, her eyes patient and ancient.

"Why are you seeking the wolves?" she asked eventually.

"We lost a trait –" I began, just as Amari said: "I killed the last of his kind –"

We stopped, blinking at one another.

Berchta offered a thin smile. "You want to restore Tenacity to the world. And you did the world a favour by removing the hunter from it."

Amari leaned forward. "Is it possible? Can the trait be restored?"

"It might be," Berchta said, her voice like the first hint of spring on a cold winter's morning. "If someone still carries the wolf's essence in their blood, it might be coaxed to the surface. The wolf might return, and with it, what was lost."

My blood turned to ice. Norton had been the last werewolf. If there was someone else, how would we even find them?

I turned toward Amari and found her already watching me, a strange light in her eyes.

"Ambrose," she said slowly, a smile tugging at her lips. "I know someone who might help."

"Who?" I asked. And then it hit me. "Oh no. No, no, no. We are not turning my sister into a werewolf."

"We can at least ask her."

"No, we can't," I said, backing away. "She's just a kid. She's already had her brush with death. And now you want to risk her life all over again? Absolutely not. She's been through enough already. If that's the only way forward, then maybe the world doesn't deserve saving."

Berchta stood, brushing off her skirts, and offered me my cup back with a raised brow. "Thank you for the tea. I must take my leave, and so should you. The *Schwarzwald* is no place for cowards."

"I'm sorry," I said quickly, heat rising to my face.

"That was uncalled for. It's just… The last werewolf we met… Well, let's just say he wasn't exactly a nice guy."

"And when he was a man?" Berchta asked, one eyebrow arched. "Was he nice then?"

"I…" I faltered. "Probably not."

"Then what makes you think it was the wolf that turned him into a monster?"

I opened my mouth to respond, but no answer came.

Berchta's voice turned cold. "Go."

A trail of elderflowers bloomed at the edge of the clearing, forming a winding path through the trees.

Amari rose and slung her pack over one shoulder. "Come on, Ambrose," she said gently. "We've done all we can here."

I grabbed my backpack, my chest still tight from the conversation. The thought of Cassie – of what we might ask her to become – twisted in my chest like the lamia's grip – tight, unrelenting, and laced with guilt. I'd already failed her once. Was I really about to gamble with her humanity just to save the rest of the world?

I glanced back one last time.

Framed by the fire's glow and the shadows beyond, Berchta looked like a queen of the wild, unfathomable and immeasurable. Her gaze found mine, unreadable and ancient.

Then I turned and followed Amari into the trees, each step feeling heavier than the last.

⁂ ⁂ ⁂

We were still somewhere underneath the trees when something changed. Beside me, Amari shivered as if she had just walked through a freezing waterfall, and when I looked up, I could see the sun an orange streak against a pale blue sky peaking through the leafy boughs overhead. My internal clock was all out of sorts, and hunger gnawed at my temper like a rat on a rope.

I couldn't get out of the woods soon enough.

Apparently, Amari felt the same. She reached for my arm, her jaw clenched so tightly I was sure I could hear her teeth grind together, and I barely had time to shield my eyes before her Word swept us away.

※※※

It was raining when we landed in Hyde Park – a fine, icy drizzle that soaked us to the bone within seconds. Amari's lips tightened as we dashed for cover beneath the broad canopy of an oak tree, breath misting in the air. Shivering, we fished our rain jackets out of our backpacks.

"We should talk to Cassie right away," Amari said, tugging her hood up.

I shook my head. "It can wait until tomorrow. I want some food in my belly and a night in my own bed. The world can do without Tenacity for one more day."

She sighed. "I wouldn't say no to a long soak in a hot bath."

Something in her voice made me glance over. She stood hugging herself, and for the first time since I'd known her, she looked small. Vulnerable.

"Oh," I said, the pieces falling into place. "You don't have anywhere to stay."

"Of course I do," she replied quickly. "London has plenty of hotels."

"Nonsense." I waved her off. "You're staying with me. No excuses."

She opened her mouth to protest, but I was already walking.

"Come on. Let's get out of the rain."

Amari hesitated – then smiled, almost sheepishly – and followed.

We made our way through the park at a brisk pace toward my flat in Bayswater. I fumbled with the keys at the door, half expecting her to offer a Word to unlock it, but she said nothing. When the key finally turned, I ushered her inside.

The place looked… acceptable. Mother would have found plenty to criticise, of course, but the books were back on their shelves and the dishes still stacked neatly in the drying rack where I'd left them before leaving for Germany. It would do.

I dropped my backpack with a relieved grunt. Amari kept hers slung over her shoulder as she hovered awkwardly near the door, still damp and uncertain.

"Sorry, make yourself at home," I added, waving her inside. "You can hang your coat on the rack over there."

Hesitantly, she took a slow lap around the apartment, as if seeing it for the first time. Her eyes scanned the room like she was unsure how to fit in.

"You can have the bedroom tonight. I'll take the couch. The bathroom's through there – and yes, it has a tub. Take your time."

"Are you sure? I don't want to impose…"

"Positive. I'm ordering takeout. Curry okay?"

She nodded, eyes already drifting toward the bathroom like a moth to a flame. The door shut behind her, and a moment later I heard the rush of water filling the tub.

By the time she emerged in a cloud of lavender and steam, I had eaten, and her food had gone cold. She wore a leopard-print kimono with a towel coiled around her head and the sort of blissful expression usually reserved for spa brochures.

"I found some bath salts under the sink – hope you don't mind," she said.

"Sarah wouldn't, I'm sure," I replied, suppressing a smile. I was eager for a shower, too. It felt like the entire Black Forest was caked underneath my fingernails, and I couldn't wait to scrub it off.

Amari glanced at the couch, where I'd stacked fresh pillows and a blanket. "You really don't mind taking the couch? I know you were looking forward to your own bed."

"I'll survive. Besides, my mother would never let me hear the end of it if I let a lady sleep on the couch while I took the bed."

"And mine would probably have a heart attack if she knew I was spending the night in a bachelor's flat," she laughed. "But I'll be out first thing tomorrow. After we've talked to Cassie."

My mood dipped. "Do we have to?"

"Yes," she said firmly. She warmed her curry up in the microwave and then sat down across from me at the dining table. "If Cassie says no, we'll need another plan. But right now, she's our best shot at setting things right."

I must have grimaced, because she placed a hand on my arm. "You know I'd do it myself if I could."

"I know. And so would I. It's just…"

"I know," she said gently. "I don't like it either."

I exhaled. "Let's say she agrees… Then what? How do we – what did Berchta say? – *coax the wolf to the surface*? What does that even mean? Is she supposed to go on a soul-searching yoga retreat and poof – werewolf?"

Amari gave a tired shrug. "I don't know. I'll have to do some research. Shame I don't have access to my own books anymore."

"I could ask –"

"No," she interrupted sharply. "I don't want

anything from James."

She stabbed at a piece of chicken, then paused. "Do you think he's taking good care of them?"

I didn't need to ask who she meant.

I considered it. "I don't think he cares the way you did. Do," I quickly corrected when she glared at me. "But he's fascinated by them. Obsessed, even. He's in his element studying them, and he knows the Council would be furious if anything happened. So yes, I think he's doing his best."

Amari looked away. "And you don't think... No. Of course not." She rubbed at her eyes, her voice catching.

I reached across the table and rested my hand on hers. "They miss you, Amari. Kentigern Mor said so himself. Even the asrai hinted at it."

"She did?" Amari gave a small, self-conscious laugh.

"Absolutely. You were a great Keeper. And after this – after we restore the trait – we'll find a way to make things right again. Father's just a steward. You're the heart of the Repository."

She nodded. "Thanks, Ambrose. You're a good friend."

Her eyes cleared a little, some of the old spark returning. "Tomorrow morning, you talk to your sister. I'll head to the British Library and see what I can dig up."

"Sounds good," I said, though I doubted it. Father had practically lived in that library during his years as a scholar. If there were any leads, he would have found them already.

Amari toyed with her curry for a few more minutes before finally pushing the plate away. "I'm just not that hungry. I think I'll call it a night. Thanks again for letting me stay here."

I waved her off and we cleared the dishes together. She disappeared into the bedroom a moment later, shutting the door with a soft click.

Yawning, I stepped into the shower and finally scrubbed off the last of the Black Forest's grime. When I eventually collapsed onto the couch - warm and clean – for the first time in days, I felt like maybe – just maybe – there was hope.

But the scent of elderflower still clung faintly to my skin, and the thought of Cassie being our only chance stayed with me long after the lights went out.

※※※

Amari was already gone by the time I woke up the next morning. She'd left a note on the kitchen table saying I should call her as soon as I'd spoken to Cassie.

The sight of it filled me with dread.

How could I possibly ask this of my sister? Of anyone, really. The world was fine without Tenacity, wasn't it?

I turned on the news to distract myself. *Rescue mission abandoned due to low morale*, the headline read. I stared at the words for a long second. Then I shut it off before my own morale could plummet any further.

With a sigh, I picked up my phone and typed a message to Cassie.

-- Hey! I need to talk to you. Can we meet up? --

And then, before she could respond:

-- But if you're busy, no worries, whenever you have time… --

The last time I'd seen Cassie was just before my trip to Germany. She'd come back from the

Repository still shaken after being turned to stone. Furious, too, that Father wouldn't let her stay and help care for the creatures. Typical Cassie: determined to throw herself headfirst into danger, even when it wasn't wise.

But for once, Father and I agreed.

The memory of her frozen face – wide-eyed, terrified – still woke me some nights. And I was about to ask her to risk something even worse.

The weight of it made my stomach twist. Sitting around waiting wouldn't help, so I hopped into the shower, letting the hot water pound against my skin. I scrubbed at my face and braced a hand against the wall, mentally rehearsing every possible version of the conversation – what I could say, what I shouldn't, what Cassie might say in return.

What if she laughed in my face?

What if she said yes?

When I stepped out, the phone was blinking. A new message.

-- I'm at the Tate. You'll know where to find me --

I did indeed.

Swallowing, I zipped up my jacket and grabbed my keys.

I stepped into the crisp morning air and sent a quick text to Sarah to arrange lunch. That meeting, at least, I could look forward to.

I didn't know how Cassie would respond. But if the lamia incident had taught me anything, it was this: it's her life. Her choice. All I could do was lay out the facts – the risk, the need, the consequences – and hope she chose the right path.

Whatever that might be.

※※※

Art galleries, like old cathedrals, always filled me with a strange mix of awe and reverence, though I've never understood a single brushstroke.

My footsteps echoed softly against the polished wooden floors of the Tate Britain as I passed silent worshippers in their own private rituals of appreciation. The filtered afternoon light streamed through tall windows, casting golden shafts across gilt frames. The air smelled of old varnish, dust, and something cinnamon-sweet from the nearby coffee shop.

I found Cassie exactly where I knew she'd be – standing before *The Lady of Shalott*. She was still, arms folded loosely, her focus entirely on the painting. The image was as striking as ever – a young woman in a boat, drifting downstream, her eyes fixed on something beyond the viewer, something just out of reach. Her hair spilled like spun gold over the edge of the boat, her tapestry abandoned beneath her. She was beautiful and tragic and caught in a fate she hadn't chosen.

Cassie had loved this painting since she was fourteen. I used to tease her it was because of her crush on Sir Galahad – knight of the pure heart, rescuer of damsels. But she'd surprised me. She'd said the Lady of Shalott was cursed to view the world only through reflections, never able to experience life directly. It reminded her of how she felt growing up, caught in the periphery of our family's complex relationships, and everything that was beyond her control.

That was the moment when I first realised my beautiful, headstrong sister was much more fragile than she pretended to be. She'd been hiding behind her outward appearance of confidence, and she was brave, yes – but also breakable. I'd promised myself then I'd always protect her. I would be her Galahad, whether she wanted one or not.

As I approached, she glanced over her shoulder and offered a faint smile.

"You said you wanted to talk?" she asked.

I nodded, gesturing to the bench in the middle of the room. "Yes. It's... important."

I looked at the painting instead of her. At the Lady, caught in her doomed drift. Was I doing the same to Cassie – setting her afloat on something she couldn't escape?

"You know how you gave up your studies and –"

"If you're going to tell me *again* that I'm wasting my potential –"

I held up both hands. "No lectures. Promise. But – have you noticed lately that things are harder than they should be? That... I don't know, you're more easily frustrated? That things stall?"

Cassie's frown deepened, but after a moment, she nodded. "Yes. I thought it was just me."

I leaned closer, lowering my voice. "You remember how Amari explained mythical creatures are tied to traits? That when a creature dies out, the trait goes with it?"

Cassie's eyes lit with recognition. "She said something like that, yes. I wasn't really listening at the time – I was kind of overwhelmed by... you know, griffons. But wait... That's what the Repository is for, isn't it? To protect the traits?"

I nodded. "Exactly. And when Norton died..." I hesitated. "We lost Tenacity."

Cassie blinked. "*Norton*? As in the homicidal werewolf? The guy who nearly killed both of us?"

"Same one."

She exhaled sharply. "And you're saying there are no more werewolves now? I have to tell you, that makes me feel more relieved than anything else."

I shook my head. "Norton killed the last of the wolves that bit him. When he died, the line ended."

Cassie's brow furrowed. "So, what? Are you thinking of becoming one?"

I looked away. "Not me. I don't have traces of his DNA in me…"

I hesitated. Her expression had shifted – not just confused now, but afraid. Defensive. Like I'd handed her a curse.

"You think *I* –? Just because I was scratched?"

"It doesn't have to be a full transformation," I said quickly. "But there might be… a hint of something in you still. Something dormant. And if there is, you might be able to –"

"To *what*, Ambrose?" Her voice rose. "Turn into a monster? Because the world lost its mojo?"

"It's not about being a monster," I said, trying to keep my voice calm. "It's about restoring something essential. You're the only one who might be able to do it."

Cassie stood abruptly, eyes flashing. "No. Absolutely not."

"Cassie, please. No one's *making* you. I just needed you to know. You can take time to think –"

"Oh, but the world doesn't *have* time, does it?" Her voice cracked. "You've taken your problem and made it mine."

"That's not what this is."

But she wasn't listening. "You don't care what it'll do to me. You just care about fixing the world."

"That's not true."

Cassie stepped back, voice trembling. "Don't follow me. I need some time to think! I need to *breathe!*"

Before I could say another word, she was gone, pushing past a startled couple who glanced at me like I'd kicked a puppy.

I gave them a weak smile. "Family drama."

They drifted to a different corner of the gallery.

I sank back onto the bench, the ghost of the Lady of Shalott watching me with silent judgment.

Cassie was right about one thing – the world didn't care who had to suffer to fix it.

I could only hope Amari would find something in the Library's endless shelves – some old myth, some forgotten clue, *anything* – that would spare Cassie from being the one to pay the price.

※※※

My heart lifted at the sight of Sarah's familiar smile. She was waiting for me in Trafalgar Square, two takeaway coffees in hand. A lion loomed behind her, crouched in perpetual stony stillness beneath Nelson's Column. I couldn't help but remember that night we'd climbed atop it, pretending to ride a griffon into the clouds.

That had been the night of Norton's first murder. The start of everything.

I pushed the memory aside with a shudder.

"Bad day?" Sarah asked, stepping in for a hug.

"You could say that," I murmured, breathing her in. Her citrusy scent cut through the rain-damp air and loosened something in my chest.

She pulled back, and I met her gaze – moss green, just as I'd always suspected. For a fleeting second, things felt normal again.

She handed me the coffee. "Want to talk about it?"

I took a sip, scalded my tongue, and grimaced. "Sure. But don't say I didn't warn you."

We walked along the edge of the square, past the fountains and toward a quiet spot near the National Gallery. I told her everything – about Tenacity's absence, and the strange, prickling emptiness it left behind, about our journey to the Black Forest, and the White Lady's suggestion.

And then I told her about Cassie. How I'd asked her to consider becoming a werewolf.

Sarah stopped walking.

"You *what?*"

I turned to face her. "It's not like I had a choice…"

"You asked your sister to become a *werewolf?*" Her voice rose, drawing glances from nearby tourists. "Have you completely lost your mind?"

"Sarah, listen –"

"No! No, Ambrose, I won't listen to this. You, of all people, should know what those creatures are capable of. Have you forgotten what Norton did? I had to scrape the victims off the pavement. I had to go tell their families what happened. And now you want to unleash another one on the city? You want it to be your *sister?*"

"She wouldn't be like Norton –"

"You can't know that!" she snapped. "You think she's going to stay gentle and thoughtful and clever once there's a beast clawing inside her every full moon?"

"She's already partway there," I said, softer than I meant to. "Norton attacked her. She might be the last link to that line. If there's even a chance she can take it on and restore the trait –"

"Tenacity is just a word, Ambrose!"

"No, it's not. You've felt it too, haven't you? The way people are giving up. The rescue crews turning back. You've said before your work is piling up and you don't even care anymore. That's not laziness. That's something deeper. Something we lost."

Sarah was silent, jaw clenched, eyes stormy behind her glasses.

Finally, she whispered: "It's not just your hidden world at stake now. If this goes wrong, normal people will pay for it. *I'll* pay for it. The next body could land on *my* desk. Don't ask me to watch that happen again."

I didn't know what to say. She looked away, blinking too quickly, and I could see the weight of it – Norton's trail of devastation, the helplessness she'd carried, the fear of reliving it.

"I'm not asking you to be okay with it," I said quietly. "But I needed you to know. Because if Cassie says yes... I'll need help keeping her safe. And keeping others safe, too."

Sarah shook her head slowly, then exhaled through her nose.

"Unbelievable," she muttered. "How did I ever let you get me mixed up in this?"

Despite everything, a flicker of warmth sparked between us. She gave me what was left of her coffee. "Drink this. You look like hell."

I took it like a peace offering. "You're not wrong."

She hesitated. "I still don't think this is a good idea."

"I don't either."

"But if she does go through with it..." Her eyes met mine. "You *watch* her. Every day. Every minute. And if I see even the *slightest* sign she's losing control, I won't hesitate."

I nodded. "I wouldn't want you to."

Her hand brushed mine, brief but not cold. "Just promise me we're not creating another Norton." Then she turned toward the station.

And I was left with the rain, the roar of distant traffic, and the certainty that I'd just made everything far more complicated.

※※※

The gym was unusually quiet for a Tuesday evening. A few scattered groups lingered near the machines or loitered by the vending area, but most

149

weren't even pretending to break a sweat. On the squash courts, a handful of players hit balls without urgency, the rhythmic thwack of rackets softened by the lack of drive. It was the kind of night where no one bothered to keep score.

"Ambrose! Over here!" Daniel waved me toward the last court. His freckled face lit up with the same reliable warmth I'd come to count on. Just seeing him here, unchanged by recent events, brought a surprising wave of relief.

"Busy tonight, isn't it?" I asked, glancing around at the underwhelming activity.

He grunted as he stretched his arms. "Busy, maybe. Motivated? Not so much. It's like everyone just gave up halfway through their reps and decided mediocrity was enough."

"A Tenacity thing, probably," I muttered. "Want to keep it light tonight?"

Daniel gave me a mock-scandalised look. "Not a chance. I'm going to trounce you, like always, and then you're going to buy me a pint for my troubles."

I chuckled. "Sounds about right."

I winced as I laced up my trainers, my ankle still a bit sore from Germany. A good excuse if Daniel did happen to beat me.

His smile dimmed. I followed his gaze… and saw Caitlynn.

She drifted towards us across the gym floor, dressed for yoga in soft, flowing fabrics. Her red hair was pulled into a loose bun, her feet bare, and her eyes… unfocused. Dreamy. She moved as though half-asleep, her hands trailing slightly in the air, brushing at something unseen.

Daniel was at her side in a heartbeat, gently catching her hand.

Her expression sharpened the moment he touched her. She smiled and whispered something to him. Then she looked straight at me and nodded.

He led her over carefully, his hand steady at her elbow.

"Ambrose," she said, stopping in front of me. "It's good to see you."

"You too. You look well… Everything alright?"

She gave a lilting laugh. "I'm fine, thank you. Though I think my brother's been hovering more than usual."

Daniel gave an unapologetic shrug.

"But there *is* something," she added. "A favour."

"Of course. Anything."

She sighed, but her tone was wry. "Not you too."

I blinked. "Sorry?"

"You and Daniel, always worrying. I'm fine. What happened… happened. And I'm still me."

She shook her head and softened slightly. "I didn't come to scold you. I just wanted to ask if you'd get Cassie to call me. She's not answering my texts. Or my calls. I miss my best friend."

There was real pain in her voice, and it caught me off guard.

I rubbed the back of my neck. "She's avoiding everyone right now. But I'll talk to her. I promise."

"Thank you." A flicker of her usual brightness returned. "That's all I ask."

Then her gaze shifted, suddenly unnervingly distant.

"Cait?" Daniel said quietly, alert at once.

Her breath caught, and she stiffened. Her pupils dilated.

"Under the trees," Caitlynn whispered, her voice thin and eerie. "Bare feet. Wind in her hair. There's howling. And blood. And teeth – her teeth."

She blinked once, slow and unfocused. "To bring back what was lost, she must lose herself."

Then she shuddered and looked around, confused. "Wait… What just happened?"

I exchanged a glance with Daniel.

"You had another one," he said gently, placing a hand on Caitlynn's shoulder.

She sagged against him, suddenly even more pale and fragile than before.

She looked at me. "That was Cassie. I *saw* her. But it wasn't like last time. It wasn't fear. It was power. Wild and real and –" She broke off. "But it could be wrong. The lamia's visions sometimes twist the truth."

"Still," I said, recovering from the chill her words had left behind. "Thanks for telling me."

She smiled faintly. "Now go. Get beaten by my brother."

Daniel gave her a quick hug and sent her off toward the yoga studio before turning back to me. "She's okay most of the time," he said. "But when the visions hit… I don't know. It's like watching a stranger inhabit her skin."

"Have you thought about sending her home?" I asked quietly. The words clung to me like sweat beneath my shirt: *To bring back what was lost, she must lose herself.* I didn't know if it was prophecy or just another twisted vision, but either way – it didn't bode well for Cassie.

Daniel's jaw tightened. "Plenty of times. Ma's begging for it. But it's not what Caitlynn wants."

He lifted his squash racket and tried to smile. "Right. You ready to get flattened?"

I rolled my eyes. "As ready as I'll ever be."

And true to form, he wiped the floor with me. But I didn't mind, and I couldn't even blame my bad ankle. For a little while, the rhythm of the game drowned out the future I didn't want to face.

Amari was setting the table when I walked into my apartment.

"I'm sorry," she said quickly. "I know I promised I'd be out of here this morning, but I don't have anywhere else to go yet."

"Of course," I said. "You're welcome to stay as long as you need." I glanced at the table, eyebrows raised. "What's all this?"

She laughed. "I thought the least I could do to thank you is to feed you. Sit down – I'll bring the food in a minute."

I shrugged out of my jacket and took a seat. The smell coming from the kitchen was nothing short of divine – warm, rich, and unmistakably homemade. A rare occurrence in my flat.

Amari returned carrying two heaped plates and set one in front of me before sitting down across the table.

I eyed the contents, intrigued.

"I was feeling homesick," she said, pouring us each a glass of Coke. "This sausage is called *boerewors*, the white stuff is *mieliepap* – kind of like polenta – and the tomato-and-onion relish is *sheba*. I wasn't sure if your palate was quite ready for *chakalaka*," she added with a grin.

"It smells amazing," I said, then took a bite, and immediately wished I'd known about this food years ago. "Why have I never had this before?"

"I'm glad you like it," Amari said, already halfway through her plate. "And... I found something in the library."

I paused, fork suspended mid-air. "Good news?"

"I found a reference to the bracelet Norton used. It's called a *sire bracelet*. It allows a werewolf to shift voluntarily outside the full moon. Apparently, if someone carries the werewolf trait, they can use it to transform, too."

I nearly choked on a mouthful of *mieliepap*. "So what, you just slip on the bracelet and – bam – instant werewolf?"

"Theoretically, yes. If the person has the trait." She gave me a knowing look. "Magic's like that. Intent and belief matter more than logic and steps."

"Okay," I said, swallowing the last bite. "Let's assume that's true. We still have one problem."

Amari arched a brow.

"Cassie said no. I asked her. I tried everything I could think of, but... she refused."

Amari's face fell. "Then I'll give it a shot."

"You?"

"Who knows? Maybe something rubbed off from Norton while he was in the Repository."

I raised my eyebrows.

"Ugh, not like that," she laughed, making a face. "It's a long shot, I know. But what other ideas do we have?"

"At the moment? None," I admitted.

"Then we have one other issue," she said. "We don't *have* a bracelet."

"What about Norton's?"

"It was in my desk when I fled the Repository. James probably has it now."

"I could ask him for it."

Amari's expression turned stormy.

"Why wouldn't he give it to us? I'm sure he's just as keen as we are to get the trait back into the world."

"Maybe," she said. "But think it through. What would he do with the person who turns into a werewolf?"

My stomach twisted. "He'd... probably lock them up."

"Exactly. That's what *I* would've done, to protect

the trait. Your father has different priorities. Not too long ago, he was happily working for a man who sold creatures to the highest bidder. A werewolf would be... valuable."

"You think he'd sell them?"

"I don't know what he'd do, but I wouldn't want my fate to be in his hands. And if the werewolf was Cassie...?"

I clenched my jaw. "He always wanted to keep her out of this world."

"He'd try to stop her from changing," Amari agreed. "And if he couldn't stop her, he'd try to control her. You know I'm right."

I leaned back in my chair, bile rising in my throat. "So we're *not* going to ask him."

"No," Amari said firmly.

An idea struck me. "We might not have to. I think I know where we can find another bracelet."

Her eyes lit up. "Where?"

I hesitated. "I know you're not the Keeper anymore, but some secrets aren't mine to share."

She narrowed her eyes at me. "You've been holding out on me?"

"I never said I'd tell you *everything*," I replied, laughing. "I gave you what you asked for. And in the case of a certain irritable dragon, what *he* asked for. The Council didn't need to know about the rest."

Amari huffed. "I thought you believed in the Repository's mission as much as I did."

"And look how that turned out."

She ducked her head shamefacedly.

"Anyway," I added. "Let's just say I might know a guy – and leave it there."

"Fine," she said with an exaggerated pout. "But maybe one day you'll trust me with the whole truth."

"I do trust you," I said, getting up and reaching

for her plate. "But I'd lose other friends if I told you about this. You cooked, so I'll do the dishes."

Amari smiled, handing over her plate. "Fair enough. And while you're busy, I'm calling dibs on your bathtub."

I grinned. "As long as you leave me some hot water."

She sauntered off and I walked into the kitchen, chuckling to myself. A dirty frying pan and a pot crusted with *mieliepap* sat waiting for me, and as I filled the sink with soapy water, the weight of everything we still had to do pressed down on me like a second gravity.

Normally, I'd be eager to head out to track down the bracelet, chase the next lead, *do something*. But tonight?

Tonight, I was letting the dishes be my excuse not to leave the apartment.

I sighed, rinsing suds from my hands. We were running out of time – and I was dragging my feet. But tonight, for once, I needed to feel normal.

Tomorrow would come soon enough.

✕✕✕

The smell of bacon and eggs coaxed me out of sleep, mouth-watering and far better than any alarm. I blinked blearily at the morning light spilling through the windows and sat up slowly on the couch, stretching out muscles stiff from a night spent in the wrong place.

Amari was already at the table, toast in one hand and her phone in the other.

I helped myself to a plate – eggs, crispy bacon, a stack of toast – and sat down across from her, wondering how to convince her to stay another night if this is how mealtimes were going to go down.

"Look at this headline," she said, angling her phone toward me as I poured myself a cup of freshly brewed coffee.

I leaned in and squinted: *Hundreds of Construction Projects Abandoned Mid-Build.*

"You think that's part of the Tenacity fallout?" I asked, chewing on a piece of bacon.

"I'd bet on it," Amari said grimly. "Lack of motivation. No follow-through. It's showing up everywhere. And it makes me wonder how my Procurement Specialists are doing. If even half of them are still taking commissions, I'll be shocked."

I looked at her more closely. "You're thinking of stepping in?"

She nodded. "I'll need to. While you go after the bracelet, I should check in on a few of them and make sure they're not doing business with the Council until I've sorted this Keeper's fee disaster."

"Do you have a plan?" I asked, mouth still full.

She gave a small, tired laugh. "One thing at a time. But I'm not sending any more creatures into the Repository until I know they'll be safe. For now, my people will just have to turn a blind eye."

I smirked. "Didn't think I'd ever hear you say that."

"Neither did I." She tore off a bite of toast, her expression shifting from bitter to resolute. "But I'll make the Repository a haven again. Either that, or I'll burn it to the ground."

I paused, mid-sip of coffee, and raised an eyebrow.

She caught my look and grinned. "Figuratively speaking. Probably."

Then she went back to scrolling, as if she hadn't just casually threatened to upend a centuries-old institution.

I wanted to laugh, but the thought gnawed at

me. I wasn't thrilled with how things were going under my father's leadership either – but tearing everything down? That felt like a step too far. Stavros was proof enough that we couldn't just let mythical creatures roam free. They weren't *evil*, but they were powerful, unpredictable, and dangerous in the wrong circumstances. If we lost another one – if another trait vanished because someone killed a creature – what then?

I pushed the last bite of toast into my mouth and stood. "Alright, I'd better get moving. I'll text you once I have the bracelet, and we can figure out the next step from there."

Amari nodded without looking up.

I was halfway to the bathroom when I paused and glanced back at her.

She looked so calm sitting there, like the world wasn't quietly caving in around us. Maybe she was just better at hiding it. Or maybe she'd carried that weight long enough that it had become part of her.

Although the thought of Amari as a werewolf still scared me, it frightened me even more to have the fate of humanity resting on my sister's shoulders instead. And if I could carry that weight for either of them, I wouldn't hesitate. Not if it meant saving them.

Even if it meant becoming a monster like Norton.

Maybe especially then.

※※※

I stopped by Sainsbury's to buy half a dozen croissants before heading toward St Paul's. It was a beautiful summer's day, the grand cathedral's dome gleaming white against a vivid blue sky. Warm air carried the mingled scents of coffee and fresh pastries, and sunlight lit the intricate carvings on the cathedral's stone façade.

The front steps were packed with families snapping photos, children pointing excitedly, and couples looking upwards in awe. Chatter and laughter filled the square, underpinned by the toll of church bells.

For a moment, it felt almost normal.

I cast a glance over my shoulder, then slipped down a side street and stopped in front of an unremarkable brown door wedged between an empty coffee shop and what used to be an electronics store, now transformed into something that looked vaguely like an antiques shop.

A plank was nailed crookedly across the door. Not a good sign.

I set the bag of croissants to one side and looked around before tugging on the plank. It came away more easily than expected, sending me stumbling backwards, awkwardly holding on to it like a burglar caught in the act.

I dropped it next to the steps and tried the door. Locked. My heart sank. I didn't love the idea of breaking into Stan's pawnshop – much less of having an irritable *domovoy* on my hands – but if I was going to find what we needed, I had to try.

I whispered the Word, and the latch clicked open.

Scooping up my tribute of baked goods, I stepped inside. The mouldy corridor was darker than I remembered – no flickering lightbulb overhead this time – so I turned on my phone's flashlight and made my way carefully down the stairs.

At the bottom, the steel door was already open.

I passed through into what used to be the front room of Stan's pawnshop – and stopped short. It was empty. Not a piece of furniture, not a single

159

item of clutter. Not even a scrap of old newspaper had been left behind. If a tumbleweed had rolled past, I wouldn't have been surprised.

Already dreading what I'd find, I crossed to the second set of reinforced doors. They were locked, but yielded to my whispered Word.

Nothing but dust bunnies and stale air greeted me. The back room was just as empty as the front.

Last time I was here, it had been packed with magical odds and ends, including at least three werewolf bracelets. But they were all gone now.

I looked down at the croissants. "Guess I'll be eating all of you myself, then," I muttered.

Why would Stan have left? Did he – like so many others probably did recently – just give up on his business and moved on? Or was there something more ominous behind this disappearance?

I made my way back upstairs. A man blocked the doorway at the top, holding the discarded plank in one hand and glaring at me like I'd just insulted his grandmother. He smelled vaguely of incense and furniture polish and had a bushy moustache that made him look like a grumpy walrus.

"Oi," he barked. "What do you think you're doing?"

"Looking for the previous tenant – Stan."

"The pawnshop guy?" he grunted. "Long gone. Place has been empty for weeks."

"You know where he went?"

"Nope. None of my business." He squinted at me, then jerked his head toward the shop next door. "I have a few of his bits and bobs. Took over some of the stuff when he cleared out. If you're looking to buy, maybe we can make a deal."

That piqued my interest.

"What kind of shop is it?" I asked, eyeing the

mismatched display in the window – porcelain dolls, a chipped gramophone, a dusty old oil painting, and a pineapple-shaped lamp.

"Second-hand everything," he said. "If you want something decent, you'll have to dig."

A few minutes later, I was elbow-deep in a dusty bin labelled '*Assorted Wristwear*'. I nudged aside a few cracked bangles, something that looked like it had been braided from human hair, and then my fingers brushed something cool and hard.

I pulled it out – a bracelet strung with sharp, yellowed teeth.

A werewolf bracelet.

My heart kicked into gear.

"Found something?" the man asked as I placed it on the counter.

"How much?" I tried not to sound too eager.

He squinted at it and shrugged. "Fiver."

I handed over the money without hesitation.

"You know what it is?" he asked.

"Jewellery," I replied casually, pocketing it.

He snorted and shook his head like he couldn't believe someone would actually pay money for it. Then he handed me a receipt and wandered off to rearrange a shelf of porcelain swans.

Back outside, I found a spot on the cathedral steps and pulled a croissant from the bag. As I munched, I rolled the bracelet between my fingers, the teeth gritty and uneven beneath my touch.

Cassie's refusal still sat like a stone in my chest. But now that I had this... maybe she wouldn't have to be the one to make the sacrifice.

I pulled out my phone and called her. Straight to voicemail. I sent a text instead, asking her to call me so we could talk things through. Or if not me, then at the very least, to call Caitlynn. The message remained unread.

Still, the bracelet felt like a win. A small one.

But enough to keep going.

I sent a quick text to Amari. We needed to test this bracelet as soon as possible.

※※※

Hyde Park shimmered in the afternoon heat, the summer sun slanting through the trees and casting lazy shadows across the grass. A group of tourists laughed by the Serpentine, a child chased pigeons near the path, and a couple jogged by, earbuds in and oblivious to the world.

Amari and I veered off the main walkways, cutting across a patch of lawn and into a quiet, overgrown thicket near the edge of the Rose Garden. It wasn't exactly a hidden grove, but it was as close as we were going to get to privacy in central London.

I glanced around, taking in the soft sway of the branches overhead, the way the light dappled the grassy floor.

Under the trees.

Honestly, I'd have preferred to avoid trees right now – but that was where Caitlynn had seen it happen in her vision.

Bare feet. Wind in her hair. Teeth.

She'd described Cassie, but Cassie wasn't here. She hadn't answered my calls. Hadn't even read my message.

And standing here now, watching Amari pull the werewolf bracelet from her pocket, I couldn't help but wonder – what if the vision wasn't about Cassie? What if it was about Amari?

I knew from experience that the lamia visions couldn't always be trusted. They twisted things. Interpreting them was half guesswork, half instinct.

Maybe Cassie was never meant to be the one.

Amari caught me watching her. "You okay?"

I nodded. "Just thinking."

"Don't overthink it," she said, holding up the bracelet. The curved teeth glinted in the light.

"Ready?" she asked.

"No," I replied. "But let's do it anyway."

She grinned and slipped the bracelet onto her wrist. Nothing happened. She held it up, twisted it around, even muttered a Word under her breath. Still nothing.

"Have you tried thinking wolfish thoughts?"

She shot me a flat look. "That's helpful."

She closed her eyes and took a deep breath, shoulders tense with effort, lips moving soundlessly.

Nothing.

After a moment, she sighed and slipped it off. "Your turn."

I took the bracelet, hesitated, then clasped it around my wrist. The teeth bit coolly against my skin. I half expected a jolt of pain or a surge of energy. What I happened instead was a pigeon relieving itself on the branch above us.

"Fitting," I muttered.

I closed my eyes and focused, heart pounding. I tried to picture myself running on all fours, fur bristling, howling at the moon. I tried to feel something ancient and wild rise inside me.

I felt... a mild cramp in my foot.

I exhaled sharply and slipped off the bracelet. "Well, that was anticlimactic."

Amari slumped down on the nearest bench. "Maybe it's defective."

"Or fake."

Before either of us could spiral too far into frustration, Amari's phone buzzed. She checked it, brow furrowing.

"One of my Procurement Officers," she said.

"The one stationed in France."

She read the message silently, then slowly looked up at me. "Well. That explains it."

I raised an eyebrow.

She handed me the phone. The text read:

-- Only bracelets made from the sire's line carry active transformation power. The rest are just souvenirs now. Sorry, thought you knew. --

I stared at the screen for a long moment.

"So that's it," I said. "We need Norton's bracelet."

"Which means…" Amari said, exhaling through her nose as she stood up again and brushed off her trousers. "We're going to the Repository."

I grimaced. "You sure you're ready for that?"

She didn't answer right away. Her gaze drifted toward the skyline beyond the trees, jaw tight, lips pressed together.

"No," she said. "But we're doing it anyway."

I gave a half-smile. "That's the spirit."

※※※

Amari's touch lifted from my arm, and I heard her mutter a silent curse. We were standing high in the mountains, the imposing bronze doors of the West Gate looming over us.

"It's true, then," she said with a resigned sigh. "I'm not the Keeper of Exotic Animals anymore."

She'd once told me only the Keeper could Travel within the Repository's walls. My heart ached for her. She had chosen to leave the Repository, but this was the first time she truly confronted the consequences of that decision. I'd had time to accept the change. For Amari, this must feel like the moment the Repository finally shut its doors on her.

Before I could say anything comforting, she stepped forward and pressed her hands to the gates. They creaked open. Wordlessly, she nodded, and I followed her into the bowels of the mountain.

"What's the plan?" I asked in a low voice as we descended the long corridor. Shadows stretched before us, and I suppressed a shiver, remembering what had slithered through them not too long ago.

"I left the bracelet in the top drawer of my desk. Assuming James hasn't moved it, all you need to do is sneak into my office and get it. Then we walk back out like nothing happened," Amari said.

"And what will you do?"

"There's something important I hid here before I left." Her eyes shone with determination. "I'm going to retrieve it."

"Alright. Where do we meet afterward?"

"Outside the West Gate. If it gets dark and I haven't returned, go down to the village. Wait for me in the *Der Geflügelte Affe* hotel. They do a fantastic schnitzel," she added with a brief smile.

She suddenly froze, pressing a palm against my chest. Voices echoed from ahead.

"Go," I whispered, stepping in front of her. "I'll draw them off. Meet you later."

She nodded and darted away just as I rounded the corner and nearly collided with two of Father's goons. One of them slammed me against the wall, wrenching my arm behind my back. The other levelled a gun at my head.

"Whoa, whoa!" I said. "Is this how you treat guests?"

"Identify yourself!" the guy holding the gun barked. "No civilians are allowed in this facility without prior authorisation."

"I have clearance," I grumbled. "Ask Clint. He knows me."

"Clint's gone," the guy said flatly, but the other man loosened his grip.

"Wait a second," he said, peering at me. "It's the boss' son."

The gunman's whole attitude shifted. "Apologies, sir. We weren't expecting you."

"Quite alright," I muttered, adjusting my jacket. "But good to know you're alert. Now, can someone show me the way to the Keeper's office? I still get lost in here."

"Right this way, sir," the gunman said, all business now.

As they escorted me through the labyrinth of corridors, I risked a glance back and caught a quick thumbs-up from Amari before she slipped out of sight.

They took me straight to Amari's – no, Father's – office. I thanked them and watched them disappear around the corner before trying the door. Locked.

I whispered the Word. The latch clicked. I slipped inside and shut the door behind me.

The room still felt like hers, even though the fire was out and the scent of coffee lingered like a ghost. Father's papers were spread across the large mahogany desk, and that awful photo of Cassie and me stared down at me from the bookshelf.

But to me, this will always be Amari's study.

Mindful that I could be discovered at any moment, I hurried over to the desk and yanked open the drawers, looking for the bracelet. Not in the top one. Or the middle. The bottom drawer held nothing but Tupperware filled with dead bugs. My heart sank.

I scanned the room. Unless the bracelet was

hidden inside a false book, there really wasn't anywhere else it could be.

A sound at the door sent my heart lurching into my throat.

Panicked, I rounded the desk and dropped into one of the visitor's chairs just as Father entered the room.

"Ambrose!" he exclaimed, both surprised and pleased. "How did you get in? I'm sure I locked the door."

"You did," I said smoothly. "Amari showed me how to Open locks a while ago. Sorry for barging in uninvited."

He seemed to accept that, smiling as he took his seat. "You're always welcome. Something on your mind?"

"Cassie," I said, cursing myself for blurting it out.

His smile faded. "Is something wrong?"

"Not really. Well, maybe. Did you know she dropped out of university?"

He sighed. "I'm not surprised. With Tenacity gone, I imagine she found it hard to stay focused."

"You know about that?"

"It was a reasonable deduction," he said with a wry glance over his glasses. "We know a trait disappeared, and with this sheer inability to get anything done lately, it's safe to say Norton's contribution to the world was probably dogged persistence."

I gave a grudging nod. Never underestimate Father. "Any thoughts on how to get it back?"

Father laughed. "Not unless you want me to go full Lycaon and serve my own son up as dinner to the gods. That's how the curse started, you know."

I grimaced. "Hard pass."

He chuckled. "Thought so."

I hesitated. "Hey… Whatever happened to

Norton's bracelet? The one made from wolves' teeth. Amari said it let him shift without the full moon."

"Ah, that," Father said, removing his glasses to clean them. "I tried it myself."

"You tried becoming a werewolf?" I asked, startled.

"Strictly in the name of science. But no changes – no longer canines, no extra hair, no heightened aggression." He slid over a paper covered in diagrams and notes. "A total failure."

I skimmed it. "So it's useless."

"Completely," he agreed. "At least, to someone who isn't a werewolf already."

"Where is it now?"

Father shrugged. "I had no further use for it, so I sold it."

I stared at him. "You what?!"

He had the decency to look sheepish. "It's not technically a creature part, so the Council didn't care about it. But there's a little museum in the village at the foot of the mountain. A cabinet of curiosities, really. They were very interested."

I sagged in my chair. "Great."

"Don't worry about your sister," he added, abruptly shifting subjects. "She'll adapt, like we all will. Humans are resourceful."

I wasn't sure I agreed, but I nodded anyway.

"Mind if I visit Stavros while I'm here?" I asked.

"Go ahead. He's still in the holding cell. I'm still trying to figure out how Amari made those enclosures. Haven't cracked it yet."

"What about the kitsune's old enclosure?"

Father's eyes lit up. "Yes! That wily fox never returned after Rome. Excellent idea. Though perhaps the airavata would be better suited. Bigger, needs more space."

"True. And he's been confined even longer."

He rubbed his chin. "I'll check both options. Although moving them won't be easy."

"Still worth a shot," I said, standing. He was already lost in logistical calculations, so I took the opportunity to excuse myself and slip out the door.

I wondered if Amari had found what she came for. She knew this place better than anyone. With any luck, she was already waiting at the Gate.

But first, I wanted to check on Stavros – just to make sure he was alright.

After that, we'd need to go pay that little museum a visit – and, hopefully, retrieve the last piece of the puzzle.

Assuming it was still there, of course.

✳ ✳ ✳

Somehow, the holding cell looked smaller than I remembered.

I paused just outside the barred gate, staring through at the massive figure within. Stavros lay curled on the floor like some ancient statue, majestic and marvellous. His eyes, a deep, molten gold, opened slowly and fixed on me.

He didn't rise, but I knew he remembered me. There was no trace left of his physical injuries – apart from the dead snake tail - but it seemed strange for him to be asleep this time of day. Guilt twinged inside my chest. Perhaps it was his way of dealing with this cage.

"Hey," I said softly, stepping closer. "Didn't mean to wake you."

The chimaera blinked. One of his goat's horns knocked lightly against the stone wall as he shifted his weight. The air felt heavier somehow, as though the creature's very presence pressed on the boundaries of the room.

"I can't stay long," I said. "Just wanted you to know I haven't forgotten about you."

Stavros rumbled – a low, reverberating sound that felt like it rolled through my bones more than my ears. Not threatening. Just… acknowledgement.

"They're trying to find a new home for you. A proper one. Not this tiny cell. It might take time, but we'll get you out of here. Somewhere you can run again."

I didn't know if he understood. Maybe he didn't need to. Maybe it was enough just to be remembered.

"I'll come back," I added, pressing a hand against the cell's bars.

Another blink. Another quiet rumble.

As I turned to leave, his tail thumped the ground once – almost like a farewell.

"I'll see you soon, Stavros."

※※※

I stepped out of the Repository and onto the stone platform overlooking the valley. The Alps stretched wide and wild beneath me – lush green meadows, jagged snow-dusted peaks, and the village below, nestled like something out of a fairytale.

I sat on a sun-warmed rock and let my thoughts churn. If Father was right, and the bracelet was useless, were we wasting our time? But without it, we had nothing. Cassie had vanished, Amari was risking everything, and I was juggling hope like it was a hot coal I didn't want to drop – too painful to hold, too dangerous to let go.

The gate creaked behind me. I tensed.

"Success?" I asked, relief washing over me

when Amari stepped out, clutching a satchel tight against her side.

"Yes," she said. "And you?"

I shook my head. "Not exactly. But I know where to look next. Let's get out of here."

She nodded, her knuckles white on the satchel strap.

"Schnitzel?" she offered, raising an eyebrow.

"Thought you'd never ask."

✕✕✕

It was close to pitch black in the little village at the foot of the mountains. The waxing moon peeked out from behind the clouds every now and then, casting an eerie, almost otherworldly glow over the wooden houses and cobbled streets.

I nearly jumped out of my skin when Amari's hand brushed my shoulder. I was crouched in a side alley overlooking the quaint Museum of Folklore, which was barely more than a one-room tourist trap.

"Here." She pressed something soft and dark into my hand.

I squinted at it. "A balaclava?"

"Hard to find in the middle of summer, but the ski shop had a few left in their off-season clearance bin."

I grunted. "Doesn't this make it more obvious that we're up to no good?"

"We'll only put them on inside the museum," she said. "Just in case there's a CCTV camera. Highly unlikely, but I'd rather not end up as local folklore ourselves."

"I'm surprised you thought of that."

She shrugged. "It's not my first time breaking and entering."

"Wait, *what?*"

She grinned. "Don't worry, Ambrose. We won't get caught this time."

"*Caught*? *This* time?" I spluttered, stumbling after her as she crossed to the museum's front door. It opened so smoothly under her touch you'd be forgiven for thinking she had a key. I slipped inside after her and pulled the door shut behind us.

"Mask on," she whispered, pointing to a blinking red light in the corner.

My stomach dropped. I was going to go to jail for this.

I fumbled with the balaclava, tugging it over my head. It smelled musty and clung to my scalp like a damp sock.

"We'll have to move fast. Spread out," Amari said as she flicked on her flashlight and vanished between the exhibits.

I turned on my phone's flashlight and scanned the room. It was crammed wall to wall with oddities – half flea market, half fever dream. The place looked like someone had ransacked every myth, fairy tale, and fantasy book, and then tried to cram the results into a single room.

Jars lined one wall, filled with murky liquids and questionable relics: a blackened 'witch's hand,' a fish's fin labelled as a mermaid scale, and a toy frog claiming to be a real water sprite. Further along, a moth-eaten tapestry hung beneath a plaque that boldly declared it had been woven by the Norns themselves.

In the centre of the room, a glass case displayed a cracked leather book, its title scrawled in faded ink: *Incantations and Curses*. It looked ancient, until I opened it and saw the crisp printed font of a twentieth-century reprint. On the back wall, mounted antlers were labelled 'kelpie horns', their stubby, lumpy shape giving the lie to any claims of magical origin. Beside them sat a glass dome enclosing a miniature 'fairy ring' – a circle of painted pebbles around a single wilting toadstool.

I had to admit, I loved the absurdity of it all. This was a collection of the myths and legends I'd loved since childhood – delightfully fake and enthusiastically curated.

Then I spotted it.

A large gilded frame held what was proudly labelled as a 'genuine vampire hunting kit' – wooden stakes, a silver cross, and a vial of supposedly holy water that was probably just the normal tap variety. Beside it, a clutter of teeth and claws were laid out reverently. Each had a hand-written tag: *Dragon's Tooth, Troll's Fang, Werewolf's Claw.* They looked like castoffs from a Halloween clearance bin.

But resting on a red velvet cushion next to the werewolf claw was a bracelet strung with jagged teeth.

"Norton's bracelet," I breathed. "Over here!"

Amari joined me in a flash, her eyes locking on the display.

"Go ahead," she said.

I hesitated. Apart from the solar simulator I'd *borrowed* in Paris, I'd never actually stolen anything before. That one barely counted – I'd sent them some cash later to cover its cost and their insurance would've taken care of the rest. This felt… different. This was real. If I took this, I'd be crossing a line… and asking my sister to do the same.

But there was no more time for moral debates.

The front door rattled violently. Angry voices barked in German from outside.

"Damn it," I muttered.

I smashed my elbow through the display case, flinching at the sound, and reached for the bracelet. My fingers closed around the familiar toothy circle just as the door burst open.

A rotund man with bushy eyebrows barged in, rifle raised.

"*Was zur Hölle –*" he spluttered, just before Amari whispered a Word and light punched the air out of the room.

⁂

"What the hell!" I echoed as the white light faded and the familiar comfort of my living room rushed in to take its place. I ripped the balaclava off, hair crackling with static, heart pounding like a war drum. "Did you *see* the size of the gun that guy was aiming at us?"

Amari looked pale and shaken as she tugged off her own balaclava. "He wasn't bluffing either. That thing looked military grade."

I tossed Norton's bracelet onto the coffee table and collapsed onto the couch. I needed a minute. Maybe ten. My limbs still felt as shaky as a bowl of custard.

"You'd think that guy was guarding the Crown Jewels," I muttered, trying to calm my breathing. "All that firepower for a bunch of fake creature parts."

"At least we have what we came for," Amari said, sitting on the adjacent couch and reaching for the bracelet.

She held it up, turning it this way and that under the overhead light. Then she slipped it onto her wrist. For a moment, she simply stared at it, almost expectantly. She squeezed her eyes shut and visibly focused, brows drawing together.

Nothing happened.

A few more seconds passed. Still nothing.

She looked at me, disappointed. "Maybe James was right."

I held out my hand and she passed it over. It was heavier than I thought it would be, the teeth strung along the cord dull and yellowed like old bones. It felt wrong in my palm – primitive and barbaric.

I slipped it on and tried to steel myself.

Think wolf. Think rage, think strength, think persistence.

Against my will, Norton clawed his way into my thoughts – his growl, his eyes, the violence that followed in his wake.

And then I thought about Cassie, and how I might be asking her to bear this burden next.

Still… nothing. No itching beneath the skin, no pull of the moon, no sudden wildness in my blood. Just a cold band of teeth around my wrist and a deeper ache settling in my chest.

I exhaled slowly and peeled it off again.

"So, it's true," I said quietly. "It won't work for everyone."

I dropped the bracelet back onto the table with a dull clack. The sound echoed too loudly in the silence between us.

"Cassie really is our last hope," I added, though I hated saying it out loud.

Amari didn't answer. I didn't blame her.

"You think we should've taken something else?" I asked after a pause. "To throw them off the scent? Father's going to know exactly what we were after when he hears about the break-in."

Amari tilted her head, lips curving faintly. "Don't worry. I grabbed a few other things while you were stealing the big prize."

My brows lifted. "You *what?*"

"There were a couple of genuine artifacts hidden in all that junk," she said, her mouth pulling into a thin line. "Nobody will know we came for the bracelet in particular."

I laughed, more from nerves than anything else. "You're full of surprises, you know that?"

She rose to her feet. "Mind if I crash here again tonight?"

"Of course not," I said automatically. Though as she padded toward my bedroom, I couldn't help wondering if I'd ever get to sleep in my own bed again.

"Goodnight, Ambrose," she said, disappearing into the room and closing the door.

I sighed and kicked off my lucky white trainers as I pulled a blanket over myself. The couch had been bought for aesthetics, not comfort, which meant it was hard as hell. I shifted until I found the least uncomfortable position and stared up at the ceiling.

We were still no closer to restoring Tenacity. No closer to saving Cassie from the weight I was about to drop on her shoulders.

Maybe Father was right. Maybe this was just how the world worked now and the rest of us would have to learn how to keep going without the things we'd taken for granted.

Adapt or fall behind. That was the human way, wasn't it?

But deep down, I didn't want to accept that.

Not yet.

※※※

The bell jingled as I stepped into Daniel's shoe shop the next morning. Caitlynn looked up from behind the counter, where she was carefully stitching the sole back onto an expensive-looking loafer.

"Morning," she said, her voice calm but eyes shadowed. "Daniel's just stepped out for coffee. Shouldn't be long."

"Actually," I said, stepping closer, "I'm here to see you."

"Oh?" She set the shoe aside and gave me her full attention, though I noticed the subtle tension in her jaw as if bracing for something unpleasant.

I ran a hand through my hair. "You know how you sometimes… lose track of reality?"

"You mean my visions," she said quietly.

I nodded. "How do they work? Do you remember them? Or do you just… wake up in the middle of the street with no idea how you got there?"

She gave a small, humourless smile. "Both. I remember what I see, but sometimes I lose the thread of where I am." Her hands trembled slightly as she picked at a stray strand on the counter. "It's like being halfway inside a dream – one foot in reality, the other in a world that no longer makes sense."

"Does it happen often?"

She hesitated, and when she spoke, her voice had a quiet fragility to it. "Not like they used to. After the hospital, it was relentless – every time I closed my eyes, I saw something else. Someone else. I'm better now, but… it never feels safe. Like I'm always on the edge of slipping away again."

My heart twisted at that. She hid it well. Most people wouldn't have noticed, but she was still scared. Still trying to survive it.

"Is there nothing you can do to control them?" I asked gently.

"If there is, I haven't found it yet." Her eyes met mine, tired but steady. "I'd trade them away if I could. Especially the ones that aren't true."

I nodded solemnly. "You haven't seen anything about how to restore Tenacity, have you?"

She shook her head. "It doesn't work like that. I don't choose what I see. It's more like the visions choose me."

Just then, the bell jingled and Daniel entered, holding two cups of takeaway coffee.

"Oh hey," he said. "If I'd known you were coming, I'd have brought one for you too."

"Exactly the kind of situation where seeing the future would be useful," I said with a grin, then winced, realising the irony.

To my relief, Caitlynn laughed. A genuine one, though it faded quickly.

Daniel gave me a wry smile. "Just for that, I'm not sharing mine."

"That's alright," I shrugged. "I have somewhere to be, anyway. Might as well return this to where I found it." I pulled the bracelet from my pocket. "Not much use for it."

Daniel's eyes widened. "That Norton's?"

"Yes," I said. "Amari and I were told – by the White Lady, actually," I paused to shoot Caitlynn a significant look, and she smiled in response, "that if someone already had the wolf trait, something like this could help bring it out."

Caitlynn's gaze sharpened. "It would," she said, surprising us both.

We turned to her. She looked a little startled herself. "At home, in the library, there's a book written by a werewolf. I can't remember his name…"

"Not important," Daniel said quickly.

"It's about how he turned," Caitlynn continued. "He'd been an amateur boxer. Stepped into the ring with a werewolf who hadn't declared himself. Things got rough, someone lost a tooth, and the blood mingled. Just like that, he changed."

"Sounds like a horror story," I muttered.

"Not really," Caitlynn said. "He described it more like an adjustment than a tragedy. The transformations weren't violent. He'd just become a different version of himself."

"Still sounds like a monster to me," I said, crossing my arms.

Daniel shook his head. "That's the story people choose to believe. The truth is, werewolves were just normal members of society – much like us Tuath. Indistinguishable to humans. The full moon made them… more impulsive, more physical, sure. But not murderous."

"But Norton –" I began.

"Norton was a monster," Caitlynn said firmly. "But not because he was a werewolf."

Daniel nodded. "He probably was a monster long before that wolf bit him."

My throat tightened. The idea had been dancing around the edges of my thoughts ever since the seed the White Lady had planted. "So… you're saying being a werewolf wasn't what made him bad? It just made him worse?"

Caitlynn gave a small, sad smile. "Daniel and I aren't human either, Ambrose. Are we monsters?"

"No! Of course not."

She tilted her head. "Then maybe the monster isn't in the blood."

I let out a long breath. "The man maketh the monster," I muttered.

Caitlynn smiled again, this one softer. "Norton wasn't a monster because he was a werewolf."

"He was just an arse who happened to grow fur once a month," Daniel added.

I huffed a quiet laugh. "I wish Cassie could have heard that."

"I just did," said a familiar voice behind me.

I spun around. For a second, I thought I was imagining her. That somehow my guilt had conjured her up. But no, my sister stood in the doorway, a little hesitant, her arms wrapped around herself – but real. I'd been so caught up I hadn't even heard the bell.

Caitlynn let out a delighted squeal and rushed to her. They hugged tightly.

"I'm sorry I've been so distant," Cassie said, her voice muffled in Caitlynn's shoulder. "I've been a terrible friend."

"You're here now," Caitlynn said. "That's all that matters."

As they pulled apart, something in Caitlynn shifted. Her smile faded, her eyes turned unfocused, and her grip on Cassie's hands tightened.

Daniel tensed.

Cassie's gaze flicked to me in alarm.

Then Caitlynn spoke, her voice strange and melodic, almost like it wasn't her own: "Howling under the full moon. Running wild through ancient woods, glorious and free. Reborn and crowned in starlight."

Her body sagged, and Daniel stepped forward to steady her. She blinked, and her eyes cleared.

Silence hung in the air like a spell had just been just cast.

Cassie's eyes were shimmering. She turned to me, her voice small but certain.

"I'll do it."

※※※

We'd debated whether we needed to return to the Black Forest for this, to the place where the White Lady had first given us hope. But Cassie had made up her mind. If she was going to become something new – something wild and ancient – it was going to happen on British soil.

So here we were: at the edge of a clearing in Epping Forest, just outside of London. The moon hung low on the horizon, a silver disc half-veiled by clouds, casting a pale sheen across the clearing.

Cassie paced slowly, her eyes darting towards the sky to track the moon's progress. Her shoulders were tense, her expression unreadable.

Amari sighed, then said: "Let me go talk to her." She walked briskly over to my sister.

"She's not ready," Sarah said quietly beside me.

I sighed. "She's stronger than you think."

"She's your *sister*," she retorted, her voice low but sharp. "How can you ask this of her? This isn't a like getting a bad haircut – two weeks of embarrassment and then it's over. This is irreversible."

"She *knows* that."

"Does she?" Sarah's voice softened, but she didn't let go. "She's trying to be brave. But if she goes through with this and regrets it…"

I rubbed my temples. "Do you think I haven't been asking myself the same thing every night?"

Sarah's gaze finally turned to mine, searching. "Then why go through with it?"

"Because the world *needs* us to. And Cassie… She needs something too. Something she hasn't been able to name, not even to herself. But I see it. She's been adrift for a long time now. She lost that fire in her a while ago, and she's doing this to get it back."

Sarah didn't respond right away. Then her face softened. "Just promise me you'll be there for her. No matter what happens."

"I will," I said. "Always."

I watched Amari give Cassie a hug, and then my sister walked closer.

"Everything okay?" she asked with a shaky breath.

Sarah looked at her, her shoulders tense. Then she closed the distance and hugged Cassie tightly. "You're braver than I am."

"I'm terrified," Cassie whispered.

"It's not too late to say no," Sarah replied, pulling back.

Cassie bit down on her lower lip, but then gave a small shake of her head.

She turned to me. Her eyes were wide but steady. "I don't want to lose myself."

"You won't," I promised. "Remember what Caitlynn said – you're not becoming someone else. You're becoming more of who you already are."

She smiled faintly, then nodded. "Then let's get this over with. Before I lose my nerve."

"It's time," Amari said, rejoining the group. She looked up at the moon. It had reached its zenith, its light painting the clearing in an almost mystical glow.

"I'm still not entirely sure this is a good idea," Sarah said, folding her arms tightly across her chest.

"Trust us," Amari responded, as I pulled the sire bracelet from my pocket and held it out to Cassie.

She stared at it, uncertain, then took it from me with hesitant fingers.

"I do…" Sarah began again, her voice barely above a whisper. I could hear the fear behind her words.

Cassie silently stepped away from the group, slowly walking towards the centre of the clearing. As she stepped into the moonlight, she turned back to face us. She looked nervous, but also excited. The smile she gave me was radiant and brave. It made me want to run to her, hold her close, and promise I'd always keep her safe.

But I couldn't protect her forever. This was her choice. It was time for me to let go.

She took a deep breath and slipped the bracelet onto her wrist.

For a heartbeat, nothing happened.

Cassie frowned, her hands trembling slightly as she lifted her face to the moon. Then her body shimmered, like light dancing across water. Her arms lengthened. Her face stretched into a narrow snout. With a graceful motion, she dropped to all fours, auburn fur erupting across her skin, rich and glossy as her hair had been.

And then she howled.

The sound rose through the trees, ancient and primal, and stirred something deep inside me. Goosebumps prickled across my skin. I couldn't look away.

Where my sister had stood moments before was now a creature of magic and moonlight – not a monster, not something to be feared or hated, but a stunning wolf, regal and radiant. There was something familiar in the way she moved – wild, yes, but unmistakably Cassie.

Her golden eyes found mine and held them, steady and calm.

Then she turned and bounded into the trees, her sleek form vanishing into shadow.

"Amazing," Sarah whispered beside me.

I couldn't speak. My throat was tight, and my eyes burned with unshed tears.

And then… something shifted.

It was like the world itself had been tilted off-kilter, and now, finally, had righted itself. A gentle ripple moved through the air, like reality sighing in relief. A sense of peace settled over me, warm and quiet. Like coming home after a long, uncertain journey.

I looked at Amari. Her wide eyes met mine, shining.

"She did it," she breathed. Then she broke into laughter, pumping her fists into the air. "She did it!"

I could feel it too. The trait was back. Tenacity

had returned to the world.

I pulled Sarah into a hug, and she melted into my arms, her moss-green eyes glistening. She stepped back just as the auburn wolf reappeared, padding softly from the shadows.

Cassie trotted toward us, tongue lolling like she was laughing. Her body shimmered again, and in the next moment, she stood before me – human once more, cheeks flushed, eyes shining.

"How do you feel?" I asked.

"Amazing!" she cried, then threw her arms around me, hugging me so tightly I lost my breath. "Thank you," she whispered into my ear. "Thank you, thank you, thank you."

I gently pushed her back to arm's length, just to see her – really see her.

She looked like herself. And yet, there was something different. Something freer. The wild spark that had always been in her was no longer caged. It danced in her eyes now, unashamed. And for the first time, there was joy in her that felt whole. Real.

My sister had found what she'd been looking for all her life.

I smiled.

"No," I said quietly. "Thank *you*."

PART 9.5

COUNCIL'S PRIZE

J ames Davids, Keeper of Exotic Animals, was just about to give up hope.

"Come now, old boy," he muttered, gritting his teeth. "You don't want to stay in this holding cell forever, do you?"

The airavata lifted its five trunks and trumpeted in furious protest, ears flaring like war banners. The sound reverberated down the stone corridor, rattling dust from the ceiling. The two men inside the cell with him scrambled backward through the gate, nearly tripping over themselves in their haste.

Thunder cracked somewhere above, low and distant, as the pungent scent of ozone swept through the corridor. It overpowered even the cloying stench of overripe jackfruit and unwashed elephant that clung stubbornly to the walls.

From farther down the hall, a goat bleated miserably.

"Enough," James said. Garcia and Campbell visibly relaxed. Campbell wiped his brow and stifled a yawn while James checked his watch. Later than he'd thought. Time had a way of slipping away inside the mountain.

He scrubbed a hand through his hair. Like everything else lately, this was turning out to be more trouble than it was worth. For a moment, he seriously considered washing his hands of the entire ordeal.

"If it won't let us move it," he said, turning away, "then it'll have to stay put."

He stepped into the corridor and reached for

the gate, then froze as a bell tolled – distant but clear – its chime cutting through the air like a blade.

The last time a mystical bell had rung inside the Repository, a trait had been lost to the world.

This sounded different. Higher, lighter. And instead of a chill crawling down his spine, James felt a strange sense of… alignment. Like a long-missing puzzle piece had clicked into place. A pressure he hadn't known he was carrying eased from the Keeper's chest.

"Let's try one more time, Boss," Campbell said. Garcia rolled his shoulders, sleeves tight around his biceps.

James hesitated, then nodded. "Alright. One more time."

They re-entered the cell. The airavata snorted, all five trunks shifting in warning. But this time, the men stood their ground. Campbell produced a bag of peanuts from his pocket and began teasing the trunks, grinning as he dodged them with ease. The creature huffed in annoyance but followed the treats' scent.

While Campbell distracted it, Garcia darted forward and gently took hold of one massive ear flap. He gave a sharp nod.

James moved quickly. The syringe was already primed. He stepped in close and, with practiced care, pressed the needle beneath the thin skin at the base of the ear.

"It's in," he whispered.

One trunk swatted lazily at Garcia, but the airavata's focus remained on the peanuts. A few more trumpets of triumph followed before the three men retreated.

"What now?" Campbell asked as they stood just outside the cell, watching the enormous elephant sway on its feet.

"Garcia, get the rest of the crew," James ordered. "If my estimates are right, we have an hour. But with a creature this size, there's no telling how fast the sedative will work."

Garcia jogged off toward the communal wing. James turned to Campbell.

"Go prep the kitsune enclosure. Make sure everything's ready."

Campbell gave a mock salute. "You'll be stretching your legs tonight, big guy," he said to the creature before disappearing down the corridor.

James lingered. The airavata had come a long way – from a dusty road outside Dubai, where it was spotted swiping bananas from a roadside stall. A Mazzoni contact had captured it after overhearing a child's outlandish story. Starved and barely alive, the elephant had reached Tuscany in poor shape. James had nursed it back to health on a steady diet of jungle plants, fruits, and spicy Indian vegetables. He'd grown fond of the beast and had been quite happy to see it break free that night of the blood moon market in Rome.

He'd hated seeing it confined for so long in this small cell inside the Repository.

"Don't worry," James said softly as the sedative began to take hold, the creature's five heads drooping. "When you wake up, you'll have grass under your feet again."

Not jungle, unfortunately. James had read the enclosure proposals Amari had drawn up – a tropical forest full of exotic fruits – but thanks to Flavius Regulus and the Green Grove's interference, the former Keeper's vision had never been realised. Now she was gone, and James didn't know how to create new enclosures.

The kitsune's empty meadow would have to do. A poor substitute, but he was out of options.

The airavata slumped to the floor with a final

sigh, just as Garcia returned with five more men, hauling an enormous steel trolley.

With practiced teamwork, grunting and swearing all the way, they manoeuvred the unconscious creature out of the cell and toward the main cave. James followed, nerves taut as they strapped the trolley into the pulley system designed to lower heavy loads down the stairs. Somehow, the descent went smoothly.

Whatever he might think of the muscled mercenaries he'd inherited from Mazzoni, at least they were professionals – and good at their job. This was just another day at the office for them.

"Quickly," Campbell called from within the kitsune enclosure, waving them forward. "It's waking up!"

Sure enough, one of the trunks twitched. James felt a knot tighten in his gut.

"Hurry! If you think a regular elephant with a headache is bad – try one with five, and a lightning storm behind each!"

The men shoved the trolley through the gate and into the sunlit meadow beyond. It was a strange sight – bright daylight blooming despite the late hour, casting golden light over wildflowers and soft green grass. Birds called from the trees, and honeysuckle scented the air.

"Gently," Campbell urged as the airavata groaned and one head lifted. Its legs twitched, and a foot nearly caught one of the handlers.

But they made it. The restraints were removed, and the creature staggered upright, ears flapping, trunks waving. Then it spotted the food beneath the maple tree and lumbered toward it, trumpeting cheerfully.

"It looks happy," Campbell said, grinning like a child.

James nodded. Relief bloomed in his chest. "It's

not ideal. But it'll do."

They stepped out, closing the gate behind them. The shift from the enchanted warmth of the enclosure to the chilly air of the cave was almost jarring.

"Get some rest," James dismissed the men, before turning back to Campbell. "Check on it again in the morning. I'm not sure if it'll be able to eat anything it can forage in there. We'll have to keep careful track of its diet for the next few days – see if it adapts to what's available."

"Will do," Campbell said, glancing back with a smile before disappearing up the stairs too.

James followed behind, slower, exhaustion catching up all at once. He entered his study and slumped into the chair behind his desk, meaning to jot down a few notes, but paused as the memory of the bell returned.

Something had changed.

"It's back," he whispered, a wide, disbelieving grin spreading across his face. "Tenacity is back."

His heart thudded as the realisation sank in. If the trait had returned, it could only mean one thing.

Another werewolf had been sired.

But how? Norton was long dead – James had made very sure of that. There was no one left to pass the curse on.

He shuffled through the clutter on his desk until he uncovered the calendar buried beneath the papers. Full moon.

James frowned. Somewhere out there, a dangerous creature was running loose, unchecked and unseen. He ought to send someone to track it down, to contain the threat before it escalated.

Instead, he crossed the room and opened the cupboard beneath the coffee station. From the back, he pulled out a bottle of single malt scotch.

He poured himself a glass, then sat back and swirled the amber liquid slowly, watching the cold hearth across the room.

Tenacity was *back*.

That was enough for now – and cause for celebration.

✳✳✳

Much later the next morning, after James had submitted his report on the trait's return to the Council, he was sifting through the stack of incoming papers on his desk when the headline on the local newspaper caught his eye: *Brazen Thieves Plunder Our Folklore!*

Intrigued, he pulled the latest issue of the *Alpenblick Aktuell* closer and began to read:

> *In a crime that can only be described as both daring and deeply disrespectful, the beloved Museum of Folklore was the target of a mysterious robbery late last night. The thieves – or should we say vandals of heritage – made off with several priceless artifacts, including a ceremonial wolf bracelet believed to date back to the 12th century, a horn fragment said to have belonged to the Krampus, and a medieval good-luck charm forged from fire drake scales, once used to ward off snowstorms.*
>
> *Local residents are in uproar. "What kind of person steals folklore?" asked Frau Ilse Binder (83), owner of Der Geflügelte Affe hotel. "That's like robbing your grandmother's memory! What's next, the singing toadstone from the town square?!"*
>
> *Museum curator Herr Günther Dörflinger (52), who claims to have caught the criminals in the act, reports no sign of forced entry beyond a single broken lock. "They blinded me with a spell and disappeared – vanished as if by magic!"*

Police have released a vague description of the suspects: two figures, one tall, one shorter, dressed in dark clothing. "Could be teenagers. Could be spirits. Could be Dutch," said Officer Markus Hennel, cryptically.

The museum will remain closed until further notice. Donations to help restore the exhibit (and replace the broken glass displays) can be made by putting euros in the brown boot by the bakery.

If you saw anything unusual, please contact local authorities or shout loudly near the town fountain. As always, Alpenblick Aktuell will keep you informed.

A wry chuckle escaped him. The villagers at the foot of the mountain were an... eccentric lot. He supposed their proximity to the Repository had been fuelling their collective imagination for centuries. Most of the article was nonsense, of course, but the mention of the stolen werewolf bracelet caught his attention.

That couldn't be a coincidence.

He'd told Ambrose the bracelet had been sold to the museum. And now, just a day after it was stolen, Tenacity had returned.

It had to be Ambrose.

James clenched his jaw. He'd suspected something was brewing ever since his son's last visit. Ambrose had been sniffing around for information the last time he visited, asking pointed questions about the bracelet. He'd probably been rummaging through James' drawers before he'd been caught.

But now... This was confirmation.

A flicker of pain passed through him – not quite betrayal, but close.

Why hadn't Ambrose trusted him?

Maybe it was time to change that.

He picked up his phone. It didn't take long for Ambrose to answer. The background noise suggested he was on a train.

"Is this a good time?" James asked.

"Of course," Ambrose replied, stifling a yawn. "I'm heading back into London now."

"Late night?"

"You could say that. Might've had one too many beers as well," Ambrose admitted.

"I *knew* it." James grinned. "You were celebrating, weren't you? You brought Tenacity back!"

There was a brief pause. "I had very little to do with it, actually."

"But you did bring the trait back, right?"

Ambrose cleared his throat. "Yes. I believe so."

James nodded. "How did you make another werewolf?"

"Excuse me?"

"You said you had little to do with it," James pressed. "So I assume it's not you. But I know you took the bracelet. Who is it? How did you find someone who could shift?"

A short pause, and then: "I don't know if I should tell you," Ambrose said carefully. "Sorry, but… You being the Keeper, and… it's complicated."

Disappointment burned in James' throat. "Fair enough," he said tightly. "Although, if I might add, I would have liked to have been involved. Even unofficially. The Council doesn't need to know *everything*."

"Sorry."

Trying to shift the conversation, James asked: "How's your sister doing?"

"Cassie?" There was tension in Ambrose's voice now. "She's fine. Really. Never better."

Something wasn't right.

James frowned, memories slotting into place –

Cassie's hospitalisation, the mugging gone wrong. But Ambrose had told him the truth that night: Norton had attacked her.

Realisation struck with cold precision.

"Ambrose… What did you do to your sister?"

"Nothing! I swear," his son said quickly, panic rising in his voice. "She's safe and she's happy."

"But does she also have a glossy fur coat?"

Silence.

"Ambrose?"

"She's fine."

"That's not an answer."

"Alright, yes," he admitted at last. "She's made the shift. Not a monster like Norton," he added quickly. "Just a normal wolf. She can change back and forth as she likes, with the help of the bracelet."

James' blood ran cold. For a moment, he didn't know whether he was shaking from fury or fear.

"You promised me you'd keep her safe," he said, voice low and dangerous.

"She *is* —"

"She's not safe!" James snapped. "Not anymore. Do you have any idea how valuable she's become? The last werewolf in the world. The only creature alive carrying the trait!"

He dragged in a breath. "Bring her here."

"What? No!"

"The Repository is the only place she'll be protected. The Council will have to be told, but at least here I can keep an eye on her. Keep her safe."

"She'll never agree to that," Ambrose said.

"She doesn't have to. Just bring her."

James ended the call before his son could argue further.

He sat there, breathing heavily. Then he reached down and pulled open the bottom drawer of his desk. Curled inside his nest of shredded parchment,

Nusku blinked up at him. The phoenix chick had grown rapidly – its once patchy down now replaced with radiant feathers that shimmered red and gold. James scooped him up, cradling him against his chest. The warmth soothed him, and the bird chirped softly, nuzzling into his shirt.

James absently stroked the phoenix's sleek neck. How could Ambrose be so reckless?

After everything with the gorgon – and Norton – he thought they'd agreed: Cassie should stay far away from all of this. But now she was bound to it. Irrevocably.

He needed her here, before someone less scrupulous than the Council found her. Someone like Mazzoni, whose network may still be active in the shadows. The idea of his daughter in a cage, her transformation paraded as a commodity, made his skin crawl.

No. He wouldn't let that happen.

She was headstrong – too much like her mother in that – but if he could just speak to her, reason with her… She'd wanted to stay and help take care of the creatures before. He should have agreed then.

Maybe she'd agree now.

And if not? Then perhaps there was another solution.

Perhaps there was still a way to save her.

✳✳✳

James inspected the latest batch of samples collected as Keeper's Fees: another harpy feather, a few more toenail clippings from the cyclops, a phial of basilisk bile – never in short supply – a clump of minotaur hair, and a scattering of shed salamander scales. Still no contributions from the asrai or any of the other nymphs, nor from the griffons, the unicorn, or half the other creatures in his care. Schoeman had even admitted he'd found the minotaur hair snagged on a jagged stone in its maze, not offered willingly.

James clicked his tongue in irritation. He was a scholar of myth, not a biochemist. What was he supposed to do with all of this? He had ideas, of course – whispers from old texts and theories cross-referenced from folklore. He'd played around with bits of bark and powdered-down scales, but he didn't have the skillset to turn samples into salves, syrups, or solutions.

And yet that was what the Council wanted: results. Deliverables. Products to be sold or weaponised or turned into luxury goods.

He exhaled sharply through his nose. The creatures were already valuable – *intrinsically* so. More than the fragments his men managed to collect could ever suggest. The Council's vision was too narrow, too material. James believed the world should see these creatures with their own eyes – pay admission not for bottled enchantments or creams distilled from myth, but to witness living magic. Breathing legends. That was worth more than any serum.

His phone chimed, interrupting his thoughts. An email from the Council.

TO: The Keeper of Exotic Animals
FROM: The Council for the Protection and Preservation of Cultural Creatures
RE: Progress Report

Mr Davids,

The Council has called a session to discuss your most recent report, as well as any progress you've made regarding research into the viable usage of the intrinsic abilities of creatures currently residing within the Repository under the care of the Council.

Please be available at our headquarters this afternoon, at 16:00, for this discussion.

Yours faithfully,
R Drake (Chairman)

James sighed and read the message again. Perhaps this was the opportunity he'd been waiting for. A chance to finally make them understand.

He glanced at his watch. Just over three hours. He'd have to hurry.

As he gathered a few samples and organised his notes into a binder, he found himself wishing – not for the first time – that Amari hadn't left so abruptly. Her ability to Travel would've saved him the journey. Instead, he'd have to take the blasted helicopter. He grimaced at the thought. If man were meant to fly, they'd have grown wings like the harpies.

He pushed the thought aside and focused on the task at hand. There was still time. And if he made his case well enough – if he could remind the Council what they were really protecting – maybe they'd shift course. Maybe they'd stop asking for potions and powders and start seeing what he saw: wonder, legacy, the kind of magic that didn't belong in a bottle.

He slid the binder under one arm and ran a hand through his hair.

Nusku chirped from his new perch beside his desk, feathers bright in the dull light. James glanced up at the bird and nodded. "Wish me luck."

He closed the door behind him and headed for the landing pad.

Let them keep their ointments.

He'd show them something better.

※※※

James spent most of the flight hunched over his notes, ignoring the dizzying thought of the earth so far below him. The rhythmic thrum of the helicopter blades did little to settle his nerves, but it gave him something to focus on as he circled phrases, scribbled ideas, and restructured theories with scholarly precision. Only when the helicopter banked and began its descent did he glance up, blinking at the sudden grey light filtering through the window.

Below, Brussels spread out in a patchwork of slate rooftops, green boulevards, and congested motorways. The sky was grey, clouds sweeping across the skyline, as the helicopter landed with mechanical grace on a private helipad just beyond the city centre.

James packed away his notes, straightened his coat, and climbed down the narrow steps into a waiting black car.

The drive took them through the industrial edges of the city – graffiti-tagged warehouses, rows of apartments with peeling shutters, the faded remnants of Brutalist architecture softened only by ivy and time. But as they crossed the inner ring, the cityscape changed dramatically. Wrought-iron balconies gave way to gilded façades. Cobblestone alleys narrowed and twisted between ornately decorated shopfronts. The scent of roasted coffee filtered in through the cracked window.

They stopped just outside the Grand Place, where vehicles were forbidden. James stepped out into the cobbled square, breathing in a mixture of syrupy waffles and wet stones. Tourists murmured nearby, their footsteps echoing on the stones, but he barely registered them.

The square opened before him like a theatre stage: the Hôtel de Ville's towering spire pierced the clouds, flanked by a court of baroque guildhalls with gold accents catching what little light the sky offered. He walked briskly, his footsteps tapping along the ancient flagstones, passing under carved reliefs of lions, saints, and long-forgotten patron deities.

He stopped in front of a stately stone building, one of many with windows framed by iron balconies filled with planters of bright red geraniums. There was no plaque, no inscription, nothing to set it apart – but James had been here twice before and knew exactly where to go.

Inside, the scent of beeswax polish and leather-bound tomes greeted him. He climbed the stairs two at a time, the sound of his polished shoes echoing off marble and dark oak panelling.

At the top, he turned left, passed two closed doors, and paused before the third. He adjusted his cufflinks, drew a steadying breath, and pushed the door open into the boardroom beyond.

The Council Chamber was sleek and silent, its glass table gleaming beneath a modern chandelier. Twelve figures sat around it – some old, some young, almost all sombre.

The Chairman, a well-groomed man in his thirties with expensive taste and an unreadable smile, nodded. "Mr Davids," he said. "Please, be seated."

James smoothed his lapels and took his place. He winced as his chair scraped across the floor.

Councilmember Finch cleared his throat and adjusted his thick spectacles. "Let's begin. Mr Davids, we've reviewed your report on the trait's return with great interest. It appears that the werewolf's passing did indeed mark the death of Tenacity. But as of last night, that trait has returned. Can you tell us how?"

James hesitated. He was not going to tell them the whole truth. Not until Cassie was safely back in the Repository with him. He didn't relish the idea of lying, but he forced his expression into a scholarly calm. "I don't have all the details, but my son was involved. He assures me the carrier of the trait is safe and will be brought to the Repository soon."

"Your son... Albert?" the Chairman asked.

"Ambrose," James corrected.

"Did he indicate how the trait was returned?"

"He found someone who could shift," James said carefully. "And thus, restore the balance."

"Someone?" Councilmember Ravel echoed, his heavy French accent curling around the word.

James offered a small noncommittal shrug. "I'll report back once I know more."

"Very well," the Chairman said. "Convey our gratitude to your son. And perhaps add an additional ten percent to the finder's fee when he brings the creature in, as a token of our appreciation."

James inclined his head.

Councilmember Finch shuffled his agenda. "Your update on the Keeper's Fees, if you please."

James withdrew three phials from his briefcase and set them before the Council. "This is basilisk bile," he said, lifting the first. "Highly potent. One drop can reverse petrification, as I've witnessed myself." He smiled faintly. "Though I wouldn't recommend the smell."

Councilmember Ravel laughed softly. "I've had to use it on Keeper Kerubo a few times. Pungent, but effective."

James nodded. "Indeed. This second phial contains fire salamander scales. Resistant to intense heat and almost unbreakable. I've begun drafting ideas for protective applications – perhaps body armour for firefighters."

A few unimpressed expressions met him. He moved to the third phial.

"Dryad bark. Different nymphs produce different strains. Ground finely, it may have medicinal properties – anti-inflammatory, perhaps even regenerative. But further testing is needed."

Silence stretched.

James glanced down at his notes, then back up, voice tight. "There's more I'm working on, but… I admit, I lack the expertise to develop these into actual products. I can trace their folklore, analyse their mythic context… But I'm not a chemist."

Councilmember Silvetti sniffed, as though offended by the admission. "Fairy-tale salves and peasant poultices? That's the best you can offer?"

Heat climbed up James' neck. "With respect, these aren't just ingredients. They're expressions of living magic. The creatures are already valuable as they are – more than any tonic or potion could ever justify."

The Chairman steepled his fingers. "Perhaps, Mr Davids, what you need is an assistant."

James stiffened. When the Elder Council had wanted to change their policies, they'd made him Amari's assistant. Was he being pushed aside already?

"I can manage on my own."

"A researcher," the Chairman clarified. "Someone who can take your knowledge of folklore and turn it into viable products."

James paused. Not a replacement. Someone with a different skill set.

Councilmember Silvetti spoke up. "I know someone. I'll reach out."

"Excellent," said the Chairman. "Let's continue."

Councilmember Finch consulted his notes. "Any new acquisitions?"

James cleared his throat. "We've had no new captures apart from the chimaera. Keeper Kerubo left without passing on her contacts, and her procurement team has gone dark."

Councilmember Silvetti pursed her lips. "But you worked with Mazzoni. Surely you have some leads."

"I don't," James admitted. "I'll make inquiries. If we're lucky, some of Mazzoni's agents might be willing to work under official Council channels."

The Chairman nodded. "Better that than having them freelancing in the wild."

The room murmured in agreement.

"And those creatures still in the holding cells?" Councilmember Ravel asked.

"We moved the airavata into the old kitsune enclosure," James reported. "It's adapting well, though the space isn't ideal. The chimaera, however, remains isolated. The incident with the salamanders made it clear: we cannot risk mixed habitats again."

"I agree," Councilmember Novak said, grandmotherly features belying the intensity in her brown eyes. "Then why not create a new enclosure?"

James flushed. "Keeper Kerubo left without teaching me how. I'm afraid without her knowledge…"

"Creating new enclosures is a lost Keeper skill," the Chairman mused. "Long before Miss Kerubo even became Keeper. She had no mentor – she figured it out herself."

"I'll find a way," James promised. "There must be something in the library…"

The Chairman gave a small, satisfied nod. "See what you can learn."

James glanced around. "Before we conclude, I'd like to propose an alternative revenue stream."

Several heads turned toward him.

"I know the Council seeks to monetise the abilities of the creatures," James said, carefully choosing his words. "And I agree there is definitely benefits to that – but I believe their greatest value lies not in what we extract, but in what they are."

Finch arched an eyebrow. "Go on."

"Controlled, exclusive visits to the Repository," James said. "Private, curated experiences for select guests. The rarest of encounters – myth brought to life. Not a zoo," he added quickly, sensing the recoil. "An immersive sanctuary. A celebration of living legend."

Silence.

Councilmember Ravel looked horrified. "You want tourists traipsing through the Repository?"

"Not tourists," James insisted. "Scholars. Patrons. Visionaries. Imagine what it would do for public appreciation. We've kept them hidden for too long – their magic deserves to be seen."

Some heads nodded. Others exchanged wary glances.

The Chairman remained inscrutable. "We'll consider it."

"Thank you," James said, and sat down again. He'd planted a seed, at least.

The meeting drew to a close. As the other Councilmembers filed out – some curious, some sceptical, a few visibly intrigued – the Chairman lingered.

"One last thing," he said. "The caladrius bird. Have you found another?"

James narrowed his eyes. This wasn't the first time the Chairman had asked. He filed it away uneasily.

"No. Mazzoni never told me where the bird

came from. And frankly, I've been focused on stabilising the Repository."

The Chairman stepped closer, eyes intense. "It's vitally important to me that you find another one of its kind, Mr Davids. More important than anything else. I'll handle the Council's other expectations if you can find me another caladrius."

James sensed something unspoken beneath the request, something personal. A quiet desperation.

"Understood," he said. "I'll do my best."

The Chairman smiled thinly and clapped him on the back. "Good man."

As James descended the stairs, the scent of old wood and politics fading behind him, his thoughts turned over and over: caladrius, Cassie, the chimaera, the Council's demands. He stepped back into the cobbled square, the clang of distant bells barely cutting through the noise in his mind.

The world might not be ready for the wonders he'd seen – but he would find a way to show them.

※※※

"Fascinating…" James murmured, his voice barely louder than the soft rustle of grass swaying in the soft breeze. He reached into his coat pocket and withdrew his notebook, flipping to a fresh page. He shook his fountain pen – he must remember to fill it up when he was back in his office – and began to write the scene playing out in front of him.

The airavata stood at the centre of the meadow, its bulk incongruous among the delicate greenery of the kitsune enclosure. The creature's five heads had always seemed awkward to James, but now, outside the confines of its small cell, they moved with surprising grace, each independently scanning the environment. One trunk carefully lifted a cluster of honeysuckle vines from a low branch, tucking them around the base of a tree like a garland. Another head stooped to sip from the stream, while a third tilted toward the sky, ears fanning out as though listening for a sound only it could hear.

James had expected resistance. A display of dominance, perhaps even a violent outburst. Instead, the creature had simply settled in and adapted.

He made a note of the woven vines and the way the grass seemed to grow greener and more thickly where the creature walked. The small hill, once dotted with wildflowers, was now blanketed with clusters of delicate blue-purple flowers. *Neelakurinji*, he recognised with a jolt, straight out of the hills of southern India. As though the airavata's presence had coaxed memories of a distant homeland from the soil.

Even the birdsong had shifted. Previously, the woodlands had echoed with the familiar calls of jays and warblers. Now, strange notes filled the air – liquid trills, unfamiliar melodies in complex patterns. James blinked, momentarily disoriented. The sound reminded him – absurdly – of the background music in that little Indian restaurant he used to frequent back in London.

James paused mid-sentence.

"It's reshaping the space..." he whispered. This creature was powerful enough to bend the fabric of the enclosure to its liking. He glanced around, looking for more signs of change. The trees seemed taller, their bark slick with dew, even though it hadn't rained in days. Was that a jackfruit tree peeking out between the maples?

His pen scratched frantically across the page: *Powerful enough to bend reality around itself.*

One head turned toward him, eyes dark and

deep as monsoon clouds. It blinked once, slowly, then resumed its work.

James closed the notebook with a quiet snap and stepped back, giving the creature space. It continued its slow work, braiding a few trailing vines through the low-hanging branches, flapping like prayer flags in the breeze.

A low rumble rolled across the sky. James looked up, his brow furrowed. Clouds were forming in the distance, rolling in slow and sure over the far side of the meadow.

"Airavata, the bringer of rain," he whispered, half in awe. "Perhaps... a potion or a powder, or something... to ward off droughts?"

A voice cut into his reverie.

"Boss?"

James startled. He turned to see Campbell approaching, a netted bag of papayas slung over one shoulder.

"She's here," Campbell said. "The lady from the Council. She's in your office."

James exhaled slowly, reluctant to leave. "I wasn't expecting her so soon. Very well. Let me go meet this scientist."

He slipped the notebook back into his coat pocket and brushed grass from his trousers. The weight of what he'd just witnessed clung to him like mist – or magic. As he stepped out of the enclosure and into the main cave, a knot of unease coiled in his chest.

He understood the value of scientific rigor – of logic, of process, of replicable results. But what he had just seen defied that kind of reason. The airavata didn't operate on chemical reactions or predictable patterns. Its presence altered the space around it in ways that science would never be able to explain. Not through cause and effect, but through meaning, and memory, and myth.

Could science even *measure* that?

He wasn't so sure anymore that bringing a scientist into the Repository was the right move.

Science could dissect and name.

But magic required wonder.

And James wasn't ready to give that up just yet.

※※※

She was younger than James had expected – late twenties, perhaps early thirties – with sleek, precisely styled blonde hair and a navy power suit that belonged more in a corporate boardroom than anywhere near a laboratory. When she looked up from the ancient volume in her hands, her smile was poised, polished, and just this side of smug.

"You must be James Davids," she said, her accent unmistakably Oxfordshire.

"Please refrain from touching the books," James replied, holding out a hand. "They're very delicate."

Her sardonic smile widened as she deposited the tome into his outstretched palm without a hint of apology, then turned on her heel toward the coffee machine. "May I?" she asked, already reaching for the switch. "I hadn't realised the helicopter ride would take quite so long."

"Help yourself," he said, glancing down at the book she'd been perusing – Pliny the Elder's *Historia Naturalis*. A first edition. In Latin. He resisted the urge to sigh.

"Miss…?"

"Doctor," she corrected smoothly as she poured herself a generous cup of coffee. "Dr Fiona Clarke. I believe I'm here to help you with a little research project?"

James returned the precious book to its place on the shelf before settling into his chair behind the desk. He gestured for her to take the seat opposite him, which she did without hesitation, her long, manicured nails tapping against the delicate porcelain of her cup with a rhythmic insistence that set his teeth on edge.

"How much do you know about the assignment?" he asked.

"Apart from the fact that it pays very well?" She shrugged, entirely unfazed. "Not much. I was told you'd brief me. And that it involved some… unconventional biology." Her eyes gleamed with interest.

James steepled his fingers. "Before we begin, I'll need to verify your credentials."

She raised an elegantly plucked eyebrow, as though the very idea of having to prove herself was mildly amusing. "Might I remind you, *Mister* Davids, that you called me. *You* need *me*."

"Indulge me, if you would."

With a dramatic sigh, she reached into her oversized leather handbag and withdrew a sleek folder. Her nails clicked against the brass latch as she opened it and passed it across the desk. "DPhil in Zoology from Oxford. Postdoctoral fellowship in regenerative biology. Published in *Nature*, *The Lancet*, and – if you'll forgive the indulgence – *Mythos Quarterly*. Not exactly rigorous, but they let me have some fun."

James flipped through the documents without comment. Her credentials were indeed impressive, even impeccable. On the last page, however, he found what he'd been waiting for: a letter from the Council confirming her temporary placement at the Repository. It included a small footnote – almost an afterthought – regarding her expulsion from Oxford following allegations of unethical experimentation and endangering students during unsanctioned research.

He closed the folder with a decisive snap.

"Very well," he said, setting it aside. "Let me be clear: this is not an academic post. It's not a stepping stone to tenure, nor is it a launchpad for grant proposals. You're not here to build your CV."

Her smile didn't falter, but her fingers stilled on the coffee cup's handle.

"You are here," James continued, "because the Elder Council believes the creatures under our care may possess biological properties worth investigating. Your role is to identify, analyse, and – if feasible – develop treatments or products from their freely-given samples. You'll have no access to live specimens unless I personally approve it."

She leaned back, crossing one leg over the other, entirely at ease. "Understood. And if I make a groundbreaking discovery – do I get credit?"

"That depends entirely on *what* you discover," James said, his voice cool. "I welcome innovation, but I won't tolerate exploitation. You report directly to me. No side projects. Nothing happens without my sign-off. Is that clear?"

"Crystal," she said, offering a smile now edged with steel.

James gave a single nod. "We don't currently have a functioning lab, but I've had a space cleared. Give me a list of what you'll need and I'll source it."

He paused, weighing his next words. "I'd prefer if you remained in the administrative wing, but something tells me you'll wander regardless. Come. Let me show you what we're dealing with here."

"I do love a good mystery," she said, standing and smoothing her blazer. "Tell me, Mr Davids – are you always this welcoming?"

"Only when I expect trouble," he muttered,

leading her down the corridor toward the steel security door. He paused with one hand on the handle and turned back to her. "What you're about to see may change your view of the world."

Then he opened the door.

Dr Clarke stepped out onto the observation platform, and gasped. Her cheeks flushed pink, her fingers trembled slightly on the railing. Below, the Repository stretched out in a cavernous sprawl of enclosures incorporating a variety of biomes where mist curled between verdant trees, seas sparkled with bioluminescence, and mythical creatures walked – or flew – beneath enchanted skies.

James watched her carefully. He remembered this moment from his own first time, when Amari had brought him here. But what he saw in Dr Clarke wasn't wonder. It was hunger.

"Oh," she breathed, eyes wide. "You have a unicorn."

"Una is off-limits," James said sharply. "We haven't received any samples from her, and the Council is firm: all materials must be freely given. There are plenty of others to start with."

"Of course," she said quickly, but her eyes lingered.

He didn't like the way she looked at Una.

"Come," he said, turning back toward the administrative wing. "I've had one of the storerooms near the West Gate cleared. You can set up there."

Her heels clicked in brisk staccato behind him, echoing against the stone.

As they walked, James couldn't help but glance over his shoulder. Dr Clarke was everything the Council wanted – qualified, efficient, ambitious. But something about her unnerved him. Not her confidence, nor her intelligence – but the gleam in her eye when she'd looked down into the cavern was the same gleam he'd seen in poachers and collectors.

She was here for the science, that much was clear.

But the Repository ran on something older than science. Older, and far less predictable.

And James wasn't sure how long it would take before science and myth came to blows.

※※※

After escorting Dr. Clarke to her laboratory – a sterile room she seemed unimpressed with but said would do – James gave her a swift but efficient tour of the Repository's living quarters. The modern kitchen, all sharp corners and humming machinery, smelled faintly of thyme and sterilised steel. He introduced her briefly to the lone kitchen staffer prepping for the night shift, then pointed out the communal area, the corridor leading to the dormitory rooms, and finally her own guest quarters close to his, luxuriously outfitted with a four-poster bed and a thick Persian carpet underfoot.

"I trust you'll be comfortable enough here," he said as she inspected the room, placing her designer-labelled suitcase on the crisp white linen of the bed.

"It's adequate," she said, inspecting a copy of a Ming vase standing on the desk in the corner.

"The residential area is normally quiet enough, but if you do happen to hear anything strange at night…" James said as he headed towards the door. "Don't investigate. Call me."

Dr. Clarke offered a smile that didn't reach her eyes. "Of course, Mr Davids."

James left her unpacking a row of expensive serums and skincare products onto the bathroom counter and made his way toward the main corridor, feeling strangely anxious.

He needed to walk. To think.

He found Wagner and deposited Clarke's list of requirements into the man's hands. The Requisitions Master had a knack for finding and procuring whatever was asked of him efficiently and without a fuss. The man didn't even blink an eye when he scanned the list – just nodded and picked up his phone.

James left him to it gratefully.

The Repository, quiet at this hour, felt more like a tomb than a sanctuary. The low hum of the overhead lights and his footsteps on the cold stone floor were the only sounds he could hear. The steel door at the end of the tunnel swung open silently and he gazed out at the enclosures below.

The dragon, Kentigern Mor, was taking a nap, stretched out on a little island in the middle of a lake designed to look exactly like Loch Ness. The creature twitched in its sleep, as if caught in a dream, its sinuous body curled around a tower of the picturesquely ruined castle on the island. James wouldn't dare visit the irritable dragon – it had made it quite clear that it wouldn't allow any humans inside its enclosure – so he'd have to be satisfied with this far-off glimpse of the creature. It seemed content enough.

The Keeper made his way down the stairs and opened the nearest enclosure with a Word. A sulphurous stench assailed his nose as he cast a quick glance at the salamanders, basking on heated rocks, a volcano oozing red-hot lava in the distance. James dotted down some notes in his notebook about moulting patterns before moving on.

Next, the cyclops. It lay curled up on its pallet at the edge of the cave, its single eye shut tightly as it snored loud enough to wake the dead. This one, at least, was not hesitant to pay the Keeper's Fee in exchange for treats or pampering. Amari had once mentioned that the creature was attuned to the trait of Focus, single-minded concentration. James wondered what Dr Clarke would make of its contributions.

Then, the dryad enclosure. The nymphs were nowhere in sight, their trees swaying gently in the breeze. James felt a pang of sadness for the days he'd spent drinking ouzo with them. They used to laugh with him. Now, they vanished at the sound of his boots. Still, he scratched a bit of bark from the nearest tree into a little phial and noted a few speculative uses for Clarke's research.

He bypassed the unicorn and the asrai's enclosures completely, instead going in where he knew he was tolerated, if not quite welcomed. The basilisk had already settled in for the night, and the family of griffons were nothing more than distant silhouettes high above, drifting like embers against the darkening sky of their enclosure.

Eventually, he came to rest on a jagged outcrop of rock that jutted from a crescent of sandy beach, gazing out at the cobalt sea stretching vast and unbroken before him. As the sky turned orange, a pod of capricorns breached the waves, their magenta scales gleaming in the setting sun, their bleating cries carrying on the salty breeze.

The Repository had been built to protect these creatures. And it had safeguarded them, hidden and locked away inside the mountain. But they deserved more than to merely survive behind stone walls. If people knew what lived here – if they truly understood their worth – they might rally to protect them, just as the Council had once done.

Maybe then, one day, the creatures could live

freely among humans again. Not myths anymore, but tangible proof that magic still had a place in the world.

But it wasn't just about preservation anymore. James knew many of the sentient creatures resented the Keeper's Fee, and he didn't blame them. But he couldn't let that stop him. If their gifts could be used to benefit humanity, then their presence might finally be recognised for what it truly was. A gift.

But first – they needed to be useful.

Clarke would find something. She struck him as the sort of person who would relish the challenge.

It was late by the time James returned to his study. He slipped off his coat, hung it neatly, then sat at his desk and opened his notebook again, rereading the entries from the evening's rounds. He'd always loved reading and research, but he was beginning to wonder if his new position as the Keeper was more administration than anything else.

James glanced guiltily at the pile of paperwork waiting for him on one side of his desk.

With a weary sigh, he reached over and pulled the first paper closer. His mood plummeted even further when he saw what it was – a letter from the Green Grove.

Once, he might have found Senator Flavius Regulus's insufferable pomposity amusing, especially during his time spent at the Repository constantly thwarting Amari's efforts. But now that James held the reins, the centaur's incessant interference was less comic relief and more persistent thorn. He found himself developing a grudging respect for Amari's patience.

Or at least, her self-control.

Since the Council had cancelled the Repository's

agreement with the Green Grove and introduced the Keeper's Fee, the centaur delegation had been banned from returning. Thankfully. But that hadn't stopped Flavius from sending a barrage of daily letters, each more imperious than the last.

So far, it seemed like the Green Grove was unaware of the Council's new policy, because if they did know, James was sure the centaurs would be at the West Gate, trying to break the door down.

James scanned the latest missive. The same demands, thinly veiled as diplomacy: the centaurs wanted the creatures in his custody returned – especially the airavata. And, as always, the senator listed the others that had been kept in the holding cells during his brief visit – all long dead in the aftermath of Norton's rampage, though Flavius didn't know that.

This letter had a new addition, however – an offer of sanctuary for the creatures within the Green Grove itself.

James leaned back in his chair, took off his glasses, and rubbed at the stubble along his jaw.

Where *was* the Green Grove?

Somewhere in Rome, surely. The centaurs had been instrumental during the battle of the blood moon market at the Colosseum. The two representatives he'd interacted with – Senator Flavius Regulus and Commander Gaius Aurelius Equustos – had names that all but stamped SPQR on their foreheads. Ambrose had been frustratingly vague about his dealings with them, but James doubted a herd of centaurs could travel through a major European capital unnoticed – unless they didn't have to travel far at all.

Which meant… they were probably already there. Hidden somewhere in the Rome.

But how do you hide an entire army of centaurs

inside one of the world's largest cities?

Unless they had something like the Repository's enclosures – spaces that bent reality.

From outside, each pen looked modest, entirely mundane. But inside, entire ecosystems unfurled in impossible scale. James still remembered the first time Amari had led him into the unicorn's enclosure. The lush glade, the dappling sunlight, the silence thick with magic. It had left him breathless. Even now, he wasn't entirely sure how the enclosures worked. Did they have boundaries? Would you eventually hit a wall if you walked far enough?

That might be worth testing someday.

For now, he could only wonder: could the Green Grove have its own hidden realm, nestled in the very heart of Rome?

He knew the Council was desperate to uncover its location, and even more desperate to lure the centaurs into the Repository, where they could be protected, or – perhaps more accurately – monitored.

If he could find it… If he could be the one to unlock that secret… It would cement his place as Keeper, despite the doubts Clarke's arrival had stirred.

And in the back of his mind, a new thought sparked, unsettling and bright.

If the centaurs had created such a space… Who else might have? And what else was hiding in plain sight?

✖✖✖

The tray in his hands rattled faintly as James ascended the stone corridor towards the research room James had set aside for Dr Clarke. Three samples in three sealed phials – nothing explosive or abrasive, but nothing he'd leave unattended in the break room either.

He nudged the lab door open with his elbow. Inside, the room still smelled of freshly installed wiring and industrial cleaner. The workbenches were bare, except for a single box of high-end equipment the biologist had brought with her when she came. The woman herself perched on a stool, scrolling through something on her tablet with the intense, unblinking focus of someone performing brain surgery.

"I brought you some samples," James said, setting the tray down with a clink.

She looked up, one perfectly arched brow rising. "How considerate. Shall I assume this is breakfast?"

"Not unless you have an appetite for creature byproduct," he replied dryly, lifting the first phial. "Basilisk bile. Still fresh – well, relatively speaking. Stable, but pungent. I'd advise against spilling it."

Clarke stood and approached, her heels clicking softly against the stone floor. She picked up the phial and tilted it, watching the viscous yellow fluid catch the light. "It's cloudy," she remarked.

"It tends to be, and it gets even smellier the longer it's bottled up. You'll want to run your experiments on this one first."

She smirked faintly. "Once I have equipment. At the moment, I'm working with air and optimism."

She held the phial up again. "Cloudy... But there's something suspended in it. Filamentous." Her voice dipped an octave, closer to fascination than she would have admitted.

He reached for the second phial. "Minotaur fur," he said, holding it up to the light. "Taken from the creature's shoulder. The old legends spoke of how no blade could pierce its hide. There's a stubbornness to the creature, something old and defiant. Maybe you'll find a way to turn its fur into the next generation of protective gear."

Clarke plucked the fur sample from the tray like it offended her fingers. "Lovely. It smells like someone shaved a yak in a barn fire."

"I can have it cleaned," James said, not bothering to hide his amusement.

"No need," she said with a resigned sigh. "I've worked with worse."

James raised the third container. "And this one's from the cyclops. The legends say cyclopes forged the gods' weapons – there's power in their hands, their very bones. Maybe even in their toenails." He shook the phial, letting the clippings bounce against the glass. "We've been trimming it for him. He seems to enjoy it."

Clarke shot him a look of faint distaste. She examined the fragment – thick, yellowed, with a texture somewhere between horn and granite. "And what exactly do you expect me to do with this? Grind it into powder and add it to some obscure cure-all? I've seen less questionable ingredients in traditional Chinese medicine."

James shrugged. "Who knows? You're the scientist, Dr Clarke. I just connect the dots in the old stories. Might be useful in osteo-regeneration. Or tooth enamel. I'll leave that part up to you."

"Marvellous," she said, dry as dust. "So far, all I've seen is fluff and folk remedies. Speculation. No measurable science. Just wishful thinking trapped in glass."

James folded his arms, ignoring the jab. "You'll have the full lab setup soon. In the meantime, those should be enough to get you started."

Dr Clarke carefully placed the samples back onto the tray, then leaned one hand on the workbench, thoughtful. "I'll run preliminary analyses," she said at last. "But if f I'd known I'd be working out of a magical zoo carved into a mountain, I might've packed my Bunsen burner."

"Welcome to the Repository," he muttered, turning to leave. "Just let me know if anything reacts in an interesting way."

Clarke gave him a tight smile. "I'm not promising miracles. But I'll see what I can find."

James didn't turn around, but a hint of satisfaction crept across his face. "That's all I ask."

He allowed himself the smallest smile, then continued down the hall, the clinking of glass and the faint fishy scent of basilisk bile lingering in the air behind him.

✳✳✳

Much to the biologist's delight – and Wagner's credit – the equipment Dr Clarke had requested arrived by midday. James allowed her to commandeer a few of his men to help set up the lab space, then retreated to his study to confront a more pressing problem: finding another caladrius.

After a brief search, he pulled a silk-bound, handwritten volume from the shelf behind his desk – one Amari had once loaned him. He brushed a hand over the elegant lettering on the cover: *An A – Z Compendium of Birds of Various Paradises.* The binding creaked softly as he opened it. He still remembered Amari handing it to him, her expression unreadable.

It didn't take long to find the caladrius. A two-page spread displayed an illustration of the graceful white bird perched at the edge of a bed, its dark, intelligent eyes fixed intently on the figure of a sick man beneath the covers. A florid caption beneath the image read: *Caladrius, healer of all manner of illnesses.*

Unfortunately, the accompanying text offered little more than a physical description—long-legged, snowy white, sharp-eyed.

James exhaled in frustration and slid the book back into place. His gaze drifted across the surrounding titles until it snagged on a small brown volume: *Bestia Mirabilis: A Compendium of Rare Creatures in Ecclesiastical Lore*. He pulled it out with care. The leather binding was soft with age, the pages scented faintly of parchment and candle wax.

His pulse quickened as he found a smaller illustration of the same bird – less ornate, but unmistakable. The passage read: "The caladrius is a snow-white bird said to dwell in the palaces of kings or temples of the devout. It draws illness from the sick, and if it flies away, the patient shall recover. If it turns its head, death is assured."

He returned to his desk and pulled his own notebook closer, updating the notes he'd made while the bird was still alive.

"Draws illness from the sick," he murmured. "So it won't heal injuries…"

Amari had told him as much when he'd once asked to take the bird to Cassie in hospital. At the time, he hadn't believed her. He'd assumed she was just being protective – prioritising preservation over compassion. But perhaps she'd been sincere after all.

He leaned back in his chair, staring up at the rock-carved ceiling.

Maybe Norton had killed the bird out of spite. Or maybe he'd been desperate – searching for a cure for his lycanthropy. But the lore was specific: the caladrius healed illness, not curses, not transformations. And now it was gone. Clarke might have extracted some regenerative value from its remains, but whatever she found wouldn't rival what a living caladrius could have provided.

And James had burned all the bodies Norton had left behind. He hadn't wanted any remains falling into the wrong hands.

Of course, that had been before he knew about the Keeper's Fee. Before he understood the Council's hunger for samples.

Now he needed another caladrius. And fast.

Where did one even *find* such a thing?

He reached for a map, unfolding it over the clutter of paperwork on his desk. His pen hovered over regions traditionally associated with miracle birds. Rome? Jerusalem? He glanced back at the text: *palaces of kings or temples of the devout.*

A faint rustle drew his attention. Nusku sat on his perch, preening his crimson feathers. The little creature had been quiet all afternoon, dozing while James read, but now it gave a soft chirp and flicked its tail feathers.

"You have an idea?" James asked, smiling fondly at the fledgling phoenix.

Nusku blinked slowly. Then, with the clumsy movements of a juvenile still growing into its body, he clambered down the perch and hopped onto the map, planting one clawed foot squarely on London.

James raised an eyebrow. "You have an opinion, do you?"

He suppressed a smile. If a caladrius had been flapping about the Houses of Parliament, the tabloids would have noticed.

He nudged the creature gently aside and studied the map again.

Most royal palaces were now tourist attractions. That left sacred spaces.

Limiting the search to Europe seemed practical, given the bird's mythological roots. Still, the options were daunting. He scoured the map, feeling that old, familiar weight of hopelessness settle on his shoulders.

Even so, he circled a few promising sites – places that combined spiritual significance with rulership or royal heritage. Perfect candidates for caladrius sanctuaries. With a glance at the little phoenix, now back on his perch and already drifting into sleep, James added London to the list. Just in case Nusku was right. Maybe he knew something James didn't.

He tapped the paper, deep in thought. Someone needed to check these locations. And there was really only one person he could trust with such an important mission.

He pulled out his phone and sent a quick message to Ambrose.

-- *When is Cassie coming?* --

The reply was swift.

-- *I wouldn't hold my breath, if I were you.* --

Suppressing a sigh, James forwarded the list of locations.

-- *I need you to check out these places and see if they have a caladrius. It's white, crane-like, with healing abilities.* --

His phone pinged.

-- *I don't work for the Council anymore.* --

James removed his glasses and rubbed his eyes. He knew his son didn't approve of the Keeper's Fee. But maybe that could be used.

-- *If you won't go, I'll have to send someone else.* --

A pause. Then:

-- *Fine. I'll look into it. Just need to deal with something urgent first.* --

James sat back, mildly triumphant. At least now he could tell the Chairman that someone was out searching.

Still, the Cassie issue bothered him. Even with Clarke here, the Repository was the safest place for her. He dialled her number, but it rang unanswered. He sent her a text instead.

-- *Changed my mind. Still want to come help in the Repository?* --

The message remained unread.

"Understandable," he muttered, irritated. She had every reason to be hesitant. Sprouting fur and fangs probably came with its fair share of trauma.

But she still belonged here. If she wouldn't come willingly, and Ambrose wouldn't bring her, maybe he needed to send someone else.

Then again... The thought of Clarke experimenting on Cassie gave him pause.

Did he really want his daughter reduced to a sample under the biologist's microscope?

And yet... If Clarke could reverse-engineer whatever had altered Cassie's DNA, perhaps she could undo it entirely. Cure her. Restore her humanity. And in doing so, provide James with a viable serum. A reliable, renewable source of werewolf essence.

They'd never have to fear losing Tenacity again.

Cassie could return to normal.

But perhaps it would be wiser to wait until the

biologist had proven her loyalty.

Still…

If Clarke managed that, James wouldn't just tolerate her presence at the Repository - he'd welcome it.

✕✕✕

The Keeper yawned behind his hand. His days bled into nights lately, an endless shuffle between paperwork, sample checks, and crisis management. Working as Amari's assistant had been physically exhausting, but at least he'd slept at night. Now, it felt like there simply weren't enough hours in the day to get everything done. Even Nusku was fast asleep on his perch, his head tucked underneath his wing.

James was in the middle of jotting down a quick list of Mazzoni's old contacts when his phone rang, sharp and sudden. He nearly dropped his glasses in surprise.

Ambrose.

James snatched up the call, heart lurching. The last time he'd received a call at this time of night, Cassie had been in the ICU, barely clinging to life.

"Ambrose? What's wrong? Where's your sister?"

"She's alright," Ambrose replied, voice taut. "This is something else."

James exhaled, shoulders sagging in relief. "At this hour? Can't it wait until morning?"

"No. I have a barghest on my hands, and I don't know what to do with it."

James blinked. "A barghest?" He sat up straighter, the weight of exhaustion evaporating. An actual barghest – a species of hellhound, harbingers of death. Norton had killed a hellhound destined for the Repository while it was still in its holding cell. Acquiring another so soon would be a major win – and it might just earn him a reprieve with the Elder Council.

"Text me your coordinates. I'll send a team immediately."

"I can't wait for a team," Ambrose said. "Have your men ready outside the West Gate in ten minutes. I'm bringing it to you. Bring lots of light."

The line went dead before James could respond.

Ten minutes?

Wasn't Ambrose in London?

Did he know how to Travel?

James shoved the questions aside. They could wait.

Right now, he had to rally the team.

✕✕✕

"What on earth is that racket?" Clarke asked as she sat down opposite James in the kitchen the next morning. She'd helped herself to a bowl of overnight oats and a steaming cup of black coffee. Her makeup was flawless, her power suit freshly pressed – glamorous enough that James noticed several of his men casting appreciative glances over their bacon and eggs.

He winced as another howl echoed down the corridor.

"Barghest," he muttered, taking a bite of his own more utilitarian breakfast. Ambrose had arrived in the night with the creature, handed it over without fanfare, and departed again soon after. And yes, it turned out he *could* Travel. The whole thing had left James with more questions than answers.

Clarke took a sip of her coffee and frowned,

clearly unimpressed. He didn't blame her – this stuff was for the crew. There was a reason he had his own machine in his office.

"That hardly answers my question," she said. "And judging by that awful noise, I'd guess whatever it is has one foot in the grave."

"You're not far off," James said. "It's a type of hellhound. In some legends, its appearance is an omen of death."

Her eyes widened. "And you've brought it here… why, exactly?"

James arched an eyebrow. "I thought I explained what we do here."

She drummed her fingernails on the counter, the rhythm sharp and thoughtful. "So it's here to be studied. You don't expect anyone to die? Because as the newest recruit, I have to mention that it's not what I signed up for."

He gave a dry laugh. "You'll be fine, Dr Clarke. Unless you're foolish enough to step inside its cell. You're not planning to do that, are you?"

"Don't be absurd," she said, but there was a gleam in her eye. "But perhaps you'd show it to me?"

He studied her for a beat. If she was going to be part of this place, she'd have to learn to see these creatures for what they truly were – not just test subjects, but wonders of a forgotten world.

"Come with me," he said, rising.

They left the warmth and hum of the kitchen behind. The sounds of cutlery and conversation were quickly swallowed by the barghest's eerie howls as they passed deeper through the Repository's stone corridors. James led the way, his footsteps brisk and echoing. Fiona kept pace, her heels clicking like punctuation on the polished stone floor.

As they neared the holding cells, the howling

abruptly stopped.

James didn't break stride. He knew the chimaera would be pacing further down the corridor, but he'd save that reveal for another time. One monster at a time.

They stopped in front of the cell he'd reinforced himself with a Word last night. The barghest paced within.

Even James, who'd seen it just hours earlier, paused.

The creature's hulking frame blended with the shadows, only the slight shimmer of its coat betraying the edges of its shape, almost as if blurred by smoke. The glow of its ember-red eyes was the only truly solid thing about it, and they watched James' every movement with unnerving intensity. The air smelled faintly of ash and sulphur.

Clarke stepped closer, and faltered. "Damn," she breathed. "It's... enormous."

"About the size of a Shetland pony," James said. "With a scent for blood and a taste for panic."

The barghest shifted – a ripple of shadow. A low growl vibrated through the stone-carved cell like distant thunder. Clarke stepped back, one hand half-raised toward her chest.

James said nothing. Everyone had a first reaction.

"It doesn't move like any dog I've ever seen," she said eventually, her voice steadier. "It's... wrong. Its fur, its smell – brimstone? And are those shadows *coming off* it?"

James nodded. "Possibly. Legends claim it can become shadow. I haven't tested its reaction to different light levels yet, but it might be worth installing some additional flood lamps."

Clarke's gaze remained fixed on the creature. For the first time since arriving, her guarded confidence gave way to something real. Wonder, maybe. Or respect.

The barghest's eyes lingered on Fiona for a moment longer than necessary. James noticed, but said nothing.

"How did you catch it?"

"My son is… resourceful," James said, a smile twitching at the corners of his mouth.

There was a long pause.

"I underestimated you," she said suddenly, not turning away. It took him a moment to realise she was talking to him, instead of the creature. "When I arrived here, I thought you were just some glorified zoo warden with a mythology hobby."

James chuckled. "And I thought you'd spend more time taking selfies than samples."

She laughed – short, but genuine. She extended her hand, still looking at the barghest.

"Well then. Since we're past assumptions – Fiona."

He hesitated a moment, then reached out and shook her hand. "James."

The silence returned, broken only by the soft, strange growl from the cell. The barghest had lowered its head to its paws, one glowing eye still watching them.

"I'd like to take a sample," Fiona said softly. "Saliva, maybe fur. I want to understand how it manipulates light…"

James nodded. "We'll need to tranquillise it first." He gave her a sidelong look. She was still tense, but no longer afraid. Curious. Sharp. Ambitious in ways that could be dangerous, yes, but also useful.

"Think you're up to the challenge?"

"Yes," she said without hesitation. "Let's see what it can do."

As they turned from the cell, the barghest let

out one long mournful howl.

✳✳✳

The corridor to the holding cells was quiet, save for a low, rumbling growl that vibrated through the floor like distant thunder. James approached the cell gate slowly, tranquilliser gun in hand, cautiously eyeing the barghest.

The creature paced restlessly, its large form half-lost in shadows much darker than the holding cell warranted. Its eyes gleamed red through the darkness. When it saw him, it stilled. It sniffed the air, then bared its teeth, the growl deepening.

"This might sting a little," James murmured as he readied the gun. The dosage had been calculated down to the tenth of a millilitre, based on mass, breathing rate, even hair density. No room for error.

He aimed and fired.

The dart struck the barghest in the shoulder. It flinched, but didn't cry out – just staggered deeper into shadow – a snarl caught halfway in its throat. A long, slow breath hissed from its chest before its limbs gave way and it slumped to the floor in a ripple of thick black fur and otherworldly menace.

Only once the creature's breathing slowed and evened out did James wave Fiona forward. "All yours," he said, as he swung the cell door open.

Fiona's eyes swept across the barghest's form with a mixture of fear and excitement. With practiced ease, she pulled on a pair of black nitrile gloves before stepping inside the cell.

"Keep an eye on it," she said crisply. "I don't fancy getting mauled over a bad estimate."

James nodded, watching the creature's breathing with his own breath held.

Fiona knelt beside the beast, pulled a sterile swab

from her case, and slipped it between the barghest's parted jaws. A string of viscous saliva followed as she carefully extracted it. Then she moved to the shoulder, her gloved hand gathering a clump of fur from the edge of the dart wound.

Up close, even sedated, the barghest was terrifying. Its breath reeked of ash and brine, and its fur shimmered like oil when disturbed, layers of dark shadow rippling underneath the biologist's touch. Fiona paused briefly, her eyes narrowing as she inspected the texture.

"I've never seen anything like it," she whispered. "It's almost... not fur."

"Not in any conventional sense," James agreed quietly. "It could be partially composed of whatever liminal space it moves through."

Fiona arched an eyebrow, but didn't comment. She sealed her samples in airtight tubes, then stood, brushing her hands on her coat.

"I'll be in my lab," she said, already moving down the corridor. "I'll let you know what I find."

James didn't reply right away. He watched her retreating back, then turned to look at the barghest – still and massive, its breathing shallow but steady.

Something tightened in his chest. A pang of guilt, perhaps. They'd done nothing invasive. No pain, no harm. But still... It was done without the barghest's permission.

A voice rose in the back of his mind – Amari's, maybe, or just his own: *They're not here to be exploited.*

He exhaled and deliberately pushed his doubts away.

This was how these creatures became relevant again. The world had forgotten about them, but he was going to remind it that there was still magic to be found. And that it could be used for good.

He stood there a moment longer, watching the creature breathing, sleeping peacefully, before locking the cell door behind him again.

Now he have to wait and see what science would make of shadow and teeth.

❊❊❊

James didn't hear from Fiona for the rest of the day, which – all things considered – was just as well. The quiet left him free to tackle the stack of correspondence that had been steadily multiplying on the corner of his desk, like a hydra of dull obligation – slice one envelope open and two more appeared in its place.

He'd barely finished skimming the second letter when the unmistakable crest of the Green Grove caught his eye. Flavius again. Of course.

James sighed and sank deeper into the worn leather of his desk chair, holding the missive at arm's length as though distance might lessen the sting of its tone.

Demands. Ultimatums. Appeals to morality and ancient pacts. The senator wasn't backing down. "The airavata is not yours to cage," he had scrawled. "It is sacred. It *must* be free to roam where the winds take it."

"Poetic as always," James muttered, rubbing the bridge of his nose.

His fingers itched to pen a reply – one scholar to another – layered with philosophical nuance and subtle counterarguments. But the Council had been firm: *no further correspondence.* He was not to stoke the centaurs' righteous indignation. The last thing the Council needed was a declaration of war written in verse.

Still, James couldn't help wondering what the Council's *actual* plan was. First, they'd allowed the centaurs open access to the Repository – and Flavius had roamed freely, sticking his nose in everywhere and making ridiculous demands, most likely solely to annoy Amari. Now, they acted like they didn't exist. What had changed?

A theory had been forming in the back of his mind like a slow-moving storm cloud: the Council was trying to provoke a reaction. If the Green Grove grew angry enough, desperate enough, they might make a mistake and reveal their location. Force the Elder Council's hand.

"Force mine," he mumbled grimly, reaching for another letter. Because who else would they send when the time comes to relocate the centaurs?

James scribbled a note to follow up on Mazzoni's old contacts. He was going to need all hands on deck soon, especially now that the Council was becoming more vocal about their demands for new creatures to be brought to the Repository.

Still, the thought of centaurs inside the Repository stirred something almost giddy in him. Imagine if they were enclosed and available for interaction whenever he wanted! He could learn their dialects properly. Record their oral histories. Perhaps even verify long-contested claims. *Chiron*, for instance. What if the wise old mentor of ancient myth was still alive, tucked away somewhere beneath silvered leaves? What truths might he unlock about Achilles, Heracles, Jason – stories he'd had only ever seen distorted by poets and propagandists?

His eyes drifted to the far end of his study, where the leather-bound volumes of comparative mythology sat untouched. His hand moved almost of its own accord toward a notebook, a glint of enthusiasm returning.

The sharp corner of the next envelope dug into his wrist. White. Plain. Dull.

James frowned. Wagner.

He opened it with the kind of reluctant resignation usually reserved for dental surgery.

As expected, the Requisitions Master had written a monthly report bloated with figures and spreadsheets, and politely phrased demands – delays in delivery of basilisk-proof glasses, increased costs of dietary supplements for the Cyclops, and a shortage of the Bavarian beer the men insisted on as part of their 'danger pay'. James groaned softly.

He poured himself a cup of lukewarm coffee from the machine. It had gone bitter in the time he'd ignored it – much like everything else on his desk – but he drank it anyway.

Nusku gave a soft chirp, the sound barely louder than the slosh of the bitter brew. James glanced towards him, muttering: "You're not wrong."

There were few things he despised more than procurement. Budgets. Storage audits. Line items. He was the Keeper of Exotic Animals, not a glorified warehouse manager. And yet here he sat, tallying salamander feed and justifying the import of ethically sourced chocolate for a discriminating gargoyle.

He flipped to the next page, his eyes scanning the ledger even as his mind drifted toward Fiona. What was she doing in her lab right now? Had she made progress yet? He hoped she'd have something to show at the next Council meeting, or otherwise who knows what they might decide to do next? When the Chairman had first briefed him on the Repository, he'd mentioned the Asian branch and how they managed their residents...

James shuddered. He hoped it would never come to that here.

He sighed again and picked up his pen, dragging

it toward the margin of the requisition sheet like a man preparing to sign away his soul. So much work to do, and none of it involved mythical insight or magical discoveries – just numbers and ink, and endless responsibilities.

✕✕✕

There were dark circles under Fiona's eyes when she sat down opposite James at the breakfast table the next morning. A bowl of yoghurt with fresh fruit and a strong black coffee seemed to be her breakfast of choice. Despite the fatigue, she was still as impeccably dressed as ever.

"Long night?" James asked, buttering the last slice of toast on his plate.

"More like an early morning," she replied, cradling her coffee cup. The fatigue didn't dim the spark in her eyes. "The barghest's fur contains some… fascinating properties."

James looked up, interest piqued. "Really? Care to elaborate?"

A small smile played on her lips. "Not yet. I'll share once I have something tangible to show."

He nodded, respecting the need for proof before speculation. As a scholar, he understood that better than most.

He popped the last bite of toast into his mouth and pushed his chair back. "If you'll excuse me, I think I'll join the morning rounds today. Normally I leave that to the team, but I feel like doing a few spot checks myself."

"Mind if I tag along?" Fiona asked.

He hesitated a moment, then nodded. "Alright. I wouldn't mind the company."

He gave her a few minutes to finish her breakfast before they left the kitchen and headed toward the main cave. Fiona paused at the balcony, her manicured fingers curling around the cold steel railing as she gazed down.

"Is the unicorn on the itinerary?" she asked, eyeing the twilight grove where Una grazed peacefully in the distance.

"Not today," James said. "She's been… difficult since the last Keeper left." He caught her inquisitive glance and shrugged. "Don't worry. I promise you won't be bored."

They descended into the maze of enclosures. James moved with casual confidence, his steps guided by memory. When he'd first arrived, the identical doors and unmarked corridors had confused him. Now he navigated them with ease.

Fiona, on the other hand, glanced around with a frown. "It's disorienting. The enclosures look bigger from above."

James chuckled. "Wait until you step inside."

She paused beside one of the blank doors. "What's in here?"

He frowned. "Honestly? I'm not entirely sure. It's a forest – trees so tall you crane your neck and still can't see the tops. I've seen gorillas swinging through the canopy, but they've never approached. Fortunately, it's a self-sustaining ecosystem." He hesitated. "I've yet to find any folklore referencing mythical gorillas, though."

"Interesting," Fiona murmured, and they moved on.

James stopped in front of another unmarked door. "How's your French?"

She laughed. "Abysmal."

He gave a small sigh. "Well, we're only observing today. Stay behind me, and no sudden moves."

Her brows lifted, but she nodded. James turned to the keypad and shielded the numbers as he entered the code. One of his first changes as

Keeper had been restricting access to the Words of Wonder. He didn't trust just anyone with that kind of power.

The door swung open, and they stepped through.

Fiona gasped.

James turned to see her frozen in place, hands trembling slightly, her eyes wide with disbelief.

"How…?" she breathed. "How is this possible?"

Before them stretched an uncanny replica of early twentieth-century Paris, specifically the fourth *arrondissement* and the Île de la Cité. Gas lamps cast pools of golden light across cobbled streets in the perpetual midnight of the enclosure. The towering Gothic cathedral ahead of them wasn't *quite* Notre-Dame, but it was close. Stone façades, stained-glass windows, and gargoyles perched on every corner gave the illusion of grandeur and age.

Except one gargoyle was missing from its usual post.

"There," James said, pointing to a shifting shadow passing across the pale moon.

"What is it?" Fiona whispered.

The silhouette dropped down from above, wings spread wide, landing on a nearby plinth with barely a sound. Fiona gave a strangled gasp.

"Bonsoir, Thierry. Comment allez-vous?" James said, his eyes adjusting to the gloom as the gargoyle's chiselled features came into focus.

The creature stared at them, unmoving. James felt a flicker of unease. Fiona's tension beside him was palpable.

Then, with a voice like grinding stone, the gargoyle spoke.

"What's it saying?" Fiona asked.

"It says if we come any closer to its cathedral,

we'll regret it."

James slowly reached into his coat and retrieved a slab of expensive dark Belgian chocolate, offering it with open palms.

"Nous ne sommes pas ici pour menacer votre foyer. Nous venons avec un cadeau." He glanced at Fiona. "That means –"

She waved him off. "I get the idea."

The gargoyle still didn't move. Its silence was beginning to feel more like a threat than a pause, more ominous by the second.

Finally, it spoke again. *"Gardez-le."* Keep it.

With a beat of its wings, the gargoyle rose and vanished into the shadows above without a backward glance.

Fiona exhaled loudly. "That was… tense."

"Indeed," James agreed, eyes tracking the creature as it landed on the cathedral's rooftop. It had never been friendly, but it had never been outright hostile before, either.

And it had never rejected a gift of chocolate.

He cast a sidelong glance at Fiona. Could her presence have unsettled it?

Now that the creature was gone, she seemed to relax, inspecting the enclosure with more freedom. Her gaze swept over the façades and rooftops with a mixture of awe and calculation.

"Shall we go?" James asked.

She turned back to him, a slow smile curving her lips. "Yes," she said. "Show me more wonders."

※※※

Fiona practically buzzed with energy as they exited the cyclops enclosure. James had wondered how the titan might react to a newcomer, but the one-eyed creature had been instantly charmed by the biologist. It had even blushed slightly as she carefully scraped skin from its cracked heel and sealed the sample in an airtight tube. Afterward, the cyclops had shyly presented her with a polished sheep tibia – likely from a previous meal – which she accepted with all the grace of receiving a bouquet of roses.

The Keeper wasn't sure what surprised him more – the gift, or the way the biologist had accepted it with a smile, as though touched by the gesture.

"I can't wait to run this through the synthesiser," she said, holding the skin sample aloft like a prize. "Who knows what properties might be intrinsic to the creature's DNA? Obviously, getting a sample from the eye would be ideal – its power is clearly concentrated in the oculus."

She shot him a questioning look.

James shook his head. "I'm afraid that's not possible. For one, removing the eye could kill the cyclops – or destroy what makes it what it is. And more to the point, Council policy requires that all parts be given freely. As fond as he is of you, I doubt he'd volunteer his only eye."

"Pity," Fiona said as they climbed the steel staircase toward the administrative wing, the biologist still clutching the sheep bone fondly. "Still, this will do for now. Do you think –"

James held up a hand as his phone began to ring. He checked the caller ID and straightened slightly.

"The Chairman," he murmured, before answering.

"Mr Davids," the Chairman said without preamble. "How are things progressing with Dr Clarke at the Repository? Have the two of you made any headway?"

"I believe so," James said, glancing at Fiona.

"In fact, I've just introduced her to a few of the residents, and she sees strong potential for her research."

"Is she with you now?"

"Yes, we were just heading back to her lab."

"Put her on speaker, please."

James did so, nudging Fiona's elbow and motioning toward his office. She followed without question, and he closed the door behind them.

"Go ahead, Mr Chairman," James said.

"Dr Clarke, I trust the Repository is meeting – if not exceeding – your expectations?" came the clipped voice over the speaker.

"Indeed it is," Fiona replied, flashing James a pleased smile. "Each creature I've encountered so far brims with untapped potential. I already have several lines of research I'm eager to pursue."

"And have you identified anything the Council might find... useful?"

Fiona's eyes sparkled. "I believe so, but I'd prefer to withhold specifics until I have concrete data. The synthesiser is running now, and I expect results within the hour. What I've seen so far looks very promising."

"Very well," the Chairman said. "I needn't remind you that the Council expects more than promises. We want practical applications. The era of sunken costs is behind us. Even the Repository must justify its existence now."

"Understood," Fiona said crisply. "You won't be disappointed."

"Mr Davids," the Chairman continued. "A private word, please."

James switched off the speaker setting and gave Fiona a quick nod as she raised an eyebrow, silently asking permission to make herself a coffee.

"You'll be interested to know, I've identified

five potential locations where another caladrius might be found," James said before the Chairman could ask. "My son will be investigating."

"Excellent. Miss Kerubo always spoke highly of your son, and he's proven himself capable in the past."

A pause, just long enough to signal something more serious.

"That said, while I have no doubt Dr Clarke's work will be of value, you and I have both read her file. You know she holds... unconventional views on ethical boundaries. I trust you'll ensure she operates within Council policy."

"Absolutely," James said, watching Fiona pour herself a cup of jet-black coffee. "I'll keep a close eye on things."

"Good. I look forward to your next update."

The call ended.

James lingered for a moment, watching Fiona pour a second cup. There had been a spark in her eyes when she spoke about her findings – real enthusiasm, the kind that could drive discovery. But the Chairman was right: she might need reining in. If the line between discovery and exploitation blurred, it would be his job to stop her.

A soft fluttering broke the silence. James turned to see Nusku hop from one bookshelf to another. He quickly cradled the little crimson bird in his hands and returned him to his perch – the last thing he needed was nibble marks on the ancient books.

"Is that a...? What is that?" Fiona asked, her empty cup forgotten as she stared at the bird, halfway between delight and disquiet.

"It's a phoenix," James replied, stroking the sleek feathers. "I call him Nusku. He's still young – hasn't quite figured out what he's capable of yet."

Nusku chirped softly and fluffed his wings, clearly pleased by the attention.

"And what is he capable of?" Fiona asked, quirking one eyebrow as she studied the bird.

James reached down and pulled out the box he kept in the bottom drawer of his desk. "Rebirth and immortality," he said as he fed Nusku a dead cricket.

Fiona's eyes widened. "Regenerative healing powers?"

James grunted. "I've seen him burst into flames and be reborn from the ashes. Whether that renewal can be imparted onto someone or something else remains unclear."

"And you keep him in your office?" Fiona said, a smile tugging at the corner of her mouth.

"He prefers the company," James said with a shrug, depositing the little bird back onto his perch. "So do I, if I'm honest."

"Well, you're not alone anymore, James," she said, turning back to the coffee machine. "You and I – we're going to do great things together. How do you take it?"

He blinked, disoriented for a moment, before realising she meant the coffee.

"Milk, three sugars," he said, accepting the cup with a smile.

"To a world of opportunities," Fiona said, raising hers in a toast.

James touched his mug to hers. "Opportunities," he echoed.

Although a sense of unease prickled along his skin at the way Fiona's eyes lingered on the little phoenix.

※※※

James was on his way to bed when the sound

of a far-off explosion reached his ears. The light above his head flickered and died, plunging the corridor into absolute darkness.

He froze.

Then, slowly, the lights flickered back on, throwing warped shadows against the walls. The faint scent of smoke drifted down the corridor.

For a long moment, James stood perfectly still. Then he turned on his heels and broke into a sprint, his shoes pounding against the stone floor. A sick feeling was blooming in his gut. There was only one place volatile enough in the entire Repository to produce that kind of noise.

Fiona's lab.

He rounded a corner, skidding as urgency propelled him forward. He raced up the long slope towards the lab. The acrid scent of burned metal and singed fabric hit him before he reached the door, hanging askew on bent hinges. He pushed it open and stepped inside.

The room was a wreck. Glass from shattered beakers glinted in the flickering lighting and one wall had black scorch marks where something had clearly erupted.

Fiona was sitting on the floor, looking somewhat dazed, her usually immaculate hair now frizzed and trailing a ribbon of smoke. Glass crunched underfoot as he crossed to her side.

"Are you injured?" he asked, scanning her for obvious signs of harm.

She coughed, waving a hand vaguely toward the ruined workbench. "No… Just startled. Something in the barghest sample didn't like being exposed to ultraviolet plasma. I was trying to test its mutability in low light conditions…"

"Well," James said as he helped her to her feet. "Whatever you did, perhaps don't do it again."

She shot him an embarrassed look. "I'll be

better prepared next time."

Before he could respond, a low, guttural growl sounded from the open doorway. The hair on the back of James' neck raised.

Slowly, he turned.

Two glowing red eyes stared back at them through the gloom. The scent of sulphur hit James' nostrils.

"No," he breathed. "That's not possible…"

The barghest stepped fully into view, hulking and too quiet for its size. Its fur rippled like a shadow wearing the shape of a beast. The air itself seemed to shudder around it.

Fiona sucked in a breath. "James…"

His mind raced. The barghest was a creature of shadows. The momentary power outage must have given it an opportunity to somehow slip through the darkness and out of its cell.

How do you contain a creature of shadow?

Fear dragged icy fingers down James' spine. Was this omen of death going to be the death of them?

Amari would've stopped it with a Word. But she was gone – vanished without teaching him anything useful.

He only had one gamble to play – he wasn't even sure it would work.

Slowly, without breaking eye contact, James reached into his jacket pocket and drew out a slim phial – powdered basilisk scale mixed with some gravel from the oread's mountain. Something he'd been working on. Speculation, really.

Untested.

Well, it was going to get tested now.

With a sharp bark, the barghest leaped toward them.

James smashed the phial on the floor between them, shoving Fiona backwards. A puff of silver dust flared upward. The barghest stopped in its tracks, its limbs solidifying into stone.

Surprise flashed through the Keeper. It worked!

But then the barghest's back leg twitched and an icy spike of fear shot down his spine.

"What was in that phial?" Fiona asked, standing as if she too was frozen beside him. Her hand clutched onto his coat sleeve and her breathing was shallow and raspy.

"Basilisk infusion. You know they can paralyze with their gaze? Some scholars say –"

"Now is not the time, James," she said, her voice betraying her fear.

"Right," he said, as the barghest's lips moved into a snarl. "It's not going to hold it for long. I'll distract it. You run."

"I'm not going anywhere near that thing!" she protested just as the faint sound of cracking stone released the barghest.

And then it lunged towards them.

A loud popping sound rang out as two of James' men rounded the corner, tranquilliser guns raised. One dart struck home on the creature's flank. The second hit its shoulder. The barghest faltered mid-charge, snarling, teeth bared.

Then it staggered, swayed, and collapsed onto the floor with a heavy thud.

James exhaled, long and slow. "I want that thing back in its cell and I want a pair of spotlights on it at all times."

The men nodded as they each reached for a leg and dragged the creature out of the lab.

James turned towards Fiona. She looked dishevelled, shaken, but she managed a wan smile.

"You alright?" he asked.

She gave a short nod. "Usually when I experiment on something, it doesn't come looking for me afterwards."

"You're alive, that's all that matters. But you need to be more careful. You never know what might happen in here."

There was a long pause as they stood among the wreckage, catching their breaths, the silence broken only by the hiss of cooling metal and the faint crackle of the lights.

Then Fiona said, her voice steadier now: "Point taken. I'll get this cleaned up." She glanced around the room. "At least nothing too expensive was damaged."

"It can wait until morning. Come. I think we both deserve something stronger than coffee after all of this."

He started picking his way through the glass, hearing the crunch of Fiona's footsteps as she followed.

※※※

The halls were quiet the next morning – unnervingly so. Almost as if everyone in the Repository was holding their breath, half-expecting something else to explode.

Fiona was already at work, directing James' men into helping her reassemble her lab. Her voice echoed faintly down the corridor, sharp and purposeful. James left them to it and wandered over to the holding cells.

He stopped in front of the barghest's cell.

A few doors down, the chimaera was pacing, its leonine tail lashing, the goat's head releasing a mournful bleat now and then. Was it unsettled by last night's escape? Normally, that sort of disquiet would have drawn his attention, but not today.

Today, his focus was solely on the barghest.

The shadow-hound lay sprawled in one corner

of its cell, its massive head resting on its paws. One ember-red eye watched him lazily, but unmistakably alert.

James placed a hand against the bars, his other clutching his notebook. Last night's events were already half-sketched in diagrams and rambled thoughts he didn't quite know what to make of himself. But one thing was clear: the basilisk powder had worked.

Useful in an emergency. Even against creatures who shifted in shadows.

His eyes drifted to the ceiling. The two floodlights he'd had installed after the incident shone down mercilessly, bleaching the cell of every shadow. He checked their positioning. The barghest couldn't escape again, not without dim corners to melt into.

But the fact that it *had* escaped the cell gnawed at him.

The barghest hadn't broken the gate. It hadn't clawed its way out.

It had simply seized an opportunity, evaded a door locked with a Word, and somehow appeared on the other side of the Repository.

James exhaled slowly, heart beginning to race despite the bright lighting and reinforced bars between them.

This wasn't just a creature that used shadows as camouflage. It moved through them. Traversed them like cracks in a wall. Like… doorways.

He flipped open his notebook and scribbled a quick note: *Not illusion. Not teleportation. Travel?*

The barghest stirred, shifting its bulk slightly. Its tail thumped once, heavy and deliberate. That red eye never left him.

James stared back, unsettled. He wasn't the sort to believe in omens, but he didn't like the way the creature looked at him. Something in its gaze

247

made his skin prickle.

He cleared his throat, quietly. "How do you do it?" he murmured. "What's your trick? Is it light? Angle? Heat?"

The hound gave no reply. But its eye flicked, just once, toward a narrow seam of shadow where the bars met the stone floor – too thin, surely, to mean anything.

And yet.

James' skin crawled.

He straightened, snapping the notebook closed. He'd add extra lights – broad-spectrum, overlapping fields, no blind angles. He might even rig motion sensors, though he doubted the thing would trip them. Not if it could just avoid them altogether.

He lingered a moment longer.

Fiona would find something from its biological samples – he had no doubt about that.

But his job was different. The Keeper had to understand it on a different level. He needed to learn its rules, its language, and especially its limits.

If it had any.

He gave the barghest one last look.

"I'm going to figure you out," he said softly. "Even if it kills me."

The barghest huffed and rolled to face the wall. A clear dismissal.

James walked away, notebook under his arm, the scent of brimstone still clinging faintly to his coat.

He would learn its secrets.

Learn them, and use them.

⁂⁂⁂

James adjusted his glasses with one hand and turned the page with the other. The text was dense and deeply unsatisfying — a tangled mess of Latin, half-myth, and medieval medical jargon that claimed caladrius feathers could purify the soul. He made a noncommittal grunt. "Unverified, metaphorical," he scrawled beside it in the margin.

He'd just begun cross-referencing a Saxon manuscript when the door burst open.

Fiona.

She strode in without knocking. The biologist's suit was rumpled as if she hadn't slept and a black smear streaked one cheek like war paint. Her hair had frizzed out of its neat twist, and her lipstick had worn down to a faint outline, but her eyes were alight with the kind of scientific thrill he hadn't seen since her arrival.

James blinked, his pen hovering above the page.

"I take it you've made progress," he said dryly, setting the pen aside.

"You could say that." She didn't sit, but stood there in front of his desk, vibrating with suppressed excitement. "I've had… let's call it a reaction. A very promising one."

James leaned back in his chair. "With which sample?"

Fiona's lips curled, and she tapped her fingers together. "Barghest fur. Treated with a precise balance of cyclops keratin and a catalytic thermal agent. It's not stable yet, and nowhere near ready for field use, but the compound… James, it *responded*."

He raised an eyebrow. "Responded in what way?"

She was grinning now, eyes alight with something close to obsession. "It reacted to heat. Once it reached a certain threshold, the fur fibres started to ripple. With the cyclops component added, the sample *oriented* itself. It wasn't random."

James sat up straighter. "Oriented? Toward what?"

She nodded, gesturing animatedly now. "That's the thing – it chose a direction. I ran the test in a darkened chamber, and when the conditions were right, the fibres shifted – subtly, but definitely – toward the deepest pocket of shadow. Almost as if it… saw something there."

"Night vision?" James asked, intrigued.

"Possibly," Fiona said. "But it felt more precise than that. I think the cyclops keratin gave the compound focus – a directional clarity, almost like target acquisition."

"Is that what the barghest does?" James murmured, half to himself. "Uses the shadows to reach its targets?"

Fiona nodded absently, already pacing. "I've never seen a reaction like this. I need to stabilise the coating. It has to bond to natural fibres, and right now the effect barely lasts a few seconds. But tomorrow…"

She stopped, turning to face him. A sly smile tugged at her mouth, her eyes gleaming with barely contained triumph.

"Tomorrow, I'll show you," she said quietly. "And trust me – you'll want to see it."

James studied her for a long moment. The fire in her eyes, the thrill in her voice – she was exactly what the Council had hoped for.

He nodded once. "Don't burn down the lab before then."

"No promises," she said over her shoulder as she turned and swept out, leaving the door swinging half open behind her.

James stared at the empty space she'd left behind, then slowly leaned back in his chair.

A fabric that responds to shadow… That chooses where to move…

He opened his notebook, flipped to a fresh page, and picked up his pen. "Let's see where this goes…"

※※※

"What's going on in those heads of yours?" James murmured as he watched the chimaera pace its cell. It was remarkable how resilient the beast was, considering one of its three heads – the serpent – was unmistakably dead. The chimaera moved as if the loss barely registered. Perhaps the lion and goat were more than enough.

Would the lion survive without the goat? The goat without the lion? It was a question unlikely to find an answer outside a dissection table – and the Council certainly wouldn't allow that.

The goat bleated softly, but the lion's head was silent, its golden eyes locking onto James' for a moment before dropping away, disinterested.

Stavros. Ambrose had given it that name. James still thought naming it was foolish – it implied personality, perhaps even sentience, and bred unnecessary sentiment. He'd seen nothing in the chimaera but instinct and muscle. If he stepped into that cell, it wouldn't hesitate. It wouldn't ask questions. It would just rip him apart.

He tapped his pen against his notebook, then jotted a few notes. *Raw power and resilience. Cooperation between three separate entities: power, intelligence, slyness? What intrinsic properties could potentially be of use? What trait does it embody?*

That thought stirred something. He pulled out his phone, scrolled through his messages. The one he'd sent Cassie days ago was still marked unread.

He sighed, brow furrowed. Tenacity or stubbornness, he wasn't sure which his daughter embodied more. Maybe he should ask Jenna to speak with her. His ex-wife always had a better chance of getting through. His finger hovered over her contact… Then he made a face and shoved the phone back into his coat.

He passed the barghest's cell next. It was still brightly lit, though one of the floodlights was already starting to dim. He'd need to have a word with whoever was on rotation. Letting those lights slip was the sort of mistake you only made once.

James was halfway down the steel steps when a commotion drew him toward the dragon's gate.

Garcia and two others were soaked to the bone, backs braced against the heavy door, trying to force it shut against something shoving from the other side.

"What the hell's going on?" the Keeper demanded as he approached.

"Bloody dragon," Garcia growled, gritting his teeth. "Lured us in with a scale. Dropped it, like it was bait. Then it tried to drown Santos."

Santos looked pale, shaken. Bits of pondweed clung to his hair and his soaked uniform squelched with every move.

James stepped in and helped shove, his eyes widening as something massive slammed into the other side of the gate.

"Push!" Garcia barked.

Together, they managed to heave the door shut. The lock clanged into place, and James exhaled sharply.

He turned to Garcia, jaw tight. "You should know better by now. Don't go in there unless it's necessary. I don't give a damn about its Keeper's Fee. You're no good to me dead."

Garcia swallowed his retort and gave a stiff nod. "Yes, sir."

"Go dry off. Grab something warm from the kitchen. But I want you back on rotation in thirty minutes. All three of you are on basilisk duty for the rest of the week."

The men groaned in unison, trudging off and leaving a trail of water behind them.

James slumped against the gate, scrubbing a hand over his face. He'd lost enough people to that dragon. He didn't plan on losing more.

His pulse hadn't slowed yet when he found himself before another door – one he usually avoided.

He hesitated.

Then, with a muttered curse, he turned and entered the enclosure.

A soft mist rose from the pools within. Cascading waterfalls tumbled into a moonlit lake, and the air smelled faintly of holly and frost. Somewhere in the distance, a nightingale sang.

James' chest tightened. The asrai was already watching him.

Grey eyes shimmered through the mist. Her long, pale hair floated on the water's surface. A white Victorian dress clung to her figure as she lifted herself from the lake like something out of a dream.

She took one step forward.

James retreated a pace. "That's close enough," he said, raising a hand. He didn't fancy being drowned tonight.

She smiled, fingers twisting a lock of hair. "Come to collect a fee, Keeper?" Her voice was cool and silken, the burble of a stream with jagged rocks beneath it.

His throat went dry. He folded his hands behind his back to still their sudden impulse to take her in his arms and run them across her entire body. "If you're offering," he said, voice rougher than intended.

"You can have it," she purred, lips glistening.

"If you come and take it."

James blinked. He was ankle-deep in cold water before he even realised he'd stepped forward. Swearing, he backed away quickly.

Laughter bubbled from her lips, crimson like an expensive merlot. Or a fresh bruise.

"Keep it," he muttered, heat rising to his cheeks.

He was nearly through the door when her voice followed him on the mist: "Tell the alchemist if she wants it, she can come ask me herself."

James slammed the door behind him, breathing heavily.

He wasn't sure what disturbed him more – that the asrai knew about Fiona, or that she wanted her to visit…

His socks squelched unpleasantly as he stepped into what had once been the kitsune's enclosure – and stopped cold.

It had changed.

The gentle woodland meadow had been transformed into a lush, tropical jungle. Dense foliage curled skyward in spirals of vibrant green, mist clung to the undergrowth, and broad-leafed plants shimmered with dew. Vines draped from twisted banyan-like trees, their roots sinking into rich, dark soil that steamed faintly in the heat. The air was thick with the scent of rain and ripe fruit, alive with the low hum of unseen insects and the distant cry of tropical birds. Somewhere within the verdant sprawl, the airavata trumpeted.

Then thunder cracked overhead, and rain poured down in sheets, soaking him to the bone.

James just stood there a moment, drenched and exasperated.

Then he turned, walked out without a word, and shut the door firmly behind him.

Water dripped from his coat onto the stone

floor as he stalked back into the heart of the Repository.

Was there nothing in this bloody place that wanted to make his job easier?

✳✳✳

After a hot shower, James returned to his study. He'd given up trying to coax the fireplace into life – no amount of firelighters, coal, or even gas ever seemed to catch. Magic, he suspected. Or poor plumbing.

He dropped into his desk chair with a weary sigh just as someone began pounding on the door with enough force to rattle the hinges.

"James, are you in there?" Fiona's voice – bright, breathless, and unmistakably triumphant.

He opened the door to find her flushed with excitement, windswept, and wearing a lab coat. The sleeves were rolled to her elbows and streaked with something faintly iridescent that shimmered when it caught the light.

"I've done it," she said, pushing past him without waiting for an invitation. "You have to see."

James blinked, but followed, curiosity flaring.

Fiona turned on the spot, brandishing a folded square of charcoal-black fabric no larger than a handkerchief. At first glance, it looked entirely unremarkable – matte, soft, like soot-dyed wool. But as she laid it over the back of his leather chair, the edges shimmered faintly, like heat rippling off asphalt.

"Don't blink," she warned.

She reached out and tugged it from the chair – and vanished.

James jolted upright. The chair stood empty. The space where she had been was undisturbed.

No footfalls, no breeze, not even the hint of a movement. Just… nothing.

Nusku let out a curious trill, his head cocked as shadows near the fireplace flickered, and Fiona stepped back into view. She grinned at the Keeper from across the room.

"You moved through the shadows," he said breathlessly, everything clicking into place.

"Exactly," she said, her eyes bright with excitement.

She held out the fabric. James reached for it as though it might dissolve if he touched it too quickly. It was warm, and where his fingers brushed it, a faint trace of brimstone lingered in the air.

"I started with barghest fur. Something in its biology doesn't just repel light – it navigates it. Not just camouflage. Direction. The fibres orient themselves toward the strongest source of ambient shadow when exposed to heat and pressure," she said, pacing now, flushed with momentum. "Then I added cyclops keratin, just a sliver. It sharpened the response. Gave it *focus*. Directional clarity."

James' mind raced. "A fabric that knows where to go in the dark."

"It *travels*," Fiona said. "The same way the barghest does. Through shadows. Not aimlessly. *Precisely*."

James stared at the cloth in his hands, the implications unfolding in his mind like a map. Fieldwork. Recovery. Infiltration. Escape routes where none existed. Controlled, targeted movement through a space the world didn't even know was possible.

"You're not just making a cloak," he said. "You're building a door."

Fiona's smile deepened. "Not a door," she said

softly. "A *path*."

He turned the fabric over in his fingers. It seemed to drink in the light. If the Repository had once been a vault for the past, this – this was its key to the future.

"Is it stable?"

"Only over short distances. But it's real. Repeatable. I'll refine the substrate, figure out the bonding process. With wearable tech… With control systems…" she trailed off, eyes glittering. "It's just the beginning."

James stared at the cloth a moment longer, then looked up at her. There was fire in her, yes – but more than that, *vision*. He saw now why the Council had wanted her here. And for the first time in months, something like anticipation stirred in his chest.

From his perch, Nusku let out a soft, musical note, as if sensing the shift in the air.

"This changes everything," James said, voice quiet with awe.

Fiona's grin widened. "Told you you'd want to see it."

PART 10

TWILIGHT'S TRAIL

T he hiss of the train brakes gave way to the low murmur of voices and the clatter of footsteps on the platform. I stepped down, overnight bag slung over my shoulder. After the quiet of Epping Forest, London hit like a punch to the senses.

I paused just beyond the tide of passengers, letting the noise and motion wash over me. Father's call still rattled me. I hadn't meant to tell him about Cassie – and I certainly wasn't going to take her to him. Not after seeing her run, wild and free, beneath the moonlight. I'd never seen her so happy.

Maybe Father could keep her safe in the Repository. But now that he'd started taking Keeper's Fees, I wasn't so sure. And to the Council, she'd just be another asset – something valuable to keep locked away. I couldn't let that happen.

"Everything alright?"

I turned to see Sarah descending from the carriage, Amari close behind. Amari looked tired but satisfied, her smile relaxed. Sarah, on the other hand, had a small frown carved into her brow. I never could hide anything from her.

I shrugged. "Just glad we're back."

Sarah slipped her arm through mine and drew a deep breath. "Feels different," she said quietly.

I nodded. "Like a weight's been lifted."

"I'm glad we took the train," Amari added, hitching her backpack over one shoulder. "It felt good to just watch the landscape go by. I never give myself the chance to do that."

"You know what they say about the journey versus the destination…" I said, and she shot me a grin.

Sarah gave a slow, thoughtful nod. "Sometimes the long road home is the better one." Then her expression shifted, apologetic. "But, I'd better head off. I'm on the late shift tonight, and I could really use an Advil and a nap before then."

"Thanks for coming," I said, pulling her into a hug. I turned to Amari. "Both of you."

Amari gave my other arm a quick squeeze. "You can't get rid of me that easily." She hesitated. "Speaking of…"

I laughed. "Yes, you can stay with me until you find your own place."

Amari looked to Sarah for confirmation. "If it's alright with you?"

Sarah arched an eyebrow, but the corner of her mouth twitched. "You can stay with him as long as you can put up with him. Just try to keep him out of trouble."

"Hey," I said, mock-offended. "She's the one who *gets* me into trouble!"

Sarah laughed, then gave me a quick kiss. "See you soon," she said, slinging her bag over her shoulder and heading for the station exit.

My phone buzzed. I glanced at the screen. Daniel.

-- Hey. Do you have time to swing by? Need to talk. --

I stared at the message, thumb hovering over the reply button. After the events of the last few weeks, I wasn't sure I had the energy for another crisis right now. But Daniel was my best friend. He wouldn't have asked unless it was important.

I sighed and typed out a response.

-- On my way. --

I turned to Amari. "I'll meet you later, alright? Just need to catch up with a friend. I assume I don't need to give you the keys to my apartment?"

She smiled. "I'll manage. Take your time – I have some reading I need to catch up on." She rolled her shoulders, as if working out the tension. "The Repository will still be there tomorrow. We both deserve a rest – and I could do with a long soak in a hot bath."

I chuckled. "Have fun. Here." I handed her my overnight bag. "Take this with you."

She accepted it with a nod and a final smile, then turned toward the Tube entrance. I watched her go, wondering if I should tell her she was heading towards the wrong line. Clearly, navigating the public transport system wasn't her strong suit.

I chuckled to myself. She'd figure it out.

Slipping my phone back into my coat, I started walking. Hopefully, whatever Daniel wanted to talk about wasn't as urgent as my need for a decent cup of coffee.

※※※

The bell above the door jingled as I stepped into Daniel's shoe shop. The familiar scent of leather, beeswax polish, and varnished wood wrapped around me like a warm coat. Behind the counter, Daniel looked up from a pair of hot pink stilettos.

"Hey, mate," he greeted, nodding toward the extra stool next to the counter – Caitlynn's usual perch these days. "How'd the shift go last night? Judging by this mountain of shoes –" He waved at a neatly stacked row of repaired footwear behind him. "I take it Tenacity made it back in one piece?"

263

"It went well. Great, actually," I said, perching on the stool. "You were right – she didn't turn into a monster."

Daniel gave me a smug told-you-so look. "Caitlynn'll be glad to hear that. She was worried."

"Where is she?" I asked. If she hadn't talked Cassie down from the edge, helped her believe that shifting wouldn't change who she was, things might've gone very differently.

"She's home," Daniel said, his brow creasing. "Bit under the weather. Had a vision this morning, and it left her feeling weak."

My stomach tightened. Caitlynn's visions weren't natural. They were a side effect of the lamia's bite, and it didn't surprise me they came with a cost. "Is there anything I can do?"

He shook his head. "She just needs rest. She'll bounce back." But he didn't sound convinced.

I wondered if she'd seen anything about Cassie – or about me – again. Her visions were always twisted just a little, but they carried enough truth to give a warning of what might be coming.

As if reading my thoughts, Daniel leaned forward, lowering his voice. "Actually, that's not what I wanted to talk to you about."

I raised an eyebrow. "Alright, hit me."

"There's talk in the community," he said. "Rumours of another market – a *twilight* market. I think it's coming with the new moon."

There it was. The crisis I knew had to be coming. "Are you sure?"

Daniel shrugged, setting the stiletto aside and picking up a sensible black courtroom shoe with a split sole. "Just speculation. But the signs are all there: folks going missing, creatures getting edgy, shady dealers getting shadier. There's a tension in the air – like everyone's bracing for something."

I raked a hand through my hair. "Amari's not

going to be happy about this."

"Why should she care?" he asked, glancing up. "She's not the Keeper anymore, right?"

"She still cares," I said. "And if there's another market brewing, she'll want to shut it down."

Daniel gave a half-smile and reached beneath the counter. "Well, I thought you might want this back." He set the two broken halves of the *rogatina* on the counter – the spear point dangling loosely from one side.

"You went back for it?" I asked, fingers brushing the shaft. The idea of returning to those lamia-infested tunnels made my skin crawl.

"Figured you might need it," he said with a smirk. "You know, when you go looking for that black market."

I picked up the pieces, running my thumb along the hidden switch that once retracted the blade. To be honest, I'd been glad to be rid of it before. Carrying a weapon with me had felt like… Like I was pretending to be someone I wasn't.

But lately, that someone was getting harder to avoid.

"I never knew what to do with this thing," I admitted. "I'm not exactly Gandalf – I can't walk around London carrying a staff."

Daniel cocked his head. "What did you have in mind?"

"Something discreet," I said, handing the weapon back to him. "Something I can carry without raising eyebrows."

He turned the shaft in his hands, inspecting it. "The retractable mechanism is clever." He nodded to himself. "I might know a guy…"

I raised a brow. "As long as it doesn't cost me my firstborn."

He gave a theatrical shrug. "I'll probably have to negotiate a bit, but I'll try not to let it come to that."

My eyes widened, and then I saw the wide, mischievous grin plastered on my friend's face. Bloody leprechaun. "You're impossible," I said with a grin.

"You say that now. Wait until you see the craftsmanship."

The doorbell jingled again as a customer walked in. I gave Daniel a wave and headed out into the chill.

Outside, the wind cut through my coat. I glanced up. Daniel's ever-present rainbow arched across Big Ben, glowing faintly against the dull grey clouds rolling in.

I tightened my coat. The thought of another market left a knot in my gut. I couldn't shake the sudden premonition that trouble was brewing. Something bigger than I was ready for.

❋❋❋

I found Amari curled up in the armchair in my living room, wrapped in a fluffy throw with a steaming mug of hot chocolate in her hands and a small leather-bound book resting on her lap. The fireplace beside her crackled cheerfully, casting a soft orange glow across the room.

She glanced up and grinned. "Hope you don't mind. It's just so cosy with the fire on. I've spent years in this country, and I'm still always cold when I'm here."

Shrugging off my rain-soaked jacket – the weather had caught up with me in Hyde Park – I hung it on the hook by the door and flopped onto the couch across from her. "I was wondering about that. Your office fire was always lit whenever I visited. Father never bothers with it anymore."

Amari clicked her tongue. "Doesn't surprise me. He probably hasn't figured out how to start it.

It's not a regular fire – you need a Word to spark it. Or foxfire."

"Foxfire?" I echoed, leaning forward.

She nodded, flipping through the book until she found the page she wanted. She held it up so I could see: delicate, curling script surrounded a sketch of a fox with several tails. "It's the magical essence of a kitsune. Used to be how the Elder Council communicated before mobile phones and email. According to Diana's diary, it's the only magic that could pierce the Repository's protections. That's why it was only ever allowed in the Keeper's hearth."

"Wasn't Riku a kitsune?" I asked, remembering the shapeshifting fox who'd helped us escape the Colosseum the night of the blood moon market.

Amari nodded, the firelight casting a sharp glint in her eye. "Yes. He used his magic to smuggle Caerus out of the Repository. Before I caught him." Her voice faltered, and a shadow crossed her features. "I wonder if he ever found his mate... or if someone still has her."

Guilt prickled under my skin. I'd promised Riku I'd help him find her – his mate in exchange for Father's freedom. But the kitsune had vanished that night, and I hadn't heard from him since.

"Speaking of markets..."

Amari's gaze flitted to mine.

"I've heard whispers of another one. A twilight market. On the night of the new moon."

She swore under her breath as she snapped the diary shut and grabbed her phone. "Where did you hear that?" she asked, already scrolling through her contacts.

"Oh, you know..." I said with exaggerated innocence. "I know people."

She shot me an exasperated look. "Do those people know *where*?"

I shook my head. "No. But it's probably not Rome again."

She made a low, frustrated sound as she tapped furiously at her phone. When she was done, she looked up. "I've sent word to every Procurement Officer I still have contact with. Someone must know something."

"And if they do?"

Her expression hardened. "Then I'll shut it down."

"*We'll* shut it down," I corrected gently.

That earned me a smile. "Thank you, Ambrose. I knew I could count on you."

Weariness hit me all at once. Between last night's chaos and too many celebratory pints at the pub, my body was calling it quits. I yawned deeply and stretched out on the couch, letting the warmth of the fire seep into my bones.

"Well," I said through another yawn. "Unless you get a lead in the next five minutes, I'll be here – napping."

A brief silence followed. Then Amari's voice, hesitant: "My bag's still packed. I can head out if you need your space. Let you have your room back."

I cracked one eye open. "You're not going anywhere until you're ready. Trust me, I've had worse roommates."

She didn't answer, but I heard the creak of the armchair as she slowly settled back, the soft rustle of paper as she reopened the diary.

I let the fire's glow blur at the edges of my vision. The last thing I saw before sleep took me was the memory of my sister's tongue lolling out in a wide, wolfish grin.

※※※

I was elbow-deep in breakfast dishes the next morning, only half-focused on the task while rain pattered steadily against the kitchen window. It felt good to be doing something normal for a change. The worry over the twilight market, and Father's insistence that I take Cassie to the Repository, still lingered at the back of my thoughts. But right now, at least, the most urgent thing I had to do was scrub the pot Amari had used to make porridge in – or *mieliepap*, as she insisted on calling it.

The scent of coffee still lingered in the air, and the warm water had lulled me into a bit of a daze when my phone buzzed beside the sink.

I rinsed the last plate and reached for it, expecting another update from Amari – she'd muttered something about research before she'd headed off to the British Library.

But the message wasn't from her.

-- I take one day off work, and they give me the rookie assignments when I return. Want to come with me, make it more fun? --

I huffed a laugh and reached for the dishcloth. That was Sarah's way of saying she needed moral support. Or maybe just someone to roll their eyes at all the right moments.

Whatever this assignment was, it was infinitely more appealing than sitting at home, waiting for someone to trickle through rumours of the market. And no matter what Father wanted, I wasn't about to take my sister out of the woods yet.

-- Be there in 30. --

I slung the dishcloth onto the counter, grabbed my coat, and stepped out into the grey drizzle.

Thirty minutes later, I stepped out of Notting Hill Gate station and spotted Sarah leaning against a lamppost near the exit. She had an umbrella tucked under one arm and a takeaway coffee in the other, and gave me a dry look over the rim of her cup.

"You're late," she said.

"Two minutes," I replied, returning her quick hug. "And be glad I'm here at all. I'm suddenly not overly fond of the Tube, now that I know what might be lurking in its tunnels."

Sarah paled slightly, and I decided not to press the point. "So," I said instead. "What delightful bit of crime are you dragging me into today?"

She rolled her eyes. "Break-in. Or possibly a breakout. At the Notting Hill Animal Refuge, just around the corner. Someone came in last night and left with one of the rescue animals."

"Strange thing to steal," I said. "Was it valuable?"

"We'll find out," she said, linking her arm through mine as we set off.

We stopped in front of a cheerfully painted door nestled between a row of pastel-coloured houses. A small brass sign overhead read *Notting Hill Animal Refuge & Boarding Kennel – Every Dog Deserves a Chance*. Overflowing planters flanked the place, and the scent of wet fur and lavender air freshener hit us as we stepped inside.

The reception area was quaint: a wooden desk piled with papers, a charity jar half-filled with coins, and a bulletin board covered with pictures of adopted dogs and thank-you notes. A woman in her late fifties bustled over, her pink cardigan dotted with muddy paw prints.

"Hello, can I help you?" she asked warmly.

"I'm Detective Inspector Sarah Miller, with the Metropolitan Police. This is my colleague, Ambrose Davids," Sarah said. "We're here about the break-in."

"Oh my, yes," the woman said, visibly distressed. "I'm Agatha Fitzgerald, the owner. I'm so glad you've come. It's unsettling, someone just walking in and taking a poor dog like that. I live right upstairs! Makes you feel unsafe in your own home."

"Did you hear anything when it happened?"

"No, I wear earmuffs at night. The kennels can get a little noisy at times. Red – the one they took – had a terrible howl. Neighbours weren't too fond of him. I received several complaints this morning."

"Red?" I asked.

"Because of his eyes," she said. "Most dogs' eyes look red at night, but his were particularly crimson. I figured it was something he ate. Poor thing was found in a graveyard – who knows what he dug up there."

A shiver ran through me. This didn't sound like your average rescue.

Sarah pointed to a CCTV camera in the corner. "Any footage?"

"It's the strangest thing!" Agatha exclaimed. "Nothing but static. Same with the outdoor camera by the kennels, though that one started working again late last night – too late to catch whoever took Red, though."

Sarah shot me a look, mouthing *Paris*. I nodded. We'd seen the same interference with the footage outside the Notre Dame that night I had a run-in with a gargoyle.

"Mind if we have a look at the kennels?" Sarah asked.

Just then, the door swung open and a woman

waltzed in, carrying a tiny dog in an oversized handbag.

"Agatha, darling, I *must* leave Fifi with you tonight!" she announced, pushing her sunglasses onto her platinum-blonde head.

Agatha gave us an apologetic smile. "I'll be right with you, love." She called over her shoulder: "Tristan! Can you take these good people from the police out to the kennels?" She turned to us again. "He's a volunteer, you know," she said with a fond twinkle in her eye. "Such a way with the animals."

A tall man entered from the back – early thirties maybe – with classically handsome Scandinavian features and a closed-off expression. He glanced at us, his mouth tightening.

"This way," he muttered, turning and walking out without waiting.

He may have had a way with animals, but his people skills needed some attention.

Sarah and I followed him outside into a narrow yard of modest enclosures, clean but utilitarian. Chain-link fences divided each pen, and the smell of damp fur, disinfectant, and dry kibble hung heavy in the air. The outside CCTV camera now blinked lazily overhead.

The dogs inside the kennels themselves were a patchwork of breeds and personalities. A scruffy terrier yipped incessantly, throwing itself at the fence with the unrelenting energy of a wind-up toy. Nearby, a dignified greyhound lay stretched out on its bed, barely lifting its head to regard us with disinterested amber eyes. A nervous-looking collie paced its enclosure, its sharp ears flicking at every distant sound, while a rotund Labrador snored in a corner, oblivious to the world.

One pen stood empty at the far end, its door slightly ajar. Deep scratches gouged the wall near the latch. The surrounding air still carried a sour, sulphurous stench.

Sarah snapped pictures while I stood awkwardly beside Tristan. He picked up a broom and started sweeping the walkway with mechanical precision, and I noticed the stylised globe tattooed on the inside of his wrist.

"Looks like it was a pretty big dog," I noted, nodding toward the claw marks. "Must've been a beast to do that kind of damage."

Tristan's eyes narrowed. "It was never meant to be confined. You can't keep a dog that big as a pet."

"Sounds like you think it should've been set free," Sarah said evenly.

He shrugged, not denying it.

"Are you admitting to the break-in, then?" she asked.

"No," he said sharply. "Just saying that dog didn't belong in a cage. Doesn't make me a criminal, does it?"

"No," Sarah admitted. "But it does give you motive."

He scowled. "Are you *really* with the police?"

She flipped out her badge.

Tristan grunted. "Finish up your investigation," he said curtly. "I have work to do."

"We're done here, anyway," Sarah said briskly. "Come on, Ambrose. I think we've seen all there is to see."

I followed her back into the Refuge, throwing a last glance over my shoulder. Tristan stood with his arms crossed, watching us go.

Inside, I murmured, "You think it was him?"

"Oh, I *know* it was," Sarah said. "But without evidence or a confession, I have nothing."

Agatha was standing behind the reception counter, brushing the terrier brought in earlier. The dog looked blissed out, perched on the desk like royalty.

"Mrs. Fitzgerald," Sarah said. "Apart from Red, was anything else taken?"

"Not that I know of," Agatha replied. "Besides maybe my reading glasses, but I do suspect I'm guilty on that account. They're probably around here somewhere…"

"And how long has Tristan been volunteering here?"

"A few weeks, on and off," the old lady said. "Surely you don't suspect him, love? He's such a nice young man."

I snorted quietly.

Sarah remained professional. "Would you press charges if we found out he let the dog out?"

Agatha looked shocked. "Oh, I hadn't thought about that. I just want to know what happened to Red. I hope he's alright."

Sarah's expression softened. "The kennel's latch was damaged. It's possible the dog escaped on its own. But I'd suggest speaking to Tristan."

"Oh, I will. Thank you, dears. And if you hear anything – anything at all – please let me know."

"Of course. Good day, Mrs. Fitzgerald."

Once we were outside, Sarah let her irritation show. "Can you *believe* she called the police over this? And it's obvious Tristan did it."

"Why would he free something that dangerous?" I asked. "Did you see the claw marks?"

"He's with GAIA," she said. "Eco-activists. That tattoo on his wrist is their symbol. Global Alliance for the Independence of Animals or something like that. They're always in trouble – breaking into labs, releasing pet shop animals, burning fur coats… That kind of thing. I'll bet you Tristan's seen the inside of a holding cell a few times before."

"He must really be passionate about the cause," I said, though I wasn't exactly warming to him. First

274

impressions weren't everything, but Tristan came off prickly at best. Still, maybe we weren't on opposite sides. If he'd freed Red for the dog's sake, then... maybe we were aiming at the same target, just from different angles.

Sarah sighed. "You know what I feel passionate about right now?"

I smirked. "A cup of tea?"

"A cup of tea," she confirmed.

While we set off down the street in search of something warm to lift her mood, I couldn't help but wonder if the missing dog – Red – was more than just a stray. And if its disappearance wasn't just random... but part of something bigger.

※※※

Amari looked up from her book as I stepped back into the apartment. From the way she was curled under the throw, you'd think she hadn't moved from that armchair since she'd returned home.

"Still reading Diana's diaries?" I asked, hanging up my coat.

She nodded. "Remember the Symbol you discovered – the one that let the Huntress Travel?" When I nodded, she continued: "I found a list of Symbols in one of Diana's older diaries, and I'm trying to decipher their meanings. There are more than I have Words for." Her excitement dimmed with a frown. "No luck so far."

"That reminds me..." I pulled out my phone and opened a drawing app. "Have you ever seen this symbol before?" I sketched the tattoo I'd seen on Tristan's wrist.

Amari's eyes widened. "Where did you see that?"

I filled her in quickly – our visit to the Refuge,

the break-in, and the mysterious volunteer named Tristan.

"Tristan?" she repeated sharply. "With that tattoo?"

I nodded. "You know him?"

She looked stunned. "Yes. From a long time ago – before I was Keeper. He was an animal rights activist back then. Always finding ways to sneak into places and getting into trouble for setting animals free."

"Still doing it," I said, dropping onto the couch. "I don't know what kind of creature he let loose, but it wasn't just a stray. The scratch marks it left behind were massive. According to the Refuge's owner, its eyes were bright red, and it howled all night. Woke the neighbours."

Amari's face paled. "A hellhound," she whispered. "It has to be. But how?"

A chill trickled down my spine. The kind of creature Father used to warn us about when we were kids – except those stories were meant to scare us into staying inside after dark.

"That... was in a Notting Hill kennel?"

"Where is it now?" she asked urgently.

"We don't know," I said. "And unless I convince Sarah otherwise, I doubt she's going to pursue the case further."

"Convince her," Amari said without hesitation. "If I'm right, a hellhound loose in the suburbs is a disaster waiting to happen."

I nodded and quickly texted Sarah. I'd barely hit send when Amari's phone buzzed.

She read the message aloud. "The fog walks with horns."

I blinked. "Come again?"

"That's what one of my Procurement Specialists just sent me. *The fog walks with horns*. Says he's been hearing that phrase a lot lately."

"That's not something someone would say often…" I pulled out my phone again. "Let's see what the internet has to say." A search brought up a subreddit almost immediately. "Here. Posted anonymously. Last night." I held the phone out so she could see.

Amari extricated herself from the throw and sat down beside me on the couch. We peered at the grainy black-and-white image attached to the post.

"Looks like an abandoned building," she said, squinting.

"Wait, what's that?" I enlarged the photo. "That's an old railway arch behind it. I know this place. I'm sure it's somewhere in Camden. Near the Regent's Canal."

Without a word, Amari rose to her feet and disappeared into my room. When she returned, she was dressed head to toe in black, her hair tied back, a purposeful gleam in her eye. She dropped something into my hand.

I looked down at the balaclava and groaned. "Not again."

⁂⁂⁂

"This is it," Amari whispered as we crouched behind a crumbling wall, peering at the building in front of us. It loomed grey and Brutalist, a monolithic concrete box smothered in graffiti. Tufts of grass, some waist-high, choked the surrounding lot, and rusted fencing leaned precariously nearby. It looked like the sort of place you'd avoid even in broad daylight.

Above the doorway, almost lost beneath layers of spray paint and grime, I could just make out faded lettering: *Regent's Veterinary Research Facility.*

"Come on," Amari said, darting across the

cracked road and toward the entrance.

The doors gave way with a soft metallic click and a faint groan as she pushed them open. Dust swirled in the stale air, catching in the beam of her flashlight. A narrow corridor stretched ahead, lined with closed doors, the walls stained with mildew and more graffiti.

I pulled the door shut behind me, wincing as the hinges screeched in protest. Subtle entrance – ruined.

"Someone's already been here," I murmured, nodding to a window cracked open just enough to let in the cold damp air.

"At least there's no CCTV," Amari replied, glancing up to where a plastic bracket sat empty in the corner. The camera had clearly been ripped out long ago. I relaxed slightly and tucked the balaclava into my pocket.

"You take the left, I'll take the right," I said, as we started down the corridor.

Amari nodded, then pushed open the first door on the left. "Empty," she said tightly, already moving on.

I walked over to the next door. It was locked, but a quiet Word slipped from my lips and the handle turned under my touch with a mechanical click. The room inside smelled sharply of chlorine, like an abandoned swimming pool. My torch revealed a large rectangular tank at the far wall, the water within surprisingly clear and still. Motes of dust hovered above its surface, catching the light like fairy trails.

As I stepped forward, something shifted in the shadows to my right.

Before I could react, a figure slammed into me, knocking the air from my lungs and sending us both to the floor. My flashlight clattered away, its beam flickering across the concrete.

"Where is it?" a voice snarled above me.

I blinked up into a familiar face – angular, handsome, and furious. Tristan.

"What did you do with it?" he demanded, fists bunching in my collar.

"Get off me," I grunted. I drove my knee up hard. He grunted, loosening his grip just enough for me to shove him sideways and scramble to my feet.

"Where's *what*?" I snapped, brushing dust from my coat.

"The seal!" Tristan was breathing hard, eyes wild. "I know it was here. Where did you take it? I knew you weren't really with the police – you're one of them."

"Hang on," I said, holding up both hands. "Calm down. You have this all wrong."

Just then, Amari appeared in the doorway, her flashlight cutting through the gloom.

"Hello, Tristan," she said coolly. "It's been a while."

Tristan froze. "Amari?" His shoulders slumped. "Please don't tell me you're one of them too."

She shook her head. "We're here for the same reason, I suspect. To find something that's gone missing."

Tristan exhaled sharply. "The seal. I don't know what they want with it, but it can't be good." He turned and swept his torch toward the tank. "They're always a step ahead. I get to the trail just as it goes cold."

"You've been following smugglers," I guessed. "That's why you were at the Refuge."

He gave a tired nod. "That place is a front. A drop-off spot for animals that need to change hands quietly. I doubt the old lady has any idea. But this isn't the first time something... strange ended up there."

"Like the red-eyed hound," I said, glancing at Amari. "What did you do with it?"

"I never said I did anything with it," Tristan replied, but not convincingly.

Amari stepped closer and placed a hand on his arm. "We're not your enemies, Tristan. We want the same thing. You can trust us."

He looked at her, then at me. "Is he really police?"

"Not exactly," I said. "But Sarah – Detective Inspector Miller – is the real deal."

He hesitated, then gave a grudging nod. "Let's just say the hound's somewhere safer now. And that's not a confession," he added quickly.

Amari didn't smile. "That hound could be dangerous. I need to know what happened to it."

Before Tristan could answer, a distant *creak* echoed from the front of the building.

We all froze.

Someone else was inside.

"Hide," Amari hissed, diving behind a rusting examination table.

Tristan slipped into a cupboard and pulled the door almost shut. I ducked into a corner behind a tattered lab coat hanging from a wall hook, cursing as it clung on to me like some over-affectionate aunt at a family gathering.

Footsteps approached.

Too late, I saw my flashlight still lying on the floor, its beam pointed toward the tank. A clear giveaway for anyone walking in.

Two men entered, their boots crunching over debris. One of them carried a pet carrier. Inside, a scrawny black cat lay curled tightly, its eyes milky white and glowing eerily in the dark.

They stopped short.

"Someone's here," one muttered, glaring at the flashlight.

"I told you I locked that door," the other snapped. "Come on – this thing's too valuable to lose."

They turned and bolted.

Amari popped up like a shot. "Quick! Don't let them get away!"

She made for the door, but Tristan spilled from the cupboard, blocking her path. I tangled with the stupid lab coat before finally wrenching free and racing after them. We burst out onto the street just in time to see the taillights of a black, unmarked van disappearing down the road.

"They're gone," I panted.

"And they took whatever that cat was with them," Amari muttered.

Tristan swore under his breath. "That was my best lead. They won't come back here now."

"How did you know about this place?" Amari asked, still catching her breath.

"I've been tracking them for months," Tristan said. "They use coded phrases, messages that don't mean much unless you know what to look for."

I nodded slowly. "The fog walks with horns."

Tristan's eyes widened. "Exactly."

"Give me your phone," Amari said, holding out her hand.

He hesitated, but handed it over. She punched in her number and gave the phone back.

"If you find anything else, call me. There's going to be an illegal market in a few days' time, during the new moon. I need to know where that market is. Any leads, you let me know."

Tristan stared at her, clearly overwhelmed. "Who... *are* you people?"

Amari's expression darkened.

"We're the ones who still remember why these creatures should be protected. And we're going to put an end to their trafficking."

Tristan frowned. "Then you'd better move fast. Because right now, they're winning."

※※※

"You think we can trust him?" I asked Amari over breakfast the next morning.

She paused mid-sip of her tea, considering. The steam curled gently around her face as she stared past me, lost in thought.

"I do," she said at last. "He's impulsive and idealistic, and I might not have agreed with his methods back in the day, but his heart's always been in the right place. Still…" Her brow furrowed slightly. "I don't think he realises exactly what he's up against. You do know it wasn't an actual seal they kept in that tank, right?"

"I'm guessing a selkie," I replied, buttering the last slice of toast. "And that wasn't your average alley cat in the carrier either."

"Definitely not mundane," Amari agreed, setting her mug down. "Did you see its eyes? Downright creepy."

Before I could answer, my phone buzzed. A message from Cassie.

-- Will you come meet me in the forest tonight? There's something I want to show you. --

I tapped out a quick reply:

-- Sure. Should I bring a leash? --

Her response came almost immediately.

-- Haha, very funny. In the clearing, around midnight. --

"Cassie wants to meet me in Epping Forest

282

tonight," I told Amari, just as her own phone buzzed too. "I'll probably be back tomorrow morning."

"Sure," she said distractedly, already absorbed in her screen. "Look at this – it's from Tristan."

She angled the phone so I could read the message:

-- You said to tell you if I found anything. Something's off at the Battersea Pet Crematorium. A friend of mine says they've been taking in way more strays than usual. Including a black cat late last night. --

I raised an eyebrow. "You think it's a front?"

Amari nodded, her expression darkening. "A pet crematorium would be the perfect cover for creature part smuggling. No one asks questions. No one lingers. No one double-checks the paperwork." She glanced down at the phone again. "He's sent the address. Says we can meet him there after his shift."

"Best lead we've got," I said, pushing my plate aside. "Let's go see what they're really up to over there."

✳✳✳

The crematorium was a modest brick building tucked between high hedges and a quiet road. Inside, the scent of floral air freshener did little to mask the bitter tang that clung to the air – something scorched and chemical, like burnt hair and disinfectant.

Tristan was already waiting for us when Amari and I arrived. He sat stiffly in a plastic chair beside an elderly man clutching a framed photo of a grey-muzzled dog. The old man sniffed softly behind a thick moustache, eyes glassy with grief.

"Any news?" Amari asked in a low voice as we approached.

Tristan shook his head. "Spoke to the receptionist. She was polite, but cagey. Claimed everything's logged and done by the book. One black cat was brought in yesterday, supposedly a stray from a local shelter. Records say it was cremated this morning." His voice dropped. "Supposedly."

"Supposedly," I echoed, frowning.

Amari's expression tightened. "Let's see for ourselves."

We crossed to the reception desk where a middle-aged woman in a beige cardigan was carefully adjusting a display of sympathy cards. Her hands stilled as she noticed us, and she turned with a practised smile that didn't quite reach her eyes.

"Good morning," Amari said smoothly. "We're following up on an animal brought in recently. A black cat. We'd just like to confirm the timing of its intake and cremation."

The woman's smile stiffened, but didn't disappear. "All cremations are handled by licensed technicians. We follow legal protocol, and every animal is accounted for. I'm afraid I can't release details to non-owners."

"It's part of an investigation," Amari added.

The woman blinked, assessing. "Are you with the police?"

"We work in conservation oversight," Amari said, sidestepping the question.

A twitch of amusement flickered across the receptionist's mouth. "I'm afraid I can't help you."

"Look," I cut in, flashing my most disarming grin. "We're not here to cause trouble. We just think something unusual may have happened to that cat."

Her polite mask didn't budge. "I'm sorry. It was cremated this morning. That's all I can tell you."

She turned back to the sympathy cards, ending the conversation with a graceful dismissal.

Tristan muttered under his breath. I caught only the word *bullshit*.

I glanced at the double doors behind the desk, marked *Staff Only*. Something about them made my palms itch. There was more going on behind those doors than the receptionist let on – and I wanted to find out what.

The old man in the waiting area gave me a watery glance. He adjusted the frame in his lap so the light could better catch the photo: a faded black-and-white shot of a dog that looked ancient even before colour photography.

"I could go look," I murmured to Amari. "Slip through the staff door. Just for a minute."

She shot me a sharp look. "No. Not now. We're not getting arrested for trespassing today."

"Can't you just..." I wiggled my fingers at her in a mock-mystical gesture.

Tristan frowned. "Can't she just what?"

"Never mind," Amari said flatly, giving me a pointed look. "We'll come back later. Tonight, when there's less chance of being spotted."

"I won't be here tonight, remember?" I reminded her. "Cassie. Epping Forest."

"Right," she said, exhaling. "You see your sister. Tristan and I can handle this."

I hesitated. I wasn't sure how I felt about leaving her alone with him. But she didn't need my approval.

From behind the desk, the receptionist was now watching us with vague suspicion, her fingers fidgeting with a pen.

"We should go," Amari said, already turning

toward the door.

We stepped outside, where the breeze carried the scent of roses from the adjacent memorial garden. Underneath it lingered that same bitter, metallic tang – something acrid and wrong.

"They're hiding something," Tristan said quietly as he joined us.

"No doubt," Amari murmured. "But if the cat wasn't actually cremated, where is it now?"

"And why pretend it was?" I added, glancing back at the building.

None of us had an answer. But I had a feeling the black market was involved somehow.

A truck rumbled past on the road beyond the hedge, its tyres hissing over wet asphalt. I watched it disappear down the street, thinking of the scrawny black cat and the strange, luminous eyes that had stared at me from inside that carrier.

Whatever it was… it didn't belong here. And it deserved better than this place.

✖✖✖

We'd barely arrived back at my flat – shoes squelching faintly on the floorboards after getting caught in a sudden downpour – when my phone buzzed in my pocket. I shrugged off my damp coat while Amari made a beeline for her favourite armchair and the stack of diaries waiting beside it.

A message from Father.

-- *When is Cassie coming?* --

I rolled my eyes. Not even a hello.

-- *I wouldn't hold my breath, if I were you.* --

The typing bubble blinked for a few seconds

before another message appeared – longer this time. A list of places, each more obscure than the last, dropped into the thread, followed by:

-- I need you to check out these places and see if they have a caladrius. It's white, crane-like, with healing abilities. --

I didn't respond right away. I just stared at the screen, thumb hovering over the keyboard. Then I dropped onto the couch and typed, slow and deliberate:

-- I don't work for the Council anymore. --

A pause. I knew exactly what would come next.

-- If you won't go, I'll have to send someone else. --

There it was. I could almost hear his voice in that line – calm, reasonable, and irritatingly certain I wouldn't walk away from this.

Because I couldn't. Damn him.

I sighed and typed back:

-- Fine. I'll look into it. Just need to deal with something urgent first. --

I tossed the phone onto the table and rubbed my eyes. From across the room, Amari glanced up from her book, raising a brow.

"Trouble?" she asked.

"You could say that," I muttered. "Father wants me to track down a healing bird."

She looked faintly amused. "Of course he does. The Chairman was exceedingly interested in the caladrius when it came to the Repository. In fact, I

287

think it might be the entire reason behind the Council's new obsession with creature parts."

I stood up to turn the kettle on. "What happened to it?"

Amari snorted. "Norton."

I grunted. "Of course. Well, a white, crane-like bird that heals people should be easy enough to spot, right?"

She shot me an amused look but didn't answer, already half-lost in the pages again.

I didn't like the idea of delivering more creatures into the Council's hands. But if I could find the caladrius first, maybe I could take it somewhere safe. Somewhere it wouldn't be used or dissected or hoarded like a living artefact.

Problem was, that safe place used to be the Repository. And now... there was nowhere left.

A bitter taste crept into my mouth. Guilt.

I'd taken Stavros there. I'd promised him it would be better. That he'd be protected. But he was still locked in a holding cell.

First Riku. Then Stavros. Seemed like my promises weren't worth much anymore.

I'd failed them.

But I wasn't going to fail Cassie, too.

✖✖✖

I arrived at the little village on the edge of Epping Forest later that night – too early for the rendezvous Cassie and I had planned. A blustery wind tugged at my jacket and whipped through my hair, needling icy fingers down the back of my neck. I quickened my pace toward the local pub, the same one where we'd toasted Tenacity's return a few nights back.

Every head turned the moment I stepped through the door.

So, this was one of *those* kinds of places, then. I must have been too high on success to notice last time.

Still, the pub itself was everything you'd hope for in a village like this: small, warm, and steeped in character. Thick wooden beams crossed the low ceiling, their edges rounded smooth by time and smoke. The walls were cluttered with mismatched frames: faded hunting prints, dog-eared beer ads, and black-and-white photographs of the village in better days. A fire crackled in the stone hearth, throwing flickering shadows across the scuffed floorboards.

The bar was a great solid slab of oak, scarred with age and polished by decades of elbows and spilled pints. Behind it, rows of bottles glinted amber and green in the soft light. The bartender, built like a wardrobe, moved with practiced ease, pouring drinks for patrons who murmured in low tones. The air was heavy with the scents of beer, roasted meat, and wood smoke.

I ordered a pint and tried not to read too much into the sideways glances. The bartender poured my Guinness with a steady hand but offered no small talk. As I settled in, the conversations around the room resumed, though more hushed than before.

Despite the inviting ambience, tension hung in the room like an uninvited guest. The usual hum of village chatter was muted, replaced by hushed conversations and furtive glances. Locals hunched over their drinks, speaking in near whispers, their voices tinged with unease. A group of men by the fireplace leaned in close, their faces grim, while a woman at the corner table clutched her mug tightly, her knuckles white.

I shifted uneasily in my seat as I caught snatches of the conversation drifting across the room.

"It took my best sheep last night, right out of the pen. Didn't even leave a trace."

"Old Harry swears he saw it. Said its eyes were glowing. Just standing there, watching from the trees."

"Sue's boy says he heard it howl. Says it's the sound of death itself."

The fear was palpable, crawling under the warmth like a cold draft. Even the bartender flinched every time the wind rattled the windows, glancing toward the door as though expecting a monster to burst in and claim a bar stool.

I couldn't help but wonder if the thing they were afraid of was my sister.

"Excuse me," I said, catching the bartender's attention. "Is something going on?"

He eyed me, wary. "It's nothing," he muttered, and began polishing a glass with more force than necessary.

I took the hint, but stayed put.

"Someone should go out and look for it!" one of the men near the hearth said loudly.

I turned in my seat. They were worked up, on the edge of action. If someone handed them pitchforks, they'd be out the door right after the next round.

"Maybe I can help," I offered quietly.

They turned to stare. Their eyes flicked over my leather jacket, fitted jeans, and admittedly too-white sneakers. Not exactly the rugged image of a local monster hunter. I'd never wanted a five o'clock shadow and a bullwhip more in my life.

"You?" one man sputtered, barely containing a laugh. "No offence, boy, but what exactly can you do?"

I took a slow sip of my beer, buying time. How could I possibly explain to these villagers all the things I've seen and done?

"If we need someone to file our taxes, we'll let you know," another man said, and the others chuckled.

I wiped the foam from my mouth. "I've dealt with worse than barking dogs," I said, trying to sound mysterious. What I really needed was a gravelly voice and a tragic backstory.

The bartender suddenly slammed his fist on the bar, making me jump.

"Damn it, boy," he growled. "We're talking about a barghest here! It's not something to make light of!"

"A barghest?" I repeated, testing the strange word. "What's that?"

He stared at me like I'd just asked what a sheep was.

"It's death," he said simply. "Death itself, come to walk among us."

"It can change shape, too," a woman at the back added. "Looks like a man sometimes. Then, next thing you know, it has your throat in its teeth."

I swallowed hard. Not because I believed in their barghest – well, not exactly – but because everything they described reminded me of one very real, very powerful creature. One who'd only recently started running around in these woods.

Cassie.

"How long's it been plaguing you?" I asked, trying to keep my voice neutral.

"Couple of days now," the bartender said grimly. "Ever since the full moon."

I closed my eyes briefly. It was her. They were riling themselves up to hunt down my sister.

"I'll take care of it," I said.

The room burst out laughing.

"I mean it," I said, a little louder. "I can get the creature off your hands."

It sounded a little desperate, even to me. Time to pull rank, sort of.

"I work for the Council."

That gave them a moment's pause.

"The council?" a man near the fire scoffed. "They can't even fix up that pothole in front of my house after two years of complaints. How are they going to take care of a barghest, boy?"

"Not *that* council," I said. I had to wrack my brain to remember what official name Amari had given me so long ago. "The… uh… The Council for the Protection and Preservation of Cultural Creatures."

That earned me a few wide-eyed stares. The name was long enough to sound important, at least. Hopefully, no one asked for an ID.

I stood, finishing my drink in one long gulp.

"I'll deal with it tonight. And if it's still a problem tomorrow – and you don't see me back here again – you can go right ahead and light the torches."

The fire's warmth fell away behind me as I walked to the door, aware of every gaze tracking me across the room.

I just hoped I could find Cassie before they did. I'd promised her she'd be safe. And now the whole village was sharpening its knives.

✕✕✕

Even though I knew the monster the villagers feared wasn't what they thought, the forest still felt spooky at this hour.

Epping Forest at night was a world transformed, its daytime charm replaced by something older, darker. Trees loomed like shadowy sentinels, their gnarled branches clawing at the sky. The wind threaded through the canopy with a mournful whistle, as if murmuring dark secrets. Leaves shifted and stirred restlessly, creating the illusion of unseen footsteps in the undergrowth.

Goosebumps rippled across my skin. How many dryads were watching me right now?

It was fine. I wasn't lighting any fires, and I certainly wasn't cutting down trees. These dryads had no reason to be angry with me.

Of course, there was also the possibility of this being the place where Tristan had let the Refuge's howling hound loose. Whatever Red was, it had wrecked its kennel, which didn't exactly scream 'man's best friend'. And the villagers had mentioned red eyes, which sounded like Amari's hellhound.

Still, a large dog didn't seem quite enough to terrify an entire village, no matter what was going on with its eyes.

No. Chances were, the most dangerous thing in this forest tonight was my sister. Which made her a target.

Above, the moon hung low and pale, casting a silver sheen across the forest floor. Its light filtered down in scattered patches, illuminating twisted roots like skeletal fingers and stones coated in dark moss. The wind picked up, and the shadows seemed to twitch and sway, sending cold shivers down my spine.

"Cassie?" I called out.

A chilling howl answered me, echoing through the trees – impossible to determine which direction the sound came from. I froze as leaves crunched behind me.

I spun around. A large, wolfish shape emerged from the gloom, silhouetted in silver light.

"You scared me," I said, heart pounding. "We have to go. The villagers are onto you. They're one torch short of turning you into a pub rug."

The wolf advanced slowly. It raised its head and howled.

It didn't sound like Cassie. This was deeper. Heavier.

Wrong.

Somewhere behind me, something else howled in response.

"Oh, shit."

The creature in front of me turned its head towards me. Red eyes burned through the shadows.

This wasn't Cassie.

"Shit!"

I stumbled back as the thing – a massive, hulking shape – stepped closer. It blurred at the edges, flickering in and out of shadow. The scent of brimstone hung in the air like a warning.

The barghest.

Amari had been right – it was a hellhound. A big one.

It vanished into the shadows. I swallowed. It wasn't just hidden – it was gone.

Then, it erupted from the darkness at my side, lunging. I leapt back, tripped over a root, and hit the ground hard. Its jaws snapped shut where my throat had been a second earlier. I rolled, grabbed a handful of leaves, and flung them at its face. It snarled, momentarily blinded, and I scrambled upright, backing away until a tree blocked my escape.

The barghest shook off the leaves and growled at me. The muscles in its hind legs bunched together as it readied to pounce.

It leapt.

I flinched, and then another blur slammed into it midair, knocking it aside.

A tawny wolf landed between me and the barghest, growling low and fierce.

Cassie.

The hellhound recovered quickly, saliva dripping from its fangs as it squared off. They circled each other – two predators. But the barghest was at least twice her size.

I cast about for anything – *anything* – that might help. Something that would give Cassie the upper hand. There was nothing but rocks around. I hurled one at the barghest. It dodged easily and vanished again.

Cassie turned toward me, wolf eyes confused, and then the barghest struck from a different angle.

It barrelled into her. She snapped her jaws, trying to scare it off, but it wasn't fazed. It lunged, teeth sinking into her neck, and shook her violently before tossing her aside like a rag doll.

Her wolf's form shimmered – and then she was human again, crumpled and unconscious on the ground, the werewolf's sire bracelet hanging loosely around her wrist.

Something inside me snapped.

Roaring like a lunatic, I launched myself onto the barghest's back, grabbing fistfuls of its slick, oily fur. It snarled, jaws snapping inches from my face. I ducked. It bucked. I held on. I had no plan – just panic and adrenaline.

Then it stepped into a shadow, and I fell through empty air, crashing to the ground.

It had vanished.

I spun, searching – too late. It exploded out of another shadow, straight at me.

I threw myself sideways. Too slow. It landed on top of me, snarling, its fangs inches from my throat.

Adrenaline surged. I locked my arm and shoved back with everything I had. Somehow, I kept it at bay with one hand while the other scrabbled around blindly.

My fingers closed around another rock. I slammed it into the side of the barghest's skull. It yelped and toppled sideways, dazed.

I scrambled back, frantically searching for something to trap it with. Nothing but rocks and leaves. And how do you trap something that can step through shadows?

The barghest lumbered to its feet, shaking its head. I had seconds left before it would attack again.

"Ambrose!"

Cassie's voice – ragged, but alive.

I didn't dare turn. The hellhound's glowing eyes locked onto mine.

I was out of time.

No shadows. I needed to get it somewhere it couldn't hide.

A small moonlit clearing was visible through the trees up ahead. If I could lure it there… Maybe I'd have a chance.

A howl tore through the night. The sound rattled my ribs.

I ran.

Branches whipped my arms. Roots grabbed at my feet. I could hear the barghest behind me, then gone again.

It burst out from the trees on my left.

I ducked, stumbled, kept going.

The clearing opened before me, silvered by moonlight. My lucky white sneakers hit the soft earth just as the barghest emerged from another shadow and lunged again.

I slammed my palm to the ground and shouted the Word for Opening. A pulse of heat raced through my arm. The earth shuddered, then groaned as it cracked. I jumped back as a shallow pit yawned open – broad, steep-sided, and bathed in moonlight from above.

The barghest crashed into it, skidding to the bottom with a snarl. It tried to climb up, but the loose dirt slid beneath its claws. No shadows pooled in the moonlight. No escape.

It looked up, eyes catching the light. Then it howled – loud and angry.

I wiped sweat from my brow, breath ragged.

Then I turned, and my blood ran cold.

Cassie knelt on the ground, panting beneath a steel net. Standing over her was a man I recognized: Stalker, the rogue Procurement Specialist who had once worked for Mazzoni. His blond hair gleamed in the moonlight, and a pair of twin katanas peeked out from behind his back.

"I came for the dog," he said. "But I'll take the werewolf instead."

"No!"

I rushed forward, but it was too late. He slapped his palm onto a tattoo glowing on his arm. Blue fire sparked – and then he and Cassie vanished.

Gone.

I collapsed to my knees, shaking. I'd failed. Again.

I clenched my fists and screamed into the night. The barghest answered with a howl of its own from the pit.

I staggered over to the edge. It growled up at me, pacing like a caged beast.

I reached beneath my shirt and pulled out the silver whistle. If I blew it, Amari would come.

But she wasn't the Keeper anymore.

I couldn't take it to the Refuge, and I couldn't leave it here. The villagers would come for it. Someone would die. Or worse, they'd kill it – and we might lose another trait. I couldn't risk that.

There was only one option. I pulled out my

phone and dialled.

Father answered on the first ring. "Ambrose? What's wrong? Where's your sister?"

Guilt stabbed like a knife through my body. "She's... fine," I lied through clenched teeth. "This is something else."

I heard Father's sigh of relief on the other end. "At this hour? Can't it wait until morning?"

"No," I snapped. "I have a barghest on my hands, and I don't know what to do with it."

He sucked in a breath. "A *barghest*?" Then: "Text me your coordinates. I'll send a team immediately."

"I can't wait for a team," I said, quickly calculating time and distance. If the moonlight shifted, if even one shadow fell into that pit... "Have your men ready outside the West Gate in ten minutes. I'm bringing it to you. Bring lots of light."

Before he could respond, I hung up and slumped down beside the pit.

I'd lost her. Again. And this time, I didn't even know where she'd been taken to.

The barghest paced below, its glowing eyes fixed on me.

How was I going to get it to the Repository?

I eyed the moon nervously. A cloud was sweeping towards it. I wasn't sure I had ten minutes.

I glanced down at my watch and then back up at the sky. This was going to cut it close.

I couldn't wait any longer. When the cloud began brushing the edge of the moon, I lay flat on my stomach and edged toward the pit. This wasn't the best plan I'd ever come up with, but it would have to do.

"Good dog," I murmured. I hoped I wasn't going to lose a finger this way.

The barghest lunged and I reached down and

slapped my palm against the top of its head.

The Word left my lips – and the world vanished in a blinding flash of white.

✕✕✕

The world was still white when we materialised outside the West Gate. I lifted my arm to shield my eyes against the glare of two massive floodlights. At least Father had taken my message seriously.

"Grab it! Don't let it get away!"

Five of Father's men swarmed around me, armed with nets and what looked like cattle prods. One of them yelped as the barghest sank its teeth into his arm, but two others closed in. With coordinated strikes, they herded the beast into a steel-framed cage and slammed the gate shut. The barghest snarled and snapped, but the structure held.

"Take it to a holding cell," Father directed as someone fastened wooden poles to the cage, and four men hoisted it off the ground, muscles straining under the weight. "Make sure it's secure – and sedate it. I'm not listening to that thing howl all night."

I watched it thrash against the cage, guilt twisting in my chest. It had tried to kill me, but had I just delivered it to a worse fate?

Father turned to me, eyes alight. "Well done, my boy. A barghest! Where on earth did you find it?"

"Epping Forest," I replied. "It was stealing sheep and terrifying the locals with its howling."

"An evil omen, they say," Father mused. He was practically bouncing on his heels, and I couldn't help but smile. Even after all this time surrounded by mythical creatures, his enthusiasm was still infectious. "I'd better check the ledgers. I do believe you've just earned yourself a rather hefty procurement fee."

"Oh." The thought hadn't crossed my mind. I rubbed the back of my neck, uncomfortable. I hadn't done it for the money.

"Will you take a Keeper's Fee from it?" I asked, barely hiding the accusation in my voice.

Father's expression sharpened. "The Council wants me to explore potential uses for intrinsic traits," he said with a shrug. "I try not to be invasive."

My lips pressed together. I still didn't like it.

He folded his arms and gave me a knowing look. He could always read me too well.

"Will you be staying the night?" he asked, changing tack. "Or are you planning to hop off again in a beam of light? You never told me you could Travel."

I raked a hand through my hair. "It's... something I picked up recently."

"Care to share?"

"I would..." I hesitated. How was I supposed to explain something I didn't fully understand?

"But you've promised not to," Father finished for me. "Fair enough. I imagine Amari's taught you all sorts of things she never deemed worth sharing with me."

"It's not like that," I said quickly. "She hasn't, really. And besides – it doesn't always work. Most times, I need to be in mortal danger just to trigger it. It's not like I can pop to Tesco and back when I run out of milk."

He chuckled. "So, you'll be staying then?"

I rubbed my neck again. In all the chaos, I'd managed to push what had happened to Cassie to the back of my mind, but the worry surged back now, raw and electric.

"No. There's something I need to do. But before

I go…" I hesitated. "You mentioned that when you first started working for Mazzoni, a Procurement Specialist introduced you?"

"Yes," Father said, nodding. "He used to work with the Council when Mazzoni was still a member – officially, at least. I think they had a deal on the side. When Mazzoni was dismissed, the man went rogue and started working for him full-time."

"What was his name?"

"Benji," Father said. "I never learned his surname."

I stared at him. *"Benji?"* The name sounded absurdly innocent for the katana-wielding mercenary who'd just vanished with my sister. "Do you know where he is now?"

Father shook his head. "No idea. I didn't see him often. He just dropped off creatures and left. We didn't exactly get along."

Understandable. Any relationship that started with an abduction and resulted in years of coerced work was bound to be strained.

"I'd better go," I said.

Father nodded. "Good work with the barghest." He turned toward the gate, then paused. "I know you don't always agree with how I run the Repository," he added. "But regardless of the Council's new regulations, this is still the best place for these creatures. It's not safe for anyone when they're out in the wild."

"I know," I said quietly. "That's why I brought it in."

"Good man." He clapped a hand on my shoulder. "And your sister? When is she coming?"

Panic surged in my chest. If he knew what had happened, he'd never forgive me. "I'll… talk to her," I said, trying to sound casual. "You know Cassie."

He laughed. "I do. And I know you. You'll do

the right thing." He turned and walked off, the Repository gates swinging shut behind him.

My phone buzzed. My heart lurched into my throat. Cassie!

No. Amari.

-- How is Cassie doing? --

I typed quickly.

-- We have a problem. I need to talk to you in person. But I might need a pickup first... --

Her reply came fast.

-- Where are you? --

-- The West Gate --

Light shimmered in the air before me. I squinted and pocketed my phone just as Amari stepped out of the glow.

"Seriously?" she said, arms crossed. "You know this is not a place I want to be seen."

"Then let's get out of here before someone does."

Her hand brushed my arm, and light engulfed us both.

※※※

Amari sat with her hands wrapped around a steaming mug of tea, her expression grim. "You're sure it was a rogue Procurement Specialist who took her?"

I nodded. "I call him Stalker. Used to work for Mazzoni, but I don't know who's paying him now. Father says his real name's Benji."

I couldn't sit still. Standing up, I paced once, and then forced myself back into the chair.

"I remember him," Amari said, her eyes narrowing. "He was dismissed when Mazzoni was exiled from the Elder Council. Makes sense he'd keep working for Marco after that." She tapped her finger absently against her cheek, thinking. "But how did he know to come for Cassie?"

"He didn't," I groaned. "He said he came for the barghest." I told her everything – about the villagers, the fight in the woods, the trap, and how I'd taken the creature to the Repository.

Her lips thinned, but after a pause, she nodded. "You did the right thing."

I swallowed a sigh of relief.

"I'll figure out what to do about the Repository," she added. "But for now, it *is* still the safest place for any dangerous creatures we find. We just don't have a better option. Not yet."

"But what are we going to do about Cassie?" I asked, the worry gnawing at me, as relentless as the Cŵn Annwn chasing my scent.

Amari shook her head. "I don't know. But I'll reach out to my Procurement Specialists. Someone might know something about Benji – or Stalker, as you like to call him – that we can use."

A thought struck me like a gut punch. "Do you think he'll take her to the twilight market?"

The words tasted like decay. I pictured her in a cage, labelled and priced, for sale to the highest bidder. A prize in someone's collection.

Amari hesitated, then nodded. "I think we'd be fools not to assume so."

My jaw clenched. I'd been a fool to assume those villagers were just superstitious. That mistake had cost me my sister.

Trying to shake off the guilt, I cleared my throat. "Did you and Tristan find anything at the crematorium?"

Amari huffed. "Nothing useful. Either they're legit, or someone's doing a very good job of covering their tracks. If the cat we saw at the derelict lab ended up there, it was long gone – or already incinerated – by the time we arrived."

"So… what now?"

Amari let out a breath, sharp and tired. "Tristan's people are looking out for anything suspicious. My own network's on alert too. All we can do right now is wait."

It wasn't the answer I wanted. A heavy knot formed in my gut. Wait? That's all I could do? I wanted to do something. Smash doors. Tear through buildings.

How could I just sit around and wait for someone else to tell me where Cassie might be? What if I never find her again?

As if reading my thoughts, Amari reached out and rested a hand on my arm. Her voice was low but steady. "We'll get her back, Ambrose." She said it with such earnest that I knew she believed it.

And it made me believe it too.

I had to.

※※※

Sarah looked stricken, her coffee cup paused halfway to her lips, forgotten. I winced, remembering how she'd warned me not to let my sister transform. Now Cassie had been taken – because she was the world's only werewolf.

Sarah cleared her throat. "Do you know the man who took her?" she asked, keeping her voice low. We were tucked into a corner of a bustling Kensington café, the murmur of conversation and clinking cups buffering our words.

I took a sip of my lukewarm coffee before

answering. "His name's Benji, no surname that I know of. I've always thought of him as Stalker. He's a rogue Procurement Specialist. The same man who took my father all those years ago." My voice wavered despite myself. For a second, I couldn't look at her. "I never thought he'd come for my sister too."

Sarah slipped her hand into mine – warm and comforting. There was no recrimination in her eyes, only empathy. I suddenly remembered why: she'd lost a sibling too. Her brother had vanished while traveling in the East, and that grief had driven her to become the youngest detective in the Metropolitan Police.

Her brows knit together. "Do you have a photo of him? I could run it through our databases."

I shook my head. "No. But thanks for offering."

"We'll find her, Ambrose," she said firmly, her eyes fierce behind those dark hipster glasses. "I'll put out a missing person's alert. If she surfaces anywhere we have eyes, we'll know."

Since Stalker travelled by some kind of blue fire magic, I doubted they'd catch them at the airport or on a train, but the gesture still meant something. Cassie wasn't just missing in my world. She was missing in theirs too.

Which brought me to my next request.

"You remember the blood moon market in Rome?"

"Of course," Sarah said quickly. Something sparked in her eyes – probably a memory of the last time things went sideways and she ended up storming the Colosseum on the back of a rampaging centaur.

"There's going to be another one. New moon. Just a few days from now."

She sat back, frowning. "You think it's happening again? Here? In London?"

305

"I'm not sure where yet. Tristan – you know, from the Refuge – he's been helping Amari and me. He's tracking a smuggling network moving creatures through the city. The barghest we found was just the start."

"What've you found so far?" she asked, her tone sharpening with professional focus.

"Well, the animal refuge is definitely a front. We've chased a few leads since – an abandoned research facility, a crematorium – all dead ends. Whoever's behind this knows how to cover their tracks."

She reached into her jacket and pulled out her phone. "You want me to keep an eye out."

"Anything weird. Unregistered transports, missing vet records, off-the-books collections. Even strange calls from street-level patrols. You have access I don't."

She tapped on her screen for a few moments, then looked up. "I'll let you know if anything strange crosses my desk. But Ambrose – be careful. If these people are running another black market, and they're willing to kidnap someone for it, they're serious about it. Finding them could be more dangerous than you think."

"They have my sister," I said quietly. "They might find me more dangerous than they expect."

She gave me a long, level look. "Believe me, I know how that feels. Just promise me you won't do anything stupid. Or illegal."

I didn't want to make that promise, but the worry in her moss-green eyes made it hard to refuse. After a moment, I nodded. "I'll be careful. I promise."

"Good," she said, her smile returning. "That's all I wanted to hear. Now go find Cassie – and when you do, make them wish they'd never laid a finger on her."

I couldn't help but grin at that.

I still didn't know where to start looking – but there was one thing I hadn't tried yet. One last ace up my sleeve.

But if I did it wrong, it could make things even worse than they were now.

I needed to be sure it was safe to use first.

✻✻✻

I stared at the sign hanging over Daniel's shop door: Closed. I glanced at my watch. He never closed this early.

Something was wrong.

I pulled out my phone and sent him a quick text. His reply hit me like a punch to the gut.

-- Caitlynn's sick, but you can come upstairs. --

It took me a moment to notice the second door next to the shop entrance, painted a subdued green. I pressed the buzzer, and the lock clicked open.

A narrow flight of stairs led me up to the first floor, where the landing opened into a surprisingly modern flat. From the outside, I'd expected a cramped one-bedroom flat crammed above a dingy shop. Inside, it was another world entirely.

Warm light gleamed across parquet floors polished to a high sheen. The air carried a faint scent of cedarwood. A sleek leather sofa anchored the space, flanked by shelves of untouched books. A decanter of amber liquor stood like a museum piece on a glass tray beside a single crystal tumbler – probably more for show than use. Everything, from the curated art to the cushions' impossible thread count, exuded discreet luxury.

Even the rug beneath my feet looked older

than the building and probably worth more than a year's rent on my flat – which, in comparison, now felt like a neglected broom cupboard.

"Not bad for a guy who charges twenty quid to re-sole shoes," I muttered.

Daniel stepped out of one of the bedrooms, looking sheepish. "It's a bit much, isn't it?" he said, wincing. "My grandfather bought the place before the war. It's been in the family ever since. Ma had it redone when I moved to London."

He moved to the open-plan kitchen, where marble countertops and brass fixtures gleamed like leprechaun gold, and flicked on the kettle. "Not exactly my taste."

I gave the space another glance. Impossibly elegant, designed for both comfort and quiet status. There was an understated flair to it, the kind only old money could pull off.

"It's… nice," I offered. "Very homey."

That made him smile. He shot a worried glance toward the bedroom.

"How's Caitlynn?" I asked.

His smile faltered. "Not great. I think it's the visions. Every time she has one, it drains her. Like a sickness eating her up from the inside."

A sense of helplessness tried to overwhelm me, but I pushed it down. "Has she seen a doctor?" I asked instead.

Daniel shook his head. "Who'd know what to do with her? A leprechaun with visions caused by lamia poisoning?" His voice was bitter. "She wouldn't be safe. They'd just lock her up and poke around until she broke."

I hesitated. There was one possibility, but I knew Daniel wouldn't like it.

He caught the look on my face. "You're going to offer the Repository, aren't you?"

"It is protected by a powerful regenerative spell…"

He shook his head. "The price is too high."

He was right, of course. I released a relieved breath.

"There may be another option," I said, remembering Father's recent request. "A caladrius."

Daniel's eyes widened. "They have one?"

"Had," I corrected. "Not anymore. But Father wants me to find another one. If I can… It might help Caitlynn."

A voice from behind startled us both. "What might be able to help me?"

Caitlynn stood in the doorway, pale and wan, her red hair loose around a white dressing gown. I suppressed a shiver. She looked far too much like a White Lady for comfort.

"Ambrose says he might be able to find a caladrius," Daniel told her, handing her a cup of tea as she sagged into an armchair. I sat across from her while Daniel took his place on the sofa.

Her face lit up with a faint hope. "To be free of the visions…" she whispered. Then she looked at me. "I had another one of you."

"Oh?" I asked, sipping my tea. It smelled of cut grass and tasted worse. A three-leaf clover floated towards the top of the cup. I grimaced, swallowed, and set it aside. "Anything about Cassie?" I felt hope rise unbidden.

She gave a soft laugh. "No, it was nonsense. You were eating an empanada."

My shoulders sagged. The hope died as quickly as it had sparked.

"Wait, is something wrong with Cassie?" Daniel asked. "I thought you said she was fine after the shift?"

"She was," I said. "Until she was captured." I told them what had happened in the forest, how she'd been taken, and how I had no idea where she was now. "I'm desperate," I said. "Do you think I could use that last wish…?"

Daniel's eyes went wide. "It's risky, Ambrose. You never know how the luck will turn. I wouldn't chance it – not when Cassie's life is on the line."

I sighed. He'd warned me before. Still, I didn't want to give up hope so easily. "Are you sure? What if I just wished to have her back here? Or to know where she is, at least?"

Caitlynn gave a weak laugh that didn't reach her eyes. "Wishes always come true, but never in the way you expect. There's a story about a man who wished for gold – he found himself buried under a landslide in a collapsed mine. Another wished for eternal youth and ended up trapped in a baby's body for the rest of his life."

She met my eyes, serious now. "The magic sometimes twists the wording. It doesn't care what you meant. Only what you said."

A cold weight settled in my gut. I could almost see it happening – Cassie returned to me, but… damaged, somehow. I looked away, jaw clenched.

"You're right," I muttered. "I just don't know what else to do."

"I get it," Daniel said, flicking a glance at Caitlynn. "While she was in that coma and we couldn't find the lamia… I was tempted too. But wish magic's too fickle. You never know what you're going to get. Best to trust the luck, my friend."

I didn't want to trust luck. I wanted to walk up to Stalker and punch him in his smug face. Or drop him in the asrai's pond and walk away.

"You wouldn't happen to have any ideas, would you?" I asked. "Know someone who can track a person?"

"I'll ask around," Daniel said. "But in the meantime, I do have something for you." He crossed to a shelf and retrieved an ornately carved wooden box. Opening it, he pulled something out and returned to me.

"Repeat after me," he said with a mischievous glint in his eyes. Taking my right hand, he slipped a ring onto my middle finger. "With this ring…"

I choked back a laugh. "Seriously?"

Daniel grinned.

I looked down to see a plain steel band now circling my finger, unadorned but solid. I turned my hand over. A small, smooth bezel, like the face of a signet ring, rested on the palm side.

"I don't…?"

"You know the Word for Reveal, right?" Daniel asked.

I shook my head, still confused.

"Extend your arm," he said, stepping back. Then he spoke a Word, and the air shimmered.

I flinched as the shaft of the *rogatina* suddenly materialised in my hand, fully repaired and tipped with a wickedly sharp spearhead.

"How?" I asked, dumbfounded.

I let my hands glide across the smooth shaft. The weapon was a good fit for me – not too heavy, and perfectly balanced. But holding it again stirred memories I didn't want right now. I just wished it didn't come with so much baggage.

Daniel shrugged. "Hey, I just repair shoes. This is someone else's handiwork. But it's linked to the ring, somehow. Say the Word for Conceal, and it disappears again."

He demonstrated, and the weapon vanished in a ripple of air.

"That's… amazing."

"I figured walking around with a big spear's not exactly subtle," Daniel said, clearly pleased with himself. "Even just a walking stick will get you weird looks. And good luck getting the *rogatina* on the Tube. This way, you'll have it with you all the time and no one'll even know."

A hidden weapon I'd always carry with me. I wasn't sure how I felt about that.

Would it turn me into a hunter, like Nadiya? Like Stalker? I didn't want to be like them.

But if it helped me save Cassie, I'd take it.

"Thank you," I said sincerely. "How much do I owe you?"

Daniel smiled, just a little sadly. "You don't owe me anything, mate. But there is something you can do."

"What's that?"

He glanced at Caitlynn, still pale, still a little listless. "Find a caladrius."

✕✕✕

I stared at the message again, thumb hovering over the list Father had sent me. Five locations. Five wild-goose chases, probably. But one name pulled at me every time I looked.

Monasterio de El Escorial.

According to Google, it was a sixteenth-century colossus of stone – an austere labyrinth of cloisters, crypts, and courtyards nestled in the hills outside Madrid. Steeped in history and Catholic mysticism, the place practically oozed secrets and sanctity. If a mythical healing bird had taken refuge anywhere, it would be there.

And, for some reason, it felt right.

Also, it was in Spain, which shouldn't have meant anything. Except Caitlynn's ridiculous vision of me eating an empanada had stuck with me. Nonsense on its own. But maybe that was the point. Maybe it meant I needed to go to Spain. Maybe the caladrius was waiting there.

I sighed and tossed the phone onto the couch

beside me, rubbing at the ache behind my eyes. The London night pressed in through the window, heavy and grey, hiding the stars behind a curtain of low clouds.

At the kitchen table, Amari looked up from her laptop, surrounded by three open books and a half-empty mug of tea. Loose papers curled at the corners. The lamplight threw soft shadows across her face, emphasising the dark circles beneath her eyes. She looked like she was tiptoeing the line into obsession.

"Any progress?" I asked, my voice low.

"Some," she muttered, tapping at the keys. "That paperwork Sarah sent – it's a trail of forged quarantine records leading out of Folkestone. But it's messy." She rubbed her temple with her knuckles. "I need time to follow this through. Properly. It might be our best lead before the new moon."

I nodded, the weight of urgency settling on my chest again. "We need to find them *before* the market. If we're late –"

"It'll be a disaster," she finished, giving me a weary smile. "Exactly. And we have, what? A week?"

"Maybe less," I said. I hesitated, then took a breath. "I was thinking of taking a little field trip."

Her fingers stilled on the keys. "To where?"

"El Escorial in Spain. One of the leads from Father's list of possible locations for a caladrius. It feels... promising."

She narrowed her eyes. "And if you find it?"

"They won't hurt it," I said carefully. "It's too valuable."

"Which is exactly the problem," she shot back. "The Council will use it to line their own pockets. They won't care what's best for the bird."

I hated to argue with her, especially when I agreed.

But I couldn't tell her the real reason I needed to find the caladrius – not without breaking Daniel's trust. It wasn't about the Council anymore. If I didn't find that bird, Caitlynn might not make it.

"If I don't go, he'll just send someone else," I said. "At least this way, I can make sure it's handled right."

She glared at me, jaw tight, but finally gave a curt nod. "Fine. Go if you have to. But I'm not helping you with this."

I nodded slowly, guilt and disappointment mingling in my chest. I glanced at the window again. The glass reflected only dim shapes from the room. Beyond it, the city stretched into the gloom.

"I guess I'll take the train to the airport and –"

"You're not going by plane."

I blinked. "I'm not?"

Amari gave me an incredulous look. "Ambrose, you can *Travel.*"

I grimaced. "I mean… I've *done* it. A few times. But only when I was in mortal danger. It's not exactly reliable."

She rolled her eyes and went back to her laptop. "That's just a mental block. You don't need danger – you need *focus*. Picture where you want to go. Believe the Word will take you there."

"Easy for you to say," I muttered.

"It helps if you have a strong anchor," she added without looking up. "Somewhere familiar or somewhere real in your mind."

"I've never been to El Escorial."

"Then you'd better do your homework," she said sweetly.

※※※

I was up before dawn. London still slumbered

beneath a blanket of mist and drizzle, the kind that soaked through clothes without ever turning to proper rain. Tower Bridge loomed out of the fog like the ribcage of some slumbering beast, deserted except for the occasional gull wheeling overhead on sluggish currents of air.

Good. I didn't need any eyewitnesses for what I was about to do.

The exhibition walkway between the two towers was locked, but a whispered Word and a gentle push was all it took to gain entry. The heavy door gave way with a soft creak, and I slipped inside.

I climbed the iron stairs two at a time, each step rattling beneath my feet, echoing faintly in the early morning silence. The air smelled of cold metal and old oil. By the time I reached the top level, my breath came in sharp bursts, the glass panels around the walkway fogging with moisture. The ceiling lights were dimmed, but enough ambient glow filtered in from the city to see where I was going.

At the far end of the walkway, I found the emergency hatch and pried it open. The hinges groaned in protest. I hauled myself through and onto the maintenance platform above.

The wind bit at my face as I emerged onto the very top of the bridge. The steel girders were slick beneath my feet, and my gaze travelled down to the Thames, a dizzying drop below.

I stepped to the edge of the narrow ledge, heart pounding. My fingers tightened on the cold railing.

The fall probably wouldn't kill me if this didn't work.

Probably.

I adjusted the steel ring on my finger before reaching into my jacket and pulling out the photo of El Escorial's courtyard. Immense, weathered by centuries, the sunlit fortress in the picture seemed impossibly far from this grey morning. I studied it one last time, then tucked it carefully into the waterproof lining inside my jacket and took a slow, steadying breath.

I could do this.

I *couldn't* do this.

My heart seized like a vice as vertigo gripped me. Below, the waters of the Thames churned like Charybdis waiting to devour me. This was madness.

I started to take a step back, and then Daniel's desperate face flashed across my vision. Caitlynn was running out of time.

My resolve strengthened. I couldn't save my sister right now, but I sure as hell could try to save his.

Before I could lose my nerve again, I launched myself off the ledge.

The fall tore the breath from my lungs. Wind screamed past my ears. The girders vanished above me as cold mist streaked across my face. The Thames rose to meet with terrifying speed, its black depths lurching towards me like an open maw.

I squeezed my eyes shut and forced the image of the courtyard into the forefront of my mind – every detail I could remember. The cobbles. The fountain. The light.

The Word burst from my lips just as I was about to hit the water – and the world exploded into white.

※※※

I hit the ground in a crouch, heart still thundering from the jump. The world snapped back into focus with the sharp smell of rosemary and juniper, the crisp morning air cold against my skin. My knees ached, and my palms stung, raw from the gravel-strewn courtyard I'd landed in – but I was alive.

And judging by the mountainous silhouette rising behind me, I was exactly where I'd aimed.

El Escorial.

The monastery loomed in solemn majesty beneath a washed-out Spanish sky. Stone-grey and solemn, it stretched across the landscape in a sprawl of imposing domes, spires, and cloisters, a stark stronghold set against the mountainside. The copper-tiled roofs glinted faintly in the morning light, lending a ghost of warmth to the fortress' otherwise forbidding appearance.

I straightened, dusted myself off, and tried to look like I hadn't just teleported via magical near-death experience into the middle of a UNESCO World Heritage Site.

A tour group was gathering by the main entrance, orbiting a guide with a saffron scarf and a flag sticking out of her backpack. I blended into the tail end of the group, doing my best impression of a dazed but harmless British tourist.

"This way, *por favor*," the guide chirped, switching to English with the ease of someone used to pilgrims and pensioners. "We'll begin in the lower cloisters, then visit the basilica, the royal tombs, and finally – if you have the extended experience package – the sacred aviary."

A few camera shutters clicked. An older American couple murmured to one another with quiet excitement.

"In the sixteenth century," the guide continued as we moved beneath the colonnade, "a white bird was said to have healed the sick in these very halls. Some believed it was a messenger of Saint Lawrence. Others claimed it was a divine creature able to sense sin and illness, and draw the affliction into itself. If the bird turned its face away from you…" She smiled. "Well. You may wish to make your peace."

My breath caught.

A caladrius? Could there really be one here?

Father's message echoed in the back of my mind: *White. Crane-like. Healing abilities.*

The older woman gently squeezed her partner's hand. He looked ill – pale, with dark crescents beneath his eyes and the waxy pallor of someone who'd spent too long in hospital rooms. They were definitely here for a miracle.

I paid for the upgrade at the next desk without hesitation, scribbled my name on a clipboard, and accepted a small sticker from a nun with rimless glasses. The American couple did the same.

I slapped the sticker on my chest and followed the group through a long, vaulted corridor that smelled faintly of beeswax and old stone. Velvet ropes guided us past portraits of grim-faced monarchs in heavy frames, their painted eyes seeming to track our slow procession.

I kept glancing ahead, hoping we'd skip straight to the aviary, but the guide was committed to the full experience.

"This wing once housed King Philip II himself," she said, gesturing toward an austere chamber filled with carved wood furniture and threadbare tapestries. "He governed the Spanish empire from that very chair."

The chair in question looked like it hadn't been designed for comfort – much like my couch at home. I stifled a yawn and checked the time. Still too early to duck out unnoticed.

We passed into the basilica. Vast and echoing, its marble floors gleamed beneath shafts of sunlight that filtered in through stained glass. The scent of incense clung to everything, and organ music drifted from somewhere far above. Statues of saints stared down from the arches, frozen in expressions of ecstasy or agony.

Even I paused to admire it. The basilica felt sacred in a way few places did. A fitting shelter for a caladrius.

Then came the library.

It was breathtaking.

The hallway opened into a long, barrel-vaulted chamber, where the ceiling unfurled in a painted celebration of classical learning – astronomy, geometry, music, and theology all rendered in curling frescoes. The scent of vellum permeated the air as I passed by walls lined with shelves, all crammed with tomes bound in cracked leather and faded gold. Some were chained in place, as though knowledge itself required locking away.

I drifted toward a brass-mounted globe the size of a beach ball, my fingers tracing the faded lines of a forgotten continent. So many secrets were buried in places like this – hidden, hoarded, or simply lost.

Much like the Repository.

The guide paused by a glass display case inset into the wall. A leatherbound book that wouldn't have looked out of place in Amari's office rested on a purple velvet cushion.

"This is one of our oldest bestiaries," she said. "A handwritten copy dating back to the early 13th century." She pointed at the illuminated page depicting a white bird mid-flight, golden light radiating from its wings as it hovered over a man in bed. "The caladrius. According to legend, it could cure illness merely by looking at the afflicted."

My breath snagged in my throat.

I stepped closer, heart hammering. The Latin

script curled like ivy across the page, framing the image. The bird's beak gleamed gold, and a halo shimmered behind its head. It was beautiful. Serene. Almost holy.

Excitement flared in my chest. Maybe this wasn't a wild-goose chase after all.

The group lingered a while longer, but I barely heard the rest. My eyes kept darting back to the page. This could be the cure Caitlynn needed.

Finally, we moved on.

Those of us sporting the special sticker were led through a smaller passage branching off the courtyard, across a walled garden hemmed in by cypress trees and neat hedges.

My heart galloped. This was it. I could feel it.

The aviary was a tall, peaceful structure, with light filtering down through latticed windows and filigreed iron gates. Inside, the air changed – fresher, tinged with citrus and faint traces of frankincense from some nearby altar.

Beside me, the American woman gasped. "There it is," she whispered, almost reverently, and gently guided her husband forward.

The bird perched on a low stone ledge within a circular enclosure. It had long legs, pure white feathers and a narrow beak like a blade. Its dark eyes didn't blink as it watched the couple.

The woman clutched a rosary to her chest. "I told you," she said tearfully, her voice trembling with hope. "It's a sign."

Her husband lowered himself carefully onto a bench, wheezing softly. He looked like the next breath of air would push him over.

The bird turned its head, and the couple held their breath. It watched them quietly for a long moment, not looking away. Then it preened a wing and gave a soft, rasping cry.

"That's a blessing," the woman whispered,

brushing at her eyes.

The spell snapped and a cold certainty settled like a stone in my chest as I studied the man. He was clearly still sick, his breath coming in short, sharp wheezes. If this bird had any magic in it at all, we would have witnessed a miracle right here.

It wasn't a blessing. It was just a bird – not a caladrius. Entirely mundane.

Disappointment was bitter on my tongue.

The couple gazed at it with such raw belief, such fragile hope, I couldn't bring myself to correct them. Let them have their miracle. If it gave them peace, what harm could it do?

But for me... It was another dead end. Caitlynn's vision had been wrong.

I slipped away before the tour moved on, ducking through a side corridor and out into the cool morning air.

The monastery loomed behind me, all stone and silence, watching with the impassive stillness of the centuries.

It had nothing more to give, and I had no clear lead to follow next.

✖✖✖

The Plaza Mayor wrapped around me like an ornate enclosure framed by red-brick facades and rows of wrought-iron balconies perching beneath steep slate rooftops. Beneath the colonnades, restaurants spilled into the square, their white tablecloths fluttering in the breeze. Tables were already crowded – tourists sipping sangria, street musicians competing for attention, and a few locals retreating from Madrid's restless tempo for a long, lazy lunch.

I found a spot near the edge of the square and took a seat, the metal chair wobbling slightly against the uneven cobblestones. The scent of grilled chorizo drifted from a nearby kitchen, mingling with the faint bitterness of stale espresso from the table beside me, where a couple chatted in rapid-fire Spanish.

The sky hung low and overcast, and a cool breeze stirred the pages of the menu the waiter handed me.

"I'd like an empanada, please," I said automatically, barely glancing at the options.

The waiter hesitated, his gaze locking with mine for a beat longer than my simple lunch request warranted. Then he gave a curt nod and walked away without a word.

I leaned back in my chair, watching children chase pigeons while a weathered man strummed something wistful on a beaten guitar. Across the plaza, King Philip III loomed bronze and eternal on horseback, casting a long shadow across the square. Flags stirred in the breeze. Arches framed narrow side streets while the flag of Spain fluttered from and overhead balcony.

For a moment, I let myself imagine I was just another traveller, unburdened by mythical creatures, shadow markets, or the gnawing dread of what might happen if I failed. Just a man in a square in Madrid.

The waiter returned, setting down a breadbasket, a small bowl of green-gold olive oil, and a folded piece of paper where my plate should have been.

"I'm sorry, *señor*, but we are all out of empanadas," he said a little louder than I thought was strictly necessary. His eyes flicked meaningfully toward the paper.

I raised an eyebrow. "Okay… Bring me whatever's good here, then."

So much for Caitlynn's vision. No empanada.

No caladrius. No miracle. This entire trip to Spain had been a waste of time.

I picked up the paper, expecting a different lunch menu. Instead, it looked like a flyer – perhaps advertising some local event – sparsely covered in Spanish text. My eyes skimmed it absently until one word caught me short.

Mercado.

I frowned. "What does this word mean?" I asked, pointing to it.

The waiter reached for the paper, quick and deliberate. "Excuse me, *señor*," he said tightly. "There's been a mistake –"

I pulled it back before he could take it.

We played a brief, ridiculous tug-of-war over the document until he finally relented with a sigh.

"*Crepúsculo*," I said, jabbing at the word, both baffled and annoyed by the waiter's actions. "What does it mean?"

The waiter paused. His mouth twitched.

"Twilight," he muttered, before turning sharply and walking away.

I sat back, stunned. A twilight market.

I stared down at the paper, heart kicking up a gear. My fingers moved frantically across the few lines of text, scanning for anything else familiar. There was no address, no map. But there *was* a date.

My breath caught.

Tonight.

Not next week. Not during the new moon.

The twilight market was happening tonight.

※※※

Still clutching the flyer, I left the restaurant and headed down one of the quieter side streets off the square. The din of the Plaza Mayor faded

323

behind me – children laughing, cutlery clinking, music drifting lazily through the air – until all I could hear was the sound of my own footsteps echoing off the cobblestones.

I pulled out my phone and dialled Amari.

"How's Spain?" she said, her smile audible through the line. "I hope you're not sunbathing on a beach somewhere while I'm doing all the hard work."

"Hardly," I said, glancing up at the cloudy sky. "No sun, no beach, and definitely no bird."

"You didn't find the caladrius?"

"No," I said, jaw tightening. "But I found something else. We've had it wrong, Amari. The market – it's not happening during the new moon. It's tonight."

There was a sharp pause.

"What?" she said, suddenly serious. "How do you know?"

I quickly explained the flyer, the strange reaction from the waiter, the way he'd tried to snatch it back.

"Did you follow him?" she asked.

I swore under my breath. "No."

"Well, what are you waiting for? He clearly knows something. Go ask him!"

"Right. On it."

I ended the call and turned back toward the square, slipping the flyer into my jacket pocket. When I reached the restaurant again, my table was gone – now claimed by a young family with two squirming children. The mother looked one tantrum away from snapping, but the father, surprisingly cheerful, answered my question with a lilting Scottish accent.

"Waiter? Aye, think it was that lass over there who took over for him."

He pointed toward a waitress with short black

hair, busy clearing plates from a nearby table.

I thanked him and made my way over.

"Excuse me," I said. "Do you know where the waiter is who was serving that table earlier?" I gestured to where the Scottish family now sat.

She glanced over, then nodded slowly. "Juan? His shift ended a few minutes ago. He's probably halfway home by now."

"Do you know where that is?"

She frowned. "No, sorry." A pause, then a wary glance. "Why?"

I didn't answer that. Instead, I pulled the flyer from my pocket. "Do you know anything about this market?"

She gave it a cursory glance. "A night market," she said with a shrug. "What do you call it in English? A... bug market?"

"A flea market," I said, deflating slightly.

She nodded. "Yes, flea market. That's the word." She looked past me and gave a small wave to another table, then turned back with a distracted smile. "Excuse me, *señor*. That table's ready to order."

I let her go and stood in the middle of the square, the weight of disappointment slowly pressing down on my shoulders. Another dead-end clue that led nowhere.

If Juan *did* have answers, they'd slipped out of my reach by now.

This was what came from trusting the damn luck.

I pulled out my phone as it buzzed.

-- Any luck? --

Grimacing at Amari's choice of words, I typed back quickly.

-- No, he got away. --

Her reply came seconds later.

-- Okay. I just received a new lead from one of my contacts. Meet me here in ten minutes. --

A picture appeared on my screen.
My breath caught.
It showed a courtyard like something from a travel writer's fever dream. A round fountain stood at its centre, surrounded by ornate stuccoed pillars. White marble gleamed beneath the soft shadows of carved lions that supported the fountain's edge. The architecture was a tapestry of Moorish elegance – arched walkways, geometric tile work, and sunlit stillness. Everything was bathed in warm tones, and the blue sky overhead was almost too vibrant to be real.

My heart thudded as I stared at the image. I didn't know the place, and there was only one way to get there fast enough.

I swallowed hard.

Hopefully, my luck hadn't run out just yet – because it looked like I was going to have to throw myself off another building.

※※※

The first thing I noticed when the white light faded was that my feet were wet. The second was Amari's smirk as she leaned casually beneath a stuccoed portico across the courtyard.

I looked down. I was standing knee-deep in the fountain from the picture.

Awkwardly, I waded out, trying not to damage what was no doubt an irreplaceable piece of Moorish architecture.

Amari stepped forward to help. "Well, that's one way to make an entrance – and get yourself thrown out of the Nasrid Palaces."

"Where?" I asked, dripping a puddle onto the marble floor.

"The Alhambra," she said. "It's an ancient fortress just outside Granada. My contact said someone here can tell us where the market is being held tonight."

"About that…" I began, but a group of tourists spilled into the courtyard, chattering and snapping photos. Amari lifted a finger to her lips. I swallowed the rest.

She led me through an arched doorway into a room so sumptuously decorated it felt like stepping into another world. Ornately carved stucco covered the walls; the floor was a checkerboard of polished marble; and the ceiling stretched above us in a dome of painted stars. It was unlike anything I'd seen at El Escorial – lighter, dreamier, more ancient and alive.

We descended into a small walled garden, heavy with the scent of citrus. A gentle trickle of water echoed through the serene space.

"You were saying?" Amari prompted, sitting at the edge of a fountain in the centre of the courtyard.

I pulled the flyer from my jacket and handed it to her. "I think I might've been mistaken. The waitress said it was just a flea market."

Amari scanned the text, brow furrowing. "No… You were right. *Mercado del crepúsculo.* Twilight market. And today's date." She glanced at me. "Wasn't that what your source called it? But I thought you said it was on the night of the new moon?"

I ran a hand through my hair. "He guessed it might happen during the new moon, and it had made sense at the time – blood moon market, new moon market… But – he did say it was just a theory."

I shrugged uncomfortably. "Perhaps it *is* just a flea market. Maybe we've been getting worked up about nothing at all."

Her gaze didn't waver. She shook her head. "We know they've been moving creatures around – and it's not for a simple flea market. Maybe we were wrong about the date, but the *twilight* market is still happening. I'd rather be early than too late. You were lucky to find this."

I snorted. Trust the damn luck.

Amari's eyes caught on a line near the bottom. "*Presentado por Los Cazadores del Velo…* Hosted by the Hunters of the Veil." She looked up. "I've never heard of them."

"But the name does sound suitably mystical…" I replied. "Exactly like the kind of people who'd have mythical creatures up for sale."

Perhaps it wasn't a false lead after all.

"Yes…" Amari agreed, frowning.

"So where is it?"

"That's why we're here. My contact said we'd know her when we saw her."

"Vague," I muttered. That could mean anything. A mysterious stranger in a cloak? Someone hawking magic beans in the garden?

I glanced up at the fading sky. "We'd better get started. If the market's tonight, time's running out."

✖✖✖

We spent hours wandering through the Alhambra. The place was enormous. We passed through courtyards laced with roses and marble columns, peered into domed chambers with muqarnas ceilings like honeycombs made of stone, and even explored a Renaissance palace that looked like it had been dropped here by accident. Beautiful, all of it, but useless.

By the time the sun hovered low on the horizon and painted the walls gold, we were retracing our steps when we finally found her.

She sat alone at the edge of a long reflecting pool. Perfectly trimmed hedges bordered the water. Arched colonnades framed the space in postcard perfection. Her dress was white as bone, her long black hair cascading down her back. She stared into the water as if into another world.

"An *encantada*," Amari whispered, her grip tightening on my arm. She was trembling.

"A what now?" I said quietly. Women in white never boded well – especially near water.

"An enchanted spirit. And one tied to this pool."

The woman lifted her head. Pale grey eyes locked onto mine, and I stilled.

She raised a hand, and I froze. When she spoke, her voice was equal parts sorrow and storm. I didn't understand the words, but the meaning was clear: she was not pleased to see us.

"What's she saying?" I hissed.

"She says she won't speak to anyone from the Council," Amari replied through clenched teeth. That vein in her forehead that usually spelled trouble was popping like a drumbeat. "Least of all the Keeper."

"Tell her you're not the Keeper anymore."

"I don't think she cares."

Amari broke into rapid Spanish, her voice low but intense. The encantada remained unmoved. After a moment, she pointed at me.

"What's happening?" I asked, mildly alarmed.

"She says she'll only speak to you."

I swallowed, suddenly reminded of the Serpentine in London and the asrai who'd tried to drown me in it. "Alright. Translate for me."

I stepped forward slowly, the pool shimmering in the fading light. "We're not here to hurt you," I said. "We just want information. There's a market – tonight. We need to know where it is so we can stop it."

Amari translated. The spirit's face remained unreadable. Her next words were soft, like wind on water.

"She wants to know how she can trust you."

I met the encantada's gaze. "Look closely."

She tilted her head, eyes narrowing. Her expression shifted – wariness giving way to something like wonder.

Tocado por la escarcha. Marcado por el fuego," she murmured.

"'Touched by frost. Marked by fire,'" Amari translated, then looked at me. "What does that mean?"

"Doesn't matter," I said. "She believes me."

The woman turned back toward the water and lifted a hand. A silver glint shimmered beneath the surface – a comb, resting like a sunken relic at the bottom of the pool.

An icy shiver ran down my spine. A test.

I glanced at Amari, who gave a helpless shrug. "It's up to you," she said. "I don't think she wants me to go get it."

Groaning, I peeled off my jacket like a condemned man and slipped out of my shoes. "I'm not overly fond of water," I said as I remembered to tuck my phone into one of them. Then I stepped into the pool.

Cold, but only knee-deep.

I grinned. "This won't be so bad."

The encantada watched silently, her eyes

unreadable.

I took a step. Then another. And then the ground vanished beneath me.

The cold hit like a slap. I plunged in, struggling to stay afloat. The water wrapped around my chest, then my neck. I kicked to stay upright.

"You can do this, Ambrose," Amari called out just as the first fingers of fear tightened around my throat.

The asrai's cold eyes flashed before me. Panic surged like ice through my veins. I imagined hands clamping onto my legs, dragging me down. I flailed underneath the water, trying to resurface. Every movement cost me a little bit of breath. Already, darkness was threatening at the edges of my vision.

I couldn't do this. I was going to drown.

Then, another face. Warmth. Sunlight. The azure waters of the Adriatic. The rusalka off the coast of Dubrovnik, teaching me how to swim. I remembered.

I dove for the comb, my lungs burning as my fingers closed around it.

Gasping, I broke the surface, my heart hammering against my ribcage. Amari stood at the pool's edge, relief flooding her features.

I sloshed back, water streaming off me, and held the comb out to the encantada. She took it without a word, tucking it into the folds of her gown. For the first time, she smiled.

Amari helped me out of the water, her grip steady. "Well done," she murmured.

I was soaked and shaking, one breath away from never surfacing again – but I'd done it.

Shivering, I wrung water from my shirt. "Now… about that market?"

Amari translated the white lady's words. "She says she overheard two men discussing it," Amari said.

"They mentioned the snow-covered mountains."

I sighed. "That narrows it down."

I bent down to retrieve my jacket and put on my shoes. It was going to be miserable running around in a soaked shirt and jeans.

Amari's brow furrowed. "Wait. That's the literal translation. *Sierra Nevada.* Of course! It's the mountain range just outside the city."

Hope flickered in my chest.

I turned to thank the encantada – but she was gone. Only a ripple disturbed the water where she'd once been.

"Come on." Amari glanced up at the sky. "We have a lot of ground to cover."

She touched my arm, and the world turned white.

✹✹✹

We were so high in the mountains it felt like I could reach up and brush the moon with my fingers. Above us, the night sky stretched vast and brilliant – a tapestry of stars woven through the arc of the Milky Way, shimmering against the indigo darkness.

My breath steamed in the cold air. I tugged my jacket tighter, then paused, surprised. I was dry. Bone dry, as if I'd never plunged into that icy pool.

I turned to Amari.

"I chose to leave the water behind," she said with a faint smile. "Look."

She gestured toward the view.

The Sierra Nevada rose in jagged silhouettes, its rocky ridges catching the moonlight like shards of glass. Though it was late summer, streaks of snow clung stubbornly to the highest peaks, glowing silver beneath the moon. Below, hardy scrub and twisted pines clung to the mountainside, their dark needles whispering secrets as the wind threaded through them.

We stood on a rocky promontory overlooking a flat, wind-swept plateau. The market sprawled beneath us in a riot of tents and makeshift stalls that stretched across the open ground, their silks rippling in the alpine breeze – crimson, emerald, obsidian, all vivid even under the moonlight. Smoke curled towards the sky, scenting the air with charred meat, incense, and something strange… Something sharp and acrid, like the sting of potions brewed from mythical ingredients.

"Let's go," I said, taking a step forward.

Amari's hand gripped my arm.

I turned. Her face looked ashen.

"It's real," she whispered. "All this time… I mean, I knew, after Rome, I knew there were still…" Her voice trailed off. She swallowed, her lips pressing into a thin line. "But this –" Her gaze swept the scene below "This makes it feel like everything I've done was for nothing."

I turned her to face me. "You've done more than anyone to protect mythical creatures, Amari. You gave them a safe place in a world where this –" I gestured toward the market, "happens in the shadows. We are going to stop it. Right after we rescue Cassie."

Her eyes flicked up at me. "Cassie…" she murmured, as though remembering all over again. The doubt fled her features, replaced by hard, steady resolve. This was the Amari I knew.

"Let's go save Cassie," she said, and started down the slope.

I hurried to catch up.

As we walked, Amari glanced sideways. "Frost and fire, huh? One day, you'll tell me what that means."

I shrugged noncommittally. "Maybe one day I

will."

As we approached the tents, the air thickened around us, like we were trying to wade through molasses. Breathing became harder, as if a cyclops had its hands around my throat, squeezing. I pushed past the feeling of asphyxiation and walked face-first into an invisible wall.

Beside me, Amari grunted as she hit it too.

We both staggered back, rubbing our chests and gasping until the air cleared again.

"I've read about this," Amari said, her voice low. "In Diana's diaries. Some of the markets were protected by a Word – a password, basically."

"Do you know it?"

She shook her head. "No. It changes every time."

I exhaled sharply and dropped onto a nearby rock, frustration bubbling. We'd come all this way, and we were locked out like beggars at the gate.

Amari stood at the barrier a while longer, muttering Words I didn't know. Nothing happened. Eventually, she joined me on the rock, scowling. "We need to think."

I slouched. "How can I save Cassie if I can't even *get in*?"

"Ambrose…" Amari said. "That waiter in Madrid – why did he give you the flyer? And why try to take it back?"

I frowned. "He made a mistake."

"But why did he make it?" Amari insisted. "Did you say something that made him think you were part of this?"

I racked my memory, flipping back through the brief encounter. I hadn't said anything strange. Just ordered –

I jolted upright. "I ordered an empanada."

I strode toward the invisible wall until my lungs began to tighten again, then took a breath and said:

"Empanada."

The air shimmered, and the weight vanished.

I grinned. Caitlynn's vision had been right after all.

I turned back to Amari. Her brow arched. "*That* was the password? I never would've guessed."

"Come on," I said, almost breathless with excitement.

I stepped past the threshold and into the twilight market.

※※※

Rome hadn't prepared me for this. I'd never seen anything like it.

Vendors hawked their wares beneath enchanted lanterns that glowed in hues no natural fire could produce – violet, molten gold, electric blue. Tables overflowed with jars of glittering powders, iridescent scales, and bundles of peculiar dried herbs.

The clientele was as bizarre as the wares. Cloaked figures drifted from stall to stall, their faces hidden behind masks of bone, metal, or cloth. A woman with antlers jutting from her elaborate mask argued over the price of a vial filled with shimmering liquid. A tall man in a midnight-blue coat examined a cluster of glowing feathers with a jeweller's loupe. My hands clenched when I spotted Juan – the waiter from Madrid – manning a stall that sold nothing but teeth.

Snatches of conversation in a dozen languages filled the air, mingling with the occasional snarl or growl from the creatures on display. Some were shackled to stakes. Others paced in iron-barred cells.

I froze at the sight of one: a bony, skeletal beast with a long neck and a face like a half-rotted goat's skull. It let out a bloodcurdling screech that raised the hairs on the back of my neck. At another stall, two men were arguing over an enormous, muzzled bull with boar's tusks and inward-curving horns, its scent a pungent mix of herbs and manure.

I wandered deeper into the maze of tents, each step revealing stranger sights. A pale woman with hair like flowing smoke and black, empty eyes sat motionless with an iron collar around her neck. Further on, a hybrid creature with the body of a stag, the head of a lion, and strange cloven hooves paced inside its cage.

"This is real," Amari hissed. Her lip curled in disgust. "Never in my life did I think they'd be this bold." She looked about ready to rip the mask off the nearest buyer.

I put a hand on her arm. "We can't stop all of them. Not tonight. We're here for Cassie."

A muscle in her jaw jumped, but she gave a sharp nod. "You're right. But you realise what this means, don't you?"

"What?"

She swept a hand to indicate the whole nightmarish scene. "This is an entire *industry*, Ambrose. Creatures, buyers, handlers – it's organised. They're not as rare as I thought."

"Either that," I said grimly. "Or the Council hasn't told us the full story."

Even now, I could hardly believe the scale of the market. But the two of us couldn't stop all of this. Not alone. We'd need help.

Amari nudged me. I followed her gaze.

There it was – the scrawny black cat we'd been looking for at the crematorium. It stared at us with eerie white eyes, silent and watchful.

Beside its cage, a woman caught my eye. "Interested?" she asked, beckoning me closer.

"What is it?" I asked, stepping forward.

"It's called a *matagot*," she said. "A spirit that gives its owner a solid gold coin every morning – so long as it gets the first bite of every meal. Naturally, it's very valuable. Very rare, too. But I can give you a good price."

"How much?" Amari asked through clenched teeth.

The number the woman named nearly made my eyes water.

Warmth radiated from Amari. I looked down – fire licked around her palms and the air warped with heat. I put a hand on her shoulder.

"Not yet," I murmured. The last thing we needed was to cause a scene and lose Cassie before we even found her.

Amari trembled with rage, but nodded. The flames died away.

The vendor's expression shifted from smug to alarmed. "Who are you?" she demanded, glaring at Amari.

"We'll come back," I said quickly, steering Amari away from the stall.

The vendor stared after us for a moment, then began hurriedly packing up her wares.

I kept walking, pulling Amari along. But then I saw a teenage boy with golden-brown hair and an iron collar chained to another stall. He sat sullenly beside a vendor talking animatedly to a group of potential buyers.

I swallowed hard. I knew him. The selkie who lived in the Thames – the boy Father had saved from Stalker so many years ago – and probably the seal Tristan had been trying to rescue.

I couldn't leave him here to be sold.

I started toward him, but froze as a flash of pale hair caught my eye.

My gut clenched.

"There," I growled. A tall man with two katanas strapped to his back shoved past a vendor shouting over a cart of brightly coloured potions. "Stalker."

Amari followed my gaze, her expression hardening. "Let's follow him."

I wanted to charge him right there, fists first. But Amari's idea was probably more sensible. We weaved through the crowd, keeping our distance.

Stalker moved lazily through the market, picking through goods, chatting with vendors. He didn't seem to be in any rush, or looking for anyone.

"I don't see Cassie," Amari murmured. "If she was with him... he must have sold her already."

A crimson haze clouded my vision. I knew I shouldn't – not here, not now. But I couldn't stop myself. Not after everything.

"Ambrose, wait!"

Amari tried to grab my arm, but I was already moving. I stormed up to Stalker, tapped his shoulder, and the moment he turned, I punched him in the face.

Pain shot through my hand. Satisfaction bloomed hotter. He reeled back, dazed.

"Where's my sister, you bastard?" I snarled, grabbing the collar of his sleeveless shirt, ignoring the ring of curious onlookers forming around us.

His eyes flicked to mine – unfocused for a moment – then narrowed. His mouth curled into that infuriating smirk.

"She's just a tidy deposit into my retirement fund by now."

I spat the Word and the *rogatina* shimmered into my hand. I lunged.

Stalker twisted aside, but not before the tip sliced a clean line across his cheek.

He stepped back, touched the blood trailing

down his face, and stared at it for a second. Then he turned back to me, smirk gone, his mouth a flat, dangerous line.

I lifted the spear again, heart pounding, ready to charge again.

But Stalker blurred, moving faster than I could track.

In an instant, the *rogatina* was knocked from my hands, clattering to the ground. He twisted behind me, yanked me into a chokehold, and pressed a katana to my throat.

"What are you gonna do about it?" he hissed, the blade biting cold against my skin.

A bead of sweat slid down my cheek.

"Let him go."

Amari stepped into view. The look on her face was ice.

"Keeper," Stalker said, tensing.

The word rippled through the crowd. Some people bolted. Others leaned in. They knew what a Keeper could do – or maybe they just knew what Amari could.

"I said, let him go," Amari repeated.

"You have no authority here," Stalker sneered, but I heard the fear in his voice. Felt the slight tremor in his grip. Stalker was afraid of Amari.

She opened her mouth to speak again, but he shoved me away, backing off quickly.

I whipped out my phone and snapped a photo. "There. Now every cop in Britain will know what you look like."

His jaw clenched. Without another word, he slapped his hand to his forearm.

"No!" I rushed forward to grab him, but it was too late. Blue light flared, and he vanished.

"Damn it!" I shouted.

"Ambrose…" Amari's voice was tense.

I was seething. I wanted to tear the whole place

down.

"Ambrose!"

"What?!"

I turned, and froze.

The crowd was running. But not away from us.

Amari looked pale. Rattled.

I looked down. The hair on my arm was standing on end.

"What's happening?"

"Someone's coming," Amari whispered, and then the sky tore open.

※※※

They stepped through the rifts like shadows made flesh – men and women clad in black, faces masked, only their eyes visible. Symbols flared in the air, crackling with magic. Anyone hit froze where they stood, like statues.

"The Hunters of the Veil," Amari muttered – just before ducking as a streak of white light flew past her head.

I didn't have time to react. A masked figure was already on me, sweeping my legs out with a short staff. I hit the ground hard, rolled, and spotted the *rogatina* where it had fallen. As the attacker lunged, I sidestepped – Nadiya's training kicking in – and cracked him on the back of the head with the shaft of the spear.

He dropped like a puppet with its strings cut.

Panting, I scanned the chaos. The market had erupted into madness.

A six-legged creature with a turtle shell barrelled after a fleeing vendor. The potion-seller lay unconscious in a puddle of shattered glass, his skin an unnatural green. A masked woman held two black-clad attackers at bay with a fencing sword.

I spotted Amari beside a cage. Her fingers brushed over the lock, and it snapped open.

The tusked bull burst free, charging into the fray. One of the Hunters went flying, her Symbol fizzling midair.

Amari caught my gaze and gave a grim smile.

Then her eyes widened. "Watch out!"

I ducked just in time. The same attacker I'd downed before had recovered, his staff whistling through the space where my head had been. He froze mid-swing – Amari's doing.

I staggered back, just in time for a jet of water to slam into me, knocking me off my feet. The blast had come from a blue-haired woman. A cracked steel shackle clung to her neck.

A water nymph.

Someone lunged for her, and she dissolved into a puddle, vanishing into the dirt.

"You okay?" Amari was suddenly there, helping me to my feet.

I nodded, breathless. "We need to find Cassie."

"She's not here, Ambrose," she said softly. "We'll find her. But not tonight. Right now, we need to get out of here."

"No one is going anywhere," a female voice said behind us.

A chill stabbed through me.

Amari went unnaturally rigid. A Symbol glowed on her arm.

I spun around, bringing the *rogatina* up – its tip kissing the throat of the masked woman standing before me.

Her eyes met mine – steady, dark, unflinching. I knew that stance. That presence.

"I hoped it wouldn't come to this," the Huntress said. "But this market is an abomination. Everyone here is breaking the laws of Banka-Mundi."

My stomach dropped. I knew that voice.

"Release my friend," I said hoarsely. "We're not here to support the market. We're here to rescue Cassie."

The Huntress sucked in a breath. She retraced the glowing Symbol on Amari's arm, erasing it in an instant.

Amari's stance softened as I mumbled a Word and the *rogatina* vanished.

The Huntress reached up, pulled off her mask – and Pavi's stricken face stared back at me.

"What's happened to Cassie?"

THE END

(The adventure continues with *Myth Bringer*, the final instalment of the Mythical Menagerie series.)

BONUS SCENES

ON LYCAON'S TRAIL

"Amari's boots slipped on moss-slick stones as the sun beat relentlessly down on her. From a distance, the mountains of Greece had looked beautiful – green ridges folding over each other like the backs of sleeping beasts. Up close, they were nothing but rock, pine, and a warm wind that did little to ease the oppressive heat.

Three days. Three villages. Three old men willing to share stories over bitter coffee and olive-stuffed pita bread.

So far, that's all they'd been – stories.

She'd come in search of Lycaon's descendants – others like Norton, who could change their shape and become wolves. Werewolves.

Norton.

The knot in her stomach tightened at the thought of him. He'd left a wake of devastation in his path – slaughtering every creature in the Repository's holding cells before attacking Una.

And then Amari had killed him.

She had failed him. Failed every creature who had died at his hands. Failed the world – a trait lost forever because she'd been reckless. And now, she was no longer Keeper.

That loss cut deepest of all. Who was she, if not the one who kept the creatures safe?

But she was going to fix things. It was too late for Norton and the rest, but she could still restore the trait and save the world. All she needed was to find a werewolf.

And if that meant taking on the curse herself, so be it.

If only it weren't so damn difficult. More than once, she'd been on the verge of giving up, of going home – not to the Repository, but back to her family. She knew they'd would welcome her. But they would wonder. Wonder if she hadn't been good enough to make it on her own after all. Wonder if she should have followed the path they had chosen for her instead of carving out her own.

It was the thought of that disappointment that kept her climbing this mountain.

Wiping sweat from her brow, Amari pulled out her water bottle and drank deeply. Her rucksack was lighter now – she'd given the last of her tea to a shepherd's wife that morning in exchange for directions to an abandoned chapel perched above the valley. Her last hope.

Tucking the bottle away, she followed a goat track barely wider than her boots, scrambling over rocks until the ruins came into view – clutching the mountainside like a forgotten harpy's nest. Her breath rasped in her ears as she hurried toward them.

She sank to her knees on the scraggy grass, staring at the toppled walls. The stones were old enough to remember Lycaon's name, but nothing else remained.

She waited for something. A sign. A howl carried on the wind. Even a single pawprint in the dust.

But the mountains stayed silent.

It had all been a lie. A tale told to make the world more interesting.

The knot in her stomach collapsed into a hollow pit. She couldn't do this. She couldn't go on.

She slumped to the ground, tearing at the leopard-print scarf at her neck – it felt like it was choking her. She couldn't breathe.

Leaning back against the ancient stones, Amari closed her eyes. Exhaustion coiled around her like chains and dragged her into the abyss.

※ ※ ※

A chill wind tugged at her curls, pulling her back to consciousness. Amari opened her eyes to find the sun reduced to a thin slice of orange on the horizon, the first stars winking into the darkening sky. She knew night came quickly in the mountains – bringing with it a cold that seeped bone-deep.

Sighing, she pushed herself to her feet. Her gaze drifted over the ruined chapel and empty trail. No more leads. No more ideas.

She tilted her head back, searching the dimming heavens for inspiration. The constellations were faint, barely visible against the last traces of daylight. What she needed was illumination.

Her eyes widened. Illumination.

Snapping her fingers, she flooded the world in white light.

※ ※ ※

Bat Willow Meadow lay cloaked in shadow when the brilliance faded. A cool breeze sifted through the trees, tugging at her scarf. She pulled her jacket from her pack and shrugged into it – summer in Greece was nothing like summer in Oxford.

Her gaze swept the small clearing. "Come on, come on," she murmured, heart hammering. "I need your help one more time."

Goosebumps prickled along her arms as a dozen glimmering sparks flickered to life around her. The air filled with a strange, resonant hum, and the clearing glowed in soft, otherworldly blue light.

A smile curved her lips.

One of the lights floated toward her. She reached out, almost too afraid to breathe, and touched it.

The sparks exploded into an aurora that swirled dizzyingly around her, wrapping her in ribbons of rainbow colour. Their music crescendoed into a symphony that drowned out her fear, her doubt, her guilt. Energy thrummed through her veins until her mind seemed ready to burst.

And then – a memory ignited. A conversation with Ambrose, the night he'd brought Norton to the Repository. Hybrid DNA, he'd said. From a rare strain of Bavarian wolves.

Her breath caught, and then a laugh burst from her throat. Of course.

A vibration in her pocket dragged her back to the present. She fished out her phone. The battery was nearly gone, but one notification glowed on the screen.

Ambrose had blown his whistle.

Amari looked up at the lights still spiralling around her. "Thank you," she whispered.

The colours dimmed, fading into the dark, and then the Word swept her away in a flash of white.

KEEPER'S PROMISE

Amari slipped from the shapeshifter's enclosure, the satchel clutched tight against her ribs as though Diana's diaries inside could vanish if she loosened her grip. True to his word, Reese had kept them safe. The old winged monkey had told her James and his men rarely bothered the shapeshifters anymore. The creatures had refused to make contact, steadfastly ignoring any attempts at luring them down from the lofty trees. Eventually, the new Keeper had lost interest.

That suited her just fine.

By now, Ambrose would have found Norton's bracelet in her desk drawer – if it was still there. And if not… well, then he'd be waiting for her outside the West Gate, empty-handed and impatient. Either way, she had to get out without anyone noticing, and without risking the confiscation of her satchel.

Her gaze caught on an unmarked door nearby. Una's door.

She hesitated – only for a heartbeat – then crossed the space in quick, quiet steps and slipped through.

The unicorn's grove unfolded in a wash of green

and gold, sunlight dappling through the canopy. A brook murmured softly, somewhere beyond the trees. The air was laced with the scent of dew-drenched grass and something sweeter – like apples kissed with starlight.

"Una?" Amari's voice was soft, as though anything louder might shatter the spell.

Leaves rustled, and the unicorn stepped into the clearing. The light caught her silver horn, scattering tiny rainbows across the grass. She whickered gently, and Amari's chest loosened for the first time in days.

She reached forward, fingers sliding through the silk of Una's mane. Magic clung to the strands, a faint hum that seeped into Amari's bones, untying knots she hadn't realised she'd been carrying.

"I've missed you," she whispered.

Una's warm breath brushed her cheek. Amari wrapped her arms around the unicorn's neck and held on, drinking in the scent – crisp apples and something older, wilder, undeniably magical. For a moment, the world beyond the grove didn't exist.

But she couldn't stay here forever.

She pulled back reluctantly, letting her hands trail down the unicorn's neck. "They haven't touched you, have they?" Her fingers skimmed over sleek muscle and found only one old scar. Nothing new.

"Good girl," she murmured. "Don't let them take anything from you."

The unicorn tossed her mane, sunlight glancing off the spirals of her horn.

"I have to go," Amari said, her voice wobbling despite herself. "But I'll come back. I promise."

Una gave her a gentle nudge, then turned and slipped back into the shadows, her white coat vanishing between the trees.

Amari stood there a moment, committing the sight to memory. Then she straightened her shoulders, tightened her grip on the satchel, and walked away.

She couldn't save Una today.

But she *would*.

THE COST OF YES

C assie spilled out of the Tate the way tears spilled down her cheeks – hot, relentless, unstoppable.

How *could* he?

How could Ambrose ask this of her? After everything – after being turned to stone, after nearly dying at the hands of a werewolf... And now he wanted her to *become* one.

To lose herself again – only this time permanently – and turn into a monster.

And for what? Because the world was missing something? Because she might, *maybe*, be able to bring it back? Why should she be the one to do that? What had the world ever done for her?

She pushed through the crowd without seeing their faces, barely paying attention to where she was going. Not caring where she ended up, as long as it was away from him and his unfair expectations.

Her shoes slapped against the pavement. Shoulders bumped hers. Somewhere, music pulsed from an open doorway – low, heavy bass vibrating in her chest. She followed it, not because she cared where it led, but because it was there, and she needed something louder than her own thoughts. Somewhere she could escape.

Inside, hours blurred against the pounding bass and the rhythm of strangers pressing against her as they moved with the beat. She danced hard enough to forget everything, never stopping long enough to catch her breath. If she kept moving, there was no room to think.

By the time she stumbled outside, the cold hit her like a slap. Her phone read 3:47 AM, its battery hanging by a thread. Her calves ached, and she couldn't bring herself to go back to her empty apartment.

Instead, she caught a southbound train.

Brighton greeted her as the sun rose. The last time she'd been here, Pavi had pulled her along the pier, wind-whipped and laughing, daring her onto the rickety rollercoaster. They'd eaten chips on the beach, salt stinging their lips, and dreamed about running away somewhere warm.

Now the pier boards creaked under her feet, but the laughter was gone.

She walked until the wind numbed her face, then borrowed a sketchpad from a street artist. Sitting with it in her lap, she began to draw the sea without really seeing it. The gulls wheeled overhead, screeching over nothing, their wings jagged against the pale sky. Once, she'd have caught that motion, turned it into art. Today, she closed the pad halfway through.

Had she already lost what made her, *her*?

Was Ambrose right – had Tenacity bled out of the world? Was that why her fire felt so dim?

She stared across the grey waves, turning his words over. Fear coiled in her stomach... but beneath it was something else. Not excitement. Not acceptance. But possibility, maybe.

If she said yes, she'd become a werewolf. The thought was terrifying – claws, fur, hunger, the loss of control. It wouldn't be her anymore.

And yet… it would be freedom.

When she'd dropped out of university, she'd wanted to help the world. This wasn't what she'd had in mind – she'd wanted to hunt monsters, not *become* one. But maybe this was the only way. Not just for the world, but for herself. A chance to matter.

She returned the sketchpad to the artist. His own canvas was barely more than an outline.

The last train carried her back to London, no closer to a decision.

✳✳✳

The next morning, Cassie found herself in Hyde Park. The grass sparkled with frost, the air crisp and quiet. The paths were empty of the usual early morning joggers.

She stopped at the edge of the Serpentine, watching a swan glide across the water in a clean, unhurried line. Somewhere between the ripple and the stillness, her decision settled in her chest.

She couldn't do it.

The cost would be too great. She couldn't risk losing everything again. The world would have to find someone else to save it.

Cassie swallowed back the lump in her throat. She'd have to tell Ambrose. Let him down again.

But first, she had to talk to Caitlynn. She hadn't spoken to her friend since that day she'd dragged her into danger. She needed to apologise.

That much, at least, she could still do.

CLEAN SWEEP

A mari's breath puffed white in the cold night air as Tristan struggled to jimmy the lock on the service door at the back of the pet crematorium.

"This thing's rusted solid," he muttered, shooting her a frustrated look. "Don't think it gets used much."

She rolled her eyes and nudged him aside. Muttering the Word under her breath, she heard the lock click open with a reluctant clank. The door followed with a drawn-out creak loud enough to wake the dead.

"How'd you do that?" Tristan asked as he flicked on his torch and stepped inside.

Amari didn't answer.

The sting of industrial-strength disinfectant burned her nose as she swept her own flashlight across an empty corridor lined with closed doors. She scanned the walls for a CCTV camera – no tell-tale red light blinked from the shadows. Relieved, she shoved the balaclava deeper into her jacket pocket.

"Let's split up," Tristan whispered.

She nodded. While he headed for the back offices, Amari crossed to a door marked *Furnace Room*. The heavy steel gate groaned as she pushed it open. Inside, the cremator loomed like a sleeping giant, its metal panels glinting in the beam of her light. She crouched to check beneath the machinery – just dust, an abandoned broom, and a crumpled paper cup.

Her footsteps echoed as she moved on to a side storage room. Cardboard boxes were stacked neatly along one wall, each marked with dates and paperwork. She tore one open – floral wreath stands and ribbons. Nothing more.

Tristan reappeared, shaking his head. "Offices are empty. No ledgers, no odd shipments, no animals. Nothing."

They checked the staff kitchen – bare cupboards, stale biscuits in a tin. The maintenance shed out back – mops, buckets, cleaning fluid. Not so much as a paw print.

"It's clean," Tristan said finally, the disappointment in his voice matching her own.

Amari leaned against the brick wall, exhaling a frosty sigh. "I hate dead ends."

She jumped when Tristan slammed his fist against the wall with a low growl. "We can't let them get away with this!"

"They won't," Amari said, her voice steady with conviction.

Tristan gave her a sidelong glance. "What are you really looking for, Amari? That hound at the Refuge wasn't just a stray dog. Which means this cat we're after probably isn't just a cat, either."

She let out a slow breath. "You're right. They're not ordinary animals. They're… mythical."

He didn't laugh. Instead, a small frown creased his brow. "That's not as hard to believe as it should be," he admitted. "There was something… uncanny about Red. How long have you known? About them?"

"Since Oxford," she said, chuckling at the surprise on his face.

Silence stretched for a moment before Tristan said: "You should come work with GAIA."

She arched an eyebrow. "You want me to join a group that breaks into places for a living?"

"Why not?" he shrugged. "You're remarkably good at it. You were last time, too."

She folded her arms. "I'm not sure I'd fit in."

He grinned. "You clearly care about these creatures. You don't want them locked up any more than I do. That's what GAIA's all about – freeing animals who never should've been caged."

Amari hesitated, glancing back at the silent building. "I'll think about it."

Tristan's mouth curved into a slow smile. "That's not a no."

"Come on," she said. "Let's get out of here before someone sees us."

They slipped back through a gap in the chain-link fence. Somewhere far off, a cat yowled, raising goosebumps along Amari's arms. But she knew it wasn't the one they were looking for.

For tonight, the trail had gone cold.

PLEASE REVIEW

If you've enjoyed this story, please consider leaving a review on your online platform of choice and/or on Goodreads. Think of it as word of mouth recommendation. Independent authors such as myself need reviews for visibility and social proof, and to get those algorithms to place my books in the hands of other readers.

It doesn't have to be a long and in-depth review - one sentence, or even just a star rating, will do.

It would mean the world to me. Thank you!

WANT MORE?

Subscribe to Suneé le Roux's email list to receive an exclusive short story prequel set in the Mythical Menagerie universe, only available to newsletter subscribers!

SUBSCRIBE.SUNEELEROUX.COM/KEEPEROFEXOTICANIMALS

**WHAT WOULD YOU DO IF THE WORLD'S
LAST UNICORN WENT MISSING?**

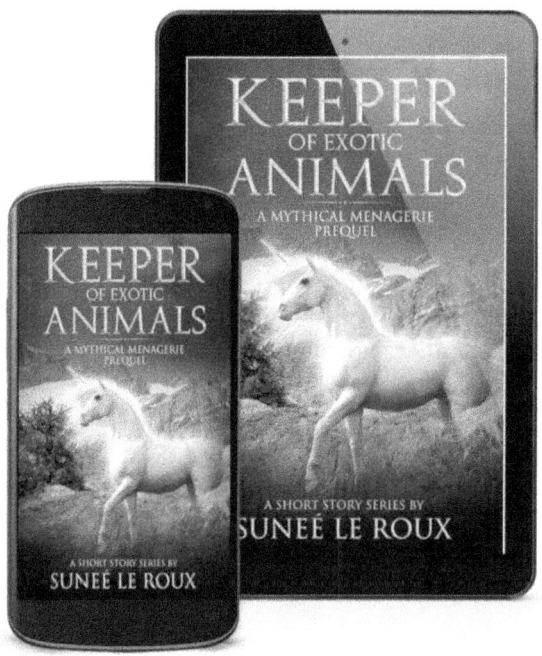

Claim your free e-book now!

ACKNOWLEDGEMENTS

Writing is a solitary endeavour that can only be accomplished with the support of many wonderful people.

A HUGE thank you goes out to my beta readers: Mari Terblanche and Thalia Fourie, who took time out of their busy schedules to read my stories, point out their flaws, and help me make it better.

Thank you my parents, Jannie and Henda, and my friends, Claudette and Schalk, for cheerleading and motivation!

Thank you to my husband Gareth, for continued encouragement and support, and for taking care of all the practical parts of day-to-day life while my head is in the clouds, dreaming up adventures for Ambrose and Amari.

And finally, thank you to you, dear reader, for reading this book and supporting this passion of mine. I hope it added a little magic to your life too!

ABOUT THE AUTHOR

Suneé le Roux is a South African author of contemporary and high fantasy stories that blend myth, magic, and adventure. She lives in South Africa with her Welsh husband and their young wizard-in-training.

She loves nothing more than to hear from readers. Connect with her here:

Website: www.suneeleroux.com

Email: contact@suneeleroux.com

Facebook: www.facebook.com/authorsuneeleroux/

Instagram: www.instagram.com/suneeleroux/

WWW.SUNEELEROUX.COM